The Developer

Stephen P. Bye

BookLocker
St. Petersburg, Florida

Hardcover ISBN: 978-1-64718-533-6
Paperback ISBN: 978-1-64718-532-9

Published by Booklocker.com, Inc., St. Petersburg, Florida.

Printed on acid free paper.

This is a work of fiction, based on actual persons and events. The author has taken created liberty with many details to enhance the reader's experience. The characters are purely fictional.

Library of Congress Cataloguing in Publication Data
Bye, Stephen P.
The Developer by Stephen P. Bye
Fiction
Library of Congress Control Number: 2020908008

Booklocker. Com. Inc.

2020

First Edition

Dedication and Acknowledgements

This novel is dedicated to my former clients and colleagues in the commercial real estate industry, far too many to acknowledge individually.

As a special memorial, this work is dedicated to Professor James A. Graaskamp (1933-1988), who provided the inspiration for my career path in real estate while I was a student at the University of Wisconsin Madison.

Thanks to my wife, Karen, who provided editorial support and the encouragement to create this story.

Preface

With over four decades in arranging capital for large commercial real estate projects, I've met hundreds of developers and property investors; and at least a thousand loan officers, appraisers, attorneys, brokers, and other real estate specialists. With that background, I created the story around a cross section of those professionals. The main character in this novel (Alexander Kellogg III) is a composite of the real estate entrepreneurs I encountered or read about. All characters in this novel are fictional, and their names are solely random.

Chapter One

Alexander Kellogg III studied his six-foot frame in the full-length mirror. He moved a bit closer, turning to view his profile. He snapped his suspenders and sucked in his stomach, which now hung slightly over the waist band. He plucked some lint from his blue pin stripe suit, which was now uncomfortably tight with his recent weight gain. He crept within a foot of the mirror to adjust his scarlet tie, ensuring the dimple was perfect. He tugged his square jaw back slightly, exposing his flawless teeth, as he rubbed his index finger over them rapidly, expecting to polish them even more brightly. Using both hands, he fluffed up his hair, so it looked thicker, rejecting the notion that it was inevitably thinning. He was also losing a battle to greying hair, demanding his stylist's weekly treatments maintain its natural black color. Kellogg was as vain in his appearance as he was ruthless in business.

Alexander Kellogg III, known as Xander, ran his real estate development company like a tyrant, demanding total allegiance from his employees and anyone he selected to do business with. He expected everyone to respond within minutes of any request, seven days a week, and at any time of the day. It was a privilege to be associated with Kellogg Development Company, although he now preferred the firm to be known simply as Kellogg, steadily building his brand over the past ten years. He also promoted a self-appointed nickname, Mr. X, much like a celebrity.

Kellogg heard a tap on his door. "It's Mike Peavy, boss…I need to speak with you immediately."

Peavy nervously stepped into the room, knowing Kellogg was notorious for 'killing the messenger' who bore bad news. "Ah…Mr. Kellogg, um…I just got a phone call from a clerk at Continental Divide Bank about the West Tower Office loan…they want a one and a half million-dollar paydown to lower their risk."

"Peavy…what the hell's wrong with that fucking lender? Christ, they should change the name to Cuntinental Bank! Get our damn loan officer over here this afternoon…what's his name again?"

"James Middleton." Peavy timidly replied as he brushed back a few strands of blonde hair that hung down to his eyebrows. He had the appearance of a meek accountant…thinly built, barely five feet tall and was balding quickly. Peavy was terrified of Kellogg and after a year as chief financial officer, he was convinced Xander lacked attention for detail.

"I remember the cocky bastard…it's a shame he doesn't have the personality of his father. The dink promised his bank would create a long-term relationship with me…now they're demanding a million and a half dollars! Why?"

Peavy lowered himself slowly on the green couch. "Mr. Kellogg, they're declaring the loan on West Tower out of balance based upon an updated appraisal…the value apparently dropped by two million dollars."

"Are they joking…the appraised value should have risen by two million…or more!"

"Boss, you only contributed two hundred fifty thousand in cash when the construction loan closed last year. The bank also generously credited you for the significant increase in the land value above your purchase price, so perhaps a demand for more equity isn't that unreasonable."

"Peavy, are you hallucinating? I created the big pop in the land value after I stole it from a church and wrestled with the City of Lakewood bureaucrats for a year to get the zoning variance. John Collin's law firm pulled a few strings behind the scenes too! God only knows who they bribed."

Peavy shrunk down in the sofa, scanning the wild animal trophies mounted on the walls. Kellogg pointed at the collection. "Peavy, how do you think I can afford my safaris to Africa, the deep-sea fishing expeditions, and the Canadian hunting adventures?"

Peavy squirmed and looked down at the green carpet. "You've already taken five hundred thousand dollars in developer fees too."

Kellogg flung a note pad at Peavy, narrowly missing his head. "Pal…without my development fees, your ridiculous salary wouldn't get paid." Kellogg slammed his fist on the desk. "What firm did the damn bank hire for the appraisal?"

"Boss, it was Allied Appraisal Group. Our property manager, Brenda Dunston, told me they inspected the building two weeks ago."

Kellogg threw his hands up. "I could have lobbied the appraiser in advance if she had alerted us. I knew that we shouldn't have hired that bimbo, but she does have a great body now that I picture her. Shit…you should have known about the appraisal too. What's your excuse?"

"I was on vacation that week."

"Peavy, I didn't hire you to take vacations! One more fuckup like this and you'll be on a permanent vacation!"

"Yes, Mr. Kellogg. It won't happen again…I'm sorry."

"I don't want to hear any of my employees using that word."

"Huh?"

"I haven't used the word sorry in thirty years…it's a sign of weakness. Now, go call that nimrod banker…I want to see him by the end of the day." Kellogg picked up a coffee cup from his desk and hurled it against the wall. "I don't have an extra million-five laying around right now!"

Mike Peavy returned to Xander's office ten minutes later. "Mr. Kellogg, I spoke to Middleton's secretary…he's playing golf at The Platte Club and can't be reached for the rest of the day."

"Drive over there right now, find Middleton, and haul his ass over here!"

"I'm not a member at The Platte Club…they won't even let me in the front gate."

"I'll call the golf shop myself." He tapped several buttons on the telephone. "Hello…Kenny Boy?"

The head golf professional, Ken Ingram, intuitively knew who was calling…only one member called him Kenny Boy. "Good morning, Mr. X."

"Fine…fine, Kenny Boy. Listen…James Middleton is out of the course somewhere. Deliver a message to him immediately to call my secretary, Phyllis. Got it?"

"Yes sir."

"Wait…don't hang up yet. Did you hear the joke about the priest…the one where the Catholic priest, Father Nelson, demonstrates his wrestling holds on the caddie?"

"Yep…that's a good one."

"Thanks Kenny Boy…see you on Thursday."

Kellogg strolled outside his office to address his attractive assistant. "Phyllis, when James Middleton calls, tell him to get here by four o'clock."

"Yes, Mr. Kellogg...do you want drinks served?"

"Hell no...unless you have some strychnine handy. Peavy, you need to be here too."

"My son has his first little league game today at four and I didn't want to miss it."

"Peavy, you'll have plenty of time for your kid's games if you miss this meeting. Do you know what I mean?"

"I think so, Mr. Kellogg." Peavy's shoulders slumped. "I'll be here."

"Good...now go over the budget for West Tower with a fine tooth comb and move some line items around to eliminate this capital call ambush from those bank shysters. You got me into this mess by recommending Continental Divide Bank as the lender, so you better get me out of it."

Peavy also knew that when there was negative news, Kellogg always used the words 'you' or 'your', blaming anyone except himself. Everything involving the firm centered on Kellogg, who always used the words 'me' and 'I'...never 'we' or 'us'.

Twenty minutes passed when Phyllis buzzed Xander's intercom. "Mr. Kellogg, James Middleton called...he'll arrive at our office by three forty-five."

Kellogg dialed the extension for Eli Cohen, his Director of Leasing. "Cohen, bring the tenant prospect list for West Tower to me...right now!"

Eli Cohen hustled down the carpeted hallway to Kellogg's office, where Xander was rearranging several golf trophies on his credenza. "Good morning, Mr. Kellogg."

"Not a good day, Cohen…our crazy West Tower lender wants a huge loan paydown. I'm meeting with our arrogant loan rep later…I want the latest detail on the tenant prospects."

Cohen handed Xander a stained yellow sheet with handwritten notes. "Sir, here's the most recent update from Reagan & Holbrook's leasing team…it's two weeks old."

"What do ya' mean…two weeks?"

"R & H updates the leasing activity every two weeks…it's expressly stated in the leasing agreement."

"Shit…two weeks is an eternity. And what's with this scribbling…I can barely read it! Can't those lazy brokers even type? What's with all the coffee stains?

"Sorry, Mr. Kellogg…" Kellogg instantly covered Cohen's mouth with his right palm. "Don't ever say sorry again! I just chewed out Peavy for that too."

Cohen coughed twice and tried to clear his throat. "My wife spilled her coffee on the leasing summary after I left it on our kitchen table."

"Cohen, how many times have I told you never take anything confidential out of this office…spies are everywhere to steal a tenant. Do you want a permanent vacation too?"

"It won't happen again."

"Tell those sleepy R & H brokers I want to see a detailed typed tenant prospect list every day. I don't give a shit what the listing agreement states. Now, give me the updates."

"They're chasing a new proposal with the GSA…"

Kellogg interrupted. "Who is the GSA?"

"The General Services Administration...the Federal government. The GSA needs eighty thousand square feet for their Fish and Wildlife division...they prefer the top two floors of West Tower on a three-year lease term."

"How long have they been working on it?"

"About two weeks now...it's very preliminary. You know how bureaucratic the government is...some flunky in Washington is the decision maker. The Bureau of Mines needs thirty thousand square feet, but they want the best space on the fifth floor for a six-year term with a cancellation option after three years."

"Why does a government agency need views? Their employees should be housed in a basement somewhere where there's no windows! Christ...and they want the right to vacate early too?"

"The Department of the Interior is planning a three hundred-thousand square foot building to consolidate several agencies, so the Mines division would likely move into that facility as well as Fish and Wildlife."

"Are we on the bid list for that project?"

"They want a developer who has built office projects of at least that scale. We can't meet the minimum qualifications."

"Call our congressman, Casper Walsh. I gave him two thousand bucks for his last campaign. He should know the right contacts back there in DC to get us in the game. Who else looks like a good tenant prospect?"

"A small gold mining company for twenty-five thousand square feet. They're not well capitalized, so we would be taking a credit risk."

"What's the price of gold these days?"

"About three hundred bucks an ounce."

"Call Stan Thompson at Bache and ask about their forecast on gold prices. If they're bullish on the price of bullion, we can get some stock warrants on the company to compensate for the financial risk."

"There are two companies involved in oil shale exploration on the Western slope, each needing fifteen thousand square feet. They're privately held, and we haven't seen any financials on them yet."

"Ask Stan about whether shale technology has any future and what the breakeven price they need to be profitable for a barrel of oil. Who else is out there?"

"Just a handful of small businesses…two accounting groups, an individual law firm practice, a financial planner, and a residential loan broker."

"We certainly don't want to break up a floor for smaller tenants yet. However, have George Clements' architectural team create a space plan for a multi-tenant floor layout. More importantly, order those two worthless brokers from R & H to come here Thursday morning. This is their first assignment with us, so they better get their asses in gear or I'll fire them. You should start sweating too, since you recommended those bumpkins."

"I have a tenant showing on Thursday morning…can we make it in the afternoon?"

"No…I've got a big golf game set up on Thursday afternoon at The Platte Club." Xander scanned the tenant list again. "Cohen…add a few large company names to this list and have Phyllis retype it. I need to impress our lacky loan rep and his braindead associates."

"I'll call Pete Simpson or Nate Allen at Reagan & Holbrook right away."

"Don't call those clowns…make up a few impressive companies, like IBM, Dupont, GE, and Xerox."

Cohen appeared confused, but slowly pivoted, disappearing down the hallway.

Xander shuffled over to his liquor cabinet, reached for a bottle of Glenfiddich scotch whiskey and poured it into his favorite glass, handblown in a Venetian factory he toured last year with his wife, Jill. He reached into a silver ice bucket, plucked six cubes, and dropped them in the fancy crystal. He swiveled the drink with his index finger, sampled it and smacked his lips. As he peered out at the passing cars on Interstate Highway 25, he pondered why he let his brother, Robert, convince him to develop office buildings. He would now need to get tough with the bank and the leasing team at Reagan & Holbrook. One by one, he chewed on the ice cubes, taking larger sips until the glass was empty.

Mike Peavy knocked on the partially open door and Xander motioned him into the office. Peavy unfurled a long sheet of paper and spread it out on the desk.

"Mr. Kellogg, I've studied our budget and see a few places to save about five hundred thousand dollars." He pointed to several highlighted red numbers. "We can eliminate some trees and excess landscaping and convert the concrete parking lot to asphalt…that's nearly a hundred thousand bucks right there. We have seven hundred thousand in unfunded tenant finish and for the common areas and the restrooms…we can order cheaper fixtures and lower grade carpeting or tile to save fifty grand. Clements' space planners can design open floor plans to lower the demising costs. Finally, we have two hundred thousand in our contingency account and can convince the bank's inspector to get by on a hundred thousand."

"Is that all?" Kellogg frowned.

"One major problem...the bank is concerned about the interest reserve and believe the Prime Rate will increase soon. We're eating through our reserve pretty quickly...trouble either way, Mr. Kellogg."

"What do those bank dummies know about interest rates? The politicians in Washington know the country can't handle higher rates. By your math, that still leaves a million-dollar shortfall. Get a copy of the appraisal report from the bank or call the appraiser directly."

"I'll be in trouble with the bank if I call the appraiser."

"So what? I want to see the appraisal report tomorrow."

Phyllis called on the intercom. "Mr. Kellogg, your wife is on the phone." He pounded his desk, becoming even more infuriated.

"All right...I'll speak to her." Kellogg reluctantly accepted the call, never wanting to be interrupted by his wife while conducting business...none of her ideas could be more important than his priorities.

Kellogg waited a minute to pick up the receiver, knowing it would irritate her. "Hello Jill...how are you?"

"Fine...do you remember the fundraising dinner is tonight?"

"Yes, I remember...you've only reminded me fifty times!"

"It's at six o'clock at the Cosmopolitan Hotel and I MUST be there early as the co-chair for the event. Be sure you bring your credit cards...I want to bid on several expensive items."

"Of course." He slammed the receiver down.

Phyllis broke in again. Mr. Kellogg…your attorney is on the phone for you." Kellogg was eager to speak with John Collins, his longtime counsel, who he nicknamed Colly.

"Colly, have the cowboys in Nebraska contacted you on the ground lease extension yet?"

"Not yet…apparently, they don't they know if they miss the ground lease renewal date, their two downtown buildings revert to your KF Trust."

"Colly, you should disappear for a couple of weeks so they can't find you…bye bye." Kellogg dropped the receiver on the handle perfectly from a foot above.

Peavy was listening intently to the conversation. "Hold on a minute, Mike…I gotta take a piss."

Peavy closely examined the animal trophies until Kellogg returned from his private bathroom. Purposely keeping his back facing away from Peavy, Kellogg picked a circuitous route around his desk, before bouncing into his leather desk chair. Peavy chuckled…Kellogg had urinated on his slacks and was surreptitiously trying to hide the wet stain.

"Peavy…that was John Collins on the phone. In 1938, he drafted an eighty-year ground lease on a downtown quarter block our family trust owns. A real estate developer leased the land and built two four-story buildings on it in 1939 and later sold them to Gus Bristol, a wealthy rancher from western Nebraska. Gus died five years ago, and his dimwit sons inherited the leasehold interests. Collins is the Trustee for the KF Trust…the Kellogg Family Trust, whose sole beneficiaries are my brother and I. Nearly forty years has passed, and the extension option date for the next four decades is quickly approaching. If the Bristol kids don't exercise the extension option in writing soon, the KF Trust will automatically get title to both buildings…after I demolish them, I'll construct the tallest building in downtown Denver on the parcel."

"Very impressive, Mr. Kellogg."

"Yes, I am a genius…now go back to your office and find more savings on the budget. Middleton will be here soon." He glanced down, noting the hands on his Rolex Cosmograph watch, which pointed to three o'clock.

Kellogg poured another scotch and stretched out on his office couch. He picked up a travel agent brochure on a Mediterranean Sea cruise. Jill had been pestering him about the trip for several weeks. A few minutes later, he fell asleep.

Phyllis startled Xander with a call on the intercom. "Mr. Kellogg, James Middleton is here to see you…he's waiting in the reception area."

He stumbled toward his desk and snatched the phone receiver. "He can sit out there for a while. Did you type Cohen's tenant prospect list?

"I'll be done in a minute."

"Bring it here when you're finished…then call Cohen and Peavy to report here for duty."

Cohen came in three minutes later, anxiously observing Kellogg scrutinizing the tenant roster.

"Cohen…nice job. IBM, Xerox, Dupont, GE, Exxon, and Texaco should really impress those banksters." He skimmed down the list. "Who's Tosco?"

"A California oil exploration company…they're working on a large shale project on the western slope."

"And Frontier Insurance Group…who are they?"

"R & H actually had them on an earlier list. They're located in a building down the street and have a lease expiring in two years…we could sublease their space if we land them for West Tower."

"Sublease their space for less than two remaining on their lease term? What the fuck are you thinking?"

"Just trying to be constructive…maybe we can get an extension or exercise an option if Frontier even has one."

"Who's the building owner?"

"Abe Friedman."

"He's a Jew. I can't deal with those people…too much endless negotiations."

"Mr. Kellogg, you're forgetting that I'm Jewish."

"Ah…well…that's why I hired you in the first place…you like to kibitz too." Kellogg chuckled, glancing at the tenant prospect list again. "This should work, Cohen."

He turned to address Peavy, who joined the meeting. "Did you find any more cost savings in the budget?"

"Nothing that would make much of an impact."

"All right…go get that creep. What's his first name again?"

"James…James Middleton."

Xander opened his closet door, using the mirror to brush his hair in place, so it was perfectly parted. He rubbed his fingers over his teeth again and dropped a breath mint in his mouth. Recalling his bathroom accident, he inspected his trousers, waving the note pad over the spot several times. He elected to sit behind his expansive oak desk, built on a pedestal six inches above the floor...Kellogg insisted on looking down at everyone seated in the room.

James Middleton, still dressed in golf attire, was escorted by Peavy into Kellogg's office.

"Good afternoon, Mr. Kellogg."

Middleton attempted to shake hands with Kellogg, although Xander remained seated, pointing the banker to a straight back wooden chair. "James, it's nice to see you. I hope you got your golf game in...how did you play?"

"I had to cut my round short after the fifteenth hole...I was one under par."

"Nice...you can finish your round when we're done here, but this meeting couldn't wait. Peavy got a call from some clerk at your bank suggesting our West Tower loan was a million dollars out of balance. There must be some mistake...that's a beautiful building. The Colorado Architectural Association will name it the best suburban office project for 1978. When we get the landscaping in and the parking lot fully paved, we'll get even more tenant inquiries...actually, Eli Cohen's phone has been ringing off the hook."

"I just heard about the loan paydown decision early this morning. The required amount is actually a million and a half."

"Why didn't you call us immediately?"

"I had an important meeting with a new bank customer and hosted another prospect for golf at The Platte Club."

"New customers, eh?" Kellogg jaw clenched before slamming his fist on the desk. "What about an existing fucking customer?"

"I should have called myself, but..." Middleton hesitated as he squirmed in his chair. "The loan documents allow our bank to order an appraisal update any time...our compliance department engaged Allied Appraisal Group three weeks ago and the report was received yesterday. The value was lower than the appraisal prepared a year ago before the loan was closed. Our audit department is concerned about the lack of leasing and the shrinking interest reserve balance too."

"I can't understand why Sanders Appraisal Services wasn't asked to provide the update. They're the most familiar with the building and the market. I want to see a copy of the Allied appraisal to check their mistakes."

"I'll try to get it released, but our compliance department doesn't want borrowers to review our appraisal reports...it can only lead to a contentious debate"

"I don't care about your policies...I want to see where they're screwing us!"

Middleton started to stammer, looking out the window. "Y...Y...Yes...I'll try my best."

Kellogg rose from his chair, standing in front of the shaken loan officer and yanked Middleton's jaw forward. "Look at me when I speak to you! Eli Cohen updated our leasing prospect list, so take this back to your clueless green eyeshade auditors. The boys at Reagan & Holbrook have really picked up the pace recently. You'll see some big company names who could lease the entire building."

Middleton studied it for thirty seconds. "This looks fairly good. I hope we can see some leases soon…or at least some letters of intent. My boss, Willard Edwards, asks me about this loan every day. If you recall, the loan extension comes up in three months and there are certain leasing hurdles required for the option."

"We'll easily meet those tests. Peavy wants to go over the budgets with you too. He feels that we can reduce several line items based upon input from our architect."

Peavy unfurled a long ledger with his handwritten adjustments. "James, here's our modified budget that will free up about five hundred thousand dollars…take this with you too."

"All right, but our bank will want to know that the quality of the building is consistent with our expectations based upon the original plans and specifications."

Kellogg snatched the ledger from Peavy and held it three inches from Middleton's eyes. "You're pissing me off! You danced in here a year ago telling us how reasonable your bank would be. I don't want to hear any more bullshit. I want a copy of the appraisal tomorrow and you need to credit us for these budget changes before the next draw. I'm not giving you more cash equity because some bumbling auditor can't get his fat ass out of his chair and drive out to see our beautiful building. I should have done this loan with Wes Wheeler at First National Bank."

"Mr. Kellogg, it IS a gorgeous building, but we need to address the lack of leasing."

"I'll bring our brokers down to your office next week and they can give your boss a firsthand report."

"I'll try to see what I can do, Mr. Kellogg."

Middleton's face was pale, and his voice trembled. He rose quickly from his chair and bolted out the door.

Peavy instantly stood up. "Mr. Kellogg...Middleton has only been at the bank for two years and West Tower is the largest loan he has originated. He doesn't have much influence."

"Are you defending him?"

Peavy shook his head.

"Peavy, let's see what happens tomorrow. Fucking bankers...all they're good for are tickets to the Bronco games, although those two Super Bowl tickets last year were decent. I need to get home and attend another rubber chicken charity dinner my wife roped me in on. I hate these things. I can't even remember what charity this involves."

Chapter Two

Xander raced down the rear stairs of Kellogg Plaza to his carport and jumped into his scarlet Corvette convertible for the fifteen-minute drive to his Cherry Hills mansion. He knew Jillian would be pacing, planning to be at the reception early to model her lavish dress and jewelry she recently bought in Manhattan.

Jillian Pike was Kellogg's third wife and their three-year-old marriage was crumbling. She had expensive tastes and travelled to Paris, Milan, and New York every year to acquire the latest women's fashions. He met her on a Caribbean cruise in 1974, when the marriage to his second wife, Colleen, was failing. Jill, a former Miss America finalist from Kentucky, was seated at a bar in the ship's casino. Exhibiting a bronze tan and sculptured body, Kellogg couldn't resist the challenge to engage her in conversation. After buying her two Manhattans and extolling his real estate triumphs, he was convinced he could take her. Later that evening, while Colleen slept, Kellogg slipped into Jill's stateroom and engaged her in an hour of intense sex. Kellogg was hooked and within months, finalized the divorce with Colleen and married Jill in an extravagant event at The Broadmoor in Colorado Springs.

Jill was involved in many charitable foundations and chairwoman for several events, which meant Kellogg had to call friends and clients to buy tables and contribute unique items for the silent auctions. Kellogg normally recycled items he bought at other charity events, always stretching the stated value more than his cost to ensure optimum tax deductions. He also offered his home in Vail at every auction, although limited its availability to offseason weekdays.

Kellogg sped through two red lights on Hampden Avenue and steered the sports car up the circular red brick drive to the massive stone residence. As he pulled toward the side entrance, Jill bolted out the door, confronting him before he could turn off the engine.

"Xander, where have you been…we should already be at the hotel now. I'm co-chair for this gala and I have important responsibilities!"

"You only want to parade in front of the guests and show off your new dress and gems!"

"Xander, you're an honorary co-chair for this too…you MUST be more punctual. This is important to me."

"Will you let me open the car door now?"

Jill glanced at her dress, noticing a smudge from the car door. "Now look what you've done! I've warned you about getting your car washed every day…this blemish better come out!"

"If it doesn't, you'll have a hundred other dresses to pick from, although it would take an hour to find a match with the thousands of shoes you've collected."

She stormed away, climbing the steps, and slammed the heavy wooden door shut, as Xander parked the Corvette in the garage. He entered the residence, bounding up the winding staircase, two steps at a time, and hustled to the master suite. A tuxedo was laid out on the bed, along with a red cummerbund, a red bowtie, and a red pocket handkerchief. He spied Jill in the bathroom dabbing seltzer water on the dress.

"Xander, I selected your tux for tonight. The red bowtie and cummerbund will match my red dress."

"How thoughtful of you, Jill."

Kellogg entered his cavernous closet to pick out a white formal shirt and a pair of cufflinks. As Jill checked his progress, Kellogg finished tying the laces on his black dress shoes. He inserted his index finger into his mouth and rubbed a scuff on the tip of both shoes.

Moments later, Xander led Jill toward his Corvette and opened the door to the convertible. "I can't possibly ride in that car…it will mess up my hair. We need to use my Mercedes."

Kellogg knew Jill had to make a grand entrance in a luxury vehicle. He was surprised she hadn't ordered a Rolls Royce and a chauffeur for the evening. He opened the Mercedes passenger door for Jill as she slid into the leather seat. Kellogg started the engine and stared at her. "Jill, I absolutely mean this…you're stunning in that gown."

Jill checked her make-up in a mirror tucked inside the sun visor. "Thank you, Xander. Can we go now?"

"I'm at your service, madam."

"Have you looked at the travel brochure for the Mediterranean Cruise yet? I want to go on in May."

"Yes…looks interesting, but I've got quite a few deals on the front burner right now. I can't possibly get away for more than a long weekend."

Jill frowned and looked away. Avoiding further conversation with her, Xander turned to a radio sports talk program.

"Why are you listening to that drivel?"

"A hot prospect for the Montreal Expos Baseball Club spoke with me last week about a job…he's being interviewed tonight."

"If he has that much talent, why would he want to work for you instead of playing baseball?"

"The owner of the Denver Bears is a friend and told the player I was the smartest businessman he knew. He figured the kid may need to work with a crafty entrepreneur in the off-season and invest in my deals when he starts making the big bucks."

Jill laughed quietly. When she first met Xander, she thought his confidence and brashness was sexy, now she found his ego tiresome. Kellogg turned up the sound to drown out any further commentary. A few minutes later, they arrived at the front entrance to the Cosmopolitan Hotel.

"Look Xander", pointing to a couple walking toward the hotel. "There's Henry and Olivia Buckingham…she's co-chairing the event with me tonight. Doesn't she look magnificent in her red, white, and blue dress?

"Yeah, maybe the hotel could hoist it up the flagpole tonight and play the *National Anthem*."

"I'm warning you…no wiseass comments about my friends, assuming they even decide to speak with you!"

The car was still slightly rolling when Jill opened the car door, ordering Kellogg to stop abruptly. Having recently clashed with attorney Henry Buckingham on a real estate transaction, Kellogg wanted to avoid any contact with him. Jill was unaware of the altercation, as he never shared anything about his real estate development business with her. Jill had loose lips and a slipup could cost him dearly. Alexander Kellogg trusted very few people.

After handing the car keys to the hotel valet, Kellogg noticed George Clements pull up in his Cadillac. A neighbor and golfing partner at The Platte Club, Clements was president of the largest architectural firm in Denver. Although sixty-two years old, he had recently married Kathy, a thirty-three-year-old stewardess, following a forty-year marriage to Maureen, who died two years ago.

Xander stalled near the hotel steps. "Hey Georgie Boy…good to see another guppy here tonight. Ready to open your fat wallet?"

"Kathy has her eyes on a few auction items. Is your house in Vail on the bid sheets again?"

"Sure is…late April and early November are great weeks in the mountains! I threw some old office furniture in the auction too…we bought new stuff when we relocated to Kellogg Plaza."

"Have you thought any further about the golf trip to San Francisco and Pebble Beach? My friend can set us up at his house in Carmel. Jill and Kathy can shop while we play golf. Fred Hawthorne, Al McDonald and their wives can join us too…four couples."

"Their wives are trolls…they're fun haters. Their definition of a great day for those women is how many crossword or jigsaw puzzles they can finish. Perhaps we can leave Kathy and Jill in San Francisco and go to Carmel alone for a few days and chase some skirts and play a few golf rounds."

"Kathy chases me around the bedroom every night...I don't need to pursue other women."

"You might consider hiring a detective to follow Kathy around. There's a lot of down time on those overseas flights if you get my drift. I dated four stewardesses for a time between my first and second marriages and joined the highflyers club with them on a few flights."

"Jill is probably like Kathy…always exploring new positions or having sex in different rooms in the house. I'll have to buy a bigger house pretty soon."

"Jill's always looking for a new angle, but it's not about sex!"

"Jill looks hot tonight in that red gown…you don't look to shabby yourself."

"Just trying to keep up with you, George. How's Clint doing at the law firm?"

"Moving up the ladder and soon to become a partner. My other son, Roger, really loves his position as a police officer and giving back to serve the community. Money isn't that important to him."

"I guess with your wealth, he doesn't have much to worry about down the road. He must be aware of all the financial benefits of your success. Congratulations, George…I'm sure you're proud of your sons' success. I only wish my son, Buster, had the work ethic and passion that Roger and Clint seem to have."

"How is Buster?"

"I'll tell you later, but I'd like to get him back to Denver and integrate him in our company…it's a family business after all."

"That seems encouraging." They strolled through the hotel entrance. "I need to find Kathy…she came here earlier. I'll see you at the Club on Thursday afternoon for our round of golf."

Kellogg spotted Fred Hawthorne, his dentist, hurtling down the hallway toward him. "Mr. X…George Clements invited Al McDonald and our wives to join your California golf vacation next month. I love Pebble Beach and so does Carrie…we're really looking forward to it."

"Well, Dr. Freddy…I may have to postpone it. I found out yesterday we have important zoning hearings coming up on a major project. I need to be around in case we need to bribe a few city officials."

"Huh?" Hawthorne was taken aback.

"Only kidding about the bribes, Freddy Boy."

"By the way, you're overdue for a teeth cleaning and a checkup."

"Yeah, I've got a little crack in one my molars too…it must from chewing ice cubes. My secretary will call for an appointment. You still have that cute dental assistant, right?"

"Yes, Pam is still with me. Now, please excuse me, Xander…I need to find my wife at the silent auction tables…Carrie wants to win a subscription to a jigsaw puzzle club…they send a new one every week."

"Wow, there will surely be a frenzy to bid on that one!"

Xander entered the expansive ballroom; it was a typical arrangement for a charity dinner with a sea of round table adorned with floral centerpieces, wine glasses and assorted plates. He noted the red flowers and napkins on the table, realizing why Jill chose to wear a red gown. Kellogg cast his eyes in a semicircular motion, hoping to spy more friends and business associates. He felt a tap on his shoulder and turned around, recognizing Lawrence Reagan, a principal of Reagan & Holbrook, the real estate brokerage firm handling the leasing on his West Tower project.

"Mr. X, good evening…so nice to see you."

"Hello Reagan…what are you doing at an affair like this? I didn't know brokers could afford black-tie events."

"Very funny, Xander! You know…R & H is a major contributor to charities in Denver. My business partner, Marty Holbrook, is on the board of the Archbishop's Orphanage Foundation, so we always buy two tables. I understand that your wife, Jillian, is co-chair for the event tonight."

"An orphanage, huh? Frankly, I didn't even know what charity I was here for…Jill never told me. I guess that's a fairly good cause…orphans probably need a safe place to go. And speaking of orphans, your two leasing brokers are lost. We gave you the leasing assignment a year ago on West Tower and they've produced nothing."

"I know they've been working hard, there's a lot of inventory out there and most tenants want to be downtown."

"Working hard...I'd say hardly working." Kellogg was pleased with his play on words.

"Nate Allen and Pete Simpson are here tonight...I'll find them so they can say hello."

"They're probably jacking off in the can. Shit, instead of getting drunk here tonight, they should be out cold calling tenant prospects."

"Mr. X, there are plenty of decisionmakers at this function...we're working for you twenty-four hours every day."

"If Ho and Hum find a prospect here, send them to Table 4, so I can cut a deal in the bar."

As Reagan spun away, Xander spotted Al and Donna McDonald, beating a path directly toward him. Blocked by other guests, he was trapped in a corner. "Xander, Donna and I are excited for the invitation to the California trip with you and George Clements. We'd like to add some wine tours in Napa to the itinerary...Jill should like that too."

"Yes, Jill is very good at whining." He laughed to himself. "I meant to say she's a member in two wine clubs."

"We haven't seen Jill tonight."

"You can't miss her...she looks like Little Red Riding Hood. Oh, I love your gown, Donna...those black and white squares could double as a checkerboard."

Donna glared at him. "My dress is actually a harlequin pattern. Grab another drink, Xander...since we're all friends, we'll overlook your condition tonight, but I know a doctor who can help with a sobriety problem."

"Excuse me, Donna...I need to speak with someone important over there."

Kellogg crossed the room where John Collins was surveying the auction items.

"Colly, I didn't know you were coming tonight." Kellogg was happy to see his friend and attorney.

"I didn't either until Margaret reminded me this afternoon...we attend this every year. The Archbishop is making an appearance any minute...the Catholic groupies will follow him around the room like sheep. They want their picture taken with him and will bid up the oral auction items to get his attention and approval."

Jill approached Xander and Collins. "It's so nice to see you tonight, John...thank you for supporting the Orphanage Fund. I hate to interrupt, but Xander and I need to welcome the guests at our table. And John, remember to bid high and bid often...it's for the children."

As they walked to their table Kellogg asked, "Who are your guests, Jill?"

"Archbishop Coolidge plus his assistant, Al and Donna McDonald, as well as Henry and Olivia Buckingham."

"Oh shit!"

"What's 'oh shit' supposed to mean?"

"You'll find out soon."

"Mr. and Mrs. Andrews round out our table guests."

"Who are they?"

"I met Nancy Andrews at my wine club. She and her husband, Franklin, are moving here from Houston, Texas. He's the CEO of an oil firm, but I'm warning you…please act appropriately and welcome them properly."

Jill led Xander by the arm to Table 4, located at the center front of the ballroom and introduced Xander to the Buckingham's. "Olivia and Henry…this is my husband, Alexander."

Henry Buckingham stayed seated and made no attempt to shake Kellogg's hand, while Xander looked away.

Olivia smiled. "Hello Mr. Kellogg...Henry and I are pleased you're a contributor to the Orphanage Foundation. We invited the Archbishop Coolidge to sit at our table tonight…Henry's on the board of directors."

"Oh, I know another gentleman on the board…Marty Holbrook."

"Yes, we've known Marty for many years. How do you know him?"

"His real estate firm is handling the leasing on one of my office buildings…I should say they're bumbling the leasing on my office building."

Jill smiled. "How nice everyone can make connections, right Xander?"

Kellogg ignored Jill's comment, noting Al and Donna McDonald's arrival at the table. Donna approached Jill, exchanging kisses on the cheek. "Hello Little Miss Riding Hood, it's so nice of you to invite us to your front table this evening?"

"Little Miss Riding Hood? I don't quite understand, Donna."

"Your husband told us you dressed as Little Red Riding Hood tonight…then he commented on my checkerboard dress."

Jill frowned at Xander, before turning to Donna and laughingly explained, "Xander knows a lot about real estate, but nothing about high fashion."

"Just making a little joke, honey." Kellogg leaned toward Al McDonald. "Al, after we spoke, I attended a temperance club meeting in the bar...I'm sober now."

"You're a funny fellow, Mr. X."

Jill continued scowling at Xander when the Andrews' couple arrived at their table. He was a tall man with the look of self-made success. She was pretty and petite with Texas style big hair.

"Hello Nancy...what a gorgeous gown."

"Thank you, Jillian. I bought it last year in Dallas. It's my favorite dress for these occasions. Your dress is exquisite, and your hair is lovely too." She grabbed her date's hand, pulling him closer. "This is my husband, Franklin, but everyone calls him Buck."

Buck kissed the back of Jill's hand. "It's so nice to meet you Franklin...I mean Buck."

"Howdy partners...happy to be with you for the roundup tonight." Buck spoke with a strong Texas twang.

Jill tugged at Xander's shoulder to engage him in the introductions. "Nancy and Buck, please meet my husband, Alexander, although he prefers Xander."

Xander stood up and reached out to shake Buck's hand with his firm grip, twisting slightly to the right. "Great to meet you both...I know a Tony Andrews from San Anton...any relation?"

"Nope."

"Buck, Jill tells me you're in the oil bidness." Xander tried his best at Texas slang.

"Yes, we're headquartered in Houston, although we're moving a large exploration division here in the next six months...about five hundred folks. We like the shale play on the western slope and in Wyoming."

"Do you have a building picked out yet?"

"We have some brokers working on options for us, although we really want to buy a building. Renting is a waste of money...real estate always goes up in value."

Jill interrupted. "Xander is constantly talking business. Nancy, I know that you're staying at the Brown Palace Hotel on your visits to Denver, but where are you looking to buy a house?"

"We've looked at several houses in Evergreen because it has a great Colorado mountain feel. Buck prefers a company location on the west side of the city, although there's more oil business networking downtown."

Kellogg instantly zeroed in on Buck's firm as a possible solution for his West Tower building, closely matching the size to house five hundred people. "Buck, I'd like a private word with you before the night is over."

"Sure, just let me know when."

Kellogg was distracted when Bill Douglas, the executive officer of Remington Properties, strolled past.

"Buck, please excuse me for a moment."

Kellogg instantly chased after Douglas. "Hi Bill, how are you? Let's talk about your site near the Colorado Boulevard interchange. I heard you're putting it on the market."

"That's just a rumor, Mr. X...you'll be the first to know if we decide to sell. That site is the last of our key pieces which will certainly define the quality of our overall development scheme. When we decide to sell, we'll pick the developer who has the best design."

"Bill, you should know that I'll hire a great architect and erect the most elegant building you would be proud to own yourself. Let's have lunch next week...I'll have my secretary arrange it."

"Can't wait, Mr. X."

The room was now buzzing with a commotion unfolding near the entrance of the ballroom. Seeing several bright camera flashes, Kellogg assumed the Archbishop had entered the ballroom. Straining his neck, he observed a large entourage following the patriarch on a circuitous path around the tables. Two photographers snapped continual photos of the benefactors, who crowded around the Archbishop for optimum positions. Colly was standing nearby to gain Kellogg's attention, as he pointed toward the Archbishop and nodded.

Needing to use the men's room, Kellogg flung the door open, spotting the two R & H leasing brokers, Pete Simpson, and Nate Allen, huddled in a bathroom stall. They quickly picked up a straw from the toilet lid, swept away some white powder on a notebook, and covertly pocketed a silver container. Looking surprised, they bumped each other trying to exit the stall.

"Hello Mr. X...how are you this evening?"

"Do in' well, boys. What are you up to... fishing for tenant prospects in the can or just trying to powder your nose?" As they approached Xander to shake his hand, Kellogg noticed a white residue around their nostrils.

"I just saw your boss out in the crowd...I'm sure he'd be happy to hear you're sniffing out some good tenant leads in here." He pivoted toward the urinals, ignoring their attempted greeting. "Please excuse me, but I don't like to shake hands with guys who just came out of the shitter."

After several seconds of silence, Simpson finally blurted out a comment. "Have a good night, Mr. X…we look forward to our meeting next week."

Kellogg continued to urinate. "You'd better get cracking on the leasing front!"

When Kellogg returned to Table 4, Archbishop Coolidge was seated along with his envoy. The Buckingham's had made introductions to everyone at the table but ignored Kellogg as he noted the empty chair between Donna McDonald and Olivia Buckingham. The Archbishop nodded at Kellogg, who circled the table. "Hi, Archbishop Coolidge…do they call you Archbishop Cool?"

"I'm usually called your Eminence or Archbishop Coolidge." He chuckled.

"My name is Alexander Kellogg III…they call me Xander and sometimes Mr. X."

"Mr. X is a strange name."

"Xander is spelled with an 'X'…just like one of those popes in Rome."

"I understand. This is my Envoy…Father Xavier." He pointed at a priest seated to his left. "His name begins with an 'X' too. Should we call him Father X?" The Archbishop smiled, his gracious manner was well known, even when speaking with fools.

"Sounds perfect. I'd like to meet sometime…I understand the archdiocese owns some great real estate. I'm a developer, so when you decide to sell any property, I'm your man." Kellogg snagged a business card from his suit pocket and placed it on the Archbishop's charger plate, although Father Xavier instantly picked it up.

Jill stood up instantly. "May I have a word with you, Xander."

"Not now, Jill...I want to speak with Mr. Andrews." He rotated around the table, signaling in the direction to the bar with his right hand. "Buck, will you join me in the bar upstairs?"

Buck shot up from his chair. "Absolutely, I'm not much of a wine drinker...I need a real drink."

"Let's go to Trader Vic's...the Polynesian décor is not typical for Denver, but theme restaurants are the trend these days. They're famous for a cocktail called a Mai Tai...it's too sweet for me though."

Kellogg pointed to two lavender colored stools at the side of Trader Vic's bar where he knew their conversation wouldn't be overheard.

"What do ya' drink, Buck

"Bourbon on the rocks."

Kellogg motioned to the bartender, an older man who furthered the Hawaiian theme by wearing white slacks, a loose fitting multicolor floral shirt and a yellow lei around his neck.

"Gentlemen...how about a Mai Tai right from the shores of Hawaii? I make a tasty one."

"Are you kidding me? That's a chick drink...I'll have a scotch whiskey...Glenfiddich. My pal here will have the best bourbon you have in stock."

The bartender looked confused.

Kellogg pointed at the back bar. "Charlie...should I write that down for you?"

"No sir…just trying to decide on our best bourbon."

"Just pour the most expensive one in stock."

Skipping any informal chitchat, Xander turned toward Andrews. "Buck, I'm a big real estate developer and built a beautiful five-story office building off the West 6th Freeway exit in Lakewood. From your employee count, it would be a perfect size for your operations. There's a small bank tenant on the first floor, but you could arrange the space plan for the balance of the building to suit your needs. It has great views from the top floors."

"Sounds interesting, but our leasing brokers are trying to convince us to locate downtown near the Petroleum Club…a lot of big oil deals go down there."

"The Petroleum Club is only a ten-minute drive from my building. Which brokerage firm is representing you?"

"I believe the name is Reagan & Holbrook…we actually have the top partner, Holbrook, working on it."

Kellogg bristled in his seat, his blood pressure rising. Ever the cool negotiator, he remained calm. He quickly picked up his glass, gulping the last bit of scotch. "Holbrook, eh…never met him, but I know his partner."

Kellogg reached inside his tuxedo for his business card, pressing it on the teak wood bar. "Buck, my firm is Kellogg Development Company…Kellogg is a premiere real estate brand in Denver. I have a contracting division too, so we could do all the tenant finish work and get you squared away in the building quickly. We know all the right people to pull the building permits too and a terrific space planner."

"Andrews reached into his suit pocket, displaying a glossy white business card. "Our COO in Houston is coordinating the leasing decisions…I'll write his name on the back." He searched his pockets for a pen.

Kellogg motioned to the bartender. "Hey Charlie...got a pen?"

The barkeeper plucked a black ballpoint from the back counter and placed it on the bar top. Andrews jotted down his executive's name on the card and handed it to Kellogg, who immediately examined it…an oil derrick image was etched in the top left corner, with Andrew's name and title of President & Chief Executive Officer printed in the center of the card. The cities of Dallas, Midland, and Oklahoma City were listed below his Houston headquarters' phone number and address.

"Your building sounds interesting but let us not get ahead of ourselves. We would need to establish a price that works for both of us…Holbrook could provide an opinion of value."

"We have an existing appraisal we could provide immediately." He hesitated a few second and motioned the bartender over. "Charlie…I'll take that whole bottle of bourbon my friend is drinking."

"Xander, you must know the bartender well since you know his name."

"Nope…I just like to use the name Charlie for strangers, but maybe I should address him as Don Ho with that getup." Kellogg chuckled, leaned forward, and lowered his voice. "So, Buck…don't mention my trophy office building to Holbrook yet. I'll need to speak to my investor partners to determine if they might consider a sale. Most of them are relying upon a steady cash flow from the rents…and certainly the value appreciation."

After the bartender poured the bourbon, Andrews instantly picked up the shiny glass and held it in front of his face, sported a giant smile, exposing a full mouth of brownish teeth. "Cheers!"

As Andrews raised his glass, Kellogg tried to look away but was captivated by the apparent chewing tobacco stains. "How about a cigar, Buck?"

"No thanks. I hate to admit this, but I like to chew. My old man got me hooked when I was twelve. Nancy tells me I need to get these damn teeth capped, but I told her it was just a waste of money."

"Yeah…dentists are all a bunch of terrorists. My guy, Fred Hawthorne, is only good at hiring cute receptionists. By the way, do you play golf?"

"Yup…I belong to two country clubs in Houston."

"I'm a member at The Platte Club…it's the most exclusive golf club in Denver. I could pull a few strings to expedite your membership…normally there is a five-year waiting list, even if a guy can make the cut but I can tell you would be a great addition. What do you shoot?"

"My handicap is about a twelve. I've heard great things about The Platte Club. I'll be commuting between Houston and Denver, and it may be strategic to have a connection like that for entertainment here."

"Let's have another drink and toast to it."

Chapter Three

Kellogg and Andrews abandoned the entire charity event, each polishing off a bottle of liquor at Trader Vic's lounge as they shared stories about hunting trips and building their respective businesses. Kellogg staggered as he rose from his bar stool, snagging the edge of the bar to remain upright. Andrews propped him up, as they stumbled toward the exit. After a few steps, Xander tripped on the carpet and fell face first on a cocktail table, splattering drinks over a man and woman, who instantly vaulted up to avoid the spill.

"Scuse me." Kellogg belched loudly and clumsily balanced himself on the table. He looked up, realizing the traumatized couple was Al and Donna McDonald. While Al dabbed his shirt and tuxedo jacket with a handkerchief, Donna rubbed her arms with a napkin.

"You're a drunken fool, Xander." McDonald held up his right fist, ready to punch Kellogg.

Kellogg burped again, searching a pocket for his money clip. Struggling to open it, Kellogg finally managed to snag a five-dollar bill and cast it on the table.

"Al Boy…here's a clean green napkin."

"Xander…look what you did to Donna's dress!"

Kellogg rubbed his eyes. "She can exchange it for a chessboard tomorrow."

McDonald grabbed Kellogg by the lapels of his tuxedo, shoving hm backwards into Andrew's arms. Buck pulled Kellogg aside, directing him toward the stairs. It took Kellogg several minutes to negotiate the steps, hanging tightly to Andrews' shoulder and the bannister.

Upon reaching the ballroom, Kellogg stumbled through the maze of tables knocking over several chairs. As he approached Jill, he tripped and fell, hugging his face to the carpet.

Jill's face was as red as her dress with anger. "Get up, you slob…you have some explaining to do."

"Why?" Bracing himself with a chair, he struggled to his feet. "Jill dear…this is my best buddy, Buck."

Jill glanced at Nancy Andrews and threw her arms in the air in disgust. "Nancy, what can I say…please accept my apology."

"Think nothing of it, Jillian…Buck does this all the time." Nancy lightly padded Jill's arm.

Although Buck wavered to maintain his balance, he was more coherent than Kellogg. "Xander just needs more practice to catch up to us Texans."

Jill was furious, turning to Kellogg. "The valet is pulling the car around…you're in no shape to drive, so I'll have to. Can you walk to the car or should I get you a room here tonight?"

"I'm fine…I love being chauffeured."

Jill sighed, briskly marching with Nancy toward the lobby. Andrews wrapped his right arm around Kellogg's waist, skillfully supporting him with each step. After five minutes, the pair reached the hotel lobby entrance and descended the stairs, one step at a time. Kellogg finally recognized the Mercedes 450SL parked a few feet away, where Jill sat impatiently in the driver's seat. A reluctant valet awkwardly helped Andrews tuck Kellogg into the passenger seat.

As Buck pointed his right thumb up, Jill smirked, turning the key to start the ignition. "Ya' all have a great evening…nice meeting you, Mrs. Kellogg." Buck slammed the passenger door shut.

Kellogg opened one eye with his fingertips and glanced at Jill. "Dear…why don't you drive?" Kellogg suddenly opened the car door and leaned out, vomiting on the pavement. Jill pulled him back into his seat, as the valet covered his mouth with his left hand and firmly closed the door.

Jill glared at Kellogg. "You're a drunken mess…now tell me why you called me Little Red Riding Hood?"

Kellogg launched into the first verse of the tune recorded by Sam the Sham and the Pharaohs.

"Shut up…you made a joke out of Donna's dress too!"

Kellogg took a deep breath and swallowed. He slapped his face several times, futilely trying to get some control of his speech. "It's a dress for all occasions. She can wear it to a dance and play checkers, tic tac toe, or chess on at the same time."

"That's a designer dress…she bought it at a trendy fashion store in Chicago. You're not funny at all Xander…you embarrassed me, you insulted my friends and left our table guests for the whole night." Jill threw her head back in a gesture of disgust. "I also understand that you had a furious argument with Henry Buckingham about some business and insulted him several times. Olivia told me all about it tonight."

Kellogg was quickly regaining his speech. "He represented a landowner on a deal I was putting together and interfered with the negotiations. I demanded to know if someone took the bar exam for him. I also congratulated him for cheating on the bartender's exam to pass the bar."

"Why do you continually need to insult people? I have worked so hard to build a social circle of nice people beyond your cronies at The Platte Club. How can you behave like this?"

Kellogg closed his eyes as Jill had drove away. Several blocks from the hotel, Kellogg peered out the side window as they passed City Park.

"Hey, there's our old family home. Why are you driving this way…are you lost?"

"I thought it might be good for you to go back to your roots. You're getting a little big for your britches. Your brother told me how poor you were growing up…and humble until you started making big money in real estate."

Kellogg rested his head back, closed his eyes again, and began to sort through his family history. Over the past six decades, the Kellogg family had seen its share of success and failures. Xander's grandfather, Alexander Kellogg I, was a rancher, who owned several thousand acres in eastern Colorado at the turn of the century. He struggled with finances, due to the volatility of agricultural and livestock prices, and the stress resulted in a fatal heart attack at the age of forty-seven. Xander's grandmother struggled to remain in the ranching business until her death in 1920, when Xander's father, Alexander II, took over the family affairs. Known as Junior, his father sold the ranch and homestead in 1925 and moved to Denver, where he began to purchase houses and a few small commercial properties.

Junior and his wife, Julia, lost their real estate holdings after the Great Depression, taking on a significant amount of debt. Xander recalled hearing stories of bank officials and the police serving foreclosure notices to his father. Junior's family was ultimately evicted from their home after a contentious bankruptcy process and were forced to move in with Julia's parents for several years. The years of fighting creditors took a toll on Junior, who killed himself in 1939, when Xander was eight years old.

Undetected by creditors prior to his bankruptcy, Junior transferred a quarter block of downtown land fronting Seventeenth Street to the KF Trust, whose trustee was John Collins, an attorney and confidant of Xander's father. The strategic parcel in downtown Denver was leased to a developer who built two four-story buildings on the site. The ground rent enabled the family to buy an older four-unit apartment where they lived in one of its small two-bedroom units. The income from the other three apartments and the ground rent paid for the family's needs, as well as the tuition for Xander and his brother, Robert, to attend the University of Colorado in Boulder.

Although Robert was three years older than Xander, they closely bonded growing up, using a toy grader and frontend loader to engineer roads in the family garden and inserted wooden boards as bridges. Julia bought them a building block set, where they competed creating unique designs. In high school, Robert and Xander learned to make minor repairs in the apartments as well as maintaining the grounds and parking lot. Julia, a part time bookkeeper for John Collin's law firm, taught Xander accounting, so he became responsible for maintaining the apartment's books. Eventually, Xander prepared the family tax returns.

After graduating from college in 1953 with a business degree, Xander served two years as an accounting clerk in the Army. Returning to Denver in 1955, he worked as a property manager for a portfolio of small apartment buildings, owned by John Collins. Gaining valuable experience, Xander began to purchase four-unit and eight-unit apartment buildings in 1960, primarily through estate liquidation sales. He managed the properties himself, screening each tenant personally. He relied on old trusted high school friends, who renovated and repaired the buildings. Robert left college after three years and began working in the construction industry and started a general contracting business in 1959, focusing primarily on office buildings.

Based upon the lessons learned from his father's loan problems, Xander financed his apartment acquisitions conservatively, relying primarily on cash equity raised by John Collins and his wealthy friends. By 1972, there was mass overbuilding of new apartment and condominiums projects in Denver, financed by aggressive real estate investment trusts and East Coast money center banks. Using Collins' connections, Xander began to purchase several defaulted mortgage notes, gaining title to the properties through aggressive foreclosure actions, as well as suing borrowers for deficiency judgements. Some of the projects were halted prior to construction completion while Xander waited patiently until the banks capitulated, struggling with vast construction problems and engineering deficiencies. Xander ultimately decided to add Robert as a fifty-percent partner in Kellogg Development Company in 1974, trusting an experienced contractor to complete the unfinished work and to erect additional apartment buildings on the vacant parcels slated for future phases.

The timing of the apartment acquisitions was perfect, as Denver's population soared in the mid-70's. The portfolio of multifamily buildings was fully leased, and cash flow increased significantly. However, John Collins, who was nearing retirement, wanted to liquidate the portfolio of eight larger projects and invest the profits in US Treasury bonds, fearing the economy would soon fall into a recession. Alexander debated with Collins about his decision since the long-term capital gain tax rate was forty percent. In addition, Kellogg's property management fees, covering all the business overhead, would quickly evaporate. Ultimately, Xander relented, respecting the family's lengthy relationship with John Collins.

By early 1978, all apartment projects had been sold, netting Kellogg Development Company six million dollars in after-tax profits. With apartments trading at a premium, the brothers focused their attention on developing office buildings. Their first endeavor was building a series of small professional office buildings near downtown Denver and the Cherry Creek area. Finding success, Kellogg Development ventured into the suburban market, developing a seventy thousand square foot, three story building, which Xander named Kellogg Plaza. Through a series of introductions, the pair partnered with ten physicians, developing three medical office buildings adjacent to the Swedish Hospital campus and two near Porter Hospital. Robert expanded the construction business for owner-users, including a dental building for Fred Hawthorne's practice.

Their office development activity was ramping up quickly and the generous development fees were addicting. In late 1977, Xander elected to proceed on the development of a two hundred thousand square foot speculative five-story office building, called West Tower, located in the western Denver suburb of Lakewood. Except for the parking lot and landscaping, the building was complete and tenant finish work was progressing on a five thousand square foot space leased to Continental Divide Bank. Xander also had several vacant sites on his radar screen for future office developments.

Kellogg finally opened his eyes as Jill stopped the Mercedes abruptly in the driveway, nearly striking his chest against the dashboard.

Jill muttered. "Wake up, dirt bag…we're home."

Kellogg growled, managing to find the door handle. He pushed the car door open, leaned out, and vomited again on the red brick driveway.

Jill was still livid. "You can sleep in the car all night for all I care…and by the way, the Archbishop expressed his thanks for your generous twenty-five-thousand-dollar donation. Henry Buckingham challenged you to match his gift and I knew you would not want to be outdone, so I put it on your American Express card. Good night!"

Xander crawled out of the Mercedes and knelt on the brick pavers. He twisted his head watching Jill open the front door and slam it behind her. The lights in the house progressively flicked on…first on the first floor and then to second floor bedroom area. He collapsed to the pavement, trying to launch more poison from his stomach. He struggled to crawl into the back seat of the sedan and tucked himself into a fetal position. Just before passing out, he murmured to himself, "Shit…I'll never drink alcohol again."

Chapter Four

A stream of blinding sunshine pierced Kellogg's eyelids as he huddled in the back seat of the Mercedes. He awkwardly turned his left wrist, attempting to read his Rolex watch…six-twenty. He glanced at his soiled shirt and tuxedo, covered in a crusty yellowish-brown pattern…his black shoes and trousers were splattered with similar spots. His head was exploding, as if being pounded with a sledgehammer. He rolled his tongue over his teeth, feeling a molar had cracked off, rubbing his finger repeatedly over its rough edge. Rolling over, he noticed the back door was ajar and the overhead car light was on, apparently burning all night long.

Kellogg's memory of the previous evening was clouded, although he suddenly recalled the discussion with Buck Andrews about their office space needs and something else about a twenty-five thousand credit card charge. He checked his left pant pocket…clumsily extricating Buck Andrews' business card, nearly bending it in half. He lifted it to his bloodshot eyes and turned it over, studying Rusty Affenson's name scratched out in blue ink. Xander sat upright in the backseat and whispered to himself, "It's almost seven-thirty in Houston…he'll be in his office soon."

After last night's episode, he feared Jill would shoot him with one of his prized pistols if he attempted to enter the house…she would have a perfect excuse, fearing an intruder was breaking into the house in the early morning darkness.

Xander crawled out from the car, positioning himself on the cool brick driveway on his hands and knees. He firmly grasping the door handle, pulling himself slowly to his feet and steadied himself against the car door. Still dizzy, he stumbled toward the garage, following the red brick pathway to the side door. Bracing himself on the door frame, he knelt to retrieve a key hidden beneath a flower planter box. He wriggled the key repeatedly into the door lock and after several attempts, finally realized he was inserting it upside-down. Successfully opening the door, he reached for the light switch and shuffled over to the Corvette, spotting the key in the ignition. He reached for the door handle, opened the heavy door, and clumsily collapsed into the bucket seat. He started the engine, stepped on the gas pedal, and threw the gear into reverse. A loud crash followed, shattering the morning's silence. Kellogg jammed his right foot against the brake, his neck smashing against the headrest. Momentarily stunned, he cranked his neck to the right to observe the damage. The wooden planks on the garage door were shredded, and the steel frame was hanging gingerly from the supports.

Kellogg muttered, "Shit...who closed the garage door?" He shifted the car into a forward gear, nursing it ahead six feet and shut off the engine. He struggled to lift himself from the seat, gradually pulling himself out with his left arm, and shuffled over to the Buick Regal sedan, parked a few feet away. He opened the driver's door and leaned in, unable to locate the key in the ignition, the console, or above the sun visor. Kellogg staggered to the new black Chevrolet C/K truck but couldn't locate the key either. Resigned to drive the Corvette, Kellogg climbed back into the convertible and flicked the button to close the black rag top cover. He revved the engine twice and threw the transmission into reverse, smashing through the remaining sections of the garage door. Parked in the driveway, he surveyed the area, now filled with debris. He glanced up at the house, noticing the curtains part in the second-floor master bedroom window. He instantly looked away and thrust the gas pedal to the floorboard, the tires screeching as he zipped down the drive.

Five minutes later, as Kellogg sped along Hampden Avenue, he heard the faint sound of a siren. Glancing in the rearview mirror, he observed a police car quickly closing. He reluctantly coasted the Corvette to the curb as the policeman parked the squad car several feet behind. After the officer exited his car and drew closer to the driver's side of the Corvette, Xander recognized Roger Clements in the sideview mirror. Xander cranked down the window, rolled his head in a counterclockwise motion and glanced up at Roger, who towered three feet above him. Blinded by the sparkling sun, Kellogg shaded his eyes with his left hand, before securing his sunglasses.

"Mornin' Roger…you're working early today…what's up?"

"Hello, Mr. Kellogg…I didn't know it was you at first. You look like hell."

"My head is killing me, and my tooth is cracked for some reason…I didn't sleep too well last night either."

"Mr. Kellogg, I clocked you driving fifty-two…the speed limit posted is thirty-five miles per hour. Your rear license plate is missing, and the rear reflectors are also broken?"

"Shit…I accidentally backed into the garage door this morning and didn't even notice the plate was ripped off. It's probably sitting on the driveway…I'll pick it up later before I take the car to the shop." Kellogg slipped out of the Corvette, sauntered around the front fender, bent down, and pointed. "Roger, the front plate with my custom print, MRX007, is still attached."

Clements checked the license plate to be certain. "I get the Mr. X, but what about 007?"

"Seven is my lucky number and friends say I look like Roger Moore, the James Bond actor."

Officer Clements squinted at Kellogg's face. "Perhaps a little …so Commander Bond, you need to get this taken care of right away. I'll call a wrecker service and have the car towed in."

"Geez Roger…can you give me a little slack? I'm late for my morning work-out at The Platte Club."

"Look, Mr. Kellogg…I'm going to give you a break by not giving you a speeding ticket, so I suggest you take my advice." Officer Clements adjusted his cap and tightened his square jaw.

"How about I give you ten bucks and we just forget about it?" Kellogg grinned as he reached for his wallet.

Officer Clements instantly detached the cuff links from his belt. "Stop…my dad has known you well for a long time, but I won't be bribed, no matter how much you offer me. I can restrain you right now for resisting arrest if you want to push this further."

"Oh, come on, Roger…I was just joking with you." He winked. "Okay, call the wrecker service …and a taxi too."

"Jump in my patrol car and I'll drive you to The Platte Club."

"Roger that, Roger…I appreciate it." Kellogg laughed heartily, although Clements' face remained grim.

As Kellogg walked around the back of the Corvette to inspect the damage, Clements called for the wrecker service. "The tow truck will be here in a couple of minutes…they had one in the area." He looked at Kellogg's face again. "Sir, if you're not feeling well, do you want me to call your wife?"

"Hell no…although it's okay for you to call her a bitch."

"Hmmm…I've never met her. She's that bad, huh?"

"Worse…she has no sense of humor!"

"I really liked your old wife...Colleen, right?"

"Roger...Colleen was my second wife and we were married nearly fifteen years. After we divorced, she got a law degree and is doing pretty well from what I hear."

"I didn't know you had another wife before Colleen."

"Yeah...a colossal mistake. Her name was Janice and we fell in love during college and got married when we were only twenty-two after she got pregnant with Alexander IV...I mean Buster. Our marriage only lasted two years. She works for a title company now and I heard she has a big gambling problem."

"That's too bad. I haven't seen Buster for a few years...how's he doin'?"

"I haven't spoken to him in six months, but he'll be calling soon when he needs some dough again. He's nearing the end of his probation for a marijuana possession conviction in California. He's twenty-four now, so he may grow up one of these days. It was probably a mistake sending him to college out there. All he did was fuck around and hang out at the bars. Last year, I set him up as an intern at a real estate brokerage firm in Los Angeles, but they let him go after he was habitually late for meetings. I'd like to get him back here in Denver and get him involved in the development business, but I'll have to convince my brother, Robert."

"Good luck...I hope that it works out for both of you."

The wrecker pulled up and the driver maneuvered the tow truck in front of the Corvette. Kellogg flipped the car keys to him. "Hey Charlie, haul this over to Harv's Auto Repair...tell Harv Mr. X will call later. Be careful...that's an expensive car!"

"Yes sir." The overweight driver saluted him and bent down to attach a hook to the car chassis, brushing the metal chain against the front bumper.

"I said be careful, chubby!" The tow truck driver ignored him.

Roger Clements grabbed Kellogg's shoulder, pointing to the police cruiser. "Jump in the front seat and relax…the fellow is doing his best." Officer Clements plugged his nose with his fingers. "Peeuw…it appears you had another accident the way your clothes smell."

"Yeah, a few more shots than I could handle last night…I must be losing it. I'll clean up and change clothes at the Club."

Kellogg twisted in the front seat, trying to find a comfortable position in the patrol car. "Jesus, Roger…they sure don't make these car seats very cozy." He rolled down the window for some fresh air.

"Our guests typically sit in the back seat, which is even worse."

As they pulled away, Kellogg looked back, seeing the Corvette hoisted off the ground.

Five minutes later, the police car slowly approached the gated entrance into The Platte Club, passing the vacant guard house.

"Roger, just pull up at the front entrance."

"I hope that your day gets better, Mr. Kellogg."

"Thanks again, Roger…and let's forget about my little ten-dollar gift offer."

"I already have."

Kellogg slammed the car door and hopped up three brick steps to enter the clubhouse. Upon opening the large oak doors, he encountered The Platte Club general manager, Rex Wilson, who wore a blue suit and his traditional bowtie.

"Good morning Mr. Kellogg. You must be privileged to get a ride in a squad car"

"Hi there Rexy Boy…I am incredibly special. My car broke down and the police officer, George Clements' son, gave me a lift."

Wilson studied his suit and shoes. "Hmmm…it looks like you have some special stains on your clothes and shoes."

"A clumsy waiter spilled his tray all over my tuxedo last night. You know…hotel waiters aren't as good as the Platte Club staff."

"Must have been a long night…you don't look too well."

"Looks can be deceiving…one of the best nights ever. I gotta get in the locker room to shower now. Can you call a taxi for me, Rexy Boy?" I need to go to my office near Belleview Avenue and I-25 in thirty minutes."

Kellogg took a left turn and hustled down the hall to the men's locker room. Rounding the corner of his locker row, he nearly bumped into George Clements.

"George…why are you here so early? I almost crashed into you."

"I'm here early for a massage…I really need it after Kathy jumped me last night." Clements scanned Kellogg's black-tie outfit. "Christ…why are you still wearing your tuxedo and what's that crud on it?"

"Jill got drunk and threw up on me."

"Wow…I saw her at the end of the party last night and she seemed fine. Kathy and I congratulated her on such a successful event. It was generous of you and Henry Buckingham to kick off the appeal by giving twenty-five thousand each. It really opened everyone's hearts and wallets for the orphans…we only gave ten-thousand."

Kellogg now remembered what Jill had told him about the donation "Shit…I really donated that much?"

"You didn't…but Jill used your bid paddle."

"Maybe I can retract the bid…I spent the entire gala at Trader Vic's with the husband of her new friend from Houston. They came over to our house after the event…it was a hell of an afterparty. Boy…Texans can really drink. We polished off a few bottles, but Jill obviously couldn't keep up, although I held my own."

"I don't know about that…you look like shit. Your eyes are bloodshot, and I can see a piece of your tooth is missing."

"Fuck…is it really that noticeable? I'll call Fred Hawthorne later…he'll get me in right away. I knew there was a reason to check out his gal Pam again…what a body!"

"Yeah…she's pretty cute."

"Last night Dr. Freddy was pumping me about our trip to Monterrey. Why did you tell him about it…I had to make up an excuse?"

"I thought you had already invited him."

"No…he's boring and his wife is even worse. I'd like to talk more but I need to get cleaned up and to the office. Where's the damn shoeshine boy…he needs to scrape this shit off my shoes."

"I saw a sign on his door that he would be out today. Have a nice day, Xander."

"Great…just the time I need the little turd." Kellogg quickly showered and shaved and tossed on a golf shirt, khaki trousers, and a pair of white tennis shoes he stored in his locker.

Kellogg arrived at his office at eight-thirty. Phyllis was getting organized as he raced by her desk. "Honey, I need two cups of strong black coffee and five aspirins…my head is ringing like a bell."

"Right away, sir."

Kellogg pulled Andrews' business card from his wallet and hastily picked up the phone receiver and started dialing. After two rings, the receptionist answered in a distinct southern twang. "Andrews Oil…how may I help you?"

"Can I speak to Rusty Affenson?"

"I'm sorry sir…he's in a meeting."

"Interrupt him…Buck Andrews told me that he would take my call at any time. My name is Alexander Kellogg from Denver…Xander Kellogg."

"Please hold the line, Mr. Kellogg."

Kellogg waited impatiently for several minutes, tossing his business cards, one by one, toward a small garbage.

"I'm sorry, Mr. Kellogg…he says he doesn't know you, but will try to call you later today."

"Listen miss, I want to speak with him NOW…get him on the phone!"

"Please wait, sir."

Kellogg now paced back and forth around his desk, stretching the phone cord to its maximum length. After three minutes, he placed the phone on a speaker mode, so he could examine his tooth in the mirror.

Finally, the receptionist reported back. "Mr. Kellogg, he's still tied up on an important conference call and will call you in an hour."

Kellogg was exasperated as he picked up the receiver. "You didn't even try to interrupt him, did you...what's your name?"

"Dixie."

"Well Dixie...fuck YOU!" Kellogg slammed the phone receiver down which bounced across the desk on to the floor. Phyllis came through the open office door carrying a tray with two cups of coffee, a glass of ice water, and five tablets artfully arranged on a small plate. She placed the tray on his desk and picked up the receiver and hung it back on the cradle.

"That's not a nice hang up, Mr. Kellogg...here are your beverages and five aspirins."

"A bimbo receptionist kept me on hold for ten minutes...TEN MINUTES...can you believe that? If a guy named Affenson from Andrews Oil calls me, put him right through. Now, order Eli Cohen to come here right now."

Thirty seconds later, Eli Cohen knocked on Xander's door.

"Enter." Kellogg glanced at Cohen. "Have those R & H broker clowns ever mentioned a tenant prospect called Andrews Oil Company...they're out of Houston."

"Never...why?"

"I'll tell you later. That's it...get to work!"

Phyllis rang over the intercom. "Mr. Kellogg...your wife is on the phone."

"Which one?"

"Jill...she sounds agitated."

"Damn it...why did you tell her I was here?"

"Because you're here sir and you didn't warn me otherwise."

"Okay, put the call through." Xander tossed all five aspirins in his mouth and slugged them down his throat with two gulps of water. He took a large sip of coffee, sat back in his chair, and picked up the receiver. "Good morning dear...how are you?"

"I feel great, dumb ass...but our driveway is full of wood debris, the frame around the middle garage door is shattered and your Corvette license plate is laying in the flowers. How can you be so stupid...were you still drunk this morning?"

"The car accidentally was in reverse and I thought that the garage door was open...I already have the car in the shop. Aren't you concerned if I was hurt?"

"Are you kidding? I hope that you broke your nose after embarrassing me last night in front of all my friends, especially Nancy Andrews...I don't know her that well."

"Forget about her...I made a long-lasting friendship with Buck, which may be valuable...more money for your next fling in Paris. How about dinner at The Platte Club tonight to celebrate your successful event?"

"Are you joking? Last night, Donna McDonald told me you've had dozens of trysts with Jackie Jones at your apartment building...you even keep a unit for her, so I fired her today."

"Donna is a liar...Jackie's the best maid you've ever hired."

"How many extramarital affairs have you had since we've been married?"

"None…are you going to believe me or a lady who wears checkerboard clothes and who's idea of a good time is to do jigsaw puzzles?"

"You're a cheating bastard…I'm changing the locks on the house, so don't bother coming home. I found one of your prize pistols and will shoot you if you try to break in. I've called a lawyer and I'm filing for divorce."

"You'll soon regret that!"

"I regret I didn't file the papers sooner…how could I be so stupid all this time?"

Kellogg slammed the receiver against the wall, causing Phyllis to rush in the office. "What's wrong now?"

"Shit…another marriage down the tubes. Oh well…she won't get any assets under the prenuptial agreement. I just checked it last week. I'll only pay her three thousand a month…a grand for each year we were married. I'll call John Collins to initiate an eviction process to remove her from my house."

"You're always planning ahead, Mr. Kellogg."

"How about joining me for dinner tonight at The Platte Club?"

"I have a date tonight."

"Yeah…with ME!"

"No, a real date this time. I met a guy a few weeks ago and I want to get to know him better."

"It won't last…let me know when you're ready to fly with me to Acapulco again. Can you call Linda Melrose? I need some clothes fast…and phone Fred Hawthorne's dentist office to get an emergency appointment set up after lunch for my cracked tooth. One more thing…pick up the business cards scattered on the floor…a few landed in the garbage can too."

"Yes sir." She pivoted across the room and began to collect the cards.

Kellogg stood up abruptly, gazing into the mirror at his tooth. He snatched a stick of gum, chomping on it repeatedly for a minute. He reached in his mouth with his fingers, pulling out the whitish glob and pushed up against the molar, expecting it to cover the damage. After shaping it several times with his thumbs, he gave up, flinging the gum ball in the trash can.

The intercom buzzed. "Mr. Kellogg…you have a one-thirty appointment at Dr. Hawthorne's office and your son is also holding for you…he's calling collect."

"I knew that I would be hearing from him soon." Kellogg closed the office door and picked up the receiver. "Buster, my lad…how's it going?"

"Not that great, Pop…I need money fast. Please wire me two thousand bucks this afternoon…I'm three months in arrears on my apartment rent."

"Haven't you've been staying in a halfway house during your probation. Why do you still need an apartment?"

"For all the crap I've been collecting out here…do you expect me to move it all into a self-storage unit?"

"How much longer will your probation last…I want you back in Denver."

"The probation is actually over...it was revoked this morning." He paused. "I was arrested for selling grass to an undercover cop...it's total bullshit! A friend of mine set me up to reduce his own sentence. It wasn't fair...he took advantage of me."

"You're selling that stuff now...what were you thinking?"

"I didn't want to ask you for more money, so I thought I'd make a few hundred bucks peddling pot to some of my buddies...I know a guy who grows it."

"You're a fucking moron, Buster...you should know better."

"I know I let you down again, Pop. But please, can you wire the money now...it's actually for my bail."

"You're pissing me off...stop lying to me. I don't want to hear any more. I'm placing you on hold and you can tell Phyllis where the wire needs to be sent."

Xander pushed the hold button. "Phyllis, pick up the line...Buster will give you instructions to wire him two thousand from my private company account. Then call Peavy to invoice two grand for the next draw on the West Tower loan as a miscellaneous consulting fee and direct it back to my personal account next month."

"Yes sir. The gentleman from Houston has been holding for you a couple of minutes...I believe his name is Affenson."

Kellogg snagged the receiver immediately "Mr. Affenson, how's it going down there in Houston today?"

"No, this is Dixie Oliver...the lady you wanted to have sex with, Mr. Kellogg. It might be difficult trying long distance, but I'm always up for a challenge. Hold for Mr. Affenson, please."

"Ah...ah...okay then."

"Mornin' Mr. Kellogg." Affenson drawl was so thick and elongated that Kellogg had to place the receiver tightly against his ear.

"Howdy there, partner…thanks for getting back to me so soon."

"Buck told me that you were a real bubba who likes to get right to it. I heard you had some phone sex with our gal, Dixie. She likes that kind of dirty talk…I guess she's used to it hanging around wildcatters all these years."

"She's sounding better all the time. So, Mr. Affenson…can I call you Rusty?"

"Sure, as long as I can you Mr. X."

"Why not…most of my close friends do. Buck must have spoken to you…did he mentioned my office building we just built on the west side of town…it's called West Tower?"

"Yep…sounds interesting. I've had two building tours in Denver with our brokers. Where's your building located?"

"Right on Union Boulevard off the 6th Avenue Freeway…it's a terrific location with great views from the top floors."

"Yeah…I remember driving past your building last week with Marty Holbrook. I saw the R & H leasing sign and asked about it, but he said the building was fully preleased. I got the impression he wanted us to locate in a newer office in downtown Denver where R & H has another listing."

"Which building is that?"

"It's called the 1010 Building…the one with a glass atrium at the top. We lease a thousand square foot office there now on a short-term basis."

"Yes, I know the project. I thought Buck wants to buy a building…the 1010 building is not for sale as far as I know.

Rusty…my property is not fully preleased, although I've got a stack of letters of intent on my desk to lease the building twice over. My partners want to keep the property for cash flow, but based upon Buck's interest in buying a building, I've already spoken with two of my investors this morning who would entertain a purchase offer."

"I'll call Marty Holbrook and inform him right away."

"Let me call Marty…I know him well. We can cut through a lot of crap, just to see if we're in the ballpark on price and timing. If Marty calls you, don't mention this conversation…okay?"

"No problem…my jaws are scaled."

"Great…have a super day, Rusty. I'll call you back soon…and say hello to Dixie for me."

Kellogg promptly called Cohen directly. "Eli… do you know who provided the equity for the 1010 Building downtown?"

"I heard all of the major brokers at R & H provided the capital for the developer, Abe Friedman…why?"

"Never mind." Kellogg abruptly hung up and quickly dialed John Collins.

"Hello Mr. X."

"How did you know it was me?"

"The phone number that you called is dedicated only to you."

"Great idea…I just got off an interesting call. I discovered Marty Holbrook from R & H is representing a Houston company that's relocating to Denver. Last week, he told their COO West Tower was fully leased when they drove past. That's an outright lie…he obviously knows it's nearly all vacant. Holbrook is pushing the firm to locate in a downtown building where several R & H brokers hold a major equity stake. I know the Texas company could be interested in buying West Tower. I want to terminate my listing agreement with R & H, so I can deal with the Houston firm directly."

"That's very risky, Mr. X. Reagan & Holbrook would have a good case against you, as well as the company, for collusion by avoiding the payment of a brokerage fee."

"But not when Holbrook is playing games…right?"

"Ethically, you're correct, although a judge or jury may not see it that way. You're on some thin ice here, plus the company would be exposed to litigation too."

"What if some time passes to delay a closing date?"

"The listing agreement may protect the brokers for a defined period after registering a tenant or buyer."

"Holbrook hasn't presented our building to the company and even told them West Tower was fully leased…we have a great argument."

"Maybe, but I'll have to review your listing agreement to provide more advice…can you fax it?"

"These fax machines are unreliable and too messy…we'll run the agreement down to you quickly. One more thing, Colly…Buster was arrested overnight for selling dope and called for bail money. Can you call your lawyer friend in Los Angeles again and get him on the case right now? Thanks."

Xander paced back and forth in his office when Phyllis interrupted. "Your tailor is waiting in the lobby, Mr. Kellogg."

"Show Linda to my office…but there's one more thing, Phyllis. Earlier, you told me that Mr. Affenson was holding, but when I picked up the phone, I heard a receptionist's voice…never make that mistake again!"

"Yes, Mr. Kellogg."

Kellogg sauntered over to the mirror again to fluff up his hair and scrape his front teeth with his fingernails. He opened a drawer, locating a tin container of mints and popped two in his mouth. After hearing a knock at the door, Kellogg escorted Linda Melrose, his personal tailor, into the office and closed the door, securing the lock. He wrapped his hands around her thin body and immediately kissed her lips for three seconds, before she gently pushed him away.

"Darling…not feeling romantic today?" Her blonde hair glistened in the sun shining through the south facing windows.

"I was very busy this morning, Mr. X…but I rushed over here after your secretary said you were in a bind for some new clothes."

"My bitchy wife locked me out of the house again, so I won't be able to get to my stuff for a few days. Can you do a few quick measurements and pick out a few new outfits at Moss and Charles Custom Clothiers? You can bring them tonight when I meet you for dinner at The Platte Club."

"I'll arrange for the clothes to be delivered tonight, but I can't make dinner…I'm meeting a new client at an airport hotel at six o'clock…a referral who only has two hours between connecting flights."

"It's ironic you help people buy clothes, but make more money removing them." Kellogg chuckled. "Get the tape out…I might have added a half inch since you last measured me."

"Okay, let me stand behind you."

"No…this time, just kneel in front."

"If you insist." She pulled her skirt up slightly, bent down on her right knee, and extended the tape around his waist, securing it in front. "Closer to thirty-six inches now."

Kellogg reached down and began to unzip his fly. "I've also added a half inch to my equipment since you last measured it too."

She jumped up instantly. "Not today, Mr. X."

He groaned. "Come on, Linda…what's the problem? I've paid you well over the years."

"Yes, you certainly have and thank you…what wardrobe should I select for you?"

"One black suit, a blue pinstripe with narrow stripes, and a grey one with matching vests. I'll also need a blue blazer with charcoal grey slacks, two pairs of khakis, four white and two blue cotton dress shirts. You can select the colors and patterns for five ties. Pick out a pair of brown loafers and black dress shoes…size 11D…socks, handkerchiefs, and matching belts. Also, order a couple suspenders and make sure the trousers include buttons for them."

"How about underwear?"

"You should know by now I often don't wear any, but just for a change, add six pair of white boxer shorts."

Linda scribbled feverously. "What else?"

"A quick blow job would be nice."

"Not today, Mr. X." Looking exasperated, she unlocked the door, opened it, and strutted down the hallway. Kellogg gawked at her long legs until she was out of sight. She was beautiful and smart with an ingenious cover for her call girl business as a tailor.

Having skipped breakfast, Xander was starving.

"Phyl...if Robert is in the office today, call him to see if he is available for lunch."

"I heard his voice earlier...I'll check."

Xander picked up the phone receiver and phoned John Collins again. "Colly, get a court order so I can evict Jill from my house...she's filing for divorce. I checked our prenup...she must vacate the house within twenty-four hours upon serving me with divorce papers. I'm expecting they'll be delivered any minute."

"Sorry to hear that, Mr. X."

"Not as sorry as I am. I shouldn't have surrendered to her constant begging to get married three years ago."

"I have a copy of the prenuptial agreement in our files. I'll review it and ask a clerk to run it over to Judge Watson's office this afternoon. He owes me a favor, so I'll request a quick turnaround."

Phyllis poked her head through the open door. "Robert said that he could have lunch...drop by his office when you're ready to go."

"Thanks...please call The Platte Club for a lunch reservation in twenty minutes. I'll be at Hawthorne's dentist office right after lunch and back here by three."

"Have a nice lunch, Mr. Kellogg."

Xander meandered through the hallway maze, where the operations for Kellogg Construction Company was housed on the opposite end of the third floor. He strolled into Robert's office, which also overlooked I-25.

"Hey Robby Boy...what's new?"

"Just the normal shit dealing with our lazy subcontractors…I'm not sure why we keep using those union shops. We're running four weeks behind on two medical office buildings and our doctor partners are getting pissed."

"I need to see Fred Hawthorne a little later with a tooth problem…how's his dental building progressing?"

"Our concrete guy is late too…we need to get the foundation work done soon, before it turns cold."

"I'll just tell him that we're ahead on timing…dentists are the most gullible people I know. Let's get to lunch…we'll need to take your truck though. I had a little accident with the Corvette this morning trying to back out of the garage."

"What about your other three vehicles?"

"The keys were missing…I slept in the Mercedes last night after Jill drove home from a fundraiser at the Cosmopolitan Hotel. I was drunk and she locked me out of the house. She's filing divorce papers later today."

"I always thought she was a bit aggressive."

"It was time to get rid of that slut. She's not like Gwen…how long have you two been married now?"

"Coming up on thirty years in December."

"Congratulations…I'll start hunting for spouse number four soon."

"From all the stories I've heard about your extramarital affairs, it seems you're working on wives ten and eleven."

"As they all say, variety is the spice of life."

"You might be more careful…your pecker might fall off one of these days."

They hopped into Robert's Chevy C/K truck and were off to lunch at The Platte Club.

Chapter Five

Robert Kellogg drove his pickup truck into The Platte Club entrance, veering left past the guard house into the main parking lot.

Xander pointed toward the porte cochere. "Robby Boy...use the valet."

"I'll have to pay a tip, so I'll park it myself."

"You're always worried about spending a couple bucks. I expense tips as miscellaneous business expenses and Peavy buries them in my loan draws."

Robert shook his head, signaling his disapproval.

"Robby Boy...park in the remote lot," directing him to the right. "The club members will be pissed if a mud-covered truck is parked near their cars. I'm not sure trucks are even allowed here unless they're related to some official construction work. Look...there's a spot behind those bushes where it should be out of sight."

"Xander, just tell those smug pricks the truck belongs to a landscape guy."

"The Club requires all maintenance vehicles to be perfectly clean before they're allowed to enter the grounds. The guard must have taken a break, or he wouldn't have let you past the gate."

After Robert parked, they walked around the side entrance to the clubhouse, where Rex Wilson intercepted them. "Mr. Kellogg, you should know that trucks aren't allowed on the grounds unless they are a pre-approved service contractor... it's covered in mud too!"

"Relax Rexy Boy, this is my brother Robert, who runs our contracting division. He's preparing a bid on some renovations to the pool and the tennis courts. I told him to park the rig in back, so the members couldn't see it."

"You better hope not...I could be fired, and you could be expelled as a member. I haven't heard about any construction projects."

"I guess you don't know everything, Rex. If someone is pissed about the truck, tell them to speak with me. We're having lunch, so escort us to a nice table in a private area of the dining room."

"Of course, sir."

Wilson directed them to a table where Kellogg could look out toward the eighteenth green and Mount Evans. "This will do Rexy Boy...tell our waiter I'll have a Glenfiddich scotch on the rocks. How about you Robby Boy?"

"An iced tea, please."

"Your waitress' name is Chanelle...she just started last week. I'll give her your drink orders."

Xander raised his eyebrows at Robert. "Chanelle, huh? Her name sounds romantic."

"Are you already adding her to your future spousal trial list?"

"I'll let you know when she arrives. Other than the delays on the medical buildings, how's everything going at the construction company?"

"Pretty well...we're bidding on three shopping center projects, two large apartment developments, and a hundred thousand square foot warehouse for AM Products, Al McDonald's manufacturing company."

"Al McDonald, eh? He's a good friend…I just saw Al and his lovely wife, Donna, last night at the Archbishops' Orphanage Fundraiser although he didn't mention the project. How are my nephews doing?"

"Terrific! I knew that they would make great contributions to Kellogg Construction Company. Bobby's degree from CU in Spanish has really helped…our non-union subs are hiring more Hispanic workers every month and he can communicate more effectively with them than the veteran foremen. Skip's accounting experience has created some breakthroughs in our bidding process and tightened up on our costs."

"Great to hear…families are such an important part of our history and why I decided to bring you in under the Kellogg flag four years ago. Mom and Dad would be proud of what we've built. I want to bring Buster back and involve him in our operations somewhere."

"We've been over this before, Xander. I like Buster, but he's doesn't have any work ethic and his substance abuse issues will be a huge distraction."

"He's only guilty of having a few too many beers now and then…who hasn't done that?"

"It's more than that…I understand he was arrested for smoking pot and expelled from three community colleges. He also blew the internship your arranged at the brokerage firm in Los Angeles."

"Who told you that?"

"Your former wife, Janice…I saw her at the Western States Title office when we I dropped off the last batch of lien waivers."

"Janice is lying about Buster to get back at me. She was a lousy mother and now has an acute gambling addiction…maybe hard drugs too. Robby…Mom would have wanted all her grandsons to be involved in the family business. Please keep an open mind…we can give Buster a six-month probationary period for you to get comfortable with his progress."

"Only if you don't interfere and let me be the sole judge of his accomplishments."

"I agree. It may take time to convince him to come back to Denver…he's hooked on surfing, although the ski season is fast approaching."

"I recall the championships he won for his high school ski team."

A stunning waitress suddenly appeared at the table carrying two glasses. "Good afternoon, Mr. Kellogg…I have your drinks."

Xander studied her slender frame and her dark brown hair, pinned back in a ponytail. He gazed at her face, focused on her high cheekbones, then moving to her sparkling brown eyes. "You must be Chanelle?"

"Yes, sir."

"It's my privilege to meet such a beautiful young woman…are you a model?"

She blushed. "No."

"I understand you're new here…it's so nice to have you at The Platte Club."

"Thank you…our family recently moved to Denver from New York City and I work to pay my tuition at the University of Denver."

"What part on New York? I know the City well. I get there frequently to see my bankers on Park Avenue."

"We lived in White Plains…the Westchester area, just north of the City."

"I've played golf nearby at Winged Foot and Quaker Ridge."

"I've never played golf, so don't know those places...have you gentlemen decided on lunch?"

"I didn't see your name on the menu, but I'd like to order out." Xander flashed a grin.

"I beg your pardon...I don't understand." She took a step back from the table.

"I'd like to take you around and show you the sites of Denver. I'm developing several major office buildings that will change the skyline of the City." Kellogg pointed out toward Mount Evans through the expansive glass windows.

"Thanks, but college keeps me very busy...plus the hours working here."

"I'll keep my calendar open for you...any time." He turned to Robert. "Robby Boy, let's both have the BLT special and a cup of French Onion soup." Robert nodded.

"Is that it, Mr. Kellogg?"

"We'll discuss dessert, although I've already decided what I'd like to order."

"I'll be happy to write it down now."

"Chanelle, please let me know when you have a day off."

She smiled and turned away.

Robert chuckled. "Brother, I haven't seen you close up in action since high school, but your performance was smooth...real smooth. I don't know how she can resist you. Of course, she's only about twenty-one and probably hasn't heard those clever up pickup lines before."

"Don't be so certain…New York City is in the fast lane."

"Yeah…but Denver is still a sleepy cow town to most folks."

"Not for long Robby Boy…the mining and oil exploration business will put Denver on a high growth trajectory. That's why I'm talking to Bill Douglas at Remington Properties for his prize office site on Colorado Boulevard and patiently waiting to control the leasehold interests on the buildings over our Seventeenth Street parcel. Buster can help us with our new projects…we'll need all hands-on deck."

"You were always the dreamer, Xander, but please don't lead us into a nightmare. I hope you've got something up your sleeve on West Tower…I learned the bank made a capital call."

"Where did you hear that?"

"Who doesn't know with all the shouting from your office this morning."

"I'm going to fire the person who started that false rumor." He abruptly halted conversation when Chanelle appeared with the lunch order. "Hello again…beautiful."

Chanelle carefully arranged the plates and soup bowls on the table. "Would you care for freshly ground pepper on the soup?"

"Yes, Chanelle…that would be perfect." She leaned in over the table and cranked the handle of the pepper container. "Please let me know when."

Xander gently put his left arm around her waist and tugged her slightly closer. "Not quite yet…honey."

She twisted away from his grip. "I assume that you've had enough pepper, sir."

"Almost…but you can get me another scotch and a refill of his iced tea. Hurry back." Xander smiled, noticing she was staring at his mouth.

"Yes, Mr. Kellogg." She glanced at Robert, as if asking for his help, but scampered away without looking at Xander again.

Xander pointed at her. "I can tell she's already in love with me."

"Yeah…right! Your broken tooth is definitely a romantic attraction…I'm certain she's eager to date a hillbilly."

"I'm getting it repaired right after lunch. So, we're set with Buster coming aboard then?"

"Only on my terms though. Now…tell me about your office development plans."

"Later…when I have the details nailed down.

Chanelle appeared with the drink tray. This time, she leaned in from the opposite side of the table where Xander was seated. After securing the glasses, she carefully dropped a small leather folder on the table containing the bill. "Thank you, Mr. Kellogg…have a nice day."

"Thank YOU, Chanelle. I'm sure that we'll see one another soon…very soon."

She nodded and faded away into the dining room.

Xander snatched the folder and quickly scribbled his initials and scrolled 007, the member number he had recently arranged with the Club. "I'll leave her a twenty-dollar bill as a gratuity…that will really impress her."

"As if she wasn't already awestruck?" Robert smirked.

Xander slammed down his drink and addressed Robert, "Can you drop me at Fred Hawthorne's office over on Hampden and I-25?"

"I'm going the other way...I need to check on a few problems at our projects near Swedish Hospital."

"It's only be ten minutes out of your way, Robby Boy." Xander threw the balance of the scotch down his throat. "Let's fly."

Xander popped a breath mint in his mouth before turning the door handle to enter Dr. Hawthorne's office. The receptionist and dental assistant, Pam Carter, greeted him immediately...her glowing red hair was even more striking than he recalled from his last appointment. "Good afternoon, Mr. Kellogg...we heard you have a slight problem."

"Hello gorgeous...it's been too long. I was chewing on some ice last night and cracked a molar." Kellogg tried to kiss her on the cheek, although Pam stepped back, pointing down the hallway. Quickly skipping ahead, she reached the exam room and gestured toward the chair. "Please get comfortable, Xander...there are buttons on the side to adjust your back and neck."

"I'd be more comfortable if you'd jump on my lap, Pam."

"Not today, Mr. Kellogg."

"Not interested in joining me on my next trip to Vegas on my new private jet?"

"I'm seeing someone now. Look...we had a few nice times, but that's history."

"Never say never."

Pam gathered a paper patient bib and leaned over Kellogg to secure it around his neck. He instinctively pulled her closer with his right arm, her breasts pressed tightly against his chest, while simultaneously reaching around to squeeze her right buttock with his left hand. She instantly thrust her forearm against his neck and with her muscular physique, causing Kellogg to start choking. Between breaths, Kellogg pleaded for water. Pam rushed to the sink, quickly filling a paper cup and threw it in his face. She turned to refill the glass when he stopped coughing. "Just get me a towel...I got the message."

Pam hurled the bib at him. "Put it on yourself!"

As she abruptly departed, Xander dabbed his face with the protective cover and placed the clasps around the back of his neck.

Fred Hawthorne knocked weakly on the door frame and entered the room. "Good afternoon Mr. X...have you sobered up yet? You were certainly a mess last night...Al McDonald told me you crashed into his table at Trader Vic's."

"I tripped on the torn carpet...they need to replace the lumpy padding too. I'm contemplating suing them...I hurt my knee on the table too."

"Did you have an accident with your tooth? Let me peek...open wide." Snatching the mirror instrument, he peered around Xander's mouth. "It's too damaged to save...I'll have to pull it and replace it with an implant. I'm booked today, so we'll have to schedule an appointment later...it looks like a molar on the other side is cracked too. You know...I've warned you before about chewing ice cubes."

Kellogg slammed the arm rest. "Can't you fix the broken one today...I have a lot of important meetings coming up and I can't afford to look like a carney."

"Well, I could construct a temporary cap if you have a couple of hours. I have other patients scheduled and would need to work you in after hours."

"Tell the other patients you're cancelling their appointments…they can't be that important."

"I can't afford to hurt my reputation…a couple of them are friends too."

"I guess you don't want to join George and me on that Monterey trip next month then."

"You just told us last night that you couldn't go because of some important hearings on your next big project."

"Well…I found out this morning the meetings will be postponed a few weeks."

"I'm sorry, Mr. X…I can't do it."

"How about tomorrow morning then?"

"You should know I take Wednesdays off."

"Great, then you'll have plenty of time for me."

"I had previous plans…Carrie and I are driving to Estes Park."

Kellogg snatched the front of Hawthorne's dental coat to pull him closer. "Fuck Estes Park…fuck your day off…and fuck Carrie too, if you still can! If you can't open the office, we're going to shut down the construction of your medical building immediately. It's already running late…problems with the concrete guy."

Hawthorne spun from Kellogg's grip. "You do you think you are…you can't do that! I've given my landlord a notice for a moveout date and have a huge rent penalty if I hold over on my lease" He thought for a few seconds. "I'll sue you for non-performance under our construction contact."

"Go ahead…we can just use the force majeure clause as our defense…you know, things beyond our control, Freddy Boy."

Hawthorne stared out the window for a minute. "All right, I'll open the office for you at seven o'clock...we can leave for Estes Park a little later than we planned."

"That's too early...I can be here at eight-thirty."

Hawthorne threw the mirror instrument on the tile floor, the glass shattering with fragments scattering across the exam room. "Be here at eight o'clock at the latest."

"You need to keep your anger under control, Freddy Boy...that's very unprofessional!"

Pam overheard the commotion and rushed in. "What happened, Doctor Hawthorne?"

Kellogg interrupted. "Doctor Fred had a silly tantrum."

Hawthorne turned to Pam. "I need to take care of Mr. Kellogg's teeth in the morning, so can you come in by seven-thirty?"

Pam scraped her shoes against the tile floor to corral the glass fragments. "I had some other plans tomorrow, but I'll work around them if you need to."

"Honey, I knew that you wanted to see me again tomorrow." Kellogg winked at her.

Ignoring his comment, Pam bent down to pick up the instrument pieces as Kellogg twisted his head for a better view of her backside.

Kellogg whipped off the patient bib. "Pam, honey...how about joining me for dinner at The Platte Club tonight?

"Are you kidding?" She shook her head.

"The Colorado Mine Company, then?" She scowled.

"Well, how about tomorrow night?" She glared at him witheringly.

"I take that as a no, Pam. Can you call a taxi for me? I don't have my car today."

"Several cabs are normally lined up at the Marriott Hotel down the street...it's a short walk. I'm sure you'll enjoy the exercise."

"I was hoping to spend a little more time with you."

She sneered at Kellogg again. "I'd rather have a root canal."

Kellogg noted two women seated in lounge chairs as he whisked through the waiting area. He turned his head slightly, recognizing Olivia Buckingham, and looked away quickly. She called his name, but he plowed ahead, pretending not to hear her. As he closed the hallway door, he heard Olivia's comment to the other woman... "He's the cad I was telling you about earlier..."

Kellogg arrived at his office around three and hustled to Phyllis' desk.

"Do I have any messages?"

She shuffled a stack of pink notes. "I organized these by importance."

Kellogg tapped his foot, getting impatient.

"John Collins called twice, and Linda Melrose phoned about ten minutes ago. Eli Cohen came by and your brother Robert called from a pay phone somewhere...he sounded frantic. Oh, I almost forgot...Mr. Affenson called from Houston."

Kellogg snatched the pink slips from her fingers and immediately sat down at his desk, deciding his first call was to John Collins.

"Hello Mr. X…I looked over the prenuptial agreement. You were right…Jill needs to vacate the house twenty-four hours after serving you with divorce papers. Have they arrived?"

"No…not yet."

"Let me know when. I cannot petition Judge Watson until I can attach the official divorce filing…I checked on the procedure after our earlier call."

"What about the West Tower R & H lease agreement?"

"I see they are protected for a leasing commission for up to a year after the termination date, provided they disclosed the tenant's name in writing. However, the section regarding a commission for a sale to a perspective tenant or buyer, was crossed out and initialed by you, as well as Lawrence Reagan of R & H. His signature was acknowledged by their notary."

"Excellent…so, I could terminate the agreement and be relieved of any commission obligation?

"R & H could establish the company as a prospective tenant before you officially notify them about the termination, but I can't see any reason you would owe them a fee if the Texas company purchases the property. However, I cannot opine to the company's obligations to Reagan and Holbrook for a commission without thoroughly reviewing an original form of the company representation agreement."

"I understand Colly…I'll be in touch."

Xander desperately pushed four phone lines, unable to get a dial tone. Irritated, he yelled out the door at Phyllis, "Honey…I can't get an outside line for a long-distance call."

Within five seconds, Phyllis confirmed line three was available.

Rather than calling Rusty Affenson's direct number, Kellogg methodically dialed the main number for Andrews Oil, hoping to speak with Dixie again.

"Andrews Oil, how can I direct your call?"

"Is this Dixie?"

"Yes it, is."

"Xander Kellogg here...from Denver. I spoke to you earlier this morning."

"Oh yes...How could I ever forget?"

Kellogg decided to violate his core philosophy. "I want to apologize for my inappropriate comment this morning. I lost my temper...maybe I could make up for my indiscretion and buy you dinner the next time I'm in Houston."

"Well...that depends on how big you are."

"You mean my height?"

"Maybe...I stand nearly six feet in high heels. I don't like to date small men."

"You won't be disappointed...I can assure you. Dixie, I'd like to talk to you further, but I need to speak to Rusty Affenson immediately. Can you find him?'

"Hold on, Mr. Kellogg."

A few seconds passed, when Affenson answered. "Hello again, Mr. X. Marty Holbrook phoned and wants us to make an offer to buy the 1010 Building. He and Buck Andrews discussed it over lunch at the Petroleum Club today."

"Rusty…have you closely reviewed your agreement with Reagan & Holbrook?"

"Not since we signed it three months ago…why?"

"Do you recall if their company representation agreement incorporated the payment of a brokerage commission in the event you bought a building, rather than leasing one?"

"I'm certain it does…it's fairly standard language."

"Shit…what if you terminated the agreement now?"

"The agreement has a clause that protects them for up to a year after they disclose a specific property to us…again, standard language."

"But they haven't disclosed West Tower though."

"Not to my knowledge."

"Rusty, could you send me a copy of your agreement with Reagan and Holbrook?"

"Our in-house counsel needs to sign off on that."

"Please ask him and get back to me as soon as possible."

"Okay, Mr. X…but it will have to wait until tomorrow. He's left the office for the night."

"Could you call him at home?"

"If it's that important."

"More important than you know."

"Where can I phone you tonight?"

"If there's no answer at my office, call The Platte Club's main number…303-555-1000. I'm having dinner there at six-thirty and

I'm staying in one of their suites for a few days while my house is being remodeled…thanks Rusty."

"So long, Mr. X." The phone clicked.

Kellogg instantly dialed Eli Cohen's extension. "Cohen…Phyllis told me that you were looking for me earlier."

"Pete Simpson called to tell me they have a new tenant prospect…an oil exploration firm from Houston. He didn't mention the company's name but wants to set up a tour of West Tower tomorrow. I told Pete I would get back with him to schedule a time."

"Stall him if he calls back…come up with some excuse until I can check something out."

Xander had barely hung up when Phyllis interrupted with a call from Linda Melrose.

"Hello Cutie…change your mind about dinner tonight?"

"No, Mr. X…but I wanted to let you know I got your wardrobe order coordinated with Moss and Charles. Three tailors are working on the alterations for the suit jackets, vests, and trousers based upon your measurements…they'll be ready by six o'clock. Do you want to try them on?"

"I don't have time…they'll fit perfectly knowing your attention to detail. Have Moss & Charles deliver the clothes to Rex Wilson at The Platte Club by six o'clock…Rex will know where to store them."

"I'll take care of that…good afternoon, Xander."

"So long, sexy." He dropped the receiver on the cradle.

Phyllis interrupted once again. "Mr. Kellogg, Robert has been holding for you."

"Hello Robert…it was great having lunch with you today."

Robert was upset. "Did you threaten Fred Hawthorne we would stop construction on his building?"

"More or less."

"And tell him that we had delays because of our concrete subcontractor?"

"More or less."

"I specifically told you not to disclose that to him," Robert said angrily.

"I had to use some leverage to get my tooth fixed…he was giving me the run around. I can't go around looking like a hobo."

"Xander, you're a dumb shit…I'll have to get some extra crews there tomorrow so he can see some progress."

"He and his old bag are driving to Estes Park right after he repairs my tooth…he won't have time to check."

"Look…Hawthorne tracked me down after your little confrontation and now I have some major damage control to maintain. He said you attacked his assistant too."

"He means Pam…she loves my romantic games. I've had her on a couple trips to Vegas with me…she was playing hard to get. We always fool around a little, even in Hawthorne's office. Redheads have a hotter strain than most women."

"If I was standing next to you right now, I'd punch you in the mouth…you'd have a much larger tooth problem than a cracked molar."

"Hawthorne will forget it soon. As I told you, dentists are gullible, and Hawthorne proves it."

"He also mentioned that you insulted Mrs. McDonald last night at the gala and fell on their table in Trader Vic's when they were having a nightcap. I hope Al McDonald doesn't remove us from the bid process on his warehouse for your behavior. Xander, I have enough problems with our suppliers and subcontractors...I don't need more distractions caused by your antics."

"Robert...I'll call McDonald now. Last night, he was begging for an invitation to my Pebble Beach trip next month with his wife. I'll personally extend the invitation, so we'll be set."

"I need to go."

Xander muttered to himself, "Jesus, what else can go wrong today?"

Phyllis interrupted again. "Rusty Affenson is holding."

"Is it really him or is it his secretary?"

"It's Mr. Affenson."

Kellogg grabbed the receiver. "Rusty, what did your attorney say?"

"I'm sorry...he won't release our agreement with Reagan and Holbrook."

'Why not?"

"I didn't ask him why...he reprimanded me for even asking him in the first place."

"If I fly down there tomorrow, could I read it there?"

"I don't think that would be a good idea, Mr. Kellogg."

"Shit! I need to speak to Buck right away…where can I reach him?"

"I believe he always books a suite at the Brown Palace Hotel when in Denver."

"The Brown Palace, huh? Okay…I'll try there."

"I don't think he'll override our counsel's advice."

"I have to ask him something else…Rusty Boy. I wouldn't go around you."

"All right then…good night."

Kellogg shouted out to Phyllis. "Call the Brown Palace Hotel and ask for Buck Andrews' room…I mean Franklin Andrews."

Kellogg started to count the cars driving past his window overlooking I-25. He was up to fifty-nine when Phyllis phoned. "I found Mr. Andrews at The Brown Palace in the Ship Tavern…he's holding on line one."

Kellogg pick up the receiver and clicked the blinking button. "Buck, how are you doin' today…buddy?"

"Great…just ordered my first bourbon since lunch."

"I spoke to Rusty Affenson a couple times…he told me you had lunch with Marty Holbrook at The Petroleum Club."

"I had a tasty buffalo steak…rare."

"Did you happen to mention our West Tower conversation last night to Holbrook?"

"No, although I did tell him we closed down the Hawaiian bar."

"Hmmm...he must be putting two and two together then", Kellogg thought aloud.

"That's four from where I come from...what are you driving at?"

"Never mind, Buck...go back and enjoy your drink. We'll talk soon."

"Adios, amigo."

Kellogg instantly dialed John Collins. Before Collins could even greet him, Xander launched into a rant. "Colly...the fucking Texas guys won't release their brokerage agreement with the R & H assholes."

Collins interrupted. "Hold on, Mr. X...take a deep breath and calm down."

A few seconds passed before Kellogg continued. "The oil company COO says their representation agreement includes payment of a brokerage fee in the event they buy a building. My inhouse guy, Cohen, just told me the R & H broker called about an oil company from Houston they are representing...I believe it's the same firm. I told Cohen to stall them on a West Tower tour R & H wants to schedule tomorrow. I'm terminating my Reagan & Holbrook agreement this afternoon to avoid any possible conflict, even though I'm not obligated to pay them a brokerage fee if the Texas company buys West Tower."

"That sounds fine. R & H has made a poor effort at leasing, so they shouldn't be shocked when you terminate...but if they collect a fee on a sale from a buyer, what do you care?"

"Any fee to R & H will likely reduce the purchase price by the same amount, so I take a hit. I don't want those broker scumbags making a dime when they purposely excluded my building on the company's search to purchase a building. I'm going to convince the Texas company to terminate their agreement with Reagan & Holbrook before they officially identify West Tower."

"Good luck with all of that, Mr. X."

"Colly…you should know by now that I don't need to luck to navigate a tricky situation."

"I forgot. Right-o…goodbye."

Kellogg unbuttoned his golf shirt…his blood pressure rising as he called Eli Cohen.

"Cohen…type up a termination letter on West Tower right now and fax it over to those worthless R & H brokers. Check the language in the listing agreement so the wording is perfect. It's after four o'clock already and they must receive it by the end of the business day…five o'clock. Now, get cracking and have Phyllis help you with the fax machine…I can't take any chances you screw that up."

"Should I phone the R & H brokers to let them know we're transmitting a fax to cancel their listing?"

"Hell no! I don't want those slimy brokers to pull off something sneaky at the last minute."

Xander now pulled the golf shirt out, hanging down to his thighs. "Phyl, track down Franklin Andrews at the Ship Tavern at the Brown Palace again…I need to speak with him urgently."

Xander kicked his office chair and impatiently waited for Phyllis as five minutes passed by.

"Mr. Kellogg…I have Mr. Andrews on line one again."

"Mr. X, you're interrupting my second bourbon...this better be important!"

"Buck, this may be the most important decision you'll make today. I'm certain we can cut a deal to buy my West Tower office building...it's a match made in heaven. You'll have a prominent sign at the top for everyone to see for miles."

"It sounds like it would suit our needs and the location works for me too, but you're getting over your skis, Mr. X...that's what folks say in the Rockies, right?"

"Maybe, but those crooked brokers from Reagan and Holbrook are going to collect a half million-dollar commission from you if you buy my building. If the brokers were out of the picture, I could reduce the price a bit and we both win. Call Rusty Affenson and order him to terminate your agreement with R & H in the next thirty minutes."

"What's the rush...I'm playing gin rummy now. I'll call him tomorrow...Adios." He promptly hung up.

Kellogg was beside himself, pacing around his office, pounding his fist against his forehead. He seized a yellow pad with his right hand and threw it against the window, bending the vertical blinds. He slumped in his leather chair and closed his eyes. Three minutes later, Eli Cohen knocked on Kellogg's door.

"Chief...I've drafted the R & H termination letter. Do you want to review it before I ask Phyllis to type it up?"

Kellogg shook his head. "No...just ask her to get it done quickly." He checked his watch. "It's already four twenty-five."

Phyllis tapped on his office door fifteen minutes later. "Mr. Kellogg, the letter is ready for you to sign...I've already notarized it."

"Thank you, Phyl…hand it over." He perused it for few seconds, placed it on his desk and scribbled his classic signature on the document, highlighting the 'X' in the name Alexander. "Now, fax this to the guys at Reagan and Holbrook immediately…we only have twenty minutes to spare."

"I'll get the fax drum rolling…it takes a few minutes to warm up."

Kellogg reached for the phone, calling Mike Peavy. "Peavy…do you have your car here today?"

"Sure do, Mr. Kellogg."

"You have to drive me to the Brown Palace right now."

"Ah…ah…well…I guess I could do that."

"Let's get going…I'll meet you in the parking lot in two minutes." Kellogg abruptly hung up.

Kellogg strolled around the parking lot for five minutes, waiting for Peavy, who finally emerged through the rear entrance. Motioning Kellogg to the far end of the parking lot, Peavy strolled toward a dirty yellow Plymouth Volare station wagon.

Kellogg was perturbed. "What took you so long, Peavy?"

"I had to call my wife and then cleared off my desk to lock up. You warned me about leaving important items out where the cleaning crew might steal them and sell to your competitors."

"That's right…you can't trust anyone. Why did you park in the corner of the lot far away from the other cars?"

"We bought this Volare last year and I don't want anyone to dent it…hop in."

Kellogg opened the door and peered inside. "Peavy, there are stains all over the seat…my trousers will get soiled."

"My infant daughter was in her car seat yesterday so I could see her. She chucked up some milk, but I forgot to clean it up."

"Get me something like a towel for me to sit on."

Peavy scurried to the rear cargo area and produced an old green golf towel. "Here you go, Mr. Kellogg." He carefully folded the towel and arranged it on the seat.

"The towel has dirt all over it…I'm not sitting on that!"

Peavy scratched his head. "I guess I had a few chunks of mud on it from my last golf round." He reached in the rear seat and handed Kellogg a tan floor mat. "No one sits in back except the kids and their feet don't reach the floor…it's clean."

Kellogg inspected the mat, reluctantly arranging the cleanest side to sit on.

Peavy inched the car backwards out of the parking space, swiveling his head around several times, checking for other vehicles.

Kellogg was getting more impatient. "Jesus, Peavy…what are looking for? There's only three other cars in the entire lot!"

"Just being extra careful…this car has a blind spot."

"You should be so lucky to get in an accident. This bus, or whatever you call it, is a joke. Get a cool car, like my Corvette next time and a better color…this looks like baby shit. I want all my employees to portray a successful image." Kellogg pointed forward to the first street intersection. "Run that red light…it's turning yellow."

Peavy slammed on the brakes, causing Kellogg to lurch forward, instantly bracing himself with his hands against the glove compartment. "What are you doing, shithead…I told you to run the light."

"I can't break the law, sir." Peavy glanced over to Kellogg. "You should wear your seatbelt too."

"Peavy…laws are meant to be broken, but don't get caught. Seatbelts are for wimps."

As Peavy resumed driving, Kellogg motioned in the direction of the freeway entrance ramp. "Get on I-25 and cut up on Broadway to downtown. I don't have much time, so hurry."

"What's up, boss?"

"I have an oil company from Houston interested in buying West Tower. I have to meet with their CEO and cut the deal before Marty Holbrook weasels in on a commission."

"Holy cow…when did this all happen?"

"In the last twenty-four hours." Kellogg glanced over at the speedometer." Peavy, step on it… you're only driving fifty-five."

"That's the posted speed limit, boss."

"What did I just tell you about bending the law? Push this crate to seventy-five…if it even goes that fast!"

Peavy's face turned red with sweat dripping down his forehead. He gently pushed on the gas pedal until the speedometer read sixty-five.

"Change lanes, Peavy. Get around those pokey drivers…they're sheep."

Peavy gripped the steering wheel tightly until his knuckles were white. He leaned forward over the wheel, making a violent turn into the right lane, causing Kellogg to bang his head against the side window.

"Christ...I should have driven myself. How did you ever pass a driver's test? Stay in this lane...the Broadway exit is coming up in a mile." Xander rubbed his temple repeatedly with his right hand.

"Yes, sir." Peavy steered the car off the ramp onto Broadway.

"All the stoplights are timed all the way to downtown if you keep it steady at thirty-nine...change lanes if anyone gets in our way."

Peavy glanced over at Kellogg, looking irritated, knowing the limit was thirty miles per hour.

"Relax, Peavy...I know the Denver Chief of Police."

Eight minutes later, Peavy stopped at a traffic light a block away from the Brown Palace Hotel. "Peavy...drop me at the front entrance to the Brown and keep driving around the block until I come out. I don't know how long this will take, but you'll need to drive me to The Platte Club when I'm done."

"I might run out of gas circling the block...can I park it somewhere?"

"NO...and don't waste time looking for a gas station either...I might only be a few minutes. And whatever you do, don't run out of gas."

As Peavy slowed the car near the entrance to the Brown Palace Hotel, Kellogg bolted from the car and yelled back at Peavy. "Pick me up right here."

Kellogg raced up the stairs and through the revolving doors, futilely attempting to push them faster than allowed. He scampered to the Ship Tavern and surveyed the room. Catching his breath, he spied two customers seated at the long bar and a handful of patrons scattered at the tables, although Andrews was not in sight. Kellogg shaded his eyes, trained on a balding man who faced away, seated alone at an oak table where two drinks and a deck of cards were stationed. Kellogg retreated a few steps, cranking his neck for a better angle, recognizing Marty Holbrook. Kellogg instinctively spun left, hustling toward the men's room. As he reached to push the door, it magically opened, causing Kellogg to lose his balance, awkwardly falling into Andrews' arms.

"Whoa…Gotcha again buddy!"

"Obedient door there, Buck…it automatically opened when I gave it a command."

"Tell me how that works sometime…I gotta get back to my bourbon and the gin game with Marty Holbrook. I'm up a couple hundred bucks so far. Hey…have a drink with us."

"Stop Buck…we need to talk right here about my office building. When you buy it, Holbrook can't get paid a dime…he's a sleazy asshole."

"You can speak to the asshole right now…that's the way we do it in Texas…no bullshit."

Kellogg took two steps back and rubbed his chin for a few seconds. "You're right Buck…let's go." He followed two paces behind Andrews into the Ship Tavern.

Andrews pointed to a chair. "Grab a seat there, Mr. X." Andrews reached for his drink. "Boys…you must have met before, right?"

Holbrook swiveled his head around and sprung up from his chair, extending his right hand at Kellogg. "We actually have not. I'm pleased to finally meet you Mr. X…what an honor!"

Kellogg gripped Holbrook's small hand as hard as he could and twisted it slightly until Holbrook finally grimaced. "Holbrook…we've actually never met, although I know your partner, Reagan, and two of your lazy brokers."

"Thanks for listing West Tower with us."

Kellogg checked his Rolex watch…it was five-twenty.

"You previously had the listing agreement on West Tower, Holbrook."

"I beg your pardon…what do you mean?"

"I cancelled it…we faxed a termination letter to your office about a half hour ago."

"Ah…ah…why did you decide that, Mr. Kellogg?"

"We wanted to be in compliance with the terms of the listing agreement."

"Did you call our brokers or my partner, Lawrence Reagan?"

"I didn't want to waste my time…your feeble brokers apparently didn't want to waste their time to lease my great building either."

"Look Mr. X, please allow me to arrange a meeting with our team and your staff first thing in the morning. Lawrence told me earlier today we found an excellent prospect who's interested in West Tower. They actually want to set up a tour tomorrow." Holbrook glanced over at Andrews, who shrugged his shoulders.

"It's too late Holbrook…your crack team should have found that prospect a few months ago."

A waiter dressed in a ship's captain uniform interrupted the debate. "Can I get you something to drink, sir?"

"Sure, Charlie…I'll have a scotch on the rocks…Glenfiddich if you have it."

"Are you other gentlemen ready for another round?"

Andrews raised his hand. "I'll have another bourbon…Marty, how about you?"

"Yes…another gin and tonic."

Andrews plunked down in his chair, picked up the card deck, and began to shuffle. "Marty, do you want to switch from gin to blackjack?"

Holbrook glared at Andrews. "Didn't you hear me…I just ordered another gin and tonic," he said irritably.

"I meant blackjack…the card game. Haven't you ever been to Vegas?"

"I don't feel like playing cards anymore, Buck…I need to call Lawrence Reagan. How much do I owe you?"

"Two hundred bucks!"

Holbrook reached for his wallet and pulled out two C-notes. "Here you go, Buck…but I expect you'll pick up the bar tab."

Andrews seemed irritated. "Can't be more than twenty bucks…I guess I can handle that, Marty."

Holbrook instantly stood up and reached to shake Andrews' hand, although Buck waved him off. "Buck, I'll call you later to set up the tour we discussed…good afternoon." He ignored Kellogg and quickly headed toward the hotel lobby.

The waiter appeared with the drink order and carefully arranged the three glasses on the table. "Anything else I can bring, gentlemen?"

Kellogg pointed at Holbrook. "That guy walking out the door may need a crying towel."

The waiter seemed confused. "I'm sorry?"

"Forget it. Charlie…bring me the bar tab for all the drinks."

Andrews hoisted his glass and toasted Kellogg. "You have class, Mr. X. Holbrook is poised to make a few hundred thousand from the commission if we buy a building and can't pick up a little bar tab. That pisses me off…that's not how 'bidness' is done in our parts."

"Buck…I told you that Reagan & Holbrook is a bullshit operation. Did he disclose he and his brokers are the major investors on the 1010 Building he's pushing you to buy?"

"Hell no…that REALLY pisses me off!"

"That's why I wanted you guys to terminate the agreement with R & H. Your inhouse lawyer is holding it up."

"I'll call him when I'm done with this drink…what price are you asking for your office building?"

Kellogg hesitated, scratching his head. "Twenty million…about a hundred a square foot."

"We'll pay for our own finishes and get our Houston architect involved…we want a first-class image. I'll speak with Rusty Affenson to see what his budgets looks like.' He checked his watch. "Sorry, Mr. X…I need to run and meet Nancy at Baby Doe's for dinner."

"Enjoy your evening, pardner."

"Adios."

Xander slumped down in his wooden chair and lifted his glass of scotch, toasting himself. "Well done, Mr. X."

The waiter appeared, placing a leather folder in the center of the table. "Did you say something, sir?"

Kellogg quickly scanned the thirty-dollar tab and snatched a money clip from his right pants pocket. "Here's a fifty, Charlie...keep the change."

"Thank-you...can I get you anything else?"

"Yeah...go out that door and see if a guy is parked in a baby shit yellow colored station wagon."

The waiter returned in a minute. "There sure is...the driver told me he was out of gas."

"Call me a taxi for a ride to The Platte Club."

"Several cabs are always lined up near the front hotel entrance...our doorman will assist you."

Kellogg sauntered toward the hotel lobby, deciding to leave Mike Peavy sitting outside, wondering how long he would wait. He muttered to himself, "what a chump?"

Chapter Six

Xander Kellogg arrived at The Platte Club at six o'clock, immediately registering at the front desk for his suite. He quickly headed to the rear hallway elevator lobby, punching the button for the third floor. Distracted on West Tower, he hadn't noticed that the arrow pointed down, becoming annoyed as the hydraulic mechanical system moved the cab slowly to the basement and finally up to the third floor. When the elevator door opened, he was shocked to see Linda Melrose and Bill Douglas standing four feet from the platform.

"Well...hello Linda. I thought that you had an appointment at the airport."

Linda shrunk back a few steps into the hallway. "Hi Xander...yes, I do." She forced a laugh and changed the subject. "I hope you like your suits...have you seen them yet?"

"No...I'm just heading to my room now. Where are you two going?"

"D...d...driving home to have dinner with my family." Douglas was noticeably nervous, looking away at the wall.

"How about you, Linda?"

"I...I...have a...a...an appointment at six at Stouffer's Airport Hotel." From her stuttering, Xander knew immediately she was lying.

Kellogg checked his watch. "You're, late sweetheart...it's already six-ten."

"Really?" She looked down at her wrist to verify the time. "My watched must have stopped."

"Bill…when can meet to discuss your prime office site?"

Douglas was still looking away. "Have your girl call my secretary tomorrow and we'll set a time."

Linda entered the elevator cab with Douglas trailing a step behind. "Good night, Mr. X." The elevator door closed suddenly, striking Douglas' right arm, causing him to drop a room key on the platform. Before Douglas could react, Kellogg instantly snagged it, noting Room 302 stamped on the copper surface. He held the key a foot in front of Douglas' eyes, before placing it in Bill's right hand.

"Thanks, Alexander." Douglas' voice crackled.

Kellogg chuckled as he strolled down the long corridor to Room 303. He inserted his key into the lock and twisted the knob to the left to open the door, immediately seeing a stack of clothes arranged on a brown couch. He turned to the left and opened the closet to inspect the suits and trousers. Seconds later, Kellogg heard a tap on the door and peered through the peephole, surprised to see Rex Wilson.

"Mr. Kellogg…is everything to your liking? I stacked some of apparel on the couch, assuming you would decide where to store it."

"Did my tailor, Linda Melrose, bring the wardrobe up here?"

"Who's Linda Melrose? A man from Moss and Charles Custom Clothiers delivered the clothes to the lobby around five-thirty and I brought them to your room."

"Thanks for your help, Rexy Boy. By the way, did Bill Douglas book a room on this floor tonight?"

"Yes, I believe I saw his reservation."

"Well…it looks like I'll be dining alone tonight. Can you select a nice table and have the new cute waitress Chanelle wait on me?"

"Yes…I'll take care of it, Mr. Kellogg."

Xander picked out a grey suit, holding it in the full-length mirror. He attached the blue suspenders, matching them with a blue shirt, a plain dark blue tie, and a pair of black wingtip shoes. Xander hustled to the dining room, spotting Wilson near the maître d podium.

"Mr. Kellogg, I have a private table near the windows."

"Wherever…as long as Chanelle is taking care of me."

"I heard she felt ill and left a few minutes ago."

"That's very disappointing. So, who has my table now…the old hag, Doris?"

Wilson nodded.

"That's perfect…from Chanelle to Doris…that will ensure a quick dinner and an early night."

Xander awoke at seven o'clock, scraping his tongue over his cracked tooth again and again. He rolled over, closed his eyes and fell asleep, immersed in a vivid dream where Jill pressed his '45 handgun to his left temple. Covered in sweat, he suddenly shot up and screamed. Wiping his brow on the sheet, Kellogg squinted at the clock, which read seven forty-five. He reached for the telephone at his bedside and called the valet.

"Yes, Mr. Kellogg…how can be of assistance?"

"I need a taxi in forty-five minutes."

"Yes sir…do have a have a preferred cab company?"

"Don't call High Plains Cab Service…I took one of their filthy taxis last night and have to get my trousers laundered."

"I can pick those slacks up to have them cleaned and back to your room by four o'clock."

"Good idea, buddy. What's your name?"

"It's Sam, sir."

"Well then...slam...bam...thank-you Sam!" Kellogg hooted, always proud of his clever wordplay.

"Very crafty, sir."

Kellogg took a leisurely hot shower until the bathroom was shrouded in steam. He checked the contents of the Club supplied toiletry kit, organizing them on the counter. He spent an extra minute brushing his teeth in anticipation of the appointment with Dr. Fred Hawthorne and another opportunity to romance Pam.

Strolling through the lobby, Kellogg noticed a Mountain Taxi parked outside The Platte Club entrance. As he approached the heavy door, the valet opened it.

"Good morning, Mr. Kellogg."

"You must be Sam...I haven't seen you here before."

"Sam I am...I started last week as a valet. I'm graduating from Metropolitan State in December with a business degree but prefer to land a job in commercial real estate. I'm hoping to land a position with Gabbert Financial, the mortgage banking division of Gabbert and Company."

"Here's two bucks, kid...my dirty pants are hung over the desk chair in Room 303."

Sam hustled ahead and opened the back seat of the taxi. "Sir, I wiped the back seat in case there was dirt or stains."

"Spic and span…thank-you, Sam."

"Yes sir…have a nice day."

Kellogg rolled into the center of the backseat of the cab as Sam carefully closed the car door. He studied the taxi driver, who was grotesquely overweight and didn't appear to have a neck. The cabbie wore a red stocking cap and a tattered army jacket. From the image in the rearview mirror, Kellogg could see the cabbie's two front teeth were missing.

"Where to sir?"

"My dentist's office…it's located on Hampden Avenue. Pal…with your missing teeth, it looks like you could use a trip to the dentist too."

"Where on Hampden…it runs the length of the city, you know."

Kellogg bristled and shifted his seat position. "I know, Charlie…the building is located on Hampden, a couple of blocks east of the I-25 freeway interchange. I don't have the address, but I'll show you when we get there. Do you know where I-25 is?"

"I do." The cab driver snarled, signaling his annoyance. "Can you put your seatbelt on, mister?"

"No thanks…seat belts are for pussies."

The cabbie grunted. "Chastity belts are for pussies too."

"Hey…that's pretty funny!" Kellogg chuckled for a few seconds, rolling up his left white shirt sleeve to adjust the cuff link to check the time…eight-thirty.

"Step on it, Charlie…I'm already late." Kellogg could feel the car lurch ahead slightly.

"My name isn't Charlie…it's Dusty."

"I call strangers Charlie…like buddy or pal. It's nothing personal, Dusty."

"I spent six months on the Cambodian border during the Vietnam war, so the last name I ever want to be called is Charlie."

"Charlie was the nickname for the Vietcong…right?

"Yep…and a few other names our artillery unit called those zipper heads."

"Well, at least we won that war."

"Are you fucking kidding me? We lost sixty thousand soldiers and countless kids scarred for life with physical and mental problems, and millions of Vietnamese perished…their country was contaminated with Agent Orange too."

"The USA had to stop the spread of Communism. The war was completely justified after they attacked us in the Gulf of Tonkin," Kellogg countered.

"Right." He smirked. "Have you ever read *The Pentagon Papers*?"

"That's the book describing the Pentagon Building in Washington…right?"

"No…look it up sometime. By the way, I took shrapnel from a grenade blast from about ten feet away and my mouth reconstructed twice…that's why a couple teeth are still missing."

Kellogg elected to end the conversation for several minutes.

"Dusty…stop! There's my dentist building…pull over in this driveway. Hey…thanks for your service!" He threw a ten-dollar bill at Dusty and jumped out of the cab.

Kellogg bounded up the stairs into the medical office building and down the hallway to the Hawthorne Dentistry Office. He slung open the door, where Fred Hawthorne stood with his arms folded, tapping his foot. He pointed to a wall clock. "It's nearly nine o'clock, Xander...I expected you an hour ago."

"My cab driver picked me up late and got lost finding your building...where's Pam?"

"We assumed you changed your mind, so I told her to leave."

"Christ...she's the only reason that I still come here."

"Thanks for the vote of confidence, Xander. You know...she's a great assistant and I'd like to keep her, so please reign in your charm offensive. Let's get started...Carrie's here to help me. You may recall she was my first dental assistant when I started my practice way back."

Hawthorne escorted Xander to Room 2, where Carrie held a patient bib. "Hello Xander...you won't try to pull me on top of you when I attach this...will you?"

"You never know, sweetie." Xander shifted in the chair, feeling his face redden. "Did you win the bid on the 'Jigsaw Puzzle of the Week' at the charity event on Monday night?"

"No...that sneaky Donna McDonald cheated and outbid me by five dollars."

"What a shame!"

"I got even though...I won the 'Crossword Puzzle of the Week' bid."

"She must be crushed."

"Yes...but we're still close friends."

"Carrie, you got the better deal though…she can give you her old jigsaw puzzles, but she can't use your crosswords after you've filled them out."

"Yes, she can…I agreed to fill them out in pencil and erase the words when I'm done."

"How creative…recycled crossword puzzles! Why not use pens with disappearing ink?"

"By the way, it was a wonderful charity event…please congratulate Jill for us," Carrie said.

Hawthorne stood over Kellogg, holding a syringe filled with Novocain. "Your brother was very apologetic about your threat to shut the construction down on my building."

"Well Freddy Boy, my ultimatum worked…that's why we're all here together this morning. In case you didn't know, I talked Robert into assigning another construction crew today to get caught up…we'll be back on schedule next week, so relax."

Hawthorne was still upset, and Kellogg suddenly feared he might get even. "Don't poke me with that needle in my penis…I can't afford to have THAT frozen."

"I'll relax after I move in my facility before my current lease expires." Hawthorne inserted the needle into both sides of Kellogg's gums. "It will take a few minutes to freeze before I begin the extraction."

Kellogg knew Hawthorne was an avid student of history. "Fred…have you ever heard of something called *The Pentagon Papers*?"

"Sure…haven't you? A Defense Department consultant named Daniel Ellsburg smuggled out thousands of classified documents about our military and political intervention in Vietnam to suppress the expansion of Communism after World War II. Ellsburg released the documents to the New York Times and Washington Post in 1971. They clearly showed five Presidents lied to the public about our involvement in Vietnam."

A staunch Republican, Kellogg was always quick to blame the Democratic Party for any problem. "I'm sure that Kennedy and Lyndon Johnson were the biggest culprits. Who were the other three Democrats who covered it up…Jimmy Carter, Truman and FDR?"

"It all started with Truman, but Eisenhower had a role, as well as Kennedy. However, the real villains were Johnson and Robert McNamara, LBJ's Secretary of Defense…both knew the war was not winnable. For years they deployed several hundred thousand troops to Vietnam and spent a trillion dollars on a losing effort."

"But not Nixon…he campaigned to end the war and actually pulled it off."

"Xander, you have your facts all wrong. Nixon also knew we couldn't win but couldn't accept the embarrassment of a defeat under his watch. He accelerated the war and ultimately capitulated under public pressure and pulled the troops out in 1972. You're really off if you believe Jimmy Carter had a role in this…he was elected President in 1976, well after the war ended."

"My mouth is getting numb…I'm having a problem talking, so get started and let's get this over with."

Hawthorne cranked up the drill. "Open wide."

Beginning to sweat profusely, Kellogg tightly gripped the arms of the dental chair, his body becoming rigid.

Hawthorne chuckled. "Relax, Xander…you always act so cool. What's wrong?"

Kellogg could only mutter two indistinguishable words with his gums frozen, a suction tube wedged under his tongue, and Hawthorne's hand pressed against his jaw.

Kellogg attempted to get his mind off the dental procedure by recalling pleasant memories. His thoughts drifted to his last flings with Pam, Linda, Phyllis, and the early years of marriage to Jill. The replay of the good old days of his marriage to Jill was quickly overcome with anger recalling her pending divorce filing. He had initiated divorce actions for his first two marriages, but this one was different. Dwelling further into their three-year relationship, Kellogg concluded Jill had developed mental problems. He congratulated himself for his brilliance by drafting the punitive conditions set forth in the prenuptial agreement.

Kellogg's eyes zeroed in on the wall clock, reading ten-fifteen. The Novocain was wearing off, allowing him to finally speak clearly. "Doc…are you done? I urgently need to get to my office."

"Another five or ten minutes, Xander. Carrie and I are late for our trip to Estes Park too…we wanted to have lunch there."

"You still can…just drive faster or eat a late lunch."

"We would have been there by now if you would have been here on time."

Carrie weighed in. "Xander…you seem to be habitually late for everything based on what Jill tells me. She must be saint to live with you."

"More like the devil." Kellogg snagged his money clip. "Carrie…here's fifty bucks. Have a nice late lunch in Estes Park and order a bottle of champagne on me."

"Thank-you…that's very generous."

"Freddie Boy probably made a few hundred bucks off this procedure today too."

"Xander, you'll get the bill in a few days…we need to get another appointment set up after I receive the implant from the dental lab, but you're good to go now."

"Give me a mirror…I want see how my tooth looks."

Carrie grabbed a small mirror from the counter and held it toward Kellogg, who snapped it from her grip. Holding the mirror at several angles, Kellogg compressed his lips to examine the temporary tooth, tapping on it slightly. "Will this hold?"

"Yes, as long as you don't chew gum or anything like taffy. I suggest that you favor the other side of your mouth when eating and certainly don't chew any ice."

"Got it Fred." He leaped from the chair and stepped toward the door. "Carrie, can you call a cab for me?"

"Call one yourself…there's a phone on the receptionist desk…or better yet, walk two blocks to the Marriott Hotel…there'll be a line of cabs there."

Kellogg wanted the fifty dollars back but shrugged and left the office without saying another word. He bounded up the street, reaching the hotel in five minutes. He spotted a Mountain Taxi parked second in the line behind a High Plains cab. Approaching closer, he spied Dusty leaning against the driver's door.

"Dusty…how about giving me another lift?" Kellogg reached to open the rear door of the taxi.

Before Dusty could answer, the High Plains Taxi driver limped toward Kellogg and grabbed his shoulder. "Hey man, you need to use my cab…I'm first in line!"

"Get your fucking hands off me." Kellogg shoved the cabbie backwards, who tripped on a curb, falling awkwardly on the grass.

Kellogg tumbled into the back seat of Dusty's cab and locked the door. The High Plains driver struggled to his feet and stumbled forward, desperate to pry the door open. Dusty squeezed into the front seat and started the engine. As the taxi pulled away, the High Plains cabbie released his grip on the door handle and extended his right fist at Kellogg.

"That guy's crazy!" Kellogg twisted his neck seeing the driver still shaking his fist. "Take me to my office at Belleview and I-25."

"You know…that cabbie, Charlie Jackson, is a good dude. I see him nearly every day in the taxi lines. You're lucky that he didn't get ahold of you…he has a black belt in karate."

"That crippled little prick? I pack a pistol in my belt for assholes like him…he's the lucky one."

Dusty adjusted the rearview mirror, trying to verify if Kellogg's was lying. Xander tightened his suit jacket to cover his belt, hiding the imaginary gun.

"Remember our chat about '*The Pentagon Papers*'…I checked it out. Man, that LBJ was really a SOB…Robert McNamara too."

"Both of 'em should be tried for treason."

"Jimmy Carter too…right after he took office, he gave amnesty to all those draft evaders. Now, he's bending to those OPEC ragheads in the Middle East. We should invade them and take their oil fields…they held us hostage with their oil embargo when the price of gas was exploding!"

"So…you think we should invade another country again and start another war like Vietnam?"

"Absolutely!"

Dusty remained silent until the taxi reached the I-25 and Belleview Avenue interchange. He had heard this kind of talk before, primarily from guys who had never served in military combat. "Where to now, sir?"

"Take a left." Kellogg pointed to his headquarters on the east side of the freeway." That's my building...I named it after me...Kellogg Plaza."

"What a surprise!" Dusty coasted the taxi to the front office entrance. "The meter reads two-fifty."

"Here's a five...keep the change. Dusty...what else do you do when you're not driving cab?"

"I work as a bouncer at a couple of strip clubs and handle security for a bookie who owns those joints."

"Chubby Morrison, perhaps?"

"Why...do you know him?"

"I make a few bets through him now and then. I'm surprised I've never seen you when I picked up my winnings."

"I just like to blend in."

"You're hard to blend in anywhere, except at a fat people's convention." Kellogg chuckled. "How can I reach you if I need to hire you sometime?"

"I'll write down my phone number." He pulled a pen from behind his ear and scratched a few numbers on a yellow pad.

"Thanks...what's your last name."

"It's just Dusty."

Kellogg bolted from the taxi and hopped up the steps into Kellogg Plaza. A minute later, he loped toward Phyllis' desk.

"Phyl…call Harv's Auto Repair to see if my Corvette is fixed."

"Mr. Kellogg, Eli Cohen has been asking for you all morning and a certified letter was delivered a few minutes ago from the Buckingham Smith Law Offices…I signed for it."

"I know what that is." He snatched the letter out of her hand. "I need some coffee too."

Kellogg ripped open the envelope. As he expected, it was a divorce filing. He quickly scanned the front page noting the reason Jill cited was cruelty and irreconcilable differences. He spat on the document, crumpled it, and tossed the papers into the waste basket, just as Eli Cohen knocked on his door. "Chief…Lawrence Reagan called me five times already this morning, demanding to meet with you immediately."

"What about?"

"Obviously, the cancellation of the leasing agreement on West Tower…he mentioned a conversation you had with Marty Holbrook last night."

Phyllis interrupted the conversation. "Mr. Kellogg…Sally Tuttle, the front desk receptionist told me three brokers from Reagan & Holbrook are here to meet with you. Should I arrange to have coffee served?"

"Show them into the front conference room, but no coffee…I'll be there in a minute. Cohen…grab a copy of the termination agreement and meet me in there."

Kellogg stopped in his private toilet to relieve himself, purposely dribbling urine on his right hand and exited without washing it. As he entered the conference room, Reagan reached for a handshake, slipping on Kellogg's moist palm. Using his left hand for overlapping support, Kellogg firmly grasped Reagan's hand for several seconds.

"So nice to see you at the Bishop's Orphanage Fundraiser the other night, Mr. X."

"That was quite a night…I made a couple great business connections, including Archbishop Coolidge. He's planning to sell the excess church sites to me."

Reagan looked bewildered as Pete Simpson and Nathan Allen followed Reagan's lead with handshakes as well. In unison, they greeted Kellogg. "Good morning…Mr. X."

"Howdy boys…did you find any tenant leads for our building in the men's room that night?"

"We have a white-hot prospect…here's an amendment to our listing agreement." Simpson slid a sheet of paper across the table. "We discovered that a large oil and gas company from Houston is moving a few hundred folks here in six months and they're interested in taking your entire building."

"What the company's name?"

Simpson pointed to the amendment. "Andrews Oil."

Reagan glanced at the two brokers. "They want a lease with an option to purchase."

Kellogg shook his head. "I would never agree to sell it…my partners want to own the building long term. With its excellent location and design, the building will triple in value in ten years."

Simpson stood up. "We'll talk them out of the purchase option."

Kellogg smiled. "Boys...you're too late. I cancelled the listing agreement yesterday based upon your incompetency...you've had plenty of time to help me and you struck out."

Nate Allen pleaded. "But we found a perfect tenant for you!"

Reagan held up an ink stained piece of thermal paper. "Mr. X, we received this messy fax around six o'clock. We couldn't read it, although Marty Holbrook called me at home last night after your conversation at the Brown Palace, so we assume this was an attempt to terminate our listing agreement on West Tower."

"You don't have to assume...it IS a termination agreement. We faxed it before five o'clock...prior the end of the business day, as defined in the document."

"Not according to our machine...the printout reads five fifty-five PM."

"Lawrence...we went off daylight saving time on Sunday. Did you reset the time on your machine?"

Reagan seemed confused, staring at the brokers. "I'm sure we did."

Kellogg checked his watch. "I have a lunch appointment, fellas...have a nice afternoon." Kellogg abruptly sprung from his chair and pivoted toward the conference room door.

Reagan raised his voice. "Expect a call from Henry Buckingham, our attorney."

Kellogg stopped in his tracks and turned. "Tell that incompetent asshole to save his breath and call my lawyer, John Collins...I'm sure he knows him."

Kellogg pranced to his office, where Phyllis intercepted him. "Boss, your car will be ready after twelve o'clock."

"Great...call a taxi in thirty minutes to take me to the body shop."

Kellogg poured a half inch shot of scotch into his coffee cup, slamming the drink down quickly. Seconds later, Eli Cohen knocked on Kellogg's door again.

"Chief… those brokers are really pissed. They claim that the fax was illegible, and the brokerage agreement is still in effect." He cast his hand forward. "Here's the amended listing agreement with Andrews Oil on it."

"Did you ask why they never mentioned Andrews Oil until yesterday?"

"Their defense was the company had only been interested in locating downtown."

Phyllis interrupted the conversation. "That gal from Andrews Oil is calling again for Rusty Affenson."

"I'll take the call." He glanced at Cohen. "Talk to you later."

Kellogg picked up the telephone receiver. "Hello gorgeous!"

"Who told you?"

"The word's out all over Houston."

"Please hold for Mr. Affenson, Mr. Kellogg."

"I'd rather hold you, honey."

After a moment of silence, Rusty Affenson picked up. "Hello, Mr. Kellogg…how are you?"

"Everything's great…how are you doin' today, Rusty?"

"I just got off the line with Marty Holbrook…he's pretty upset about the West Tower situation. He accused you of a conspiracy to defraud them of their leasing commission if we commit to your building."

"Rusty…we're clearly in the right to terminate our agreement with R & H. My attorney opined to it."

"My counsel had a call from a Denver attorney whose name is Buckingham. He claims you have a horrible reputation with a long history of reneging on contractual agreements. I'm pretty upset too…you promised not to go around me and speak directly with Buck."

"Rusty, I was out of moves and had to. Buck saw right through that phony broker…Marty Holbrook. It's true I run a tight ship…but I've never lost a lawsuit."

"Our counsel is trying to reach Buck right now. We may have to back away from your building entirely…we don't want to be a party to a lawsuit, especially when we're hoping to build a solid reputation in Denver."

"Buckingham and those brokers are blowing smoke. They're trying to steer you into buying the 1010 Building, where they have a large personal equity stake."

"Are you positive on that?"

"Absolutely…they should have disclosed that to you…any ethical firm would have done so."

"Well, that could change things…you'll hear back from us soon."

Kellogg scampered down the stairs, encountering a High Plains taxi parked outside. He reluctantly opened the rear door and slid into the seat, noticing the driver was the cabbie involved in the shoving match an hour ago. Recognizing Kellogg, the driver turned his head and extended his fist again. "It's you…fuckhead!"

Kellogg studied the cabbie's tattoos on his neck and forearms. "Relax Charlie...Drive me to Harv's Auto Repair Shop? It's located on Dahlia Street, just south of Evans Avenue."

"How do you know my name is Charlie?"

"Dusty told me...he said you're a good guy. I didn't mean to shove you earlier, but I don't like anyone putting their hands on me. Dusty's a friend of mine...that's why I picked his taxi. We both served in Vietnam and I wanted to talk to him about some Veteran's Day stuff."

"You look a little old to have served in Vietnam."

"I didn't mean to infer Dusty and I were there at the same time. I served as an advisor in Vietnam during the Eisenhower administration after I graduated from college." Kellogg thought his quick thinking was credible.

"I was in 'Nam' too...the Marines in 1969 and 1970."

"Those years were the most intense, weren't they?"

"Yeah...I lost a lot of buddies in my platoon."

"I know how it is...I lost a few friends in the Korean War too, although I was assigned to the headquarters far from the front lines. I had flat feet, so they didn't assign me to a combat unit, even though I volunteered."

As the taxi sped along I-25, Kellogg pointed to the right. "Charlie...I'm negotiating to buy that vacant piece of land there and develop three one-story office buildings."

"Oh yeah...why?"

"Because it has great visibility at a freeway interchange. I can make a lot of money on it."

"Do you need a property survey?"

"I will if I buy it."

"I drive cab to supplement my regular job...I just got my license to be a registered surveyor." He handed a business card to Kellogg, who cradled it between his fingers.

"Jackson Surveyors...is your last name Jackson?"

"Yeah...Charlie Jackson."

"I'll give your card to my assistant...we have a dependable surveyor but might need a guy for an emergency turnaround."

"I appreciate anything that you can do...what's your company?"

"Kellogg...didn't you see the name on my building?"

"I thought the cereal company was a tenant there...I've seen some of your construction signs around the city."

"Hey...there's the auto shop. Drop me in front...here's ten bucks."

"Thanks."

Chapter Seven

Racing down I-25, Kellogg was delighted to drive his convertible Corvette again, his meticulously groomed black hair rippling in the breeze. Arriving at his office, he dispatched Phyllis to a nearby fast food restaurant for an order of three cheeseburgers, fries, and a chocolate malt.

He retrieved the crumpled divorce papers from his wastebasket, flattening them on his desk. After perusing them further, he picked up the telephone and dialed John Collins. "Colly...the divorce papers were delivered this morning. I'll have Phyl messenger them to you this afternoon, so have your judge buddy prepare an eviction order right away."

"Mr. X, I received the papers directly from Henry Buckingham's office...your wife must have told him I would represent you. I already sent the prenuptial agreement and the divorce papers to Judge Watson. Hopefully, I'll hear from him later this afternoon."

"Buckingham is representing her, huh? I thought he only handled real estate cases."

"Apparently not."

"Shit...I want the eviction mandate by the end of the day!"

"I received a call from Henry Buckingham concerning the validity of your termination of the Reagan & Holbrook listing agreement on West Tower. I'm researching court rulings on fax machines to state our position. Are you positive your fax was sent before five o'clock?"

"Yes…I believe the time conflict was created because the R & H brokers didn't reset their machine to standard time on Saturday night."

"I also spoke to Matthew Morgan, Buster's criminal defense lawyer in Los Angeles. He got his bail reduced and is formulating a defense for his marijuana arrest."

Mike Peavy knocked on Kellogg's door. "Got to jump, Colly…that all sounds good."

"Hello Peavy…have you found any more cost savings on West Tower?"

"No sir…but what happened to you last night at the Brown Palace? I waited for you until six o'clock until I ran out of coins for the meter. While I looked for you in the hotel, I got a parking ticket. I decided to leave but couldn't start the car, since I was out of gas. I hiked six blocks to a filling station and when I returned, my car was gone. I called the police, discovering it was towed to the impound lot. I took a taxi there and didn't get home until nine o'clock."

"Wow…that's bad luck, Peavy."

"I'll include the cab fare, towing charge, and parking ticket in my next expense report."

"Peavy…you gotta be kidding. I'm not approving that! You should always keep plenty of change in your car for parking meters and never let your fuel go below half full."

"Well…ah…that's not fair."

"Life is a series of learning experiences and you just learned a new one. For the record, I went outside the Ship Tavern after my meeting and couldn't find you…I took a taxi to The Platte Club. Have a nice day, Peavy."

Phyllis carried Kellogg's lunch order, along with a glass of ice water on a tray into Kellogg's office.

"Here's your lunch, sir. I took the wrapping off the burgers and emptied the fries into a bowl. There's a spoon for your malt and plenty of ketchup in the small dish for your fries."

"Very nice…can you call Bill Douglas' secretary and see if he can play golf with me tomorrow afternoon?"

"Of course."

Kellogg wasted little time scarfing down his lunch when Robert entered his office without knocking. "Hey Robby Boy…what's happening?"

"Al McDonald called me this morning and said we weren't getting the job to build his manufacturing building. He said you were rude to his wife and disrupted their table in one of your drunken escapades."

"His wife deserves to be insulted…she's spreading malicious rumors about me! I did fall on their table at Trader Vic's, but I apologized and gave them five bucks to replace their drinks. I tripped on the torn carpet, losing my balance…I didn't have much to drink."

"McDonald told me the drinks spilled on her dress and the dry cleaning didn't take out the stains."

"She can sell it to a chess or checker player."

"You're a joker, Xander."

"Yeah…I tell a good joke. Relax, brother…I'll call Al and smooth this over."

Robert quickly left the office, slamming the door behind him.

Kellogg reached for his Rolodex, finding Al McDonald's phone number, and hastily punched the telephone buttons. Before the receptionist could complete a greeting, Kellogg interrupted by blurted out, "Connect me with Al McDonald… right away."

"Whose calling?"

"Mr. X."

"Sir…what's this about?"

"None of your business, honey…he knows me."

After a minute, McDonald answered. "Hello Kellogg…have you sobered up yet?"

"Pretty much, McDonald…I understand you spoke to my brother about your building."

"Yeah…we eliminated Kellogg Construction from the bidding because of your behavior the other night. Donna had to throw her dress away."

"I'm willing to buy her a new dress…anything would be an improvement on that ridiculous fashion design anyway."

"That's not the issue…I can't risk anyone with an alcohol dependency problem to be involved with construction our new facility. You might hook up the sanitary sewer line with our water intake."

"My brother, Robert, oversees our construction group. I have nothing to do with his projects…he's a straight arrow and does great work. Look…do you still want to go on our trip to San Francisco?

"Yes, but not with you. George Clements, Fred Hawthorne, and I are trying to schedule it."

"Here's my offer, buddy. I'll pay for a three-day vacation in San Francisco for you and Donna with a suite at the St. Francis Hotel and hire a chauffeur to drive you to the wine country for a day. You can use my private jet too…so how does that sound?"

"What's the catch?"

"Kellogg Construction builds your manufacturing building…we'll agree to match the lowest bid, provided you show us the full details on the competition."

"I'll consider your offer, but you must swear to stay away from anything that's connected with the construction."

"No problem, pal…Robert has total control. How about it…is it a deal?" After few moments of silence, Kellogg abandoned a core negotiation strategy and reluctantly offered another enticement. "I'll even include a new dress she can pick out there…there are several women's fashion stores around Union Square. What weekend do you want to go?"

"Okay, Xander…I agree. Send me the details for a trip the first weekend in December."

"Great…we'll build you a great facility and you'll have a super holiday too. Bye-bye."

Kellogg strolled out of his office to Phyllis' desk. "Phyl, arrange for my jet the first Thursday afternoon in December with a return on that Sunday to and from San Francisco. Then call the St. Francis Hotel for a suite for three nights as well as a limo company for a wine tour to Sonoma and Napa for that Friday. Use my name for the reservations and bill Kellogg Construction."

"Yes, sir…anything else?"

"Find a high-end women's fashion shop or department store near the St. Francis and arrange a hundred-dollar gift certificate…invoice Kellogg Construction Company too. I'll tell Robert."

Kellogg briskly strolled to Robert's office. "I have good news, Robby Boy. I just spoke to Al McDonald…we're building his facility."

"How did you do that…threaten him with a hitman?"

"Almost…I agreed to let him use my private jet to San Francisco for a weekend, plus a couple extras. Phyl will make the arrangements so we'll have a lid on the cost."

"I guess we can afford that."

"I also agreed that we would match the competitor's low construction bid as long as we could see the details."

"What?"

"Don't worry…if it looks like we are losing money on the job, you can cut corners on the materials or markup a few change orders…make sure our contract gives you flexibility. He probably won't have any oversight from an independent inspector anyway."

"What about the architect, Clements Architectural Associates?"

"George's firm? Well, he certainly won't create a problem for us."

"Xander, you know I don't play games like that. My construction company has a well-earned reputation for honesty and quality workmanship."

"Let me take care of it, Robert."

"Then I'll really need to worry."

Xander skipped away to his office, congratulating himself on another victory. "Hi Phyl, how about dinner tonight?"

"No…I told you yesterday I have a relationship now, but I arranged for Bill Douglas to play golf with you tomorrow and most of the details are already set for the San Francisco trip. Also, John Collins called you twice."

After instructing Phyllis to track down Buck Andrews again, Kellogg dialed Collins. "Colly…talk to me."

"Mr. X, we have good legal standing on the fax issue…there are a few cases confirming fax transmissions are an acceptable form of notice."

"Good…any update on Jill's eviction decree?"

"I haven't heard back from the judge yet."

"Keep on him…I need access to my house. I'm driving to western Nebraska on Friday to hunt pheasants and I'll need my pickup truck."

Eli Cohen was at Kellogg's door again. "Chief…Pete Simpson took some guy from Andrews Oil through West Tower this morning."

"How could a R & H broker get in without our permission, especially now that their listing was cancelled?"

"They convinced Brenda Dunston I gave them authority to show the property without my presence."

"I'm calling Rusty Affenson in Houston to see what he knows."

Not having a moment to flirt with Dixie, Kellogg dialed Affenson's direct line.

"Hello…Rusty Affenson."

"Good afternoon Rusty…this is Xander Kellogg."

"What can I do for you, sir?" Kellogg sensed coolness in Affenson's tone.

"Someone from Andrews Oil toured my building this morning with those sleazy R & H brokers. Do you know who that was?"

"Other than Buck, the only Andrews' employee in Denver today is Billy Norton, our land man…he's working in our temporary office downtown."

"Check it out with your guy, Norton. Have you spoken to Buck about Marty Holbrook's bullshit?"

"Yup…he's trying to arrange a call with our outside counsel."

Phyllis entered Kellogg's office without knocking. "Sir, I called the Brown Palace Hotel…Franklin Andrews apparently checked out this morning."

Kellogg instantly called Affenson again. "Rusty…Mr. X again. Where can I reach Buck?"

"I don't know…he's going elk hunting the rest of the week with his Texas buddies."

"Where's he staying?"

"We don't know…sometimes he totally gets off the grid."

"Who's in charge of your company when he disappears like this?"

"I am."

"Since you're running the show, YOU can talk to your outside counsel about Holbrook."

Kellogg abruptly hung up and turned to Phyllis. "Call every hotel, motel, and lodge that has a phone number in the mountains and see if Andrews has a room reservation."

"Where should I begin?"

"Start in Vail and work backwards alphabetically."

"Yes sir." Phyllis rolled her eyes believing the mission was impossible.

Kellogg reluctantly called his home, allowing the phone ring repeatedly until Jill finally answered.

"Jill…this is Xander."

"What the hell do you want?"

"Never better…thanks for asking. I got the divorce papers and my attorney is reviewing them."

"The sooner we can resolve this amicably…the better for both of us."

"I agree." He cleared his throat twice. "Have you spoken to your friend Nancy Andrews today…I need to speak with her."

"No, I'm not even sure she'll talk to me again after your drunken behavior."

"Does she stay anywhere other than the Brown Palace?"

"I have no idea."

"By the way, you might want to call for a room at the Brown Palace yourself."

"Why would I do that?"

"You'll need a place to stay after I evict you from my house."

"It will be my house after the divorce is settled."

"You seem to have forgotten about the terms of our prenuptial agreement. You have twenty-four hours to clear out after papers are served. You'd better get packing...the clock is ticking."

"You must be joking...I'm calling my attorney right now."

"Yeah...call Henry Fuckingham...I mean Buckingham."

Jill abruptly hung up.

Kellogg approached Phyllis, who looked frazzled. "I've called five places in Vail already with no luck."

"See if you can find a phone number for Andrews' residence in Houston...his wife might be there and tell us where Buck is."

"At once, sir."

Kellogg returned to his office and poured a glass of scotch. He grabbed three golf balls from a 1977 championship trophy bowl and a putter leaning against his desk. After placing a goblet on the carpet across the room, he and began to practice putting, using the glass as a substitute cup.

Phyllis stood in the doorway. "I found the phone number for the Andrews residence in Houston but there was no answer."

"Keep calling and the mountain hotels too.

"Yes sir...Mr. Collins is holding."

"Why didn't you tell me right away?" Kellogg grabbed the phone receiver. "Colly...what's up?"

"Judge Watson will sign the eviction decree by six o'clock...my clerk will pick it up first thing in the morning."

"Why not tonight? I don't really want to spend another night at The Platte Club."

"This takes time, Xander...we need to take the eviction notice to the Cherry Hills Police Department for service and they couldn't do it any sooner than tomorrow anyway."

"Very well...let me know when they plan to broom her. I want to witness the moment personally."

Right-o...Good night Xander."

"And a good night to you, Colly."

Mike Peavy knocked on Kellogg's door. "Chief...James Middleton called from Continental Divide Bank. His boss, Willard Edwards, rejected my budget revisions and demands the payment by Monday."

"What if I refuse?"

"They'll put the loan into default."

"How did they respond to our tenant prospect list."

"They wished us success in signing some leases soon."

"What about their appraisal?"

"They also rejected that request. I called Allied Appraisal and spoke with the owner, Greg Bottoms. He told me they were under strict orders from the bank not to release the appraisal under any circumstances."

"Greg Bottoms, huh...have I ever met him?"

"You met him briefly at the reception for Kellogg Plaza."

"Why was he invited to our extravagant party? I want his phone number."

Peavy handed a slip of paper to Kellogg. "Here it is, sir, I expected you would want to speak with him directly."

A lady answered Kellogg's call. "Allied Appraisal."

"I need to speak to Craig Button."

"Greg Bottoms?"

"Sounds right."

A few moments passed. "Hello…this is Greg Bottoms. How can I help you?"

"Good afternoon Mr. Bottoms…this is Alexander Kellogg, it's nice to speak with you again."

"How are you, sir?"

"Not very well, I'm afraid. I understand you were recently engaged to prepare an appraisal of West Tower for Continental Divide Bank."

"That's correct."

"Why didn't you speak with us when you were engaged?"

"The bank clearly instructed us to avoid any contact with Kellogg Development Company, except for onsite personnel to arrange the building inspection. Your property manager was very accommodating and gave us a tour of the entire property."

"You must have made a major error in your valuation…West Tower building is magnificent. I have a buyer in the wings offering a price two times the loan amount."

"If you can send us an official signed contract or letter of intent, we'll review it and determine if we can increase our appraised value."

"I want to see your appraisal NOW! I paid for the damn report!"

"I'm sorry, Mr. Kellogg, but we're under strict orders from our client…unfortunately, we cannot share it you."

"Bottoms…my company will never engage you again for an appraisal assignment and I'm going to run you out of the business. I have a lot of influence around this city."

"I'm sorry you feel that way, Mr. Kellogg."

"Bottoms…your name suits you well since your business will soon hit bottom. I'm used to getting what I want…it doesn't pay to cross me!"

Kellogg flung the receiver down on the floor in anger and marched to Peavy's office.

"Peavy, review the loan documents and determine if the bank can put us in default even though we're current on our loan payments."

"Sir, we're current on the loan payments because they come directly from the interest reserve account. However, it's being depleted quickly…enough for two more payments. We should have enough company liquidity to handle interest payments for several months after that."

"Peavy…I'm not using the company's cash."

"I read the documents, Mr. Kellogg. Based upon a third-party appraisal, the bank can demand a paydown or additional collateral if they deem their security to be out of balance. However, they need to notify us by a certified letter, and we'll have thirty days to comply after our receipt of it."

"Okay…we have more time then. I'm going to get West Tower under contract with the Houston oil company. Allied Appraisal will update their value when they see some written evidence to get the bank off my back."

"That's great news…I'll let the bankers know right away."

"Not yet." Kellogg left Peavy's office and approached Phyllis, who was on the phone. She shook her head.

"Keep calling, baby."

Kellogg was getting more impatient and called Rusty Affenson again.

"Rusty…Mr. X here…have you reached Buck yet?"

"We have no idea where he is…I contacted his wife and even she doesn't know."

"How about your guy in Denver…have you spoken with him yet?"

"Billy Norton was the person Pete Simpson took through your office building…Billy's wife is Simpson's sister. Last night, Billy had dinner with Simpson, who lured him into touring the building, telling him Andrews Oil was planning to locate there."

"That's just great!" Kellogg slammed his fist on the desk in anger.

"I also talked to our in-house counsel, who spoke to our outside corporate law firm. I'm afraid we're committed legally to Reagan & Holbrook for representation for a lease or a purchase."

"Shit!"

"Last week, Buck asked me about my budget for purchasing a building in Denver."

"What's your number?"

"No more than fifteen million, including our fit-out costs."

"That's a little short of our appraised value of twenty million. The 1010 Building would certainly cost far more than fifteen million."

"Yes, but several floors of that building are leased and there is an attractive long-term loan that we could assume. What's the size of West Tower?"

"Roughly two hundred thousand square feet…a price of a hundred bucks a foot."

"We're planning to have five hundred employees in Denver, so even with a generous layout of three hundred square feet per employee, we only need space for a hundred fifty thousand square feet…West Tower is a larger than we need."

"Perhaps…but you'll have room for expansion and or can sublease the balance of your space in the interim. I have a number of leasing prospects that could easily fill the void."

"Why haven't you decided to move forward on those deals?"

"I've been holding off for a single building user…we've had plenty of inquiries from other oil companies and several government units."

"I'll speak to Buck when he comes up for air."

Kellogg couldn't recall the outstanding loan balance on West Tower, so he punched Mike Peavy's extension. "Peavy...how much do we owe on West Tower?"

"About thirteen million, but we still have around two million yet to fund for the site improvements and interior finish costs, as well as the contingency items we discussed earlier. The loan commitment is for fifteen million, seventy-five per cent of Sanders Appraisal Services' original valuation of twenty million."

"Yeah...I remember now. Can you guess where Bottoms' value landed?"

"Hold on a second." Peavy punched in a few numbers on his adding machine. "Eighteen million.' He paused, waiting for Kellogg's response. "Don't hang up yet...ten minutes ago, I received the certified default letter from Continental Divide Bank from a courier. I signed for it, so the thirty-day meter starts today.

"Shit!" Kellogg cast the receiver on the floor again, cracking the mouthpiece section.

Phyllis heard the commotion and entered Kellogg's office. "Hmmm...looks like you need a new phone."

"Replace this flimsy telephone equipment...get me one that isn't so cheap."

"I'll look into it, sir. I'm exhausted...I tried thirty places in the mountains looking for Andrews and no luck."

"Just forget it Phyl...he's in hiding and doesn't want to be found. You can take off...have a pleasant evening."

"Oh, I almost forgot...George Clements called. He wants you to meet him for drinks and dinner at The Platte Club. He left his home number...here it is." She handed him a paper slip.

"Good night…I'll use your phone since mine is broken."

"Go ahead…see you in the morning." Phyllis collected her purse and car keys, making her way down the hall.

Kellogg sat on Phyllis' chair, grabbed the receiver, and dialed Clements' home.

"Georgie Boy, I hear you're lonesome tonight…Kathy must be flying."

"She's on a flight to New York and then on to London…she won't be back for a few days. Unless you and Jill have other plans, join me for dinner at The Club tonight at six-thirty."

"I have plans for Jill, but it won't be dinner with us…I'll fill you in later."

Kellogg rubbed his eyes for a moment and opened them, staring at Phyllis' calendar. He pulled it closer, observing a handwritten note…'dinner with Nate Allen at The Broker'. The number seven was circled in red ink. He opened the top left drawer, digging under a pile of stationary finding a framed picture of Nate Allen. He leafed through old calendar pages, seeing Allen's name several times, and recalled Phyllis mentioned she was seeing someone. Kellogg felt his blood pressure rising, wondering if she leaked information about West Tower to Allen. Even though Phyllis had been his loyal assistant for six years, he now had doubts. Kellogg shuffled through the rest of her desk drawers, looking for more evidence that would explain R & H's sudden interest in showing West Tower to Andrews Oil. Exhausted, he returned to his office, draped his suitcoat over his arm and headed for his Corvette, anxious to get to The Platte Club.

Kellogg turned on the FM car radio. The Amborsia song, "How Much I Feel" had just started to play. He focused on the words, wondering when his marriage to Jill started going off the tracks. He had a momentary inclination of regret but redirected his thoughts to hostility, since Jill had initiated the divorce proceedings. The disk jockey announced the next tune by Foreigner, called "Double Vision." After listening to the lyrics for three and a half minutes, he decided it would be a good night to get drunk.

Chapter Eight

Kellogg sauntered into The Platte Club men's grill looking for George Clements. Rex Wilson greeted him, escorting Kellogg to a private area of the restaurant, as he always demanded.

"Good evening Mr. Kellogg…I have a nice table in the corner near the windows. Mr. Clements was seated there but apparently left for a moment. Chanelle is your waitress tonight."

"Wonderful, Rexy Boy! Can you have a bottle of chilled champagne and strawberries and two glasses sent up to my room later?"

"Absolutely, Mr. Kellogg…it will be delivered after your dinner."

A minute later, Chanelle appeared at the table when Kellogg stood and smiled. "Hello doll, I heard you were ill last evening. How are you feeling tonight?"

"Very well…thank you, Mr. Kellogg. Can I bring you a drink?"

"Glenfiddich on the rocks, honey…make it a double."

"At once, sir."

George Clements strolled into the dining room and nestled into his chair. "Xander, I took a call from Kathy…she's in New York between flights. What's the story with Jill?"

"The slut is divorcing me. Oh well…it lasted three years but placed second for my longest marriage. Next time, I'll find a wife with a sense of humor."

"Sorry to hear that…divorce is never an easy thing."

"I'm kicking Jill out of the house tomorrow…it's part of our prenup. Join me for the celebration…I'll bring the champagne to the viewing party when the police escort her out." Kellogg chuckled.

"I need to review and sign off on the final architectural plans for Al McDonald's warehouse building. He wants to start construction next month…we have to file information with the City for the building permit next week."

"We're the contractor on that job."

"We delivered some preliminary plans to your brother a few weeks ago. I'm glad you won the bid…I look forward to working with Robert and his staff again…they're real pros."

Chanelle returned with the drink order. "Mr. Clements, while you were away, I asked the bartender to freshen your drink and add more ice."

"That's so thoughtful of you, darling…thanks." Chanelle nodded at Clements, knowing he was a gentleman.

"Mr. Kellogg…here's your double scotch with a glass of ice."

"Chanelle, that's perfect…just like you look tonight." He winked at her as she blushed.

"Gentlemen…would you like to hear the chef's specials tonight?"

"Yes, sometime before the night is over." George smirked.

She blushed again. "Excuse me…would you like to hear about the dinner specials right now?"

"Sure, although you are very special, Chanelle." Kellogg smiled broadly and winked twice at her.

Chanelle ignored his comment and looked down at her note pad. "The two choices are Rocky Mountain trout with jasmine rice and roast vegetables or lamb chops with mint chimichurri sauce and vegetable couscous."

"Check back with us in ten minutes." Clements grinned again.

Kellogg turned to Clements. "Georgie Boy, I didn't look at the golf tee sheet yet…who did you get as a partner for tomorrow's match?"

"James Middleton…I heard he's a real stick."

"I've heard he's a good golfer…and good at bank stick-ups too."

"Hmmm…I don't get it."

"Just an inside joke, pal. I'll relish taking a few bucks off the little pimp…let's raise the usual stakes from ten to fifty bucks a hole."

"You're sounding pretty confident, Mr. X."

Kellogg raised his glass. "Very confident with you on my side."

Clements raised his eyebrows. "What's do you mean?"

"Georgie Boy…just miss a few putts here and there. My partner is Bill Douglas and I need him to win for goodwill. I'll arrange for Middleton to pay Douglas and I'll forgive your bet with me."

"Okay…I'll play along as a favor. Xander, you always have something up your sleeve…that's why I'll never play poker with you." He toasted Kellogg with his tumbler.

Chanelle returned. "Would you like to order now?"

Kellogg spoke first. "Chanelle, I'll have a sixteen-ounce New York Strip…rare…with au gratin potatoes and steamed broccoli…a salad with house dressing too." He winked at her again.

After scribbling Kellogg's order, she peered at Clements. "Sir, have you decided?"

"I'll have the trout, please…and a salad with house dressing. Another round for us too."

"Thank you." She grinned at Clements, turning toward the kitchen.

"She's very beautiful…don't you agree, Mr. X?"

"Absolutely a vision…I'd love to get her to my room upstairs tonight…with the ceiling mirror, I'd have a double vision."

"Why don't you simply ask her to join you…you're never shy."

"I need to be a more subtle with her…I can read her mind."

"If you're a mind reader, tell me what I'm thinking right now."

"About how you'll yip a few putts tomorrow." Kellogg simulated a jerky putting stroke with his knife.

"I don't believe you have a future as a psychic, X."

"I'll make this prediction…I'll make a great fortune in the future on my real estate developments. You should be investing in my projects."

"I would, except I'm conflicted if you engage me as an architect."

"Well…I'll use another architectural group next time." Kellogg laughed.

"That's not funny."

Chanelle returned with the drink order and the salads. "Gentlemen, can I get you some rolls or fresh bread?"

"I'd like to sample YOUR buns?" Kellogg winked twice.

Chanelle seemed confused. "Yes, I'll get an assortment of warm rolls." She quickly turned away.

"So that was subtle, huh?" Clements chuckled.

Kellogg extended his right hand, repeating a squeezing motion. "If she was standing closer, I would have squeezed her fanny."

Kellogg and Clements traded stories over their dinner, alternating between sports, car collections, and favorite vacation destinations, culminating the evening with cigars and cognac. Chanelle discretely placed the bill near the center of the table, slightly closer to Kellogg, who quickly snatched the folder.

"I've got it, Georgie Boy...just an advance appreciation for tomorrow's golf match."

Kellogg signed the tab with his customary signature and penciled a fifty-dollar tip for Chanelle. Surreptitiously, he reached in his pocket, leaving his room key in the folder.

"Drive safely, Georgie Boy." They shook hands.

"Sleep tight, X, and don't let the bed bugs bite."

"I haven't heard that in a long time...that's what my mother used to say." Kellogg stood up and pivoted toward the lobby to pick up another room key at the front desk.

The champagne and strawberries were placed in Kellogg's room as he requested. He popped the cork on the chilled bottle, poured himself a glass, and sampled a strawberry. Sipping champagne, he stripped naked, draping a bathrobe over a nearby chair and climbed into the bed. Scanning a handful of television channels, he settled on *The Tonight Show,* laughing occasionally at Johnny Carson's monologue. He checked the clock continually, wondering when Chanelle would arrive. Five minutes later, hearing a faint knock, Kellogg vaulted out of bed. Before reaching the door, he noticed a room key on the carpet. He peered out the peephole and seeing no one, sprung the door open, checking both directions. The hallway was empty.

"Shit." He closed the door, fell into bed, and flicked off the TV with the remote control.

The alarm clock rang when Kellogg instantly slammed the snooze button, his head pounding as if an anvil was striking it every second. At eight o'clock, he arose and stumbled into the bathroom. Rummaging through the toiletry kit, he discovered a packet of aspirins, tearing it open with his teeth. He popped the pills in his mouth and forced them down his throat. He leaned into the shower stall, twisting the handle to the hottest temperature until the bathroom was enveloped in steam. Kellogg adjusted the shower head allowing the intense water stream to massage his aching head. After a few minutes relaxing in the soothing warmth, he contemplated masturbating, but quickly dismissed the temptation, vowing to have sex before the day was over, even if he had to hire a prostitute.

Evaluating the new wardrobe options, Kellogg selected khaki trousers, a white dress shirt and a blue blazer. Modeling his attire in the mirror, he was satisfied the clothes were perfectly tailored. After slipping on a pair of brown loafers, he reached for the telephone to call the valet.

"Good morning, Mr. Kellogg…this is Sam…how can I be of service?"

"Bring my car up in thirty minutes, buddy."

Kellogg hurried to the reception desk, snagging a copy of *The Rocky Mountain News* from the counter. He peered into the empty restaurant, quickly spinning his head when Chanelle appeared through the kitchen door.

"You're here again, Chanelle…did you sleep here overnight?"

"No, but I assume you did. I discovered a room key in the bill folder last night and slipped it under the room door."

"Why didn't you join me…I ordered a bottle of champagne for us?" She closed her eyes. "Listen Chanelle…I really like you. I didn't leave the key there by mistake."

"Thank you for the generous tips, but…" She stammered. "You're a little old for me, Mr. Kellogg…I'm sorry."

"I'm really not that old, baby…you can give me a test drive."

Chanelle snatched a pad and pen to take his order. "What can I get you for breakfast?"

Temporarily defeated, Kellogg shrunk down in his chair. "Black coffee, orange juice, two scrambled eggs, bacon, and wheat toast…unbuttered."

"At once, Mr. Kellogg."

Kellogg leafed through the newspaper, searching for the sports section. With the hours of drinking and storytelling last night, he had forgotten about the second game of the World Series. He scanned the front page of the sports section…the headline caption displaying the 4-3 Dodger victory over the Yankees. With the Dodgers up two games to none, Kellogg pounded the table in celebration. Through his bookie, Chubby Morrison, Kellogg had wagered five thousand dollars on the Dodgers to win the World Series.

Kellogg turned to the business section; his eyes directed to an image of a high-rise office building rendering. He focused on the headline below...'Plans for Highrise Office Announced.' He scanned the article, looking for a reference to a developer's name...the second paragraph listed Abe Friedman Interests as the developer of the prime Colorado Boulevard site he coveted. Kellogg was stunned, his blood pressure rising. He crumpled the paper and flung it across the room.

Chanelle arrived with a silver carafe, cautiously pouring steaming coffee into the small cup. "Is there something wrong sir?"

"I just read that the Dodgers won the World Series game last night...I made a big bet on the Yankees."

"I'm sorry, Mr. Kellogg...maybe they'll win next year."

"That was only the second game."

"How many games do they play?"

"Maybe seven...you don't know much about baseball, I guess."

"My dad took me to a game at Yankee Stadium in the Bronx when I was twelve...it was pretty boring, but he likes to bet on sporting events."

"Yeah...baseball is a dull game, but when I bet, it's much more interesting. I shouldn't say this, but I'm bidding to buy the Brewers."

"What brewery is that?"

"The Milwaukee Brewers...they're a baseball team in the American League."

"I've never heard of them. I'll see if your breakfast is ready now, Mr. Kellogg."

"Forget it...I've lost my appetite."

Kellogg shoved his chair back and instantly shot up. He quickly strode toward the front entrance, where his Corvette was idling.

Sam opened the clubhouse door. "I have your car running with the heater on. I closed the roof since it's a bit on the chilly side this morning. Is there anything else I can do you for you sir?"

"Sure…when Bill Douglas arrives to play golf here this afternoon, can you plant a car bomb underneath it?"

"I beg your pardon?" Sam scratched his head.

"Never mind, just hide a dead fish under his car seat." He slipped a five-dollar bill in Sam's right hand.

"I'll see if the kitchen has some leftovers." Sam saluted as he opened the car door for Kellogg.

"Thanks, Sam…see you later.

Kellogg entered his office a few minutes before nine, slowly passing Phyllis' desk.

"Mornin' Phyl…how was your dinner last night with the broker?" He coughed briefly. "I meant to say…at The Broker."

Phyllis squirmed in her chair. "Wonderful…but how did you know I was there?"

"An acquaintance was having dinner there last night and told me he saw you." His eyebrows lifted as if expecting a response.

"I like going there…the complimentary shrimp bowl is amazing, and the prime rib is my favorite." She nervously reached for her purse.

"How about your date…do I know him?"

"I don't believe so." She looked away and began to light a cigarette. "I replaced your telephone with one I found in the construction company office."

Kellogg headed to his office and immediately reached for the new phone to call John Collins.

"Hello, Mr. X…I assume you're calling about your wife's eviction notice."

"How did you guess, Colly?"

"Just a hunch…we have the court order and my messenger is driving it to the Cherry Hill Police Department right now."

"I'll call their police chief…he's a close friend. I'll order him to serve the notice before eleven…I have a big golf match at one o'clock. I want to see the bimbo get kicked out with my own eyes. Do you want to join me for the party?"

"I can't…I have a pile of work here."

"I'll tell you the highlights later."

Kellogg called Chief Woodward at the Cherry Hills Police Department. "Woody Boy…have you arrested any suspicious looking characters today?"

"Not yet…but I could when I see you." Woodward giggled.

"Ha…ha. I have a trespasser in my house…her name is Jill Kellogg and I want you to personally arrest her."

"That's your wife, Mr. X…what's up?"

"I'm divorcing her. You should receive an eviction decree any minute from my attorney...a judge signed it last night. I'll meet you on my front lawn at eleven o'clock."

"I can't...I've got a full calendar today."

"Is Roger Clements on duty this morning?"

"He's in the station right now getting ready to go on patrol."

"Ask him to wait for the messenger and meet me at my house just before eleven."

"Okay...let me know when you can take me on your jet to Vegas again."

"Okay buddy," Kellogg said with a smile, anticipating Jill's humiliating eviction.

Kellogg decided to draft a sale contract on West Tower with Andrews Oil Company as the buyer. He called Eli Cohen, requesting a blank copy of an official sales contract form and inserted a purchase price of $20,000,000.00 and a closing date of December 15, 1978.

Kellogg concluded Phyllis could no longer be trusted on any matter regarding West Tower, deciding to ask Eli Cohen's secretary, Abbie Kornfeld, to type the complete contract. Kellogg instructed Abbie to place the typed document in a sealed manila envelope in his top left desk drawer. The next step would be tricky, wondering how he could obtain a copy of a signature of a senior officer of Andrews Oil to forge on the contract.

Kellogg checked his watch...time to drive to his residence to meet Roger Clements. Opening his office refrigerator, he grabbed a bottle of champagne normally used for business celebrations and slipped into the breakroom to gather two plastic cups.

Kellogg spun his Corvette over his long driveway and parked near the garage. Entering through the damaged overhead door space, he found a padded pool chair and side table, placing them on the lawn forty feet from the front door of the house. He retrieved the cups and champagne from his car, set them on the table, and snatched a cigar tucked in his blazer. Two minutes later, a Cherry Hill police car pulled in front of the house. Holding a white envelope in his left hand, Officer Roger Clements, exited the car and ambled over to greet Kellogg. "Hello, Mr. Kellogg…I see you already have your car back from the shop."

"Roger, there wasn't much damage…can I pour you some champagne?"

"Thanks, but I can't drink on duty."

"Why wasn't your siren blaring? I wanted our neighbors to check out the excitement here."

"We don't use our lights or siren for these types of things."

"You should." Kellogg took a sip of champagne, smacked his lips, and hoisted his cup toward Officer Clements.

"Is your wife home?"

"I don't know…I've been sleeping at The Platte Club the last two nights. All the cars are in the garage, so she should be in there."

Officer Clements crossed the driveway and climbed the front steps. Yanking the black doorknocker, he pounded continuously for ten seconds and after peering through the side windows, pushed the bell several times. The curtains parted in the master bedroom as Jill peered out, obviously seeing the patrol car. Kellogg waved, when the curtains closed abruptly. Officer Clements now beat on the front door with his night stick, until the front door finally opened a crack.

"Are you Jillian Kellogg?"

"Why?"

Clements was irritated. "Are you Jillian Kellogg?"

"I'm changing my name to Jillian Pike very soon."

"So...you ARE Jillian Kellogg?"

She slammed the door shut. Clements glanced back toward Kellogg, who was laughing loudly as he refilled his champagne cup. Roger resumed using his night stick, striking the door again several times. "You must open the door Mrs. Kellogg! I have a court order to evict you from these premises. If you don't comply, you will be held in contempt by the court and subject to incarceration."

The door immediately opened, when Jill snatched the order from Clements' hand, abruptly slamming the door shut again. The policeman peered through the side window, observing Jill reading the order. "Mrs. Kellogg...I'll give you ten minutes to come out." He checked his watch. "It's now eleven-ten."

Kellogg poured another cup of champagne as Clements sauntered over. "Are you sure you won't have some bubbly, Roger?"

"No thanks."

"What did the bitch tell you?"

"Nothing really...she finally identified herself as your wife. I gave her ten minutes to come out."

Officer Clements returned to his black squad car to call the police station, while Kellogg began to pace across the lawn. Minutes later, Jill threw two suitcases down the steps of the side entrance to the home, when Kellogg wandered over to greet her. Jill emerged from the house with an overstuffed bag over her shoulder and began to tug the largest suitcase over the uneven pavers toward the garage.

"Hold on there, sweetheart… where do you think you're going?" Kellogg held his hand up.

"I'm loading the Mercedes, asshole."

"Hold on, honey…all the cars are registered under my company name, so it would be grand theft if you drive one away. You wouldn't get too far with a policeman watching."

"You're a fucking bastard…how am I going to transport all my stuff?"

"A taxi?"

"I've never used a cab in my entire life…they're dirty.' She stomped on the ground with her right foot. "I'm calling my attorney."

"Yeah, call Buckingham…I'm sure he'll run right over and haul all your crap away."

Jill strutted toward the side entrance of the house, where Officer Clements blocked her path.

"Mrs. Kellogg, you cannot re-enter the house…I will arrest you for trespassing." Clements held his arms out blocking her. "I don't want to do that…please cooperate. I know this is a difficult situation for you…I have to enforce this eviction order."

Visibly upset, she slammed her handbag to the ground. "How can I retrieve the rest of my things?"

"I expect your attorney can designate someone under Mr. Kellogg's supervision," Roger explained

Kellogg interrupted. "Under my strict surveillance only, Jill...I don't trust you or your scumbag lawyer. But darling...I'll go in and call a taxi for you."

"How thoughtful...you prick. I'm suing you for everything you have!"

"Now, now, Jill...let's not get nasty."

She sat down on the steps and suddenly pulled a handgun from her purse, pointing it at Kellogg's crotch.

"You are scum, Xander...I'm going to teach you! For a big prick, your cock is the smallest I've ever seen...I'm still going to shoot it off!"

Kellogg jumped back, holding his hands over his crotch as if to deflect a bullet. "Shoot me if you have the nerve."

Officer Clements unbuckled his holster and placed his hand on the butt of his revolver.

"Mrs. Kellogg, please put that gun down on the concrete...NOW!"

Jill glared at Kellogg. "You've ruined my life and now I'm ruining yours."

"Hey...taxis aren't really that bad...wait until you have to take a bus."

Clements shouted again. "I said...lay the gun down now, Mrs. Kellogg!" He yanked his revolver from the holster.

Jill repeatedly squeezed the trigger, although the pistol had a lock mechanism, preventing the gun from firing. She finally cast the weapon on the pavement, pulled a grey scarf over her face, and began to sob.

Clements instantly bounded toward the pistol and swept it from her reach in one motion.

"Lady, you'll be happy someday with that decision."

"I tried to pull the trigger…I just didn't know how."

Kellogg bellowed. "That's why I put a safety latch on my handguns, baby."

"Call a cab for me then, asshole."

"Give me your keys, Jill."

She thrust her right hand into her purse, snagged them, and cast them directly at Kellogg's face. He ducked, catching them with his left hand.

"In case you have another set of keys, I'll be changing the locks later today."

Jill curled her mouth and spit at Kellogg, some spittle landing on his trousers.

"Charming…charming, Jill. Just to think, you were nearly Miss America. Perhaps you would have won if you had tried to spit watermelon seeds for your talent competition."

Before she could respond, Kellogg snuck through the side door into the kitchen. He picked up the telephone book from the counter, leafing through the pages for the High Plains Taxi number. "I need a taxi at 4000 Woodlawn Lane. If Dusty is on duty, I want him…tell him it's Alexander Kellogg's residence."

The dispatcher hesitated for a few seconds. "Yes…he's driving cab 21 today. I'll get him on the radio to see if he can take it…please hold."

Kellogg surveyed the kitchen, reaching for a pile of mail stacked on the counter. On top was an invitation to a gala event hosted by Franklin and Nancy Andrews. He ripped the envelope open and plucked an engraved invitation to a wine tasting at the Brown Palace, noting both Buck's and Nancy's s handwritten signatures at the bottom. Casting the invitation aside, he collected five department store envelopes and ripped them open, tabulating over six thousand dollars in billings. Kellogg had never reviewed Jill's charge accounts, knowing three thousand dollars was funded directly into her private checking account by the company every month.

The taxi dispatcher clicked back on the phone. "Sir…Dusty's cab will be at your residence in five minutes."

Kellogg scooped the department store bills in his right hand, exited the residence, and cast them in Jill's face. He pointed to the papers scattered on the steps. "You'd better work out an installment payment plan with all these stores. The three grand I'll pay you each month under our prenup won't go too far based upon your spendthrift habits…you might have to find a real job, sweetheart."

"People have begged me to work for them for years. In case you've forgotten, I have a degree in marketing from Morehead University."

"Yeah…they've heard you give a damn good blow job." Kellogg roared as he leaned back against the black metal railing.

Jill lurched at Kellogg, attempting to push him backward over the barrier. She clutched his throat, as Kellogg repelled her down on the steps. Officer Clements sprang into action, grabbing Jill's thin wrists, pinned her arms behind her back, and snatched the handcuffs from his belt. He bent Jill's forearms back and secured the restraints as she began to scream. "Sorry, Mrs. Kellogg, but I must cuff you. Mr. Kellogg...do you want to press charges against her for attacking you?"

Kellogg pondered for a few seconds. "I can think of a dozen things she could be arrested for...but forget it."

Jill twisted her body, trying to free herself. "Use the handcuffs on him...he's the criminal!"

"Please relax, Mrs. Kellogg...this will all be over soon."

"I'm reporting you to the Chief of Police...my attorney will file a complaint against you for using excessive force. What's your name?"

"Officer Clements."

"Are you related to George Clements?"

Kellogg interrupted. "Don't answer that Roger!"

"Officer Roger Clements...I knew it...another rigged scheme you set up, Xander."

Jill turned away, observing an orange taxi slowly threading up the long, curving driveway. The cab abruptly stopped, when Kellogg circled the car and motioned Dusty to roll down the window. Kellogg lowered his voice so neither Officer Clements nor Jill could hear him.

"Hey buddy...pile that luggage in your car and take this bimbo to where she wants to go. Also, I need a dancer from one of your strip clubs tonight. Here's two hundred...can you handle that?"

"When do you want the stripper here?"

"About eight o'clock."

Kellogg returned to Jill, who was now slumped on the steps. "The cabbie will drive you wherever you want after he loads your bags. Don't worry...I've got the fare covered unless you want to drive more than ten miles."

Officer Clements accompanied Jill to the cab and unlocked her handcuffs. "I trust you'll behave yourself now."

Without answering, Jill opened the rear car door, slung herself into the seat, and slammed the door shut while Officer Clements returned to his squad car.

When Dusty finished packing Jill's luggage, he pulled Kellogg aside.

"Do you like blondes, brunettes, or redheads?"

Kellogg whispered in his ear. "I don't care...pick a gal with big tits and who has a sense of humor."

Kellogg sauntered over to the police car where Officer Clements was still observing.

"Roger...thanks for your help. I'll tell Chief Woody you prevented a murder today."

"No sweat...have a nice afternoon, Mr. Kellogg."

Kellogg checked his watch. "Almost time to head to The Platte Club for my golf game. Now, I need to call my brother to get one of his guys over here to change all the locks."

While Kellogg went into the house to call Robert, Clements slipped into the squad car and drove away, feeling guilty about intervening in domestic disputes.

Xander Kellogg drove into the entrance of The Platte Club at noon, waving to the guard manning the guardhouse. The gate lifted immediately, and Kellogg steered his Corvette under the clubhouse porte cochere, where Sam was waiting to open his car door.

"Sam…my man."

"Good afternoon, Mr. Kellogg."

"Have you seen Bill Douglas yet?"

"Yes sir…he arrived about ten minutes ago."

"Don't forget about the dead fish."

"I found a couple partially frozen bass in the trash bin outside the kitchen…they should be melted soon."

"Bass…huh? Will they stink?"

"Probably…I'm not an expert on fish odors."

"Okay…here's a five spot." Kellogg flipped the car keys to Sam. "Park it in the garage today."

Kellogg jogged to the golf shop entrance, fifty yards from the porte cochere. He pushed the glass revolving door, passing into the green carpeted room and scanned the area. Kenny Ingram, the head golf professional, was manning the proshop.

"Kenny Boy…I've arrived. Where are the trumpets?"

"Hello Mr. X…I don't know about trumpets, but we have two brassies in stock."

"Brassies…old 2-woods, eh? Kellogg chuckled "Okay, I get it. Did you hear about the Polack who always wore two pairs of pants when playing golf?"

"No…why?"

"In case he got a hole in one!" Kellogg hooted while Kenny sniggered.

"Good one, Mr. X. Do you want to ride today or take a caddie?"

"I'll take a looper...I need some exercise. Who's available?"

"The kids are all back in school, so just the veterans. Moe, Clyde, and Tank are coming in soon from their morning loops."

"I'll take Moe. I worry about Tank's weight...he might not make it around for another eighteen holes. I don't want Clyde either...Clydesdale clomps around like a horse, which distracts me."

"I'll have Eddie get your clubs set up on the range."

"I'm playing with Bill Douglas, George Clements and James Middleton today."

"Middleton usually takes a caddie, and the other two always ride...I'll have Eddie arrange everything."

"See you later...I need to grab a quick bite."

Kellogg briskly exited the golf shop, taking the brick path around the practice green to the café, where Clements was finishing the last bite of a tuna fish sandwich. "Hi Xander...I just practiced several misses on the putting green. How did your eviction party go this morning?"

"Terrific...Jill tried to shoot my dick off with one of my revolvers and then tried to choke me. Fortunately, Roger was there...he handcuffed her, although I decided not press charges. Jill is mentally deranged...she desperately needs psychological help."

"X, anyone who hangs around with you too long will suffer brain damage. I'd should be careful myself, especially since I agreed to go along with your devious scheme today."

"Where's Middleton?"

"On the practice range."

Kellogg turned to Doris, who was running the café operation. "Doris, you're banished to the café today…eh? I'll have a hot dog with relish and mustard, a bag of chips, and a lemonade."

"Good afternoon, Mr. Kellogg…will that be all?"

"I'm in a hurry…just sign my name to the bill and add a buck tip for yourself."

"Coming right up, sir…and thanks for your generosity."

Doris plucked a plump wiener from the grill, nestled it into a toasted bun, and generously squirted relish and mustard from the squeeze bottles on the hot dog. She filled the plastic cup with ice and nudged the beverage lever on the refrigeration machine.

"Not too much ice, Doris!"

Doris spooned out much of the ice and resumed pouring. She clipped the plastic over around the lid and inserted a straw with the paper tip protecting the end. She plucked a cloth napkin from beneath the counter, selected a bag of chips, and carried the food to the table. Kellogg wrapped his hands around the hot dog bun, opened his mouth and chomped down, the condiments exploding on his white golf shirt.

"Fuck! Doris…you're a damn joke! Did you overload the hot dog with condiments on purpose? What a mess!"

Clements roared in laughter as Doris hurriedly grabbed a wet towel, dabbing Kellogg's shirt repeatedly.

"Get that rag off me, you moron…you're only making it worse."

"I'm very sorry… Mr. Kellogg."

"Sorry…my ass. I'll have to get another shirt out of my locker." Kellogg threw the remnants of his hot dog at her, splattering her apron. He quickly left the café, heading to the locker room.

As Kellogg rounded the corner of lockers, Bill Douglas was seated on a bench tying his golf shoes. "Hello, Mr. X…I'm looking forward to our golf match today." He rose to shake Kellogg's hand.

"Douglas…don't bother getting up." Kellogg retreated two steps. "I'm surprised you showed up after the story broke in *The Rocky Mountain News* this morning…I figured you would be pouring over architectural plans with Abe Friedman for his new Colorado Boulevard office tower."

"I've already called Friedman…the story should not have been released. Our deal isn't finalized…Friedman got ahead of himself."

"I've been trying to arrange a time to discuss your site for months and you kept ignoring me. You may recall our conversation at the Cosmopolitan Hotel and I really wanted to discuss the property when I bumped into you and Linda Melrose at The Platte Club. Frankly, you looked a bit embarrassed to be seen there with Linda. I know you booked Room 302 that night…I read the room number on your key after it fell out of your hand." Douglas stared at the floor. "Look Bill, I've known Linda for a long time and had some great sex with her over the years. She's a real pro…and not a bad tailor either. I'm sure your wife would love to hear about Linda."

"What do you mean?" Douglas squirmed on the bench seat.

"Helen…that's your wife's name, right? I've met her a couple of times."

"She wouldn't believe you!" Douglas' face was pale.

"Rex Wilson knows you rented the room and so does the Club receptionist...Helen might believe them." Douglas remained silent, shifting his position on the bench. "Bill, maybe we can still work out a deal on your Colorado Boulevard site...we'll have plenty of time to discuss it on the course today. Right now, I gotta change...Doris spilled mustard and relish all over my shirt...looks like some baby shit on me. They should send her to a convalescent home. I'll see you on the first tee."

Kellogg brushed by Douglas and turned left down the aisle, counting the rows to his locker. He made a right turn and stood in front of locker 007. Looking up, he admired the gold plate with his name, Mr. X, stamped on it. He spun the code on the lock and ripped open the double oak door. He yanked a yellow shirt off the hanger, deciding it would match his trousers. He threw the soiled white shirt to the bottom of his locker and slammed the doors shut.

Kellogg strode to the practice range, where his bag was set next to the station where James Middleton was hitting his driver. "Good afternoon James...I hear that we're playing together."

Middleton seemed nervous. "Yeah...George Clements invited me. I've never played with him, or you either, for some reason."

"George needed a low handicapper to partner with him, since we're playing for a few bucks. I have a three handicap and you're a plus one...so you're giving me four shots, two on each side. My partner is Bill Douglas...he and George are both seventeen, so they'll each get eighteen shots rotating off your index."

"How much are we playing for, Mr. Kellogg."

"Just fifty bucks a hole per player...low total team net score wins."

Middleton coughed for a few seconds. "That's pretty steep."

"James…you're a member here, so money shouldn't be a problem. In case you need a loan, your daddy can probably front you. I trust he got you in here under the legacy policy."

"You know my father?"

"Yep…Middy was my sponsor when I got into The Platte Club fifteen years ago. I got to know him when he was the CEO of Security Savings. I bought two small apartment buildings from his bank after they foreclosed on them. I haven't seen him around in years…how's he doing?"

"Not well…his mind is fading. We've had to place him in an assisted living home with memory care."

"Say hello to him for me the next time you see him. I hate to talk business on the golf course but tell your idiot bank auditors I'm sending over a copy of a purchase contract on West Tower next week. I'm selling it for twenty million…that should get them off my back for your bullshit capital call."

"We'll still need an appraisal that supports that value."

"No problem…I've already spoken to Greg Buttons at Allied Appraisal."

"My boss won't be happy to hear you've intervened when Bottoms calls him."

"I'll take care of Buttons."

Middleton teed up a ball, hammering it near the back wall of the range, just as his caddie, Tank, plodded to the station. Middleton slammed his driver into his golf bag and addressed the overweight caddie. "Tank…I hear you're toting my bag today. I'm done on the range, so clean my clubs and I'll meet you by the putting green."

"Yes, Mr. Middleton." Tank, still wheezing, stuffed a hot dog in his mouth, holding another in his right hand.

Kellogg waited a few seconds until Middleton was gone and sauntered over to the caddie. "Tank, be careful eating that dog...the mustard can attack you."

Tank wiped off his mouth with his hand, rubbing it on his white coveralls. "Say what, Mr. X?"

"I'm sure you'd like to make a few extra bucks today...I'll give you ten bucks every time one of Middleton's drives is stymied by a tree or a bush...maybe a few inches out of bounds too. You caddies typically place yourself down the fairway on at least eight holes, so get creative when he can't see you."

"Okay...like last month when you paid me fifty bucks in the big match you won?"

"You got it, Tank."

Moe loped over to Kellogg's station on the range.

"Hello Mr. Kellogg...glad to be on your bag today, sir."

"Big money game today, Moe. You know the program...right?" Kellogg winked twice.

"Absolutely." He chuckled for several seconds.

"Bill Douglas is my partner...he may need some help too. I need to hit a few practice shots now."

Kellogg launched twenty practice shots, satisfied he found his tempo and motioned Moe to follow him to the practice green. After putting ten balls, Kellogg intercepted Douglas on the way to the first tee.

"Any thoughts about our little conversation, Bill? By the way, I saw your wife drive into the parking lot a few minutes ago."

"She usually plays bridge on Thursday afternoon with her women's group. You may recall she's on The Platte Club's board of directors."

"Helen's bridge group might love to hear about Linda Melrose too."

"Shut up, or I'll quit right now!"

"Quit and you'll forfeit eighteen hundred bucks at fifty bucks a hole...including my side of the bet."

Douglas nodded his head and marched to the first tee, where Kellogg took command with the group. "Boys, I think you all understand the game today...but just in case, each team will total their net score and the low team will win a hundred dollars. If there are ties, the bet will carry over until a team wins the next hole...theoretically, someone could lose nine hundred at most. I'll keep track of the scores...any questions?"

Middleton timidly raised his hand. "I only have a hundred bucks on me."

Kellogg smirked "You'd better play well James...or else George will need to cover for you."

Clements shrugged. "Wait a second, X...I only carry a thousand on me."

Kellogg extended his hand. "I take checks...how about you, Bill?"

"Gladly...let's play."

Clements correctly called Kellogg's coin flip to lead off, clunking his drive a hundred yards on the ground, while Middleton followed by striking his tee shot into the right trees. Xander was confident the match would go his way, knowing he had inside help...the same way he ran his business. He and Douglas struck perfect drives.

The afternoon match ended exactly as Kellogg had planned…he was up five hundred bucks walking off the eighteenth green. Shooting a respectable seventy-three, Kellogg's team won fourteen holes compared to only four by the Clements-Middleton duo. Middleton struggled, posting a score of eighty-one, punished by three unpayable lies and two balls out of bounds.

After the traditional handshake ceremony, Kellogg addressed the group. "Let's meet in the Men's Grill after we hit the showers…the winners will pick up the drink tab."

Middleton yelled over at Tank, who was bent over, breathing heavily. "Caddie…I'll sign for you in the pro shop and they can pay you."

Kellogg hesitated a few seconds and followed the caddies toward the bag room. "Moe, I'll sign for you too and include a generous bonus. Nice job today…all my lies were perfect."

"Always a pleasure, Mr. X…I love your jokes too."

Kellogg pulled Tank aside. "Tank, you did good too…I counted three unpayable lies and two OB's for Middleton. Maybe they weren't all your work, but here's fifty bucks anyway." Kellogg stuffed the cash in Tank's palm as they shook hands.

"You have class, Mr. Kellogg."

Kellogg trudged to the golf shop, encountering Kenny again. "How did it go out there, Mr. X?"

"A profitable day, Kenny Boy…give me a slip to sign for Moe." He inserted a hundred-dollar tip on the bottom line, adding to the customary fifty-dollar caddie fee. "Here's twenty for looking sharp, Kenny Boy." Kellogg cast the bill across the counter.

Bill Douglas' strolled to Kellogg's locker. "Mr. X…I've been thinking about our land deal all afternoon. I'll cancel my handshake deal with Friedman. It will not be easy, but I'll use his premature press article as the reason. However, you'll have to match his price."

"Bill...I'll only pay ninety percent of what your deal was. You insulted me too often with your bullshit excuses to avoid me...not a cent more." Kellogg abruptly turned away, heading to his locker.

After Kellogg showered, he joined the group at a round oak table in the walnut paneled grill room, shrouded in cigar smoke. Dante, Kellogg's favorite bartender, was managing the bar operation. "Dante Bambino...I see my partners have ordered already. I'll have a double Glenfiddich on the rocks."

"Prego...Mr. X." Dante replied in his Italian accent.

"Some mixed nuts too, Dante...I'm starving!" Kellogg surveyed the golfers. "Shit, I'm about to sit with some mixed nuts too."

"Mr. X...we must all be nutty to hang around you." Clements bellowed.

Kellogg laughed too. "Dante...got any Cuban cigars stashed away in your secret vault?"

"I have some Romco and Julietta Number 1's especially reserved for you."

"Excellent!' He nodded to Dante and shifted toward his golfing partners. "Boys...want a cigar too?"

George spoke first. "I'll have one, Dante."

Middleton gulped his beer and thrust up his left hand, signaling his rejection.

Douglas shook his head. "I'll pass...Helen will be upset if she smells cigar odor on my clothes. Did you know she's campaigning for the board to prohibit cigar smoking in the grill?"

"Bill…did you marry a communist? That will never happen if I have anything to say about it."

Douglas ignored the comment, as Kellogg proceeded to settle the golf bet. "Fellas…let's see some green. From my calculations, five hundred smackers each. George can pay me, and James can pay Bill."

Clements reached into his sports jacket for his silver money clip and counted out five one hundred-dollar bills. He laid them in front of Kellogg, who instantly scooped them up and stuffed them in his pant pocket. Douglas glanced at Middleton, who reached for his wallet, making a quick inventory of his cash, and laid out five twenties. "Here's a hundred, Bill…I'll have to pay you the rest next week."

Clements hesitated, counted four more C-notes from his clip and plunked them on the table in front of Douglas. George swiveled his chair to address Middleton. "Got you covered today, James…your credit is good with me."

"Thanks Mr. Clements…I'll drop a check by your office tomorrow morning."

"No problem…I know bankers have access to plenty of cash."

Dante reappeared, displaying two silver cigar cylinders and a bronze puncher. "You always like to cut your own, right Mr. X?"

"Yes… but stay here and light me up. How about you, Georgie Boy?"

"I'll punch mine too."

Kellogg snipped the end of the cigar in craftsmanship like fashion. He held the cigar under his nostrils, sniffing it for a few seconds, and inserted the end in his mouth to sample the taste. "Muy bien, Dante."

"Bueno!" Dante nodded at Kellogg.

Dante circled the matchhead around the cigar tips long enough for Kellogg and Clements to set the effective drags. Clements coughed a few times. "Wow…these are pretty potent!"

"Just right, Georgie Boy." Kellogg blew two smoke rings at Middleton.

Middleton slugged down the last inch of beer in his glass. "I can't recall another round where I had three unplayable lies and two out of play…what are the odds?" He tossed a cashew in the air, snagging it in his mouth.

"James, you were in the trees quite a few times today…maybe it's Arbor Day." Kellogg chuckled.

"I can't believe my caddie found all my golf balls in those thick shrubs…they were in there pretty deep."

"Tank is a great caddie…he can find a ball anywhere." Kellogg blew more smoke rings toward the ceiling.

"I'm still mystified why we couldn't find my drive on the fifth hole…it wasn't far off the fairway. That was my worst round all year."

"Are you sure you won't have a cigar, James?"

Middleton grumbled. "I already got smoked today…in more ways than one." He abruptly stood up and scurried toward the door.

"Sore loser if you asked me." Kellogg leaned back in his chair, watching Middleton exit the room.

Douglas glanced at Kellogg. "Spoiled kid…his dad always opened doors for him. James has been trying to get us to borrow from Continental Divide Bank since he started there. We've always had a great relationship with Wes Wheeler at First National, but Middleton is pissed we haven't given him any business."

Kellogg puffed on his cigar. "I have a loan with Continental…they're giving me problems on our draws. I can't wait until we until we pay them off…I'll never work with them again."

Douglas pushed his chair back and rose. "I better get home…Helen will divorce me if I'm late."

Kellogg winked at him. "She might divorce you for something else, Bill. I'll call you on Monday about our deal. I'm going pheasant hunting in Nebraska over the weekend. Before you leave, let's flip to see who picks up the drink tab, Billy Boy."

"Hmmm…okay."

Kellogg snagged a quarter from his pocket, immediately launching it in the air. He snagged it in his right palm, turning the coin over on his left hand, immediately covering it with the tips of his right fingers.

"I'll call it, Billy Boy…tails."

Kellogg lifted his palm slightly. "It's a tail…you lose, pal." He quickly pocketed the coin.

Douglas frowned for a few seconds when Clements suddenly spoke up.

"I saw a tail, Bill…you lost."

Kellogg laughed. "Bill…you just won five hundred bucks, so relax."

Douglas motioned to Dante. "Put the drinks on my tab…number one fifty-three."

Dante acknowledged him with a nod.

Kellogg yelled out. "Dante Bambino…add the two cigars to his tab too."

Douglas shook his head as he strolled to the bar, where he signed the bill.

As Kellogg watched Douglas leave, he snuffed out his cigar and reached in his pocket. "Georgie Boy…here's your five hundred back. Thanks for playing along."

"I hope it was worth it…Middleton didn't seem very happy."

"He's a weasel…we should have played for more money, but I'll never play with him again."

"Douglas may not play with you again either…was the coin really a tail?"

Kellogg chuckled. "What do you think, Georgie Boy?"

"I know it was heads."

"It's history now…no one will ever know." Kellogg checked his watch. "I need to head home…I have a blind date tonight."

"You had better hope she's blind…one look at your ugly face and she'll run away fast."

"Very clever…Georgie Boy. I'll let you know how it goes…see yah."

Kellogg marched to the bar to shake hands with Dante, pressing a twenty-dollar bill into his hand. "Gracias, Dante…buenas noches!"

"Grazie…Mr. Kellogg…a presto."

Kellogg waved and headed out the door toward the valet station, where Sam was standing attention. "Good evening…Mr. Kellogg."

"Sammy Boy…how did the fishing trip go today?"

Sam glanced around, assuring himself that no one was around to hear the conversation. "Successful…two basses in the trunk."

Kellogg slipped a ten-dollar bill into Sam's hand. "Thanks."

"I'll get your car from the garage, sir."

Chapter Nine

Kellogg buzzed along I-25 toward the Wyoming border in his Chevrolet C/K truck in route to Scottsbluff, Nebraska. He was looking forward to the annual adventure arranged by Rich Eastman and Curt Jamison, high profile office leasing brokers at Gabbert and Company. They had also invited Kellogg's former fraternity brother, Steve Nelson, to join the group this year. For several years, Nelson had provided extensive legal counsel to Gabbert and Company, working closely with Eastman and Jamison on major office leases. As each year passed, the men spent less time stalking pheasants, instead playing poker and consuming alcohol...vast sums of alcohol. In addition, every year, Jamison hired four strippers from a local strip club to entertain the guys.

After cutting cards to determine the stripper draft order, Kellogg finished last, stuck with the ugliest woman of the quartet. He futilely attempted to bribe the others to exchange, but there were no takers at five hundred bucks, so he drank more heavily than usual. The beds in the old farmhouse were old, sagging in the middle, and the squeaky bedsprings were a distraction for Kellogg to maintain an erection. The constant laughter in the adjacent bedrooms also kept him awake when he desperately needed to sleep.

Kellogg was the same age as his fraternity brother, although Steve Nelson and the younger Eastman and Jamison seemed to have boundless energy. Kellogg attributed it to the amphetamines they inhaled constantly. Although he had experimented with speed a few times in the privacy of his home, Kellogg hesitated on the hunting trip without local police relationships in the event the farmhouse was raided. On Friday evening, Jamison unwrapped a brown package filled with marijuana and proceeded to roll several joints, passing them around the group. Kellogg declined to participate, but drank scotch directly from the bottle, partying well into the wee hours of the morning.

On Saturday evening, Nelson brought a silver tin hidden under the hood of his car. After carefully opening the container, he tapped the white powder unto a kitchen plate. He pulled four short straws from his coat pocket, placing them in front of each man. Kellogg rubbed his cheek for a few moments and pushed his straw back toward Nelson. "Nellie…thanks for the offer, but I'm not into this stuff. But look at the bright side…there's more for you guys to share. I'm hittin' the sack." Kellogg pushed his chair back and left the kitchen.

Early Monday morning, Kellogg awoke in his own bedroom, exhausted from the hunting trip. He closed his eyes, relaxing in the warm waterbed mattress in his king size bed. Feeling as if floating on a tranquil lake, his thoughts focused on Jill. The hours spent having sex with her was intoxicating, their bodies churning in the warm waves. Bambi, the dancer who Dusty delivered on Thursday night, couldn't adjust to the waterbed, so Kellogg relocated to another room, where the bed with a firm mattress.

Kellogg finally rolled out of bed, shuffled into his lavish bathroom, and turned on the steam shower. After brushing his teeth and shaving, he opened the shower door and stepped in. For a minute, the hot spray rained down on his head, relaxing him even more. As he lathered his body, Kellogg suddenly recalled Buck Andrew's fundraising invitation with his handwritten signature…the solution to forging the sales contract. After dressing in a favorite blue pin stripe suit, he hurried to the kitchen, finding the wine tasting invitation on the counter. He stashed it in his suit pocket and headed to the garage.

Kellogg quickly raced past Phyllis without uttering a word, although she managed a tardy greeting. He plunked down in his chair and opened the left desk drawer, finding the manila envelope Abbie Kornfeld dropped off. Opening it, he perused the purchase contract she typed for West Tower. He pulled Andrews' invitation from his suit pocket and practiced duplicating Buck Andrew's signature. Confident he had mastered the autograph, Kellogg signed Buck Andrew's name on the contract as the buyer's representative and scribbled his own classic signature as the seller's general partner.

After ordering Phyllis to drive to a nearby bakery for donuts, Kellogg rifled through her desk to locate the notary seal. He quickly pressed the seal under the signature lines of the contract. Using an existing document, Kellogg traced Phyllis' signature on the notary space. He quickly bolted out of his office and hustled to the copier, making three copies of the executed contract.

When Kellogg returned to his office, Phyllis was arranging coffee service on his desk, along with three donuts...one plain, one sprinkled and the third one, glazed.

"How was your hunting trip to Nebraska, Mr. Kellogg?"

"Tiring, but I had fun...those birds are hard to scare up, even with dogs."

"Is there anything I can do for you this morning?" She pointed to the papers tucked under Kellogg's arm. "Do you need anything typed?"

"A couple of things will need to be messengered later...I'll let you know." He picked up an engraved card from his desk and slipped it in her hand. "Here's an invitation from Buck Andrews I found at home. Can you respond for me? I'm attending with a date, but obviously not Jill...she's history. I finally got her evicted from my house Thursday morning. If it wasn't for Roger Clements, she would have shot me with one of my guns. Jill tried to choke me too...I knew she was upset, but I didn't think she would go off the deep end."

Phyllis put a hand to her face. "What a story."

"I need a new maid for my home during the week...from nine until five every day, except weekends. Jill interviewed a couple of candidates, but I want to start over...call an employment agency."

"How much are you intending to pay?"

"Three hundred a week should be enough."

Between sips of coffee Kellogg folded one contract copy with three creases and tucked it in a large business envelope. He licked the seam twice, pressed the seal and pasted two tape strips over the edges. He snagged a blue pen from his gold-plated set and scrolled 'James Middleton; Continental Divide Bank' on the envelope.

He leaned out over his desk to get Phyllis' attention, motioning her to come into his office by curling his index finger repeatedly. "Phyl, this package is ready to be delivered by messenger to Continental Divide Bank...get the address from Mike Peavy. Thanks, Phyl." She slowly left the office, glancing at the name on the envelope.

Kellogg was eager to speak with Rusty Affenson or Buck Andrews but hoped Dixie was greeting callers.

"Good morning...Andrews Oil." He recognized her voice immediately.

"Dixie darling, it's Xander...how ya' doing, baby?"

"Just peachy...and you?"

"Miss talkin' to you, darlin'…when can we meet?"

"Anytime, stud…just tell me when."

"I'm working on it, but it's pretty hard right now. Is Rusty or Buck in the office?"

"They're both here…who would you like to speak with?"

"I'll take Buck…so long, sugar."

"Hold one moment."

Buck cleared his throat twice. "Good mornin' Mr. X…how ya' doin'?"

"Terrific…Buck. We were trying to track you down last week…how was your hunting trip?"

"Pretty good…I hunkered down with some of my Texas buddies at a ranch near Grandby. I like to get off the grid now and then."

"I know what you mean. Say…have you and Rusty had time to discuss a price for my building?"

"We were just meetin' on it. We're a little more cash strapped than I thought. You've got some tough ranchers up there in Colorado and Wyoming…leasing land for drilling is more than we budgeted, the price for rigs is escalating, and we decided to drill in Louisiana and New Mexico next year."

"What's that all mean?"

"We'll have to lease your building, but still want to buy it down the road…we'll need a purchase option."

"I beg your pardon…I didn't hear you clearly."

"A lease with an option to purchase…Rusty already called Marty Holbrook this morning to tell him."

"I thought that you were done with Holbrook given his sneaky tactics."

"Our general counsel advised us to honor our legal obligations, so we're bound by the R & H representation agreement. I don't want Holbrook to make a commission but that's bidness, I guess. If oil prices go up, like we think they will, you can still sell your building to us in a few years."

"Damn it, Buck...I don't like that."

Andrews detected Kellogg's anger. "Don't get your panties in a wad, pard...we can pursue our other options if we can't make a deal with you."

Kellogg took a deep breath. He didn't like negotiating over the phone...it was akin to playing poker in the dark. He always had to see the faces of the players he was dealing with. "Look Buck...let's not be too hasty about this. I'll tell you what...I'll fly down to Houston this afternoon and we can sort this out."

"Be my guest...I'll clear my calendar after three o'clock and we can have a few drinks and dinner at our club here. I'll ask Rusty to join us."

"Sounds good...I'll get back to you about the flight time."

"Okay then...see you later today."

Kellogg slammed the phone down. "FUCK!"

Phyllis scampered into his office. "Is something wrong, Mr. Kellogg?"

"Our jet is out of service for a couple of weeks...call Plan-It-Travel right now and get me on the next flight to Houston.

"Right away." Phyllis scooted to her desk to make the call.

Kellogg began to pace with several thoughts racing through his brain wondering how to solve this dilemma. He couldn't think clearly and opened his liquor cabinet, pouring a glass a quarter full of scotch and slugged it down in one gulp.

Phyllis shouted from her desk. "There's an eleven-thirty flight on Continental Airlines that will get you to Houston at two-thirty Central time."

Kellogg checked the time...nine forty-five. There would be ample time to drive home to pack a bag quickly, pick up the plane ticket at Plan-It-Travel's office, and get to Stapleton Airport to make the flight.

"Book it...and make sure I have a first-class seat. I'll stop by the travel agent's office to get my ticket on the way to the airport."

"What about the return flight?"

"I'm not certain, so leave it open. Call the main number at Andrews Oil and ask for Dixie...tell her I should arrive in their offices before three-thirty. Also, ask her for a recommendation on a five-star hotel near their office and have our travel agent book their best suite with a bottle of their best champagne on ice."

Kellogg seized his file on West Tower and smashed it into his brown leather briefcase. He snapped a calculator off his desk, along with a yellow pad and stuffed them into another section. Lastly, he unlocked his lower drawer and searched for a small cardboard box hidden below a stack of documents. He paused for a moment, selecting three prophylactic packets. Satisfied, he shot out of his office, waving at Phyllis as he passed by.

Kellogg raced home and parked the Mercedes in the garage, intending to drive the Buick Regal to Stapleton Airport. He sprinted into the house, bounded the stairs to his bedroom, and quickly threw a few items in a small suitcase. Returning to the garage, he attempted to start the Buick, when the engine sputtered, shook, and subsequently died. Repeating the exercise five times with the same result, Kellogg cursed, spit on the ignition key, and beat on the dashboard several times. Capitulating, he snatched his suitcase and briefcase from the Buick, tossing the luggage into the spacious Mercedes trunk.

Minutes later, Kellogg weaved through heavy traffic along Colorado Boulevard toward the Plan-It-Travel office, located in a small shopping center near the Alameda Avenue intersection. Finding the lot jammed with cars, he maneuvered the Mercedes along a red painted curb, stamped with the words 'NO PARKING-FIRE LANE'. He swung the heavy car door open, spun across the parking lot, and flung open the glass door to the office. Bunny Byers, an attractive brunette receptionist, greeted him immediately. "Hello Xander...Are you here to pick up your plane tickets?"

Kellogg smirked, rejecting the thought of offering a rhetorical comment to an obvious question. He stammered, desperately trying to recall her name. "Doll...you're just as beautiful as ever."

"Thanks, snookum...I have your tickets right here." She stood, thrusting out her hand containing a travel envelope.

Kellogg was so mesmerized with the deep cleavage created by her pushup bra and lowcut blouse; he didn't bother to look at the tickets.

"Baby doll...I gotta run to make my flight, but let's go out when I get back to Denver."

"I'll be right here...have a nice trip, love." She winked and blew him a kiss as he finally recalled her name.

"Love you too, Bunny."

Kellogg grinned and turned to exit, now recalling how stupid she acted on his three-night fling with her last year when Jill was in Europe. As he crossed the parking lot, he observed a Denver police car pull up behind his Mercedes. As Kellogg approached, a skinny patrolman sprung out of his car and pointed at Kellogg. "Is this your car, sir?"

"Yes, why?"

"You're in a no parking area…the curb is marked as a fire lane."

"Really…I hadn't even noticed. I was just in the travel agency for a few seconds to pick up some airline tickets…I'm in a hurry to get to the airport." He raised his right hand, clutching the ticket voucher in his fingers.

"I really don't care where you were and for how long…I'm writing you up for a violation."

Kellogg was irritated. "Hold on…there wasn't even a fire!"

"I need to see some identification and the car registration." The police officer pulled out a citation book and began to fill out of the form. Kellogg leaned forward, noting the cop's name was Sergeant Perkins.

"You have to be joking, Sarge!"

"Your license please, sir."

"I'm going to be late for my flight…here's a twenty. The fine can't be more than that."

"If you're trying to bribe me, I'll need to haul you in."

"Look fella…I've known the Chief of Police, Mitch Johnson, since we were kids. I have close ties with Mayor Zimmerman too…I was a big contributor in his last election." Kellogg checked his watch…it was ten fifty-five.

"I could care less who you know."

As the officer moved behind the Mercedes to write the car license number on the pad, Kellogg vaulted into the driver's seat, started the engine, and took off. He exited the parking lot, honking the car horn repeatedly, and threaded the Mercedes across four lanes of congested traffic making a left turn onto Colorado Boulevard. From the sideview mirror, Kellogg could see the officer trying to wedge the patrol car from the crowded parking lot onto the congested thoroughfare.

Kellogg abruptly turned right onto Alameda Avenue and stepped on the accelerator, reaching fifty miles per hour. He slowed slightly approaching two stoplight-controlled intersections but blew through the red lights before turning north on Quebec Street. Hearing distant sirens, Kellogg weaved through traffic, crossing lanes into oncoming cars several times, barely avoiding three collisions.

Five minutes later, Kellogg entered the parking garage at Stapleton Airport, cutting through three drive aisles marked 'NO ENTRY' to reach the short-term parking area. Finding an open space, he parked, grabbed his bag, and sprinted into the terminal. Scanning the ticketing area for departure screens, his Continental flight was posted to depart gate C-10 in six minutes. He dashed down the dingy concourse, nearly tripping on the torn carpet, arriving at the departure gate as the last passenger was boarding. Out of breath, he greeted the attractive blonde gate agent.

"Hi sweetie pie...I got here just in time. You were probably waiting for the last first-class customer." He handed his ticket voucher over.

She pulled the ticket from the folder and flipped the cover sheet over. "Mr. Kellogg, you have a ticket in the coach section...seat 23B."

He snatched the ticket out of her hand and stared at it. "There must be a mistake...my travel agent always books me in first class."

"I'm sorry sir, but the flight is fully booked. You have to board now...the door will close momentarily."

"What's your name?" Sweat poured down his forehead as he swabbed it with his white handkerchief.

"Ann Langston."

Kellogg pulled out a pen and wrote her name on the back of his ticket. "Even though you're cute, you'll be hearing from your superiors...I know a couple senior executives at your headquarters."

She stared at him momentarily, her mouth wide open. "Sir, will you board the plane now?" She motioned toward the boarding door, where an older female agent waited to take his ticket.

"Good morning sir...thanks for flying Continental today." She had a friendly smile.

Irritated, Kellogg glared at her without responding as she detached his ticket from the voucher. He quickly entered the fuselage, ignoring the first-class stewardess as he quickly passed by. He plodded down the narrow aisle, clumsily bumping a few passengers with his luggage. He reached row 23, seeing an open middle seat between two ladies, each holding a crying infant. He rechecked his seat assignment, desperately surveying the back of the plane, noting every seat was taken. He dropped his bags in the aisle and pivoted into the first-class cabin. "I'll give anyone in first class a hundred bucks if you trade your seat with me."

A gray-haired stewardess, who had the appearance of a veteran, immediately confronted Kellogg. "Sir, please take your seat now...our first-class passengers cannot be disturbed." She pointed her finger in the direction of the coach section.

He shouted even louder. "I don't care...I'll offer two hundred!" He pulled two C-notes from his money clip and waved them above his head.

An older fellow, wearing a grey cowboy hat, stood up. "I'll change seats for five hundred dollars and two free cocktails."

Hearing the commotion, the tall airplane captain, peered into the cabin and emerged from the cockpit. "Sir, if you won't be seated, I'll call airport security right now and have you removed from the plane or I'll throw you off myself." He stuck his right fist into Kellogg's chest.

Kellogg bushed the pilot's hand aside. "I'll sit down...but I'll never fly this damn airline again. Just give me a double shot of scotch, assuming you serve alcohol in coach and tell those women around me to put a cork in their kids' mouths."

The attendant glared at Kellogg. "Beverage service will begin when we level off in flight."

Kellogg turned and returned to row 23, squeezing into the middle seat and addressed the ladies who flanked him. "I don't want to hear any more crying from your babies...or you either."

Both leaned as far away from Kellogg as they could and meekly answered, "Si."

Due to heavy turbulence, the fasten seat belt sign remained lit during the entire flight and the two babies continued to scream loudly. Kellogg repeatedly punched the attendant call button, a stewardess coming to his aid two times, although finally ignored him when he tried again. After thirty minutes in flight, Kellogg climbed over the lady in the aisle seat, heading for the restroom in the tail section of the plane. Ignoring the stewardess' intercom order to return to his seat, Kellogg barricaded himself in the toilet for fifteen minutes until the first officer pounded on the door, warning him of certain arrest upon arriving in Houston. Kellogg reluctantly took his seat and cupped his palms over his ears for the remainder of the flight.

Before the plane anchored at the gate, Kellogg sprung from his seat, attempting to be the first passenger to exit the plane. However, the passengers in the first-class cabin rapidly emptied into the aisle, blocking his path. He bumped a burly man, who turned and shoved Kellogg a step backwards. "Relax, pal...where's the fire?"

"I could be off the plane by now if you'd gotten your ass in gear."

He thrust his right hand against Kellogg's upper right chest. "You must not be from round these parts." He peered down at Kellogg's shiny black dress shoes.

"No and thank God I'm not...old timer. Are you headin' to a rodeo wearing that silly cowboy hat and your oversized belt buckle?"

The cowboy pulled his coat up slightly, revealing a pistol tucked inside his belt. "Yep...and I've got this old six-shooter too."

"Don't tell me...you're going to shoot me now?"

"I should, but I'd be wastin' a bullet." The old guy turned away and departed the plane quickly.

The captain observed the altercation from the cockpit. As Kellogg approached the fuselage door, the pilot stuck his arm out to block his path. "I should detain you here and call airport security to arrest you for your insubordination."

"I have half a notion to call my buddy, Frank Lorenzo from Texas Air...he's plotting to buy your incompetent airline. The first thing I'll ask him to do is to fire your ass!"

"Go ahead...I need a vacation." The captain dropped his arm and pointed his index finger toward the jetway, excusing Kellogg from the plane.

Kellogg hustled to the concourse, locating the directional sign toward ground transportation. When he reached the taxi stand, there were at least twenty people in line. Kellogg jockeyed his way to the curb, shoving aside an elderly couple, and vaulted into a yellow taxi. He snagged Buck Andrews' business card from the front suit pocket, checking the address. "Charlie, take me to the Humble Building at 800 Bell Street."

Kellogg arrived at the high-rise office building housing the headquarters for Andrews Oil Company at three-thirty. Entering the expansive marble lobby, he located the elevator bank for the thirtieth floor. He peered below at the lobby through the glass elevator windows, anticipating meeting Dixie at the front reception desk in the next two minutes. Hearing the chime of the elevator bell, Kellogg strode out of the cab which opened directly to an office suite. His eyes were instantly drawn to the two-foot-high gold letters, ANDREWS OIL COMPANY, prominently anchored in the back wall of the office lobby. His eyes drifted downward to the receptionist, an older woman with platinum blonde hair that appeared to be painted on her head. As he approached the desk, Kellogg focused on her prominent lips, smeared with bright red lipstick.

"Well, darlin'...you must be the infamous Mr. X. I've been waiting for you all day...I'm Dixie."

Kellogg was speechless. "Ah...ah...um...Dixie...so nice to meet you." She rose, quickly rounding the large desk to greet him. He awkwardly stuck out his right hand, expecting her to shake it. Instead, Dixie smacked him on his right cheek with her wet lips.

"I wanted to give you a big Texas welcome…love."

Kellogg reached in his back pocket for a handkerchief, attempting to wipe the lipstick away. "Dixie, honey… I'd like to get to know you better right now, but I need to meet with Buck Andrews before it gets too late in the day."

"Sure… they'll be plenty of time later. After I spoke to your secretary Phyllis, I personally made a hotel reservation for you at the Savoy Houston on Main Street. I ordered a nice bottle of champagne for us too." Dixie winked and then smiled, exhibiting what appeared to be a set of false teeth.

"That's great…that's great…how thoughtful. If I can get my business done with Buck, I'll fly back to Denver tonight, so I may not need a hotel room after all." Kellogg looked down at her pink boots.

"Xander, I'll store your luggage behind my desk and tell Buck's secretary you're here. We set up a conference room for you to meet…it's down this hallway." She pointed to the left. "Please come with me and I'll show you the room."

The scent of Dixie's perfume was overwhelming, so Kellogg trailed a few steps behind her, providing a better angle to detect her thigh saddle bags. She led him to an oak paneled corner conference room with panoramic views of the downtown Houston skyline. "Isn't this a beautiful view, Xander? Your hotel is just off to the right there…only two blocks away."

"Very nice…but the high-rise buildings I'm planning in Denver will have unparalleled views of the Rocky Mountain Front Range." Kellogg glanced down at Dixie's flat chest. "We have flat plains east of Denver, so I'll orient my building orientation to the west, so most tenants will enjoy views of the beautiful mountain peaks."

"I've never been to Denver, but I've seen photos." Dixie rolled back a wall, revealing three levels of liquor bottles and an assortment of glasses. "Help yourself...there's beer in the frig too."

"Can I use the phone here to call my office in Denver...I'll be happy to pay for the long-distance call."

"Don't worry, hon...pick up any line that isn't lit, dial nine and then straight out."

Kellogg lifted the receiver and punched line seven for a dial tone and carefully pressed the numbers for Phyllis' direct line."

"Hello, Phyl, X here...what's cooking?"

"A policeman was here looking for you. Apparently, you led the cops on a chase this morning."

"Yeah...a cop wrote me up for parking in a fire lane. I didn't have any time to waste or else I would have missed my flight. On second thought, I should have missed the flight...it was the worst plane ride ever. Never book me on Continental Airlines again! Another thing...call John Collins and have him see what he can find out about my charges...he has contacts in the City attorney's office. I can't afford to get to get arrested when I get back to Denver."

"Mike Peavy is anxious to speak with you. I'll transfer you...hold the line."

"Hello...Mike Peavy."

"Peavy...it's Xander Kellogg. I'm in Houston trying to get the sale buttoned up with Andrews Oil. You wanted to speak with me?"

"I thought you should know right away...James Middleton called after they received the copy of the sales contract on West Tower."

"Great...so they're already backing off the capital call, right?"

"Not exactly…they want to see an original copy of the purchase contract with a corporate seal imprint from Andrews Oil…a corporate resolution authorizing the transaction with a seal stamp too."

"You've got to be kidding me."

"No…and I got a lecture from Willard Edwards, Middleton's boss, for contacting the appraiser directly."

"Awe…fuck them."

Kellogg waved at Buck Andrews and Rusty Affenson, who entered the conference room.

"Peavy…I'll call you later…got to hang up now." Kellogg dropped the phone into the cradle.

Buck extended his right hand. "Welcome to Houston, Mr. X…and say hello to Rusty Affenson."

Kellogg briefly shook Andrews' hand and pivoted toward Affenson, who wore a tan suit with a bolo tie.

"Super to finally meet you, Rusty." As he studied Affenson's thick brown hair, Kellogg grasped his hand and twisted it tightly to the right.

"Good afternoon, Mr. Kellogg." His tone seemed overly cool. "How was your flight down?"

"I'll never fly Continental again…they must be related to that horrible bank in Denver. The airline apparently has a slogan… 'We'll really move our tail for you,' but the stewardess crew sat on their tails the entire flight. I could never get a drink…the worst service ever."

"We have just about any alcohol you'd ever want here in the cabinet." Rusty pointed to the collection.

"I had to call my office, so I didn't have time to grab anything, but I'll have the usual…scotch on the rocks.

"Mr. X, I'll call my assistant in here to serve us." Andrews picked up the phone. "Bobbie Sue…come in the corner conference room and help us with some drinks, please."

"Xander…have you checked out these great views from our building?"

"Yes…Dixie was just pointing them out. The views are nice, but not as terrific as the Rocky Mountain panorama you'll have in our West Tower building when you buy it."

At that moment, a tall, slender blonde woman entered the room. Kellogg was awestruck, studying her perfect body shape, enhanced by her short skirt and tight sweater. His eyes finally drifted to a huge diamond wedding ring on her left hand.

"Bobbie Sue…a double scotch for our guest here and I'll take my favorite bourbon. How about you, Rusty?"

"Just a beer…there should be a Lone Star in there."

As Bobbie Sue bent down to pull a beer bottle from the cooler, Kellogg moved left three steps to get a better view, as her skirt revealed more of her legs. She stood, reached for a bronze bottle opener on the counter, and easily snapped the lid off with a flick of her slender wrist.

"Would you like it in a chilled glass, Mr. Affenson?"

"The bottle is fine…thanks, Bobbie Sue." She wrapped a napkin around the bottle and handed it to Rusty.

"Sir…what type of scotch do you drink?"

"Glenfiddich Single Malt, honey."

"Yes…we always keep it in stock. Would you prefer it straight up or on the rocks?"

Kellogg was already smitten with her. "The rocks, please." Kellogg studied Bobbie Sue's movements as she prepared his drink. Using a tong, she plucked five cubes from a silver ice bucket, carefully poured the scotch, and wrapped a napkin under the glass. As she took a few steps toward him, he reached out his left hand to take the drink. "Thank you, Bobbie Sue…I'm Alexander Kellogg from Denver."

As she awkwardly extended her right hand, Kellogg lightly touched her fingers and slowly drew her hand closer to his face. He bent slight and kissed the back of her palm. "I love the charm of Southern belles…it's wonderful to meet one so beautiful."

Bobbie Sue pulled her arm back gently and her lips parted with an innocent smile.

"Nice to make your acquaintance, Mr. Kellogg." With her distinct drawl, he assumed she was a Texas native.

Buck Andrews interrupted. "Bobbie Sue takes care of us very well, Mr. X. Just so you don't get any ideas, she's happily married to a Houston Oilers' football player."

"Oh really…what's his name?"

"She doesn't want it known publicly…it's our little secret. However, he could kick your ass and then some."

"I played a little college football myself and work out every day, so I can hold my own with most anyone."

"Let's sit down and talk about your Denver office building. We have a six o'clock reservation at my club for drinks and dinner. Bobbie Sue, that's all I need from you right now…Thanks for your help."

As she strolled toward the door, Kellogg bellowed, "Hope to see you again soon, Bobbie Sue."

She turned, smiled briefly, and extended a slight wave toward him with her left hand. Kellogg took it as a signal for an invitation to a future rendezvous, rather than Bobbie Sue's reminder she was very married.

Kellogg took a seat at the long oak conference table, opposite of Andrews and Affenson, so he could look directly at them. "So…you guys can't scrape up twenty million to buy my building, eh?"

"Mr. X, as I told you on the phone this morning, Rusty says we're pretty extended with our capital commitments in the next twenty-four months."

"Do you need a loan or something…I can help you out with that."

Affenson took a swig of his beer and set the bottle down on a coaster imprinted with an oil derrick image. "Mr. X…I've gone over our budgets five times. Buck really wants to buy a building, but we need to manage our total debt levels to satisfy the covenants on our bank loans."

"Rusty…I've discovered banks are run by a bunch of morons. A little creative accounting can easily fool those knuckleheads."

"Maybe Denver bankers are stupid but our lenders in Houston are pretty astute."

"Maybe you should switch banks. I've bought foreclosed real estate projects from the biggest banks in New York City…those white shoe boys ain't that smart, even though they all have those Ivy League college degrees." Kellogg pointed out the window as if directing them to observe the New York City skyline.

"Mr. X, I always follow Rusty's advice to a tee. We've had a few close calls over the years when oil prices dropped or where we've hit a bad streak of hitting dry wells. We're sticking with our banks here. We wouldn't mind being a tenant in your building...it sounds like it would fit our current plans and the location works well for me. If our projections are correct with oil prices maintaining a level of forty bucks a barrel or more, we'll buy your building in two or three years."

"I already have other offers to buy it, so I can't even guarantee I'll be your landlord for too long."

"That all right, Xander...we'll want a right of first refusal, so we can deal with that possibility."

Kellogg studied every eye movement from Buck...he rarely blinked and is body was always rigid. From years of experience playing poker, it didn't appear that Buck was bluffing. "I guess I could live with that if you're on a short time leash."

"Rusty has been working on some estimates for rent and the cost of our tenant improvements, so he can take over now."

"Thanks, Buck. I project our space needs as a hundred fifty thousand square feet. We built our office space in this building for twelve bucks per square foot. Marty Holbrook told us that would be ample for costs in Denver, so that's about two million...give or take."

Kellogg slammed the table with his fist and jumped up. "Marty Holbrook...what the hell does he know about tenant finish costs...he's just a low life broker!"

"Please sit down, Mr. Kellogg. I've met with Marty many times and I'm convinced he knows tenant finish costs since he exclusively negotiates large office leases."

Kellogg fell back into his chair and took a drink of scotch, as Affenson continued. "Listen Mr. Kellogg...our expected rate of return is twenty per cent on our capital costs, so that's four hundred thousand a year on two million…and that equates to just under three bucks a foot in annual rent."

Kellogg could feel another shot coming. "So?"

"So…that's a deduction of three bucks off the gross rent."

Kellogg snagged the calculator out of his briefcase and punched in some numbers. "I guess I could live with fifteen bucks a foot on your space."

"Marty says the asking rent is fifteen gross, but since we're taking most of the building, I figure that we should get a discount…say twelve bucks…and subtracting the three dollars for our tenant finish costs, our offer is nine bucks a foot."

Kellogg abruptly jumped up and shoved his chair back, which hit the wall.

"Fuck Marty Holbrook…he's a whore! You can't trust anything he says. He's trying to punish me because I cancelled his listing agreement."

"We hired Reagan and Holbrook to represent us and that's what they're doing. If it makes you feel any better, I've talked to a lot of real estate folks in Denver about our needs and they've confirmed those numbers, so don't blame Marty Holbrook."

Kellogg turned away, desperately trying to regather his composure. After a few seconds he leaned over the table facing Andrews and laughed.

"Boys…I don't know the laws in Texas, but theft is a crime in Colorado."

"I imagine bidness is bidness in Colorado, just like it is in Texas, Xander."

"C'mon guys…let's be reasonable. First, my construction group can build it for ten bucks a foot…not twelve, so that's a million and a half…and timesing that by twenty percent, is three hundred grand a year. Dividing that by your space size comes out at two bucks a foot…a lot less than three!"

Andrews kept quiet for a few seconds and then spoke. "Look, Mr. X…we don't want to get our green eye shades out and nitpick every penny. Let's be practical here…we'll pay you ten bucks a foot, but we're going to hire our own tenant finish contractor."

Kellogg didn't reply…staring at Andrews for a minute, expecting him to offer another concession.

"Kellogg…are you in trance? Do we have a deal or not?"

Kellogg slugged the last bit of scotch down his throat and began to chew on an ice cube. He stopped chewing feeling a small pebble was in his mouth. He reached in his mouth immediately detecting a molar cracked off again.

"How about it, pal?" Andrews seemed to be getting impatient.

Exasperated, Affenson threw up his hands, rose from his chair, and stepped toward the door.

With no options, Kellogg yelled out… "DEAL! I'll get my lawyer working on a lease draft."

Andrews stood, extending his hand toward Kellogg to cement the verbal agreement. Kellogg hesitated briefly and gripped Buck's hand as firmly as he could until Andrews pulled away. Affenson spun back into the office and shook hands with Kellogg too.

"Let's have another drink to toast our agreement…I'll get Bobbie Sue back in here."

"Great…that's the best idea I've heard in the last five minutes. But Rusty, before you call her, you need to explain something."

Affenson raised his eyebrows. "What's that, Mr. X?"

"The first time we spoke on the phone, you said that Dixie was good looking and liked to talk dirty."

"Dixie does talk dirty and for all I know, may have been beautiful at some point in her life."

"Yeah…but you said your receptionist was attractive."

"Bobbie Sue is our receptionist and my secretary…you've already seen how gorgeous she is."

"You mislead me, Rusty. Dixie is planning to meet me at my hotel tonight…she's at least a double bagger."

"What's a double bagger?"

"A woman who is so homely you need to place two bags over her head in case the first one falls off when having sex."

Buck interjected. "Mr. X…Dixie may be a two at ten o'clock but could be a ten at 2 AM when the bar closes."

"Maybe for you guys, but my standards are higher…believe me."

Andrews snickered and pushed the intercom button. "Bobbie Sue, we need another drink order in here."

"Yes, Mr. Andrews…in a moment."

A few seconds later, Bobbie Sue bounded through the conference room door smiling brightly. "Do you gentlemen want the same drinks I made earlier?"

Andrews quickly answered. "I do, darling. Mr. X…how about you?"

"Anther Glenfiddich with ice, please."

"Of course, Mr. Kellogg."

"Call me Xander." Kellogg stood next to her. "I'd like you to join me for some champagne tonight in my hotel."

"Thank you for the offer, but I don't drink alcohol."

"You can just watch me drink…I'll order caviar for us."

"I don't eat meat either, especially a baby calf."

"Caviar isn't a form of meat…it's a delicacy consisting of fish eggs."

"I'm sorry, Mr. Kellogg, but I can't possibly meet you. My husband wants me home at night…he's very possessive."

Andrews decided to intervene. "Bobbie Sue, thanks for your help…good night. I'll see you in the morning."

Bobbie Sue pranced away, her hips noticeably swaying.

"Mr. X…let's drink up, so you can get to your hotel and check in. We'll meet you at the Houston Petroleum Club at six o'clock. It's located up on the forty-third floor of this building."

"Where's the Savoy Hotel?"

"That's where you're staying, eh?" Affenson chuckled. "It's just a couple of blocks from here."

"Dixie booked me there…is it a dump?"

"You'll be fine in Dixie's hands."

"I'm not so sure, Rusty. Can I hang around here for a few minutes to call my office?"

"Sure…make yourself at home. Can I get you another drink?"

"No, but you can call Bobbie Sue back to serve me."

"Give up on her, Xander. There's no hope there, believe me...I've even tried myself. See you at six, buddy," as Buck laughed.

After Andrews and Affenson left the room, Kellogg strolled to the phone and called Phyllis again. "Phyl, Xander here. I need you to call the main number at Andrews Oil and speak to Dixie again. Tell her my wife had a serious car accident and is in the trauma unit at Swedish Hospital. Dixie knows I'm still here in the office and will give me the message. Then, call our braindead travel agent and see if they can get me on a plane back to Denver tonight. I'll call you back in fifteen minutes...and thanks."

"Got it...I'll call Bunny, our agent at Plan-It-Travel.

"Oh yeah...Bunny the dummy!"

Kellogg surveyed the room observing a long credenza, deftly backing toward it, ensuring no one was watching. He turned slightly and opened the top drawer, spotting a stack of blank sheets of Andrews Oil Company stationary. He snatched a dozen pages and swiftly slipped them in his briefcase. He rifled through the other drawers, hoping to find something else of value, but was startled by a voice at the door.

"Can I help find something for you, hon?"

"Ah...um...just trying to find a pen, Dixie. Mine just went dry."

"There are two pens on the conference table."

"Oh...I didn't see them."

"Mr. Kellogg, I'm sorry to give you terrible news, but I just took a call from your secretary. Your wife has been in a bad car accident and is in emergency surgery at Swedish Hospital in Denver."

"What? When did it happen?"

"I'm not sure, but apparently in the past two hours. I didn't know you were married."

"If you'll excuse me, I'll call my secretary again and get the details."

"Of course, please let me know if I can do anything for you."

"Yes, thank you."

Dixie remained in the conference room, as Kellogg raced to the phone and pounded the dial pad. "Yes, Phyllis…I just got word Jill was in a serious car accident."

"I spoke to Dixie and expect that she just told you".

Irritated that Dixie remained standing nearby, Kellogg had to improvise. "Yes…yes…that serious? When did it happen?" He paused for two seconds. "Really…who called you?" Two more seconds elapsed. "Chief Woodward from the Cherry Hills Police Department, eh?" Another pause. "What time is that flight back to Denver?" Kellogg waited again. "Yeah…I can make it back to the airport by seven. I'll go straight to the hospital when I arrive in Denver." Three seconds passed. "Thanks so much for your prayers, Phyl."

Kellogg dropped the phone receiver. "Dixie, it's pretty bad. I need to get back to Denver right away. I have a flight reservation at eight o'clock, so I'm disappointed that we can't meet tonight. Please cancel the hotel reservation right away."

"Oh well…how about a rain check?"

"Absolutely…I'll let you know when I'm back in Houston. Can you tell Buck I can't make dinner?"

"Yes, I'll let him know." Dixie departed.

Buck returned to the conference room within three minutes. "Xander, I understand you have a family emergency in Denver and need to fly back immediately."

"My poor wife, Jill, is in a coma...she was in a terrible car crash."

"My God...I'll call Nancy right away. She's in Denver now and will surely want to go to the hospital as soon as she can see Jill."

Kellogg stammered for a second. "Um...um...oh yes...Nancy. I have a flight back at eight o'clock, so I need to skip dinner. I hope you understand. I'll call you tomorrow to firm up our discussion on the lease."

"There's no rush on that...I trust that you'll want to be with Jill at the hospital."

"Well, business goes on. Please tell Nancy I'll call her about Jill's condition. Is she staying at the Brown Palace?"

"Yes, until Thursday when she returns to Houston."

Buck, if you'll excuse me, I need to call my office again before I catch a taxi."

"Certainly...I'll pray for Jill."

When Buck was out of sight, Kellogg dialed the phone again.

"Phyllis, thanks for your help before."

"I was a bit confused when you kept interrupting me."

"I'll tell you later why I had to do that. Where's my ticket for the flight?"

"Pick it up at the Continental Airlines customer service counter at the Houston airport."

"Not Continental Airlines again!"

"That was the only flight to Denver tonight we thought you could make."

"Did Bunny book a first-class seat for me?"

"I don't know…I requested one though."

"I'll deal it when I get to the airport. Did you call John Collins about my car chase problem?"

"Yes, and you should call him."

Kellogg glanced at the wall clock, which showed five forty-five.

"I need to grab a cab now…traffic is a mess here and it may take a while to drive to the airport. See you tomorrow."

Kellogg arrived at Houston International Airport at seven o'clock and immediately dashed to the Continental Airlines check-in area. Seeing a long line for the customer service counter, he circled around several passengers in a shorter line and interrupted an agent's conversation with an older woman.

"Charlie…I need to pick up a ticket for my flight to Denver."

The agent frowned and turned toward Kellogg. "Sir, you need to go to the customer service counter…under the sign over there." The agent pointed to the long line.

Three people in the line yelled at Kellogg to move along. Ignoring their grumbling, he attempted to bluff the agent. "Look pal, I'm a Continental Club member…I shouldn't have to wait in line with my status."

"Sir...there is no such club at this airline." The agent raised his voice. "Please go to the other area where I instructed you. You're holding up the line for these customers who need to purchase tickets."

A well-built younger man stepped forward and pinned Kellogg against the counter, positioning his face two inches from Kellogg's nose. He tapped Kellogg's shoulder with his index finger. "Get the hell out of our line, jackass."

Kellogg instantly reacted by shoving the guy backwards. "Fuck you, man."

After two other men grabbed Kellogg arms, Xander twisted away from their grip and without looking back, stomped to the customer service counter. Counting twenty passengers, he decided to restrain himself from jumping ahead. Kellogg impatiently checked his watch every two minutes as the line moved slowly. Exasperated, he finally bypassed four people and decided to exercise more diplomacy, noting the older female agent's name tag read Clara.

"Clara, my flight leaves in twenty minutes...I'll miss my flight unless I get my ticket now. Please help me."

"Where are you flying to, sir?"

"Denver."

"The departure time for your flight has been delayed until eight-thirty. You'll have plenty of time...please get back in line."

Kellogg's tone changed. "Your lousy airline can't even keep a schedule? I'd be out of business if I ran my company that way!"

"Sir, occasionally there are simply delays beyond our control...I'm sorry."

"Clarabell…you're another clown in the Continental circus." Kellogg turned and strutted back in line.

After twenty minutes of bouncing from one leg to the other, Kellogg finally reached the counter.

The agent grimaced and looked down at the desk. "Good evening, sir…you're going to Denver, right?"

Kellogg looked smug. "Oh…I guess you remember me. I sure hope to get to Denver sometime tonight. Are you looking for volunteers to pilot the plane?"

"No, we always have two pilots."

"My name is Kellogg, Alexander Kellogg…the third. My travel agent in Denver arranged a first-class ticket."

Clara sorted through a stack of tickets. "It's not in this pile." She opened a drawer and grabbed another handful, as Kellogg tapped his fingers on the counter. "It isn't here either. Hmmm…what's your name again?"

"Kellogg…K…E…L…L…O…G…G…exactly like the cereal company!"

She shuffled through the stack again and stopped after reading the name on the third ticket from the top of the stack. "Oh…here it is. I must have missed it the first time…I love your Frosted Flakes."

Kellogg muttered under his breath, "Jesus…no wonder it took so long to get through the line." He spoke louder. "Where's my gate?"

"Mr. Kellogg…you're on Flight 18, which now departs at nine o'clock from Gate 66 on the B Concourse." Clara pointed to the right.

"Nine o'clock…another delay? With my luck, it'll probably crash…when will it arrive in Denver?"

Clara pulled her reading glasses on and scanned a computer screen. "Twelve forty-five."

Kellogg counted on his fingers. "That's almost a four-hour flight!"

"Of course, the flight has stops in Dallas and Albuquerque."

"You must be joking!"

"No sir…those propeller planes are a bit slower than newer jets, so that adds more airtime too."

Kellogg couldn't believe what she said. "Propellers? I had no idea major airlines even flew those planes anymore. Well, at least I have a first-class seat…I'll have more time to drink."

"There aren't first class seats on those models and there's no beverage service either." Clara glanced down at the ticket. "But you have a nice window seat…5B. You can look out the window and enjoy the views."

"How can see anything in the dark?"

"The lights of the cities are electric."

Kellogg snatched the ticket from her hand and dashed down the corridor toward Concourse B. He scanned the front of the ticket voucher, noting Gate 66 and Flight 18, written in red ink. He studied the nearby concourse map, although couldn't locate Gate 66. He shuffled over to a flight screen. noting the Denver flight number was 66, departing gate 18. He cursed at Clara's obvious blunder and strolled to a nearby bank of pay phones to call John Collins. He deposited a dime into the device and dialed zero.

"Operator."

"I need to make a collect call to John Collins at 303-234-5678…tell him the call is from Mr. X."

"Mr. X?"

"Yes…X, as in exceptional."

"Exceptional starts with an E, sir."

"Okay, X as in Xander."

"Zander starts with a Z, sir."

"Do you work for Continental Airlines?" Getting pissed, he took a deep breath and exhaled into the receiver and screamed. "X…as in XRAY!"

"Hold please."

In a few seconds Collins answered the call from the operator.

"Will you accept a collect call from Mr. X-ray?"

"What?"

"Will you accept a collect call from Mr. X-ray?"

"I don't know anyone named Ray, but I do know a Mr. X, if that's who you mean. Yes…I'll accept the call."

"Hold a second please." Kellogg heard a click.

"Hello, Mr. X…is that you?"

"Yes, Colly. Holy shit…I must be trapped in the land of the stupid. I can't believe people can be this dim."

"From what I heard earlier you must have lost your marbles too. How could you be so crazy to run away from the Denver police?"

"An idiot cop tried to give me a violation for parking in a fire lane when I picked up my plane ticket. I couldn't have parked there for more than two minutes, so no harm was done. I offered the guy twenty bucks on the spot…probably far more than the parking ticket would cost me."

"They put an all-points bulletin on you and ultimately found your car in the short-term parking area at Stapleton Airport. They ticketed you for a parking in a loading area, as well as leaving the scene of a crime."

"A crime…for parking in a fire zone and loading zone?"

"I spoke to my contact in the City Attorney's office and that's how they classified this. I worked out a deal where you plead guilty to resisting arrest and two parking tickets. You'll have seven points posted on your driving record and be on probation. If you have another infraction, your driver's license will be suspended."

"That doesn't sound too bad, Colly. How much will the tickets cost me?"

"Only twenty bucks each, but I promised my friend in the mayor's office that you would make a thousand-dollar contribution for his next election."

Colly was unaware of Kellogg's connection to Mayor Ivan Zimmerman, so Xander played along as if he didn't know him. "Shit…that's a lot. Maybe you can get the mayor to extend some influence when I need my next zoning variance."

"Listen, Mr. X…a young deputy city attorney, Franklin Kennedy, was assigned to your case and wanted you arrested when you returned to Denver and immediately taken to jail. He was pushing for a five thousand-dollar bail bond too."

"Thanks, Colly…good job. Where's my Mercedes?"

"It was towed to the pound, so there's another twenty-five bucks to retrieve it."

"Colly, this may be one of the worst days in my life. These Texas oil guys are some tough sons of bitches. They can't buy West Tower due to their capital constraints and some other bullshit reasons, so the best outcome for me is to lease it and give them an option to purchase."

"How long is the lease term?"

"We didn't even discuss that, although the purchase option will last two or three years, and they'll also have a right of first refusal if another buyer comes along."

"Sounds like they drive a hard bargain."

"They're double teaming me with that prick, Marty Holbrook, to screw me on the rent too."

"Speaking of Holbrook, I took a call from his attorney, Henry Buckingham, about the listing cancellation. They're pursuing all legal options against you."

"Fine…I'll beat that fat ass."

"What floors are the oil company leasing?"

"Ah…ah…um…I guess we didn't nail that down either. We agreed on a rent of ten bucks a foot and they'll use their own contractor to build out the space. I would have nailed down the other details over dinner, but I had to leave in a hurry to get back to Denver."

"What was the emergency?"

"I'll tell you later if I ever get back. Our fucking travel agent booked me on a flight that has two stops. On top of that, it's a damn prop plane that's been delayed by sixty minutes already…and there's no beverage service either! Oh…I forgot to tell you the good news."

"What's that, X."

"I have a window seat, so I can enjoy the views according to Clarabell"

"At night? Who's Clarabell?"

"The ticket agent clown…don't you remember Howdy Doody?"

"It sounds like you need a drink."

"I see a bar across the way…I better get over there before they run out of booze. Good night."

Kellogg dashed across the hallway to the bar, where a bartender was stacking glasses on the back bar. Kellogg pulled out a stool and straddled the padded seat.

"Buddy Boy…how about a scotch on the rocks?"

The bartender pointed to a clock over the bar. "I closed down at eight o'clock…twenty minutes ago. I'm just cleaning up."

"So…just reopen the bar. It won't take but a few seconds to pour a drink."

The bartender looked up and down the corridor. "My supervisor came by a few minutes ago and collected all of the cash out of the register…it's all locked up and so are the liquor cabinets."

Kellogg yanked a tiny utility tool from his briefcase and displayed it to the bartender. "This gadget can jimmy any lock and I won't need any change, so forget about the register."

"I'm sorry, mister…I can't afford to lose my job."

"Add a little thrill in your life and take a risk. If you get fired, I'll hire you…I own a couple of restaurants around town."

"Which ones?"

Kellogg scratched his head. "Ah…ah…The Colorado Mine Company and The Broker."

"Must be new…I haven't heard of either."

"They've only been open for a few months."

"Thanks for the offer, but I really can't help you…there's a bar in the main terminal that's open until ten o'clock."

"Shit…I don't want to walk all the way back there. I should carry miniature bottles in my briefcase. Why don't you have the World Series game on your TV set?"

"There's no game tonight…it was a day off. The Dodgers need it too since they've lost three in a row."

"The Yankees are up three to two in the Series?"

"Yeah…where have you been the past three days…in a cave?"

"I was pheasant hunting in western Nebraska with some buddies. The place we stayed at didn't have a TV set and I was having so much fun, I totally forgot about baseball."

"Well, the series is back in Los Angeles tomorrow night and Don Sutton is taking the mound for the Dodgers, so they should tie it up."

I sure hope so…I've got a lot of money riding on L. A."

Kellogg abruptly sprung up from his stool and strode back to the pay phone area. He reached into his briefcase and snagged a notebook. He leafed through several pages, finally finding the slip for Dusty's phone number. Kellogg didn't want the complication of depositing coins into the slots to call long distance and opted to make another collect call, hoping Dusty would be at his home. He deposited a dime and dialed zero.

"Operator…how can I help you?"

"My name is Alexander Kellogg and I want to make a collect call to Dusty at 303-926-3379." Kellogg didn't want to risk another mix up with his name. He heard the line ringing for over a minute when the operator broke in.

"Sir, there's no answer…do you want to try later?"

Kellogg glanced at his watch. "I'm at a pay phone…I'll call back!"

He slammed the receiver on the cradle so hard that it bounced off, landing on the floor. He spotted a few passengers entering the concourse through the Gate 18 door…his plane had finally arrived. The gate agent was standing at the podium with a dozen passengers lined up waiting to check in for Flight 66, but he decided to try Dusty on more time and followed the operator protocol again. This time Dusty answered.

"Hell, yes…I'll accept a collect call from Alexander Kellogg,"

"Hello Dusty Boy. Hey…I'm down in Houston airport ready to board a crate back to Denver tonight. Can you pick me up at Stapleton at one o'clock?"

"Yeah…I'm scheduled to work the strip club until twelve-thirty, so that's fine. I'll pick you up in my green Chevy pickup."

"Great, I need you to do a job for me. I'll tell you about it when you pick me up. I'm on Flight 66 on Continental Airlines that's supposed to get in at twelve forty-five."

Kellogg prepared for the worse and the flight back to Denver exceeded his expectations. He tried to get off the plane during the layovers in Dallas and Albuquerque to find a bar, but the flight attendants wouldn't let him deplane. Squeezed into the side of a fuselage for the entire flight by a four-hundred-pound man, who overlapped onto his seat, Kellogg could barely walk when the flight arrived in Denver. Although he suppressed his comments during the plane ride, Kellogg incessantly blasted the rotund fellow about his weight and body odor problem, racing past him as he headed toward the passenger pickup area.

Kellogg emerged through the revolving doors, spotting Dusty's rusty pickup truck parked nearby. Seeing an old grey blanket draped over the passenger seat, Kellogg reluctantly jumped in, expecting his suit pants were already soiled from the old cloth airplane seat.

Kellogg stared at Dusty's right hand, which was wrapped in a crude bandage." Good evenin' pal…thanks for picking me up. Did you have a fight tonight?"

"I had to throw a couple of assholes out of the club and cut my hand during the fistfight."

"Dusty…I have a little proposition for you. I need you to break into an office downtown and hock a metal corporate seal from an oil company office…I'll pay you a thousand bucks."

"When do you need this?"

"By tomorrow night."

"I don't know…sounds risky."

"Look, it's a small office…only one employee who's out of the office a lot. You might even be able to do it during business hours. The office is in a new high rise building in downtown Denver…it should be easy."

"I'll do it for two grand…half up front."

"Okay, Dusty…I'll get the cash out of my safe when you drop me at my house. I'll pay you the rest when you deliver the seal to me."

"Write down the company name and their address on this." Dusty pulled a small white card clipped to the visor and handed it to Kellogg. "I'll case out the office first thing in the morning."

"Great!" Kellogg read the inscription on the card...Chubby's Gentlemen Clubs with addresses in Aurora and Denver. He grabbed a pen from his suit pocket and printed Andrews Oil Company, 1010 16th Street, suite 410 on the back of the card and handed it to Dusty, who stuck it under the folded lip of his stocking cap.

Exhausted, Kellogg closed his eyes and dozed off. Twenty minutes later, Dusty pulled up to Kellogg's residence on Woodlawn Lane, nudging Kellogg three times before he finally woke up. Kellogg struggled to open the truck door, stumbling up the stairs and into the home. After fumbling with the safe lock for several minutes, Kellogg returned to the truck and handed Dusty a stack of hundred-dollar bills. Dusty slowly counted them and signaled Kellogg with a thumbs up sign.

"Dusty, it's been a long day...I'm beat. Call me when you have the corporate seal."

Chapter Ten

Kellogg awoke at nine o'clock, exhausted from the long trip to Houston and back. There was a lot of work to do and his first call was to Rusty Affenson. Xander now realized that Buck Andrews was only the front man for the oil company and had little influence on the final financial decisions. He quickly showered, dressed, and raced to his garage. Opening the Corvette door, he glanced over to the vacant Mercedes stall. At some point, he would need to retrieve his car from the police pound. He backed the convertible through of the shattered garage door section and sped to his office.

Phyllis was typing a letter when Kellogg approached her desk. "Good morning, Mr. Kellogg. I was wondering when you'd be in. How was your flight last night?"

He shook his head. "You mean my flight this morning?"

"Did you stay in a hotel last night and catch an early flight?"

"No...I got home around one thirty. Bumble-head Bunny booked me on a propeller plane that had stops in Dallas and Albuquerque. A fat passenger, who also stunk, squeezed me against the window. I could hardly walk when I finally got off the plane."

"Do you want me to find a new travel agency?"

"Don't bother...I'll buy a new jet that won't be in service so often. Just get me a pot of black coffee and a couple of donuts."

Kellogg reached for the telephone and dialed Rusty Affenson directly, avoiding the main number. The last person he wanted to speak with was Dixie.

"Good morning…Mr. Affenson's office…Bobbie Sue speaking.

"Oh, Bobbie Sue…great to speak with you again. This is Alexander Kellogg from Denver."

"Yes, Mr. Kellogg…can I tell Mr. Affenson what your call is pertaining to?"

"You're pulling my leg, right?"

"I'm sorry sir, I can't be touching your leg since you're calling from Denver, which is far away from Houston, isn't it?"

"Hmmm…I'm the guy you mixed the Glenfiddich scotch for yesterday afternoon in your conference room with Buck and Rusty. Don't you remember me?"

"Oh yeah… now I remember. You wanted me to drink champagne and eat calf's liver with you."

"Yup…that's me. Can you find Rusty now?" Kellogg concluded that Bobbie Sue was an airhead, in the same class as his travel agent, Bunny. No wonder she was married to a professional football player.

'Oh…yes, just a second, Mr. Kellogg."

Kellogg fumbled with the receiver for a few seconds and untwirled the phone cord, which had become knotted.

"Good morning Mr. Kellogg. How's your wife?"

"I haven't seen her since I booted her out of the house."

"I thought that she was in a bad car accident and was in a coma." Affenson said hesitatingly.

"Oh…that wife." Kellogg coughed a few times. "Sorry, I'm still groggy from the late flight from Houston. I thought you meant my first wife. So…you mean Jill, huh? Ah…Jill…she's still in the hospital. I'm about to drive over and see how she's doing, but I wanted to call you first and iron out the rest of the lease terms since I had to skip out on dinner last night."

"As Buck mentioned, we'll pay $10 a foot gross for approximately a hundred fifty thousand feet and hire a contractor Marty Holbrook recommends for our buildout. Marty said the whole building was available, except for the bank space, so we'll take the top three floors and part of the second. Our space planner can work out the details for the exact square footage."

Kellogg stayed silent, trying to stifle his anger.

"Are you still there?"

"Yep."

"Going on...we'll sign a five-year flat lease with a five-year renewal option at a market rent to be determined by an appraiser we'll choose independently. As Buck said, we want the option to buy the building after the second, third, fourth, and fifth lease year as well as a first right of refusal if another buyer steps in. Marty indicated a rough price of fourteen million, but we need to hire an appraiser to confirm. Marty recommended Greg Bottoms at Allied Appraisal Group, although I haven't spoken to him yet."

Kellogg was speechless.

"Mr. Kellogg...are you still on the line."

Kellogg was fuming. "Rusty...I told you that theft is a crime in Colorado and so is rape. You guys are fucking killing me. I can't possibly agree to all that bullshit."

"I don't care for that kind of language, Mr. Kellogg...I'm a devout Christian."

Kellogg sighed. "Okay, how about this…You guys are killing me, and I can't possibly agree to all that crap."

"That's our deal, Mr. X. If you don't like my offer, it was nice knowing you. Call us back if you want to move ahead. Have a nice day…so long."

"Yeah…you've made my day real nice." The line clicked off.

Kellogg threw the phone receiver at the wall and slumped down in his chair, contemplating his next move. He recalled Peavy had estimated the recent Allied Appraisal value at eighteen million and subtracting two million for tenant finish costs would still provide a net value of sixteen million…a cushion to meet Affenson's option price of fourteen million. Still, the proposed rent of ten dollars per square foot was five dollars below that asking rent used in the original appraisal and the difference would surely be a problem.

"Phyl, call Peavy and Cohen to my office…NOW!"

Kellogg ambled to the liquor cabinet, poured a scotch, and started chewing an ice cube…stopping instantly upon recalling the slight crack he made in his molar yesterday.

"Phyl, arrange another appointment with Doctor Hawthorne again, but no hurry this time. Tomorrow is fine but make certain Pam Vaughn is working." As usual, everything ran on Kellogg's sense of timing.

Mike Peavy and Eli Cohen entered Kellogg's office. "Good morning, Mr. Kellogg."

"I wish it were, Eli Boy…we've got a big problem. Those Texas jerks are getting coached by that buffoon, Marty Holbrook, to screw me on West Tower. They're only going to pay ten bucks flat for five years and insist on a purchase option price of fourteen million.

They're planning to build out their hundred fifty thousand feet themselves, so that saves me two million."

"That's horrible…what floors are they getting?"

"The best damn space…we'll be left with the first and part of the second floor."

Peavy looked nervous. "We sent the twenty-million-dollar contract over to Continental Divide Bank yesterday. When they learn the deal changed, they'll accuse us of fraud…that's a crime, isn't it?"

"Relax Peavy…if they discover our sale is dead, you can say Andrews Oil cancelled the contact for some technical reason. There must be a few contingencies to allow them to back out. I haven't agreed to their lease terms yet, so we still have some time."

"Not that much time, Mr. Kellogg…don't you recall the bank demand letter?"

"Peavy…if those morons call you again, transfer the call to me. I'll take care of 'em."

"I don't want to deal with Willard Edwards again."

"Get a little backbone, Peavy. Jesus…you're a wimp!"

"Maybe." Peavy hung his head.

Kellogg slammed his right fist on his desk as hard as he could, scattering the papers on his desk. The sudden noise caused Peavy to jump, although Cohen didn't flinch.

"Peavy…get tough or get out! I don't need pussies around here!"

"Yes, sir." Peavy replied meekly. He turned and left the room, although Cohen remained in the office.

Kellogg turned to Cohen. "Eli, you're dismissed…permanently dismissed."

"I beg your pardon?"

"You're fired! You recommended that worthless broker team at Reagan and Holbrook and their devious principal is now conspiring against me. R & H was supposed to be representing me and my best interest on West Tower, but instead, their screwing me by taking the side of Andrews Oil Company. Besides, you should have known about Andrews Oil too…any good broker would have sniffed out a tenant needing that much space long ago. Now get out of my sight."

Cohen pivoted, shaking his head, and left the room quickly.

Kellogg chuckled for a few minutes. He loved the position of power and felt everyone was replaceable. He reached for his Rolodex, spinning the knob for Curt Jamison's card at Gabbert and Company.

After a few rings, Jamison answered. "Hello…this is Curt."

"Curt Baby…Mr. X here."

"Hi ho there, Mr. X…what's up?"

"Are you and Rich Eastman free for lunch today?"

"We are now…our boss just cancelled a working lunch today for our brokers."

"Meet me at The Platte Club at noon."

"I'll tell Rich and we'll see you there."

Kellogg hung up, when Phyl informed him John Collins was calling.

"Hello, Colly…what's the story?"

"Good morning, Mr. X. I received a copy of the Reagan & Holbrook complaint for cancelling the West Tower listing agreement. Henry Buckingham called and wants to depose you, Phyllis, and Eli Cohen in his office tomorrow afternoon at two o'clock. He issued a subpoena on your fax machine too."

"What's the rush? There isn't even a transaction consummated they could sue us on."

"They must believe the lease with the oil company will be signed soon and want to get ahead of it, since half their commission is paid upon execution. I'll see you tomorrow at Buckingham's office. I'm preparing my paperwork to depose the Reagan and the Holbrook staff later in the week. Right-o...good-bye."

Kellogg interrupted Phyl. "You and Eli Cohen are being deposed at 2 PM tomorrow by that turd attorney, Henry Buckingham...it's about the West Tower lease cancellation. Go tell Cohen, although I just fired him for incompetency...I should have kicked him out months ago."

Phyl shook her head and raced to Cohen's office where he was boxing up his personal possessions.

"Eli, I just heard...I'm so sorry...you're such a hard worker."

"Not according to Kellogg...what an inconsiderate jerk! He's blaming me for the Andrews Oil fiasco, just because they're killing him on the lease terms."

"You and I have been called to give a deposition regarding the termination of the West Tower lease agreement with Reagan & Holbrook. It's scheduled at two o'clock tomorrow in Henry Buckingham's office. Just so we have our stories consistent, you saw me fax the cancellation letter at four forty-five that day...right?"

"Sure...I was watching over your shoulder."

"Let me know if you need anything. I'll miss you." She hugged Cohen and wiped the tears in her eyes.

Kellogg sauntered to his reserved table at The Platte Club, where Curt Jamison and Rich Eastman were already seated. Both sprung to their feet to shake Kellogg's hand. "Boys...thanks for coming on short notice...I see you've already ordered a beer."

Kellogg turned toward Doris, who was placing the ice water glasses on the table. "Doris...you owe me a new golf shirt from the hotdog accident last Thursday."

"I'll be happy to wash your golf shirt, sir...I have a detergent that will clean almost anything."

"Yeah...and probably shrink it so I couldn't wear it again. I reported your sloppiness to Rex Wilson and expect he'll be speaking to you."

"He already has. Now...what beverage would you like to order?"

"I'll have a double Glenfiddich on the rocks."

Kellogg turned to Jamison and Eastman. "Guys...I should have brought this up in Nebraska, but I didn't want to distract you with business. I knew you had your hands full handling other things." Kellogg laughed holding up both hands, emphasizing a squeezing motion. "Listen...I'm creating a brokerage operation under the Kellogg umbrella and want you guys to co-head a team of other talented brokers."

"Wow...Mr. X. That's an ambitious plan...how does Eli Cohen fit in?"

"I fired Cohen this morning...he just wasn't cutting it." Kellogg pointed his left thumb downward.

Jamison shrugged his shoulders. "No kidding...he is well liked in the brokerage community."

"I didn't like him, so that's all that matters." Kellogg pounded his fist on the table.

Jamison was curious. "What do you have in mind, X?"

"You guys will collect the traditional fifty percent cut of every individual transaction you handle for leases or investment sales, plus share half the profit of the brokerage operation with me. I've got some big projects on the drawing board."

"Can you share that?"

"I can, but then I'll have to kill you." Kellogg smiled.

"Come on, Mr. X...you can trust us."

"Okay then...but keep this confidential. I'm planning a high-rise office downtown, which should break ground next year. I'm also developing two fifteen-story office buildings on a site at I-25 and Colorado Boulevard I'm buying from Remington Properties...Bill Douglas' company."

"Wait...Abe Friedman is buying that site. We're the listing brokers so we should know. Abe already announced it in the newspaper."

"Friedman is out of the picture...he leaked the news prematurely to the press. Douglas was livid when he saw it."

"Holy shit!"

"What price was Friedman going to pay?"

"That's confidential, Mr. X."

"I heard it was a million and a half."

Jamison and Eastman stared at each other, seemingly surprised. "Who told you?"

"You just did." Kellogg laughed. "You can lease a million feet of office space I'll build on the Remington site plus the vacant space in West Tower. The downtown high-rise will be the tallest building in Denver...at least seven hundred thousand square feet there."

"You've been busy, Mr. X."

"We're also doing a few build-to-suits with my brother's construction division and you can promote that business too. I'll let you use our private jet to fly your tenant prospects to Vegas, Palm Springs, Phoenix...wherever you want to go."

"Sounds pretty compelling, Mr. X...Rich and I will discuss it tonight."

"I'll even sponsor memberships into The Platte Club if you play your cards right." Kellogg raised his glass of scotch, while Eastman and Jamison reached across the table and clinked their beer mugs with him.

"Are you guys watching the World Series game tonight? The Yanks have won three straight games, but I'm making another wager on Los Angeles right after lunch. Don Sutton is throwing for the Dodgers tonight and the game is back in California."

"Catfish Hunter takes the mound for the Yankees...I'm not so sure about your instincts, Mr. X."

"Rich, Catfish is all washed up now...he had a few good years with Oakland, but he's done. I have it on inside information."

"You know everything...Mr. X." Jamison smirked.

Everyone stood and shook hands. Jamison and Eastman departed the restaurant, while Kellogg angled toward a phone booth. He was anxious to call Chubby Morrison to wager two thousand dollars on the Dodgers to win game six of the World Series.

Chapter Eleven

Dusty, attired in his tattered blue jeans, red stocking cap, red sweatshirt, and army jacket, parked his pickup on 20th Street, four blocks from the 1010 Building. Dusty plucked the business card from his stocking cap lip to check the Andrews suite number and tucked it back in. He entered the lobby at noon, deciding to climb the stairs to the fourth floor. Gasping for breath, he emerged at the north end of the long hallway. It was eerily quiet as he shuffled down the corridor, attempting to open a series of metal doors, finding them all locked. Nearing the end of the corridor, he discovered suite 410, the only finished space on the floor. He peeked through the side glass, detecting an unlit office. He checked the corridor before slipping a jackknife from his pocket. Using his fingernail, he pulled out a blade with a crooked edge and inserted it into the door lock. He sprung the lock in a matter of seconds, opened the door, and surveyed the space. A tiny conference room was located on the left side of a small reception area and a private office to the right. Dusty peered inside the private office, noting a large wooden desk, a high-back desk chair, and a louvered door, assuming it opened to a closet. He closed the office door behind him and walked around the desk toward the closet, turning the metal door handle to inventory its contents…a pair of muddy boots, a trench coat, a winter wool jacket, a white hardhat and a red baseball cap, both with ANDREWS OIL printed on the front. He turned toward the desk and opened the two drawers on left side, seeing nothing of value. He tugged on the top right drawer, concluding it was locked, but used another knife blade to pry it open. He instantly snagged a rubber stamp…engraved with the words 'APPROVED-ANDREWS OIL COMPANY' and tucked it into his left back pocket. Dusty noted a compartment below the drawer with a tumbler code lock mechanism. As Dusty examined the lock, he was startled upon hearing the main office door handle turn. He closed the drawer and quickly took two steps toward the closet, quietly opened the door, and stepped inside. Through the louvers, he observed a thinly built man open the office door, and flick a light switch, instantly activating the overhead fluorescent lights. The fellow laid his briefcase on the desk, draped his jacket over the back of the desk chair and reached for the telephone. Dusty instantly vaulted from the closet, stripped off his stocking cap and pulled it over the employee's head, completely covering his eyes. He thrust his powerful forearms around the employee's neck as the fellow gasped for a breath. Dusty snagged a twenty-two-caliber handgun from his belt and stuck it against the victim's spine.

Dusty shouted into the employee's left ear. "Don't move or I'll kill you...do you hear?"

The fellow nodded slightly.

"Give me the tumbler code for the locked drawer."

After the employee failed to respond, Dusty pressed the gun against the victim's neck. "I want the code, man."

"One...nine...seven...eight." The employee rasped weakly.

"Very original...now, get down on your hands and knees and start praying."

Dusty placed the handgun on the desk and spun the tumbler, releasing the lock on the metal compartment panel. Opening it, he immediately spotted a red cloth satchel imprinted with the Andrews Oil Company logo. He opened the ties on the sack, revealing a shiny gold seal. He stuffed it in his left front pocket and shuffled through a stack of papers, discovering a large brown envelope beneath. Dusty ripped open the package which contained a stack of hundred dollar bills nearly an inch thick. He jammed the cash into his inside jacket pocket and picked the handgun from the desktop, clobbering the employee's head with the butt of the weapon. The victim crumpled to the floor, unconscious, as Dusty made his escape.

Dusty abruptly raced out of the office, raising the hood of his sweatshirt over his bald head, heading toward the stairwell at the far end of the corridor. Reaching the door, he glanced back at the empty hallway and descended the stairs, reaching the lobby within a minute. He calmly sauntered to the side lobby exit, avoiding eye contact with several people congregated around the elevator bank. Dusty briskly walked through the alleys toward 20th Street, calmly boarded his truck and slowly drove away. Twenty minutes later, he arrived at an old garage in the alley behind his small bungalow. Dusty lifted the rickety wooden garage door and parked the truck inside. Entering the modest home, he emptied his pockets, deposited the stamp, seal, and wad of cash on the kitchen counter. He slipped the rubber band off the stack of bills and began counting the cash, which totaled twenty thousand dollars. Dusty removed a heating vent from the kitchen wall and placed the cash, seal, and rubber stamp inside.

While Dusty was robbing the Andrews Oil office, Xander Kellogg was back in his office, deciding the tactics to employ with Buck Andrews in one last attempt to work out better lease terms. His thoughts were interrupted by a message from Phyllis. "Mr. Kellogg, Nancy Andrews is on the line for you."

Kellogg hesitated but decided to take the call, knowing he had to keep his stories consistent about Jill. "Hello Nancy...how are you?"

"Just fine, except I've been so worried about Jill. I called Swedish Hospital a few minutes ago to check on her condition, but they said she was not a patient. I said a quick prayer before calling you, fearing the worst."

"Nancy…I should have called you earlier. Her doctors recommended a special medical team, so they transferred her to a trauma hospital specializing in brain injuries."

"Oh my God! What can I do, Xander?"

"Keep your prayers coming…Jill needs a miracle to recover."

"Promise me you'll call me every day for an update."

"Yes…I'll add you to her long list of friends."

"Thank you so much…God bless you."

Kellogg decided it was time to call Buck Andrews on his direct line.

"Howdy…Andrews here."

"Howdy Buck…Mr. X here."

"How's Jill?"

"She's in a coma…I actually spoke to Nancy a minute ago."

"We're praying for Jill."

"Since you're in such a somber mood, how about a little compassion for me?"

"You mean our lease terms?"

"Yeah…it's a goddamn sin to steal. Isn't that the seventh commandment?"

"Don't blaspheme…I'm a strict Baptist and read the bible every night."

"Buck, I didn't realize I invaded your space. I'd like you to reconsider a few lease terms Affenson dictated to me this morning."

"Xander, that's our final offer…take it or leave it."

"C'mon Buck."

"Mr. X, hold on a second, please."

Kellogg paced to his liquor cabinet and back to his desk.

"Xander, I just heard someone broke into our Denver office this afternoon and accosted our man, Billy Norton. Have a nice afternoon, but our offer stands."

The phone went dead, so Kellogg threw the receiver against the wall again. "SHIT!"

Phyl came into his office to retrieve the phone, checking to see it was broken again. "Mr. Kellogg, a fellow named Dusty called and wanted to speak with you, but he didn't want to leave a number. Do you know him?"

"Yeah…close my office door when you leave."

Without saying a word, Phyllis quietly shut the door behind her as Kellogg called Dusty. "Dusty, this is Xander Kellogg. Did you a have a problem with that assignment I gave you?"

"No problem…I got what you wanted."

"I was just spoke with the CEO of Andrews Oil…someone told him their employee was beaten up."

"I barely touched the dude. He came in the office, so I hid in a closet. I surprised him from behind by pulling my stocking cap over his head and stuck my gun in his back before ordering him on the floor. That was it…nobody got hurt and more importantly, he didn't see my face."

"Jesus…I sure hope so. When can I get the seal?"

"At four-thirty in Washington Park. There's a bench on the south side of the lake near the tennis courts...be sure to bring the cash reward."

Kellogg hung up the phone and strolled to the bookshelf, moving five books to expose a small grey safe. He spun the dial on the lock and opened it, counting out ten crisp one hundred-dollar bills. He stuck the cash in an envelope and placed the packet in the inside pocket of his suitcoat.

Kellogg dialed John Collins again.

"Colly...I wanted to confirm that Phyllis, Cohen and I will be at the deposition tomorrow afternoon. Also, can you prepare a Kellogg Development Company resolution to formally authorize a transaction or something important like that? These banks are requiring more crap for our business decisions."

"Sure, I've prepared dozens of those forms in the past. What specifically can I include for your transaction?"

"I don't need anything specific. You know I make most decisions alone, although consult with Robert if I need his approval. I only need a general form we can adapt to various transactions."

"Okay, I'll messenger a sample agreement in the morning."

"Thanks...have you spoken again to the Los Angeles attorney, Matthew Morgan, about Buster?"

"Yes...Morgan believes he can convince a judge there was entrapment by the narc squad and the case will be thrown out...keep your fingers crossed.

"That's great news...let me know any update."

Recalling his discussions about the Remington Properties site with Eastman and Jamison, Kellogg decided to call Bill Douglas.

A receptionist answered his phone call. "Good afternoon...Remington Properties."

"I'd like to speak with Bill Douglas...my name is Xander Kellogg."

"Please hold."

A minute passed as Kellogg impatiently continued to hold.

"Hello Xander."

"Good afternoon...you old sandbagger. Have you spent all the money you won on the golf course last week?"

"I handed it over to Helen to buy some new clothes."

"How thoughtful? I wanted to follow up on the Colorado Boulevard site. Are you drafting the contract yet?"

"Not yet, but I called Abe Friedman and told him we weren't selling the land to him. He was furious and threatened to sue...our attorney wants me to hold up until he believes we have no liability."

"Leave the attorneys out of this...all they want is to run up legal bills. What's the price of the land with the discount I mentioned?"

"Friedman was paying a million-seven."

"Uh huh...a million-seven, eh? That seems a little high."

"Does that mean you aren't interested?"

"I'm interested in the actual price Friedman was paying...less ten percent. My sources told me it was a million-five, so ninety percent of that is a million three-fifty."

"Your sources are wrong, Xander."

Kellogg directed another veiled threat at Douglas to remind him of his rendezvous with Linda Melrose. "Bill, I need to go...Linda Melrose is calling me...bye."

Kellogg immediately dropped the receiver in the phone cradle. It was nearly four o'clock...time to head out to meet Dusty at Washington Park. Knowing he didn't want his Corvette spotted, Kellogg called High Plains Cab Service for a ride. He grabbed a pair of sunglasses, donned a black overcoat, stuffed a black golf cap in the pocket, and darted outside to meet the taxi.

After directing the cabbie to Washington Park, Kellogg avoided any further conversation with the driver. As the taxi proceeded slowly along Louisiana Avenue, Kellogg spotted Dusty seated on a green bench...his head covered by the hood of a red sweatshirt. Kellogg instructed the cab driver to park on Downing Street and wait until he returned. Exiting the taxi, Kellogg pulled the golf cap until it touched on the rim of his sunglasses and sauntered along a gravel path that circled the bench. He plunked down on the seat three feet from Dusty, who was pretending to read a tabloid newspaper.

Kellogg reached inside his topcoat but suddenly pulled his hand back as a jogger approached. He waited a few seconds and twisted his head around, ensuring no one was watching. Kellogg stealthily plucked the envelope from his coat and laid it on the bench, sliding it slowly across the wooden surface. Dusty covered it up with the newspaper and dragged it closer. He covertly opened the envelope and using his left index finger, flicked through the bills. Satisfied, Dusty folded the envelope and stuffed it in his left pant pocket. He instantly reached into his sweatshirt pocket, nabbing a cloth satchel, and placed it inside the newspaper. He pushed it across the seat without saying a word. Kellogg cupped the satchel around paper, tucking it under his right arm and set a quick pace toward the waiting taxi. After relaxing in the backseat, Kellogg opened the satchel to inspect the Andrews Oil Company seal. Pleased with his investment, he punched the taxi seat cushion in celebration.

Back in his office, Kellogg practiced squeezing the corporate seal on a blank sheet of paper, studying the impression. He finally pulled the sale contract document from his desk drawer and created the imprint of the seal near Andrews' signature line. He went to the supply room to use the copy machine but fumbled with the controls, kicking the copier in frustration, just as Abbie Kornfeld entered.

"Need some help Mr. Kellogg?"

"I've never been able to understand how these fancy machines work."

She pointed to the power button. "You need to turn the copier on first."

"Hmmm…I thought it was already set to copy."

"Sir, I wanted to speak with you anyway…I'm leaving."

"I know…it's after five o'clock…are you going home?"

"I'm leaving Kellogg Development Company…I've accepted a position with Abe Friedman Interests. Eli Cohen called me two hours after you fired him…he wants me to be his executive assistant there. I'll stay here until Friday, but that's my last day."

"I'll tell you this, Ms. Kornfeld…TODAY was your last day at Kellogg. Go pack up your things and get out. Phyllis will cut a check tomorrow for anything we owe you, although I shouldn't be that generous." He hesitated for two seconds. "I guess you Jews must like to hang out together."

Abbie was stunned, immediately turning to leave the room. "I can't believe you just said that."

Kellogg watched her depart and quickly made four copies of the contract. He returned to his office and grabbed the phone to call George Clements. "Georgie Boy…it's Mr. X. How about joining me to watch the World Series tonight?"

"I wish I could, but Kathy and I are going out to dinner."

"Have fun. I'll call you soon…I may a large office project for you to design soon. Oh…by the way, did Middleton ever pay you back on the golf bet last week?"

"Not yet."

"That figures…his dad was such an honorable guy, but he's a worthless bum."

Chapter Twelve

Kellogg stopped at a Wienerschnitzel fast food restaurant on his way home from his office and ordered three hotdogs covered with mustard and relish. After arriving home, he slipped on a Los Angeles Dodgers baseball jersey and cap he'd been given as a birthday present. After grabbing a cold Coors beer can from the refrigerator, he settled into an overstuffed chair, flipped the pop top on the lid, and unfolded one of the hotdog wrappers, creating a perfect atmosphere for watching game six of the World Series. He carefully chomped down on the hotdog, washed it down with a mouthful of beer and wiped the condiments off the corners of his mouth with the back of his left hand.

Kellogg was optimistic when the Yankees failed to score in the top of the first inning and ecstatic when Davey Lopes led off the bottom of the first with a homerun to deep left field, followed by a Bill Russell single. After thrusting his fist triumphantly in the air, his enthusiasm quickly faded when Reggie Smith and Steve Garvey struck out, while Russell was caught stealing second base.

Kellogg unrolled the wrapper off the second dog as the Yankees batted in the second inning. After leadoff batter Lou Piniella grounded out, Graig Nettles singled, followed by a walk to Jim Spencer, when Brian Doyle's double tied the score at one apiece. Kellogg squirmed in his chair when Bucky Dent singled, driving in Spencer and Doyle, putting the Yanks up 3-1. Kellogg threw the half-eaten hotdog over the television set, seeing the yellow mustard relish mix splash on the walnut paneled wall. He anxiously gulped his beer as Dodger hurler, Don Sutton, settled down by retiring Mickey Rivers and Roy White.

Kellogg was eager to change his luck, retreating to the kitchen to search for a bag of salted peanuts. After rummaging through every cabinet, he finally discovered a bag in the pantry. Returning to his den, Kellogg decided to light the fireplace, arranging four logs in a crisscross pattern on the grate. He crumpled up an old *Denver Post*, plucked a long match from a metal case and confidently struck it to light the paper. As the logs started to crackle, the Dodgers were batting in the bottom of the third, still trailing 3-1. His demeanor brightened after Davey Lopes' single drove in Joe Ferguson, who had doubled. Kellogg cheered aloud and increased the speed of peanut shelling after Lopes stole second and Russell walked, but his hopes were quickly dashed when Reggie Smith grounded into a double play.

"SHIT…Reggie Smith sucks!" Kellogg stomped on the peanut shells.

The next two innings were boring as Kellogg unwrapped the third lukewarm hotdog and polished off another can of beer. After an opening single by Piniella in the top of the sixth inning, Kellogg relaxed after the Dodgers recorded two outs. After a wild pitch by Sutton, he yelled at the television, expecting manager, Tommy Lasorda, would replace Sutton with a reliever. However, Doyle then singled, as Piniella scored. Kellogg screamed at Lasorda again, who finally replaced Sutton with Bob Welch. The next batter, Bucky Dent, singled again, scoring Doyle as the Yanks took a commanding 5-2 lead. Kellogg whipped the hotdog against the wall, creating another yellowish stain.

Kellogg was beside himself, screaming loudly, as if someone could hear him. "That fucking Brian Doyle only hit .192 during the regular season and Bucky Dent batted just .243…those guys are killing me!"

Kellogg procured another beer and resumed shucking peanuts, a pile of shells now collecting on the green shag carpeting beneath his chair. The Dodgers went down in order in the bottom of the sixth as Kellogg paced back and forth in front of his chair, the peanut shells crackling beneath his brown loafers. Kellogg snagged his fourth beer as the Yankees opened the seventh inning. After Roy White walked, Reggie Jackson belted a long homerun off Welch, making the score 7-2. Kellogg threw the full beer can against the TV, shattering the picture screen. Kellogg shouted as loud as he could. "FUCK Bob Welch...FUCK Tommy Lasorda...and FUCK the Dodgers!" He snapped off his blue Dodger cap and flung it into the fireplace, immediately igniting in a bright blue flame. "Fire those worthless bums...I hate the Dodgers!"

Kellogg stumbled over to the bookcase and cast a few books aside to access his safe. After two tries, he finally dialed the correct combination and opened the metal door, counting seven hundred dollars. With no more than three hundred dollars in his office safe, he would need to find at least six thousand dollars to pay Chubby Morrison for his bets in the morning.

On Kellogg's early morning drive to the office, KOA news radio reported the World Series final score at 7-2...he was pleased he hadn't wasted his time watching the last two innings. As a postgame interview played with Series' MVP Bucky Dent, Kellogg quickly turned the dial to a sports station. A caller promoted the idea Brian Doyle should have been awarded the MVP with his timely hitting and World Series batting average of .438. Irritated on hearing another depressing story, Kellogg immediately punched another radio button to a music station, which played Gerry Rafferty's tune, "Right Down the Line." Recalling Reggie Jackson's fateful home run near the right field foul pole, Kellogg couldn't escape reliving his World Series' nightmare. He instantly slammed the steering wheel with his fist and turned the radio off.

Entering his Kellogg Plaza, Xander immediately took a path directly to Mike Peavy's office. Without knocking on the door, Kellogg shouted at Peavy, who jumped an inch in the air. "I need ten thousand dollars...pull it from the West Tower developer fee line."

"Continental Divide Bank won't process another draw until we comply with their terms."

"Then dip into the Kellogg general funds."

"Sir, that amount exceeds the maximum withdrawal of five thousand dollars. Any amount over that will need Robert's authorization according to the company bylaws."

"Screw the company bylaws! I need it now and all in cash too...not a check!"

"Um...let me work on it."

"Work on it NOW!" Kellogg pointed his finger in Peavy's face and pivoted toward his office.

Kellogg hurried past Phyllis without say a word. He opened his safe again and slowly counted a small stack of twenty-dollar bills...two hundred-eighty dollars.

Phyllis knocked on the door. "Sir, I have your morning coffee."

"Fine...place it on the desk. What about my dentist appointment?"

"I forgot about it...I'll call now." She left quickly before Kellogg launched a tirade.

Kellogg's telephone rang, a rare occurrence, as only a few acquaintances knew the private number. He picked up the receiver without saying a word. The caller had a gruff voice. "This is Chubby...I need the seven thousand by ten o'clock this morning. As you know, Kellogg, I demand all bets are settled within twelve hours from the outcome of a sporting event. I expect to see you in the next hour at my club in Aurora."

"I need a little more time, Chubby. I'll give you a thousand now and the rest tomorrow…but I'll pay your interest."

"That doesn't cut it. I'll send my guy over in an hour, so you'd better get creative fast and find the cash." The phone went dead.

Kellogg stared out the window toward I-25, contemplating what to do. He considered asking Robert to approve a special draw, although he had rejected every prior request, citing the virtue of fiscal discipline at the company. His thoughts were interrupted by a message from Phyllis. "Curt Jamison is calling."

"Excellent…put him through."

"Hello Curt…good morning. Did you and Rich discuss my proposal?"

"We did and we're anxious to launch Jamison Eastman Brokerage Partners."

"Great, except the name will be Kellogg Brokerage Group. Well…I guess Kellogg Brokerage Partners could work. When can you start?"

"Mr. X…Rich and I are very well known in Denver as the top brokers. Our names will bring in a lot of business and more money for you too."

"Let me think about it…I'll get back to you."

Kellogg hung up and a few minutes later, Phyllis interrupted again. "Mr. Kellogg, a messenger just delivered a letter from John Collins marked confidential. Do you want me to open it?"

"No…it has something to do with my divorce. Just hand it to me."

"Sally Tuttle, our new receptionist, says that's there's a rough looking dude in the lobby wanting to see you. He wouldn't leave a last name...he called himself Dusty. Wasn't that the name of the person who called you yesterday afternoon?"

"I don't know...I'll go see who he is."

"Very well." Phyliss was surprised, as Kellogg never greeted strangers.

Kellogg darted down the hall toward the front lobby. Since he always entered a private side door to the building, he hadn't met the gorgeous new receptionist. He stopped in his tracks and approached her desk. She stood, exhibiting a form fitting yellow dress, highlighting her hourglass body shape with her blonde hair floating midway down her back.

"Hello darling...you must be new here."

"Yes, I only started last week...my name is Sally Tuttle."

"I'm so pleased to meet you, Sally. My name is Alexander Kellogg. I'm the President of Kellogg Development Company."

"I met your brother Robert on my first day...he was so welcoming."

"Phyllis should have told me about you...she takes care of hiring decisions for all our staff."

"Phyllis has been wonderful."

"We'll have to get to know each other...I'm wonderful too."

"Thank you, sir. Oh...this gentleman says he has an appointment with you." She pointed to Dusty who was lounging in a chair in the opposite corner, his dirty boots resting on a magazine table. He wore a blue stocking cap, a stained sweatshirt with a Denver Broncos logo and torn blue jeans.

"Hi Dusty, thanks for coming over…let's step outside to talk."

Dusty grunted and followed Kellogg into the elevator, down to the building lobby, and out the front door. "I'm here to collect your bet with Chubby Morrison."

"Dusty, I don't have the money. I told Chubby I could give him a grand today and the rest in a few days."

"Look…Mr. Kellogg, Chubby isn't a guy to disappoint…I could beat the shit out of you and confiscate your car…or whatever I think is worth seven thousand bucks."

"Okay…here's the key to my Corvette." Kellogg snagged a key from his right pocket and flipped it to Dusty.

Dusty knew the money he stole from the Andrews Oil Company office would easily cover Kellogg's bet and quickly net him a five percent collection reward from Morrison. "Forget it, buddy…I'll cover for you. Pay me back sometime next week."

"Really…how…?" Dusty cut him off.

"I like to have a credit with people…I may need the favor returned someday."

"I understand…thanks."

Dusty adjusted his blue stocking on his head as Kellogg watched him drive away in his taxi. Xander returned to the lobby to engage Sally again, strutting confidently toward her.

"Sally, just let me know if you need anything."

"I will, Mr. Kellogg…I'm always available to assist you in any way too."

"I'll take you up on that…in fact, I need something typed this morning. I'll bring it by later."

"Isn't Phyllis here to help you today?"

"Yes, but I want to test your typing skills myself."

"I'm a very fast typist."

"Good." He winked at Sally and stepped away.

Back in his office, Kellogg ripped open the envelope John Collins had messengered. He quickly scanned it, determining it was perfect for his purposes. After making several copies, he selected a pencil and began to edit the document. He crossed out Kellogg Development Company and inserted Andrews Oil Company in three places, as well as incorporating language authorizing the purchase of West Tower Office Building in Lakewood, Colorado for a price of twenty million dollars. Kellogg printed Buck Andrews' name and his title of President and Chief Executive Officer below the signature line. He quickly read the entire document three times, insuring everything was covered. He opened his desk and grabbed the stack of Andrews Oil Company stationary he had swiped from their offices. He strode directly to the lobby and handed the papers to Sally.

"Sally, can you type this marked up document onto these blank sheets of stationary? I'll need five originals. Please be careful as these are the only clean sheets I have."

"Oh yes, certainly. When do you need them?"

"As soon as possible. Please don't tell Phyllis about this. I'm promoting her to a new position and am looking for a new assistant. I want to see how you perform."

"Of course, thank you sir.

Kellogg smiled at her again. "Please call me when you're done, and I'll pick up the documents."

Kellogg decided to check in with Robert, who was studying a set of building plans. "Hi there, Robby Boy...what are you working on?"

"The final plans for the AM Manufacturing warehouse. I just got them this morning from George Clements' architectural team. Thanks to your stupidity, we're going to lose our ass on this job."

"It can't be that bad."

"Stay out of my construction business!"

"I need to see Fred Hawthorne soon...how's his dental building progressing?"

"We're almost caught up, so don't mess things up again with your big mouth."

"Fine, but I need to speak with you about a couple things."

"What now?" Robert said with a sigh.

"I had to fire Eli Cohen because he fucked up on the leasing for West Tower."

"I hope you're joking...Eli's a great broker and a good family man."

"He's gone, but I made an offer to Curt Jamison and Rich Eastman to start a new brokerage company with me. They've agreed to come over but want their names included in the title of the new company...Jamison Eastman Brokerage Partners. That won't work, but I'd agree to call it Kellogg Brokerage Partners."

"Those guys are heavy hitters and will bring in a lot of business, so give them what they want."

"I'm opposed to diluting my great name identity. Kellogg is a brand in the community now."

"Start with Kellogg but include their names after yours...do it, Alexander. Don't let your ego mess this up."

Kellogg still wasn't convinced about the brokerage title as he trudged back to his office, where Phyllis was attired in her coat. "Mr. Kellogg, I'm going to lunch before the deposition. Someone from Buckingham's office picked up our fax machine and the records yesterday afternoon. I'm late to meet a friend for lunch, but I'll see you at the hearing."

When she was out of site, Kellogg checked Phyllis' calendar, noting she had another lunch date with Nate Allen circled in red ink. He turned toward his office, observing Sally Tuttle hurrying down the hallway, her brown eyes twinkled with excitement.

"I have your documents, Mr. Kellogg. I made a mistake on one, but here's the rest of them."

Kellogg inspected the pages. "Yes, this looks good...thank you. I have another special assignment for you. I need you to accompany me on my private jet to Las Vegas this weekend on business. I'll need an assistant and I'm leaving tomorrow morning."

"I've never flown on an airplane before...and never visited Las Vegas either. What should I bring?"

"Bring a couple nice dresses...we'll leave from the office around ten o'clock, so you can ride with me to Arapahoe County Airport where my jet is parked."

"I'll be ready...thank you."

Kellogg entered his office and closed the door, reading each typewritten page of the Andrews Oil resolution, verifying the correct spelling for every word and that all punctuation marks were perfect. Kellogg unlocked his safe and snatched the Andrews Oil Company seal. He carefully held a corporate resolution page steady, ensuring the seal punch was perfectly level when he squeezed it. He forged Buck Andrews' signature, carefully matching the contract form. He selected a copy of the West Tower sale contract and drew a paper clip from his desk drawer and attached the resolution form to it. He found a large manila envelope and inserted the two documents, marching directly to Mike Peavy's office, where he dropped the envelope on his desk. "Messenger this to Continental Divide Bank…this should make them happy."

"What's in there?"

"It's my ticket to get that damn bank off my back."

"I'd like to see it, Mr. Kellogg."

"Do it…that's an order! You should be worried about finding me the ten thousand bucks I need. Now…I need to drive downtown, wasting more of my valuable time for a pointless deposition for Henry Buckingham's witch hunt."

Kellogg spun away and darted to his Corvette. As he drove along I-25 to the Buckingham law offices on Seventeenth Street, he had one thing on his mind…how great Sally would look in skimpy lingerie.

As the elevator doors parted on the fifteenth floor, Kellogg stood in the lobby staring at a prominent silver-plated sign…BUCKINGHAM, SMITH & ASSOCIATES. He cast his eyes toward a gray-haired receptionist, who wore horned rim glasses. "Can I help you sir?"

"I'm here for a deposition with Henry Buckingham."

"Oh yes, I'll escort you to the conference room…please follow me."

She led him down a corridor to a corner conference room with spectacular views of the Front Range. Phyllis and Eli Cohen were already seated at a long cherrywood table.

"Would you like anything to drink sir?"

"No...I'm fine.

He turned toward Cohen. "Hello Eli...I hear you already found a new job...you hijacked Abbie Kornfeld too."

"Abe Friedman has been trying to hire me for over a year, so I made a call to him right after you fired me. He offered me a much better deal than I had with you, so I guess it worked out for both of us. Abbie was happy to get out too."

Kellogg scowled at Cohen and sat down without responding.

John Collins entered the room, slapping Kellogg's back as he passed by. "Good afternoon, everyone...it's nice to see you, Phyllis."

"Hello Mr. Collins...it's been a while." She stood immediately, leaning over the conference table to shake his hand.

Collins pivoted to his right to greet Eli Cohen. "Mr. Cohen...how have you been?"

"Never better...thanks for asking. Mr. Collins." Cohen stood, confidently shaking Collins' hand.

"Since you're all here, I'll remind to answer all of Mr. Buckingham's questions honestly. If you don't know the answer, just say that you don't know...or that you don't remember...this isn't a trial."

Cohen commented immediately. "Mr. Collins, we've been through at least a dozen lawsuits with Mr. Kellogg, so we know the protocol."

Kellogg was irritated. "Cohen, I've won every lawsuit before it even reached a courtroom. You'll be in court every week now that you're working for Friedman...his reputation for screwing people is the worst!"

"Well...at least you've given me plenty of practice over the last few years."

Before Kellogg could respond, Henry Buckingham entered the room, accompanied by a short, older woman holding a stenotype machine, which she positioned on the conference table. Buckingham briefly glanced at Kellogg, purposely avoiding him by circling the room to shake hands with Collins.

"Good afternoon John...how are you today, counselor?"

"Just fine, Henry...how have you been?"

"Busy...amazing how many people create legal problems for themselves, but it pays the rent."

"I know what you mean, Henry. I thought I'd be retired by now, but my clients won't let me."

A large man, Buckingham retreated to the end of the conference table, ignoring eye contact with Kellogg, and eased down in a chair next to the stenographer. Buckingham had a commanding presence, even when seated.

"For the record, my assistant, Martha Dodge, will type all of the proceedings today in her little machine. John, you'll receive a copy of the transcript within a couple of days."

Kellogg, Cohen, and Phyllis each identified themselves by submitting a driver's license as verification and followed the protocol, swearing they would tell the truth. After presenting the Reagan & Holbrook listing agreement as the first exhibit, Buckingham elected to question Kellogg, who acknowledged the document was valid, as well as his signature. Phyllis then confirmed she notarized it.

Buckingham next addressed Eli Cohen, who acknowledged he drafted the second exhibit, the letter cancelling the listing agreement. Kellogg verified signing the letter and Phyllis confirmed she typed it and notarized Kellogg's signature.

Buckingham now focused on the facsimile used to transmit the listing cancelation letter on Tuesday, October 10th. He held up a thermal sheet of paper and handed it to John Collins to inspect. Much of the facsimile was illegible because of a significant number of black ink smudge marks which obscured the text.

"Mr. Collins, can you read this entire facsimile?"

"Sir, I am not a deponent here, so I object to your question." Collins passed the paper back to Buckingham, who rose and placed it on the conference table in front of Phyllis for her to inspect. "Miss Williams, what time did you initiate the fax transmission?"

"About 4:45."

"AM or PM?"

"4:45 PM…in the afternoon."

"Miss Williams…how long did the fax machine take to complete the transmission?"

"Maybe five minutes…about 4:50…4:50 PM."

"Mr. Collins, I now show you the transmission receipt records for the facsimile machine at Reagan & Holbrook, where the transmission was sent from Kellogg Development Company. The time stamp shows the machine started receiving the document at 5:49 PM and ended at 5:55 PM."

Collins studied the record and showed it to Phyllis, who shook her head sideways.

"Mr. Collins…I now show you the records from the Kellogg Development Company facsimile machine, which we collected yesterday via our subpoena. The time stamp shows the machine was started at 5:43 PM and began to transmit at 5:48 PM."

Collins peered at the time stamp and showed it to Phyllis, who whispered in his ear for several seconds. "I'm positive when I transmitted the letter."

Buckingham stared at Phyllis and slightly raised the tone of his voice. "Miss Williams…please address the one-hour time discrepancy between the time stamps on both fax machines and the time you swore when you sent it."

"Um…um…I can't. But I am positive about the time I sent the fax."

Phyllis motioned to Collins, wanting to speak with him privately outside the room.

"Henry, excuse us for a minute." Collins pointed toward the door.

Collins took five paces along the corridor and turned to face Phyllis. "What is it?"

"Mr. Collins…I just realized I didn't reset the time on our fax machine to standard from daylight savings time."

"Hmmm…well, just tell Buckingham you forgot to do it."

"Mr. Kellogg will be upset and blame me."

"Don't worry Phyllis…you've worked for him for over five years. Certainly, he'll overlook one small mistake."

"Are you kidding?"

"I recommend you admit the oversight…let's go back in."

Her faced flushed, Phyllis looked at the floor as she and Collins returned. Buckingham instantly asked her the question again.

"Mr. Buckingham...I just recalled I forgot to change the time on our fax machine. However, I checked my watch when I began the transmission and swear it was before five o'clock...Mr. Cohen can verify that."

Buckingham laughed. "You've already sworn to tell the truth, so you don't need to swear again."

Kellogg could feel his blood pressure rising and his face turning red. He pressed his right palm on the arm on his chair but resisted an outburst.

Buckingham pulled out a document from his manila folder. "Mr. Cohen, do you remember Nate Allen, a leasing broker from Reagan & Holbrook, presenting you this amendment to their listing agreement? It's dated October 10, 1978 and states that Reagan & Holbrook, Inc. registered Andrews Oil Company as a tenant prospect for the West Tower Office in Lakewood, Colorado." Buckingham rose and walked to Cohen, placing it on the table so Eli could examine it. After several seconds Cohen acknowledged receiving the amendment.

"I have one last question...did any Kellogg employee deliver the original lease cancellation letter to Reagan & Holbrook, so it was received prior to the time the Andrews Oil Company registration was presented last Wednesday morning, October 11th?

Kellogg shrugged his shoulders, while Phyllis and Cohen looked at each other, shaking their heads in unison, signally no. Buckingham quickly reminded they had to provide an oral response, when they each answered verbally in the negative. However, Cohen quickly interjected...I gave them the original termination letter at the end of our meeting on the morning of the 11th."

"What about you, Mr. Kellogg?"

Kellogg could no longer hold back his anger. "Of course not! My incompetent morons were responsible." He smugly looked at Cohen and Phyllis. "Do I have to instruct you like two-year-old infants to do everything?" Kellogg couldn't believe Cohen failed to present the original termination letter to the Reagan & Holbrook group before Nate Allen presented the Andrews Oil Company tenant registration in the October 11th meeting. Kellogg sprung from his seat, heading toward the conference room door, without uttering another word. Buckingham quickly commented, loud enough for Kellogg to hear. "Thanks for coming today, sir…have a pleasant afternoon."

The deposition ended when Collins shook Buckingham's hand. "Henry…I'll see you in my office on Friday morning. I scheduled the deposition for your clients at nine o'clock."

"Yes, I'll be there."

After Buckingham and Martha Dodge left the room, Collins addressed Phyllis and Cohen. "Is there anything I need to know before I depose the Reagan and Holbrook brokers on Friday?"

Cohen spoke. "I should have mentioned this, but I watched Phyllis send the fax fifteen minutes before five o'clock."

"Not a problem, Eli. So…you have a new job, eh?"

"Yeah…I won't miss a beat."

"Good luck with Abe Friedman's outfit."

"Thanks, Mr. Collins."

"And Phyllis…good luck with Mr. X."

"I'll need more than luck to keep my job…thanks anyway."

Kellogg rushed down the hall and into the elevator, livid at what he'd heard in the deposition. He hurried down Seventeenth Street to the Brown Palace Hotel, where he left his car with the valet. As he sped back to his office, he considered his priorities. It was clear Reagan & Holbrook had legal grounds to collect a significant commission if an Andrews Oil Company lease for West Tower was consummated, so he immediately decided to end all discussions with the Houston firm. Bringing Curt Jamison and Rich Eastman into his organization was now critical, even though it would involve sharing the Kellogg name with the brokers. The forged Andrews Oil sale contract delivered to Continental Divide Bank should provide a few months of breathing room to procure another tenant, or perhaps a buyer.

His thoughts now centered on Phyllis Williams...he had to fire her, even though she had been his assistant for several years as well as an occasional romantic partner. Nonetheless, her negligence with the facsimile machine was unforgivable, not to mention forgetting to arrange his dental appointment. Moreover, he feared she would continue leaking his confidential real estate activities to Nate Allen.

After arriving at the office, Kellogg called Curt Jamison to cement the brokerage arrangement, reluctantly agreeing to the name of Kellogg+Jamison+Eastman Brokerage Partners. Kellogg told Jamison his priority was to find a major tenant for West Tower. During the conversation, Kellogg learned Rich Eastman was exclusively representing a large company seeking to lease office space in a building like West Tower. He became infuriated again, learning the Reagan & Holbrook brokers told Eastman his building was fully preleased, just as they had expressed to Andrews Oil Company. The conversation ended after Jamison agreed he and Eastman would come aboard on Monday.

Kellogg raced to Mike Peavy office to see about his progress on the ten-thousand-dollar draw.

"Peavy…where's my money?"

"Still working on it, boss. I spoke to Willard Edwards at Continental Divide Bank…he's apparently satisfied with the information I messengered this morning. However, he needs to have an updated appraisal from Greg Bottoms at Allied Appraisal before he can process the next draw."

"Call Buttons and demand he complete it by Friday."

"You mean Bottoms?"

"Of course! I also want you to fire Phyllis in the morning and find her replacement."

"What!"

"You heard me…I'm flying to Vegas in the morning and I need you to find her replacement quickly."

"There's our new receptionist Sally, although she's very inexperienced. How about bringing Brenda Dunston back here from West Tower?"

"Hey…that's a great idea. She's incredibly attractive and that's all I care about."

"What should I tell Phyllis?

"Just say we don't need her services any longer…we found someone who knows when to change the time on a fax machine."

"Should we pay her severance?"

"Phyllis has been here about five years…give her five days of pay, one day for each year. Stand over her desk when she cleans it out and be certain she doesn't take any files. Then take all her keys and personally escort Phyllis to her car."

Peavy stared at Kellogg, who spun away, quickly yelling back. "Call that appraiser, Buttons, right now."

Kellogg returned to his office to telephone John Collins.

"Hello Mr. X…just to get to the bottom line, the depositions I heard earlier are a problem and I'm not optimistic I can turn over anything new when I depose the R & H team on Friday. I want to prepare you for the inevitable…you will likely be responsible for paying the leasing commission for any of the prospects they identified, including Andrews Oil Company."

"Yeah…my two dimwits are responsible for that fiasco. Do you think I can sue Cohen and Phyllis for negligence?"

"No…don't waste your time."

"Well, I already fired Cohen and Phyllis is next. Also, I need your help is setting up a new brokerage entity…Curt Jamison and Rich Eastman are joining me next week from Gabbert's outfit. The entity will be called Kellogg+Jamison+Eastman Brokerage Partners. You can draft the typical documentation of the business terms for a brokerage company, including noncompete language if they ever leave…those guys are getting fifty percent of the brokerage company profits plus the customary fifty percent split with the company on any transactions they're involved with personally. Can you take care of the amendments for the brokerage licenses too?"

"Sure…I'll call those guys directly if I have your permission."

"You have it, Colly."

"On my way out of Buckingham's office today, Henry wanted to talk about your divorce with Jill."

"What's there to talk about?"

"Jill told Buckingham she was forced to sign a prenuptial agreement when she was intoxicated. Buckingham wants to declare it invalid on those grounds."

"Jill hallucinates a lot. She was hooked on LSD before we were engaged. And Buckingham...he's all bullshit! I didn't know until today his law firm's initials are BS Associates."

"Xander, I wouldn't go around telling stories about her LSD trips...it would validate her argument. I'll arrange her interview with one of my trusted psychologists and order other medical tests."

Kellogg interrupted. "Any update on the downtown land from those sleepy Nebraska farm boys?"

"No...be patient."

"Colly...I discovered another crime Reagan & Holbrook committed. Rich Eastman is representing another large tenant prospect. The R & H scum told him West Tower was fully leased. Can't you do anything about those lying pricks?"

"I know a lawyer on the ethics committee of the Colorado Association of Realtors and a senior guy at the State Division of Real Estate. I'll call them to see what options are available. Also, I'm having a fundraiser for Casper Walsh at my house Sunday night. His congressional election is coming up again next month."

"Another one already? It seems like I donated to his election last week. Sorry, I can't make it...I'll be in Las Vegas having some fun."

"We'll miss you...Right-o, good-bye."

Kellogg needed to retrieve his Mercedes and called High Plains Cab Service for a ride to the police lot. Surprisingly, when Kellogg opened the door to the cab, he recognized the driver.

"Hey…isn't your name Charlie?"

"Yeah…Charlie Jackson. You were one of my fares last week. I picked you up here and took you to an auto repair shop on Dahlia Street."

"You do property surveys part time…right?" The driver nodded. "I need you to take me to the police lot where they impound cars. Do you know where it's located?"

"Yeah…just off Brighton Boulevard, near 38th Street."

"Good. Hey…I have a couple complicated survey jobs coming up. I assume you'll want to bid on them. I'll tell my finance guy, Mike Peavy, to call you."

As they passed the Colorado Boulevard interchange at I-25, Kellogg pointed over at his future office building site. "See that vacant land parcel over there? I'm about to buy the site and build two exquisite fifteen-story office buildings."

"That's a terrific piece of land!"

"I only buy the best. I made a million bucks on two apartment buildings on the east side of the University of Denver campus…they're coming up on the left." Kellogg thrust his hand out, pointing toward the properties. "They were cash cows, but I decided to sell them when they became a nuisance to manage. I only want big deals now, although I still own The Eldridge, a twenty-four-unit apartment building near Washington Park."

"What's your company's name again?"

"KELLOGG…Kellogg Development Company." Kellogg scoffed.

In a few minutes, the taxi pulled in front of the police impound lot. Kellogg flung a twenty-dollar bill into the front seat. "Keep the change, buddy."

Kellogg shot out of the taxi, heading toward a narrow sidewalk that penetrated an eight-foot-high chain link fence, topped with two feet of barb wire. A tiny dilapidated cinder block structure was the only building on the site. As Kellogg entered the door, he observed a slender policeman hunched over a counter.

"Come for your car?"

"Yeah…it's a black Mercedes sedan towed here on Monday."

"We get a lot of black Mercedes in here, asshole…describe it."

"Is there a problem, officer?"

Kellogg stared at the cop, finally recognizing the policeman from the travel agency parking lot. "Look man…I explained I was late to catch a flight, so big deal…and all because I innocently parked in a fire lane?"

"You must be a big dick around here to get out of an arrest warrant like that."

"I know a lot of important folks, Mr. policeman."

"I need to see some identification." The cop snagged a document from a drawer, slamming it shut, while Kellogg pulled out his driver's license from his wallet. He extended it toward the officer to read.

"Our records show the car registration is under Kellogg Development Company."

"Yeah…I'm the CEO and President."

"Prove it." The officer's tone seemed hostile.

Kellogg rolled his eyes and hunted through his suit pockets for a business card, apparently leaving his gold-plated card case at the office.

"I left my business cards somewhere."

"That's too bad."

"With my wardrobe, doesn't it look like I'm an executive who would own a Mercedes?"

"Look, pal…we get some luxury cars here owned by drug dealers and pimps who dress like movie stars."

Kellogg strained to read the officer's badge. "What's your name again?"

He grumbled. "Sergeant Perkins."

"Well Sarge…I'm calling your Chief of Police, Mitch Johnson. Where's your phone?"

The officer chuckled. "There's a pay phone over there on the wall."

"What's the main number for the police department downtown."

"I forgot."

Kellogg sneered and placed a dime into the slot and dialed zero. "Operator, I want to report a shooting…please connect me with the main Denver Police Department."

Perkins laughed again.

"Yes…please connect me with Mitch Johnson….my name is Alexander Kellogg."

"Hold one minute for Chief Johnson." Kellogg tapped his foot and pretended to shoot the sergeant using his index finger of an imaginary pistol.

Mitch Johnson picked up the call. "X-man…how are you?"

"Hello Johnny Boy…I've got a problem. I'm standing in your shithole office at your car pound on Brighton Boulevard. There's a Sergeant Perkins here who's giving me a hard time with my identification to pick up my Mercedes."

"Oh…I heard about your little run in with my officer on Monday. Mayor Zimmerman even called me to go light on your crimes."

"I wouldn't exactly refer to them as crimes…no one got hurt. Can you speak to this prima donna here so I can pick up my car?"

"Sure…put him on."

"Sarge…the chief wants to speak with you." Kellogg smirked and pointed to the receiver.

Perkins stood up and shoved his chair backwards, walking slowly around the side of the counter and snagged the phone receiver. "Sergeant Perkins here."

"Sergeant…this is Chief Johnson. Give me a brief description of the fellow with you."

"The guy produced a driver's license with the name of Alexander Kellogg III, but the car is registered under Kellogg Development Company. He's arrogant and is wearing a silk suit with a narrow yellow tie…silver cuff links and fancy black shoes. He's a little over six feet tall. His hair is dark but looks fake…like he's wearing a toupee."

"That's Alexander Kellogg all right…let him take the car."

"Yes, sir." He slammed the receiver into the telephone cradle and returned to the counter. "Twenty-five dollars, Mr. Kellogg the turd…I mean third. The car is parked in the back row."

Kellogg whipped the cash across the counter at the cop.

"Sign this release form…it says you won't hold us responsible for any damage to your vehicle." The sergeant handed Kellogg a pen and put his thumb on the signature line. Kellogg scribbled his classic signature and purposely cast the pen over the counter onto the floor.

"Here's your copy." The officer pulled a key out a drawer. "Have a pleasant night…I'll open the gate when you pull up."

Kellogg snorted and bolted through the side door. Reaching the Mercedes, he noted it was covered in dust and the side panels had several long scratches. The front hood ornament was broken off and the radio antenna was bent in a 'Z' shape. Kellogg nearly passed out after opening the driver's door with an unbearable stench. Kellogg opened the trunk, discovering a dead skunk. Using the tire iron, he flung the rancid animal on the gravel and got back in the car to start the engine. He tapped the accelerator, creating intense clouds of black diesel smoke, and steered the Mercedes toward the front gate. For five minutes, Kellogg repeatedly honked the car horn, impatiently waiting for Sergeant Perkins, who finally emerged from the building to drag the fence open. As Kellogg passed through, he lifted the middle finger of his right hand, while Sergeant Perkins responded with an upward right arm salute.

Kellogg drove straight home to pack for the weekend excursion to Las Vegas. His thoughts drifted to the arrangement he had made with Mayor Ivan Zimmerman two years ago, when they met on an elk hunting trip coordinated by his childhood friend, Police Chief Mitch Johnson. The relationship with the Mayor had already proven helpful after offering a free furnished unit at The Eldridge Apartments to Zimmerman for his extramarital affairs. It was a small price to pay for political favors.

Chapter Thirteen

Kellogg was the only passenger on his private jet when it landed at Arapahoe County Airport on Saturday afternoon…his short stay in Las Vegas was a disaster. After checking into Caesar's Palace on Thursday, Sally insisted on staying in a separate hotel room, vowing to maintain her virginity until officially married. Kellogg even proposed to her, attempting to convince her it was the same as being wedded, but she rejected every pitch he tried. Irritated, Kellogg gave her thirty bucks for a bus ticket back to Denver.

Kellogg also had a streak of bad luck in the casino, consistently losing at craps, blackjack, and roulette. He even struck out in the lounges with several ladies for a one-night stand. Running low on cash, as well as maxing out his Diner's Club and American Express cards, he couldn't pay for a call girl. When the casino refused to extend his twenty thousand-dollar credit line, Kellogg called the pilots on Saturday morning, ordering them to fly him back to Denver immediately. Fortunately, the pilots scraped enough cash to buy enough fuel for the flight back.

Kellogg drove straight to The Platte Club, where he was greeted by Rex Wilson.

"Hi there Rexy Boy. Is Chanelle working tonight?"

"No…didn't you hear? Her father died suddenly on Wednesday."

"No, I've been in Vegas. That's terrible…what happened?"

"Heart attack."

"I'll send her a sympathy card…that's what they're called, right?"

"Yep…if you drop it by my office, I'll be sure she gets it."

"I'll eat in the grill tonight. I'm alone for a change and need a break after my trip to Vegas."

"Dante is manning the bar in the grill tonight."

As Kellogg strolled toward the grill, he rounded the corner, nearly bumping into Bill Douglas and his wife, Helen.

Douglas took two steps back, pulling Helen away slightly.

"Bill…we nearly collided."

"Hello there, Alexander…what's up?"

"I just flew back from Vegas after robbing Caesar's Palace again …they may never let me back."

"Congratulations!"

Kellogg stared at Mrs. Douglas "Bill, I believe I've met your wife before…it's Helen, right?" Kellogg took a step forward and kissed her on the cheek as she awkwardly leaned backward.

Her lips parted briefly, reluctantly smiling. "Yes, I believe we've met a before. I've played tennis with your wife a few times. Jill is so nice…how is she?"

"Not very well…she's having some mental issues. We're running some tests."

"Oh my God…I'd like to call her."

"It's not a good time, but I'll let Jill know you asked about her. So, Bill…I was expecting a call from you about my offer to acquire your office site."

Helen glanced at her husband. "What site is that, dear?"

"Our Colorado Boulevard property."

"I thought Abe Friedman was buying it."

"He was..." Douglas coughed and swallowed hard. "He was until he prematurely announced his office building design to the press. The terms weren't really set...it was more of a casual verbal agreement. I didn't feel comfortable about his announcement."

"Bill, why didn't you tell me? I loved his design and the buildings would have culminated the overall development envisioned by my father and our Remington family."

Kellogg interrupted. "Helen, my project will be ten times more magnificent. Isn't that right, Bill? I'm sure Helen also wants to learn more about my plans...the stuff we discussed here on Tuesday evening."

"I didn't know you were at The Platte Club last week."

"Um...um...Alexander and I had a drink in the grill. Right, Mr. X?"

"I think so. I'm so busy, it's difficult to remember what I did yesterday. When can we ink the sale contract?"

"I'll send a draft of the contract to Rich Eastman and Curt Jamison, the brokers at Gabbert representing us on the listing. They can forward it to your rep."

"I'm handling this directly on the Kellogg side. Here's some news...you apparently haven't heard Eastman and Jamison are joining me on Monday with a new brokerage group I'm starting up."

"Hmmm...the listing agreement was signed with Gabbert and Company, so I don't know if those guys will still be involved."

"Well, you can sort out the brokerage fee splits, and I'll look forward to seeing the contract on Monday then. I'm meeting Linda Melrose for dinner in a few minutes, so I'll say hello to her from you, Bill."

Helen seemed surprised. "Who's Linda Melrose, dear?"

Bill's face instantly became flushed. "Ah...ah...she's a tailor Alexander introduced to me. I ordered two new suits from her."

"Oh, you didn't mention you were getting new suits. I've always enjoyed picking them out with you."

I must have forgotten to tell you...you'll like them, Helen."

Douglas immediately grabbed Helen's right hand and escorted her away. Without glancing back at Kellogg, he reached behind his back and extended his right middle finger.

Kellogg smirked and turned into the grill room, saluting the bartender.

"Dante Bambino...Buenas noches."

"Buona sera, Mr. Kellogg. You're confusing your languages again. Do you want the usual?"

"Por favor...and a cigaro too."

"Prego... I have a Romeo and Julietta Number 1 saved just for you." Dante sneered.

"Excelente!" Kellogg snuggled into a bar stool; his name prominently printed on a metal plaque on the back. Three years ago, he paid two thousand dollars to the Club for the dedicated chair.

"Here's your Glenfiddich sir...and some mixed nuts too."

"Thanks Dante. I'm eating here tonight, so rustle up some prime rib with a baked potato."

"Sour cream and chives?"

"You got it."

Kellogg took a sip of his scotch when he felt a tap on his shoulder. He twisted his neck to see George Clements and his wife, Kathy.

Kellogg instantly rose and kissed her forehead. "Hello Kathy...I haven't seen you lately."

"I've had two overseas flights, but I'm home for a couple of weeks to take care of my hubby." With her arm wrapped around George's waist, she tugged him closer.

"Yeah...he looks like he needs some tender care. He's been hanging out with me too much."

"Mr. X...that's a lie. There's no way I can keep up with you. Say...I have an extra opening for my ten o'clock tee time tomorrow. Do you want to join me?"

"Who's playing in your group?"

"John Collins and Casper Walsh."

"Walsh...the Congressman?"

"Yeah...he's is in town for a fundraiser tomorrow night Collins is hosting it at his house. I'm surprised he didn't ask you to attend."

"He did, but I told him I would be in Las Vegas. I'd still be there, but I nearly bankrupted Caesar's Palace, so they kicked me out early. I'd love to join you for golf."

"Good...see you there. Kathy and I just had dinner, so we're headed home. Good night."

"Have fun, Georgie Boy." Kellogg winked.

Sunday was an eventful day for Xander Kellogg. He and Congressman Casper Walsh were golf partners, each winning three hundred dollars and celebrating with several cocktails after the round. John Collins invited Kellogg to the dinner at his home later in the evening, where Walsh became even more infatuated with Xander's entertaining stories.

After several drinks, Walsh disclosed he was a major shareholder in Continental Divide Bank and had a vast background in the stock brokerage industry, currently a silent partner in a new penny stock trading firm called Sherman Grant and Blackmon. Kellogg, however, was more focused on convincing Walsh to intervene on the bidding process for the development of a proposed Department of the Interior office building Cohen had recently mentioned. Walsh, the ranking member of the House of Representatives Natural Resources Committee, bragged about his political influence by bringing hundreds of jobs to Colorado, as well as playing a pivotal role in the developer selection on two recent government building projects in Denver. Before the party ended, Kellogg pledged ten thousand dollars for Walsh's reelection campaign and convinced Casper he had the credentials to bid on the government office project to be built within the Federal Center in Lakewood.

Kellogg rolled into the office at nine o'clock on Monday morning, using the private building entrance to avoid Sally Tuttle, assuming her bus from Las Vegas had arrived in Denver by now. As he approached his office, he spied an attractive woman bending over Phyllis' former desk. He paused, stopping a few feet away to admire her shapely figure.

She stood up and glanced at Kellogg, flashing an inviting smile. "Good morning, Mr. Kellogg. I'm so happy to be back in the central office to work for you directly. I was so lonesome out in the trailer at West Tower."

Kellogg couldn't recall her name and stammered for a few seconds. "Honey…glad to have you here." He leaned over slightly to kiss her on the right cheek when Mike Peavy strolled up to greet her.

"Hello Ms. Dunston…it looks like you're settling in nicely."

"Please call me Brenda, Mr. Peavy."

Kellogg touched her shoulder. "Peavy…Brenda was just saying how pleased she's back here working with us. Sweetie, you'll be doing double duty for a while. Besides taking care of me, you'll support my new brokers, Curt Jamison and Rich Eastman…they're starting today with a new company I'm creating."

"I know them both…they brought a tenant prospect through West Tower in the past month."

Peavy interrupted "Mr. Kellogg, those guys just came in and wondering about their office arrangement. They'll need to share Cohen's office until we can figure something out."

"Peavy, you can give up your office. There should be a couple of open cubicles for you to take over…you can have your choice!"

"Are you serious?"

"Brenda can help you move your stuff. Look at the positive, Peavy…you'll be closer to the can." Kellogg pointing at the men's restroom sign a few feet away.

"That's so considerate of you, Mr. Kellogg," Peavy said sarcastically.

"Think nothing of it. So, let's all get to work. And Peavy…do I need to remind you again about the ten thousand bucks I needed last week.

Before Peavy could respond, Kellogg pivoted away toward the break room. As he struggled to pour a cup of coffee from the dispenser, Eastman and Jamison entered the room. Kellogg quickly strode toward them and boldly shook their hands with his classic twist grip.

"Welcome aboard boys…we're going to make a lot of money together."

"Mr. X, we're glad to be here but your controller told us that we had to share Cohen's former office…this place seems a bit disorganized."

"I just told Mike Peavy to vacate his office, so one of you can move in there as soon as gets his shit out. Brenda Dunston is your assistant and can help you get settled. You apparently know her already."

"Is she the dimwit trying to lease West Tower?"

"That's right…doesn't she have the greatest ass you've ever seen?"

Eastman sighed. "I couldn't tell…she never got out of her chair when I escorted a small tenant prospect through the building. She didn't want to get her shoes dirty in the construction dust."

"Didn't want to get off her butt, eh? Maybe she was a stewardess for Continental Airlines before we hired her."

"She did appear to be a bit on an airhead."

"Don't worry…she's just a temp. Can you bring over your assistant from Gabbert?"

"We've already asked her…can you pay her thirty-thousand-dollar salary?

"Thirty grand? That's outrageous unless she's an eleven on a scale of ten!"

Jamison laughed. "Penny's worth every nickel."

Kellogg roared. "Penny…that's her name, huh? Does that mean she can deliver five times her salary in value?

"Maybe…she's that sharp. Her name is actually Penelope…Penelope Nelson."

"Her salary will be included in the operating expenses, so it comes off the bottom-line you guys split with me. If she's so valuable, bring her over. Also, I'm expecting a contract from Bill Douglas on the Colorado Boulevard site I told you about. You guys should be involved in the commission since you listed the site at Gabbert and Company."

"Mr. X, we resigned from Gabbert on Friday and forfeited all unearned fees including the Remington Property sale listing on the Colorado Boulevard land. However, we assumed we will receive the other side of the commission representing Kellogg as the buyer."

"Never assume anything about Kellogg Development Company. ASSUME is a word for making an ASS out of YOU and ME. You guys should have cut a deal with Gabbert before you resigned. I negotiated the sale terms with Douglas on Saturday night at The Platte Club, so the transaction wasn't even set on Friday…you guys had nothing to do with the final deal."

"Hold on there, Mr. X. Don't you recall we disclosed Friedman's price to you in confidence."

"No, you didn't…I read your minds. Besides, Douglas agreed to sell it to me at a price of a million-three, so it doesn't matter anyway."

"Really…how did you pull that off?" Eastman was dumbfounded.

"I'm a shrewd negotiator."

"Yeah…like you just screwed us out of a commission, eh?"

Kellogg smirked. "Wait a second, boys...I never promised to pay you a commission on the land sale. I only mentioned the leasing commissions you'd collect on the buildings I'm planning to build there." He hesitated a few seconds. "I'll tell you what...I'll have Douglas demand Gabbert cut you in on their commission."

"We'd like to see you pull that off, Mr. X."

"Now...let's talk about West Tower and the large tenant Rich is representing."

Eastman seemed enthusiastic. "Over the weekend, I got exclusive control of the company after our resignation from Gabbert. Have you heard of Sherman Grant and Blackmon...or SGB?"

Kellogg bluffed. "No, I haven't ...why?"

"I guess you don't invest in penny stocks. It's an exploding business and SGB is busting out of the seams in two old buildings they occupy on Eighteenth Street...between Grant and Sherman Street. They're adding twenty brokers every week and need to lease about two hundred thousand square feet in a few months. West Tower is perfect for them."

"What's a penny stock?"

"Publicly traded common stock in small companies, like all the wildcat oil exploration firms...silver and gold miners too. The shares trade for a few cents...that's why they're called penny stocks."

Kellogg raised his eyebrows. "Do they raise money for real estate development companies too?"

"Maybe."

"Is there any credit behind the firm? What's it called again...SOB?"

Eastman chuckled. "SGB…Sherman Grant and Blackmon. From what we've learned, they have rich backers who contributed significant capital when they started it up last year."

"Who are the major stockholders…will they personally guarantee the lease?"

"Otto Blackmon runs the firm although the names of the other principals are confidential. No personal guarantees were offered on the 1010 Building lease negotiations, so that's a dead path."

"Otto Blackmon, eh? Wasn't he involved in some insurance scam a few years ago?"

"Who knows? He was the past President of the Denver Chamber of Commerce and sits on three company boards. He was also campaign chairman for Congressman Casper Walsh for his last two elections. He has a great resume and knows everybody."

"Who are Sherman and Grant?"

"Nobody…it's a joke. The names come from the streets their offices are located on…Sherman and Grant Streets."

Kellogg snorted. "That's clever. What lease terms were discussed on the 1010 Building?

"It didn't progress very far, but they'll sign a five-year lease term and pay your asking rent of fifteen bucks."

"What about their tenant finish?"

"They'll want a swanky entrance and a few flashy conference rooms, but the brokers will sit in bullpen space, so the demising costs will be minimal. They want large neon signs on three sides of the building and Blackmon demands a luxury office on the top floor with a bar, a bedroom with a hot tub, and a private bathroom including a shower."

"A guy who works twenty-four hours a day…like me, huh?"

"I deal with his operations guy, Mick Poletti. I've only met Blackmon twice…he has several beautiful assistants and wears gold chains. He'll want a garage for his Rolls Royce and Maserati too."

"There's no garage at West Tower, but I guess my brother can design something if they pay for it. When can we move on this?"

"I'll set up a building tour this afternoon."

"Great…Brenda Dunston has the building keys. Let me know how it goes."

Jamison entered the conversation. "Mr. X, so we're on the same page, Rich and I are representing the Kellogg ownership side of the transaction for the three percent leasing commission under our new Kellogg+Jamison+Eastman partnership arrangement…correct?"

Kellogg hesitated a few seconds. "Okay."

Eastman quickly interjected. "And no objection for Curt and I keeping one hundred percent of the tenant rep commission of three percent…correct?"

"No…I assume we're equal partners now at Kellogg…fifty-fifty."

"Wait a second…we controlled the tenant representation before we started today…just like your rationalization on the brokerage commission for the Colorado Boulevard land sale."

Kellogg's neck stiffened. "That was different!"

Jamison stepped between Kellogg and Eastman. "Mr. X, what did you just tell us…don't assume anything?"

"Screw you guys." Kellogg bolted toward the door, but suddenly turned around and pointed his right index finger at them "Take your fucking three per cent…I hope you're happy now. Just get this deal done by tomorrow." Kellogg tugged at his tie and instantly left the room.

Jamison and Eastman toasted their coffee mugs in celebration. "Curt, I hope we made the right decision to create this partnership with Kellogg. We'll have to watch him every step of the way."

"Yeah…but he's destined to become the king of commercial real estate in Denver before too long. We'll be rich."

"I'm already rich…Rich Eastman" They laughed heartily.

As Kellogg strolled back to his office, he spotted a large envelope on his chair, noting a Remington Properties label pasted on the top corner. He quickly snagged a letter opener, ripped the edge of the envelope, and snagged the document. He scanned the first page, focusing on the items inserted in the original blank sections, verifying the price of one million three-hundred-fifty thousand dollars. On page two, he noticed the legal description of the property was a traditional lot and block identification as well as some site boundaries. He was immediately distracted, noting the transaction closing details would be handled by Western States Title Company.

He reached for the telephone and dialed John Collins. "Colly, thanks for the invitation to your party last night."

"You're most welcome. It appeared that you and Casper Walsh got wrapped up in some long conversations."

"Throw a few bucks at a politician and you can buy a lot of minutes. Listen…I'm shipping a contract I received from Remington Properties on the Colorado Boulevard site I mentioned to you. Take a glance at it and let me know if I can sign the document.

"Right away…anything else?"

"What do you know about a stock brokerage firm called Sherman Grant and Blackmon?"

"Only what I've read in the newspapers, Mr. X."

"I only look at the sports pages…what do the articles say?"

"You can read them yourself…go down to the public library where they keep back copies."

"Colly, I don't want to waste my staff's time running down there, so just tell me."

"Sorry, but I can't. I'm conflicted with anything involving that company."

"You can tell me in confidence, Colly."

"No."

"Why not?"

"I'm conflicted and that's it."

"You're a jerk, Colly. With all the work I've given you over the years and the money you've made from my real estate deals, I expect a lot more."

"Mr. Kellogg, you should know that lawyers have a code of ethics. Weren't you demanding a morals inquiry for the actions of Reagan & Holbrook?"

"That's different…they fucked me."

"Maybe, but that's not for me to decide, but I can't discuss anything about Sherman Grant and Blackmon. Also, I forgot to tell you yesterday my depositions of the R & H brokers on Friday didn't turn up anything. I issued a subpoena for their fax machine and the transmission records showed an ending reception record from your fax machine at 5:55 PM on October 10th, so Reagan & Holbrook hadn't reset their machine to standard time either. Regardless, it doesn't impact our case."

"Collins, I may have a solution to bury the entire matter and leave Reagan & Holbrook hung out to dry. But since you're conflicted, you'll be the last to know. And forget the contract review...I'll send it to another attorney. BYE!"

Kellogg slammed the receiver down before Collins could reply and promptly called Bill Douglas on his direct number.

"Billy Boy...Good morning. Mr. X here."

Douglas didn't respond.

"I just got your contract. It looks good, but I'm sending it over to an attorney to review it."

"I hope you're happy, asshole."

"Asshole? Is that how you talk to a friend?" Kellogg asked.

"I had to do some fast talking after you brought up Linda Melrose in front of Helen the other night."

"You needed a little reminder about our deal, Billy Boy, but I need one more thing."

"What's that...another price reduction?"

"Not yet, but I want you to call Vic Gabbert and tell him to cut Curt Jamison and Rich Eastman in for ten thousand on the listing commission, even though they resigned on Friday."

"And why would I do that?"

"Because Helen may want to learn more about Linda Melrose."

"Fuck you! When is this extortion game going to end?"

"When I see the title officially transfer to Kellogg Development Company on the Colorado Boulevard parcel. Let's try to close it soon. I just started talking to my banks about the loan."

"What bank are you intending to use?"

"First National."

"I have a long relationship with Wes Wheeler...I'll ride herd over him to get it closed quickly."

"Thanks a lot, buddy boy. Say hello to Helen for me."

"Say hello to Jill for us. Let us know if we can help her during these tough times."

"These substance abuse treatment centers are pretty good, but expensive."

"Really? I didn't know it was that bad...I'm sorry."

"We'll get through it...goodbye."

Kellogg immediately spun his Rolodex to retrieve Wes Wheeler's phone number.

"Wes Wheeler speaking."

"Hi Wheeler dealer"

"Hi Mr. X." Wheeler automatically knew who was calling.

"Pal...I'm buying a piece of land at Colorado Boulevard and I-25 from Bill Douglas at Remington Properties. I'll need acquisition financing now and a construction loan in a few weeks after we get our building plans set."

"I thought you would use Continental Divide Bank again. How's that relationship going?"

"Those shitheads don't have a clue. I should have used your bank, but James Middleton pressed me for business because of the relationship I had with his father at The Platte Club. You know...his old man sponsored me to become a member."

"Yeah...I remember."

"This is a bigger deal than West Tower...two fifteen-story office buildings."

"Is the property near the project that Abe Friedman is developing?"

"It's the same site...I wrestled it away from him. Bill Douglas was impressed with my development plans and wanted a legacy building on his wife's family land."

"Congratulations...how much are you looking for on the land loan?"

"A million-three."

"What's your purchase price?"

"A million three-fifty."

Wheeler laughed, pausing to enter the numbers in his calculator. "Ninety-six percent loan of your acquisition price?"

"Friedman had it under contract for a million and a half, so I'm only asking for eighty five percent of that number. Two Dallas developers offered a million eight, so my loan request is only seventy two percent...a no brainer."

"We'll look into it...send down the sale contract when you can."

"Right away...I'll need to close the purchase in a month."

"No sweat...so long, X."

Kellogg ordered Mike Peavy to his office.

"Yes, Mr. Kellogg."

"How's your new office working out?"

Peavy frowned, signaling his discontent. "I love it...only six seconds to the men's room."

"You'll get used to it in no time. I have another assignment for you...call Middleton at Continental Divide Bank. I need a loan of a million-five on the Colorado Boulevard site I'm buying from Remington Properties."

"Why would you deal with Continental again after the problems they've created for us?"

"I'll take their money again if their loan amount is the highest offer."

"I know the drill." Peavy rolled his eyes, showing his frustration.

"I forgot to ask you about the day you fired Phyllis Williams."

"You fired her...not me. I just relayed your order to her."

"Did she cry?"

"She actually laughed, as if she was expecting it. Phyllis called me yesterday...she's now Abe Friedman's personal assistant."

"I can't believe it...Friedman is raiding all of my people, but it proves I only hire the best talent."

Peavy spun and retreated to his cubicle, thinking Friedman could now learn Kellogg's inside information by hiring three former employees, all who had grievances to settle. Peavy wondered if he would be next.

Chapter Fourteen

Mick Poletti, the operations head of Sherman Grant and Blackmon toured West Tower with Jamison and Eastman early Tuesday morning. Poletti immediately committed to lease one hundred ninety thousand square feet for a term of five years at the asking rent of fifteen dollars per square foot with three percent annual escalations. However, Kellogg still had doubts about SGB's fiscal picture because of their unwillingness to provide financial statements.

Still fuming about Collins' refusal to share any background on the penny stock operation, Kellogg called Casper Walsh's Congressional office ten times to dig further. One of Walsh's staff finally returned Kellogg's call, informing him that the Congressman was tied up in meetings for the balance of the week. Even more incensed, Kellogg bolted to Rich Eastman's office when he suddenly stopped in his tracks, stunned to see a beautiful lady.

Eastman escorted the woman toward Kellogg. "Mr. X…say hello to Penny Nelson."

Kellogg smiled broadly. "You must be our new leasing assistant? I'm so pleased you joined my team."

He leaned forward to kiss her on the right cheek. To avoid his advance, she awkwardly turned slightly, forcing him to nuzzle her auburn hair. "You can call me Xander." He flirted with her for several minutes although she rebuffed his faint romantic hints, finally displaying a diamond wedding ring a foot from his eyes.

Kellogg chuckled. "So…what does that mean?"

"It's a wedding ring, Mr. Kellogg…I'm happily married."

Kellogg smirked. "That's nice...I was happily married for a time with my three former wives too. Let's have lunch sometime soon."

"As long as Rich and Curt can join us...or perhaps my husband, Steve Nelson."

"You're married to Steve Nelson, my old fraternity brother?"

She nodded. "Yes...for twenty years."

Kellogg glanced at Eastman, nearly blurting out the details of the hunting trip to Scottsbluff with her husband. Kellogg turned toward Jamison. "You guys better convince SGB to provide some financial information. I know my lender will need to see them."

"We're trying. Mr. X."

"Try harder...no financials...no lease...no commissions."

Kellogg suddenly pivoted, retreating down the hallway, where Mike Peavy intercepted him. "Boss... Greg Bottoms revised the Allied Appraisal valuation to twenty million based on the Andrews Oil purchase contract, so Continental Divide Bank agreed to fund the West Tower construction draw request...it includes a forty thousand dollar development fee."

"When do I get the dough?"

"Hopefully by Friday."

"Get on the phone and demand they cut my check tomorrow."

"I'll try."

"Don't try...get it done!"

Kellogg pondered for a moment, deciding if there was enough money to pay off his loan to Dusty and provide ample personal spending funds for a few weeks. He strutted to his liquor cabinet, pouring a scotch and selected a cigar from a humidor, tucked in a locked credenza compartment. He tilted back in his office chair, relishing his creative maneuvers with Continental Divide Bank, when he was interrupted by a call on his direct line. "Hello…X here."

"Alexander…Buck Andrews calling."

"Bucky Boy…how've you been, pardner?"

"Terrific…oil prices are looking good and two wells came in last week. I'm surprised we haven't heard back from you on our offer to lease your building."

"I've got a few other offers cooking. Your bully, Affenson, shouldn't have been such a prick on the draconian lease terms he proposed… you should call him Dracula."

"He's a bulldog all right…that's why he's Chief Operating Officer."

"Good for you."

"Another thing…Nancy spoke to Jill and learned she was never in a car accident. You're a damn liar, Kellogg. We can't deal with a fraud, so our verbal lease proposal is off the table. We have a few irons in the fire too. I'm happy we never finalized a deal…you would probably have screwed us by cutting off our power on a whim. From everyone I've spoken to in Denver, I've learned you're a slimy scoundrel."

"Fuck you, Andrews. I've heard the same about you too…and just for the record, I'm not sponsoring your membership in The Platte Club."

"That's fine with me. I wouldn't join any organization that admitted you as a member!"

Kellogg slammed down the receiver and chomped on his cigar. He instantly dialed Eastman's extension. "Rich, get the Kellogg standard lease form to the penny broker outfit right now and arrange a meeting tomorrow with that fellow Blackgammon...I need to see who he is."

"His name is Blackmon...Otto Blackmon. I gave his operations guy your lease form yesterday after our tour, Mr. X."

"Great, that's a tough lease...if a tenant even sneezes, I'll nail 'em."

"Is John Collins handling the lease review?

"Not this time...the old curmudgeon is conflicted. If Poletti makes a lot of changes, I'll get Steve Nelson involved since we got reacquainted on the pheasant hunting trip."

"Don't worry about any lease issues...I'm on it." Eastman confidently replied.

"If this has liftoff, arrange a meeting with my brother, Robert, and George Clements' architectural firm to coordinate the space plans and other bullshit features for Blackmon's suite improvements and a garage for his fucking luxury cars."

Kellogg spun his Rolodex to the "N" section, searching for Steve Nelson's phone number and dialed.

"Nelson law firm...how can I assist you?"

"I want Nellie."

"Mr. Nelson...one moment, please."

"Hello X, that has to be you."

"You got 'em, Nellie Boy. I have some work for you. I'm giving my regular attorney a little vacation, so I need you to review a purchase contract on a piece of land I'm buying and handle the closing…it's a real big deal."

"I'll clear my desk and get right on it."

"Great…my new leasing assistant will get you the details."

"That's Penny, right?"

"I had no idea we hired your wife…see ya, brother." Kellogg hung up abruptly.

Brenda shouted out "There's a call from a lady named Jillian…she seems awfully mad. Do you know her?'

"Yeah…she's on the way to becoming my former wife."

"Really…pick up line two please."

Kellogg cleared his throat twice and punched line two.

"Jillian, my dear…how's life on the road?"

"You're a piece of shit. My friends are calling me constantly about my car accident…they're all concerned about my mental breakdown too. How could you start those vicious stories?"

"I have no idea what you're talking about, honey...but I admit I told John Collins to engage a psychologist to evaluate your mental state after you tried to shoot me."

"My friends would say shooting you would be an act of sanity. You belittled me and constantly cheated on me while I tried hard to make this marriage work."

"Look…I suggest you quietly accept the terms of our prenuptial agreement and settle this divorce quickly. You can hit the dating circuit soon to trap another sucker to pay for your extravagant lifestyle."

The phone clicked. After hearing a dial tone, Kellogg called out to Brenda. "If that lady calls again, tell her I'm out. Also, every time you receive a call for me, either come into my office or buzz me on the intercom…no more screaming messages from your desk."

"Yes, sir."

Kellogg contradicted the order he just gave her. "Brenda, do you know anything about hiring a housekeeper?"

"No, I don't own a house."

"Phyllis hired an employment agency to find a new maid for my home. There must be a file there somewhere around your desk…call them and see how it's coming along."

With the construction draw on West Tower set for funding; Kellogg called Dusty to arrange for repayment of the seven-thousand-dollar debt for the World Series bet. The phone rang ten times before the ringing stopped. Not hearing a response, Kellogg was uncertain if someone had picked up the receiver. A few seconds passed before he whispered, "Is this Dusty?"

"Who wants to know?"

Kellogg spoke louder. "It's Mr. X."

Dusty finally responded. "There's trouble, Mr. Kellogg. A couple cops showed up at my door this morning…they wanted to know where I was around noon last Tuesday…the 17th…about the time I broke into the office downtown."

Kellogg remained silent.

"They found a card for Chubby Morrison's clubs on the floor of the office. It must have fallen out of the rolled-up lip of my stocking cap. I pulled down over the guy's head...the moron who interrupted the burglary."

Kellogg remained silent.

"You wrote the name of the oil company and their address on the back of the card the night I picked you up at the airport. The police are questioning everyone at the club...even Chubby. I don't believe they have any evidence or witnesses, but I'm going to need an alibi just in case. Do you know what I'm talking about now?"

"What about hair samples from your cap?"

"You may have never seen me without a stocking cap or hood. I shave my head nearly every day...I'm completely bald."

"Don't worry Dusty...I'll come up with a story if you need some cover. Listen...I have your seven thousand bucks and can pay you on Friday."

"Okay, let's meet at that bench in Washington Park again at four o'clock...in the afternoon."

"No...I'll stash it and call you with the location." Kellogg began to think about distancing himself from Dusty. He suspected there was more to the robbery than Dusty was telling him.

Kellogg instantly felt a pit in his stomach. Knowing every piece of physical evidence tying him to the robbery had to be destroyed immediately, he stared at the yellow slip with Dusty's phone number, trying to memorize it. After several failed attempts, he decided to convert the last seven numbers to letters on the phone dial to form a word he could remember. He jotted three letters for each number on a yellow pad, trying to organize them into something recognizable.

After fifteen minutes, he made a discovery…the letters formed XANDERX after the 303-area code. Satisfied, he folded the slip twice and placed it in the ash tray. He struck a match, igniting the corner of the paper, which incinerated in four seconds. Using a pencil eraser, Kellogg poked at the ashes until they turned to a blackened powder.

Kellogg opened the lower credenza drawer and snatched the copies of the purchase contract and the Andrews Oil corporate resolution. After tearing them six times, he dropped them into a metal trash can beneath his desk. He crumpled up a sheet from a yellow pad and lit a corner, releasing it on top of the document scraps. The flames shot up instantly, nearly touching the bottom of the desk. Kellogg reached for a glass of water to extinguish it when the fire suddenly subsided.

Brenda rushed into his office. "I smell smoke…should I call the fire department?"

"Forget it…just burning some old forms. The fire is out now."

She peeked around the corner of the desk at the smoldering ashes in the trash can. "I would have been happy to purge them. You should open a window." Brenda flapped her hands for a minute until Kellogg pointed to the door, suggesting she return to her desk.

Kellogg opened his office safe, plucked the Andrews Oil corporate seal from the red satchel and rubbed off his fingerprints on the metal stamp with his handkerchief. He slipped the sack into the topcoat pocket, dashed to his Corvette, and charted a course to Fred Hawthorne's dental building construction site. Upon arriving, Kellogg spotted a construction worker operating a backhoe filling dirt around the concrete basement walls. He signaled the foreman, Bobby Kellogg, and engaged his nephew for several minutes about the progress of construction. After Bobby walked away, Kellogg tossed the satchel against the wall, seconds before the workman dumped a load of dirt over it.

Kellogg decided to stop at The Platte Club for lunch, although primarily wanted to check on Chanelle. After he arranged to sit at one of her assigned tables, she approached with a solemn expression.

"Good afternoon, Mr. Kellogg…what can I get for you today?"

He immediately stood and touched her shoulder. "Chanelle…I was so saddened to hear of your father's sudden death. I was on a trip and just heard about it on Saturday night."

As Chanelle began to sob, Kellogg reached in his back pocket for a handkerchief and extended it to her, as she dabbed the tears in her eyes.

"It's so devastating for our family…he was so young. My mother decided to cremate his body and we're planning to hold a memorial service in New York to spread his ashes back there."

"Is there anything I can do?

"Thank you, but we're just trying to get through the shock" A tear dripped down her right cheek. "Our finances will be difficult…we discovered Daddy's life insurance policy lapsed and were shocked to learn he had several gambling debts. My mother has never worked, other than as a maid in England, where my father met her. We'll probably move back East to be closer to our relatives."

"Sweetheart, that's not necessary…I can help. So, your mother was a maid, huh? If I may ask, how old is she?"

"Forty-four…her birthday was last month."

"Did you get your natural beauty from her?"

"Yes…she's beautiful."

"What's her name?"

"Magdalene, but she prefers Maggie."

"I'm afraid I don't even know your last name."

"It's Donaldson…Chanelle Donaldson."

"So, her name is Maggie Donaldson. Do you have a photo of her?"

She nodded and reached into her pocket for a small wallet. She slipped out a color snapshot, handing it to Kellogg. He held it toward the light, admiring a beautiful woman with striking features and long, reddish hair.

"Yes…she certainly is stunning. I'd like to meet her sometime."

"Maybe after the memorial service."

Kellogg returned to the office and marched directly to Peavy's cubicle, as Mike spoke on the telephone. Kellogg became impatient after a few seconds, repeatedly thrusting his palm across his throat, signaling Peavy to cut off the call. Exasperated, Kellogg snatched the receiver from Peavy's hand, slamming it on the telephone cradle. "What's wrong with you Peavy…I need to speak with you immediately."

"My wife was telling me about our son's report card."

"The only important thing you can do right now is to get the West Tower contract back from Continental Divide Bank…the Andrews Oil corporate resolution too."

"Why? They're funding our draw tomorrow based upon the sale transaction."

"Those Texan double crossers called off the deal this morning…they discovered the purchase of my building violates a bank loan covenant."

"I'll call Middleton right now."

"Not yet…wait until the draw is funded and all of the checks are cashed…especially my developer fee."

"But…but…but…"

"But what, Peavy…got a stuttering problem now? Call me when you have my developer fee check."

Kellogg scurried toward his office when Brenda Dunston stopped him. "Mr. Kellogg, I spoke with the employment agency about a housekeeper. They have four candidates lined up for you to interview."

"I want to see full body color photos for each of them. I can't waste my time interviewing anyone who doesn't meet my standards."

"Certainly. Oh, I almost forgot…there's someone claiming to be your son holding on line two."

"Why didn't you tell me immediately," Kellogg said with exasperation.

"You didn't ask, sir…but I'm telling you now," Brenda responded defensively.

Kellogg rolled his eyes and walked directly to his desk where he picked up the call.

"Buster…how long have you been holding?"

"About five minutes…what happened to Phyliss?

"I canned her…my new assistant is Brenda Dunston."

"Are you certain her last name isn't Dumbston?"

"What's up?"

"Matt Morgan is a genius."

"Who's Matt Morgan?"

"He's the attorney you lined up to defend me. He worked out a plea bargain with the district attorney's office…I received probation for a year."

"Terrific…what do you have to offer in return."

"Testify against two cocaine dealers."

"You're into that crap too, Buster?"

"No, but those guys sold grass to me a few times."

"That's trouble…you need to get your ass out of California and back to Denver. I've worked out a deal with your uncle Robert for you to join the firm."

"But I can't surf in Colorado and the winters are too cold…plus I have to report to my probation officer every month out here."

"You can't surf if those guys order a hit on you…your body will be cold permanently. When you move back here, you can take up snow skiing again. Haven't you missed that?"

"Sometimes…I guess I can ski on sunny days."

"That's what I want to hear. Look…I need to run. Call me when you have the details worked out to move back here. We'll get Morgan to arrange your probation meetings here in Colorado."

"Thanks Dad…can you wire me a thousand dollars to tide me over?"

"I can arrange that next week, but no money for dope."

"I promise."

"Good...talk soon." Kellogg hung up and strolled to Brenda's desk. "That was my son, Buster. The next time he calls, let me know immediately. By the way, how would you like to join me for dinner tonight?

"Yes...I'd love to. Do you have a restaurant in mind?"

Kellogg thought for a moment, taking a mental inventory of places where the company had a credit account. "Make a reservation at the Palace Arms in the Brown Palace at six. I'll drive you from our office."

"That's sounds wonderful, Mr. Kellogg. Will you drop me back here to pick up my car after dinner."

"It depends."

"Depends on what?"

"Whether you take a cab or not."

On the drive to the Brown Palace, Kellogg decided to engage Brenda about her background.

"Brenda, I really don't know much about you. I like to know more about the people I work closely with. Were you born in Denver?"

"No...in Greeley."

"Are you married?"

"Not now...but just once. My husband was a construction worker and the marriage lasted six or seven years. We didn't have any kids."

"What did you do before you worked at Kellogg?"

"Many things really…a waitress, a bank teller, a title company marketing associate, and a few secretarial positions, including one in 1972 for Congressman Casper Walsh's office in Denver. My last position was a personal assistant for Mr. McDonald at AM Manufacturing."

Kellogg didn't think all these different jobs raised any red flags…rather he was more curious about her former employers and what she could tell him about them.

"Mr. Kellogg…I understand that you'll be single again pretty soon."

"Not soon enough…not soon enough."

"But you're dating already, correct?"

"Absolutely!"

She flashed a brief smile and asked, "Is this a date tonight?" Brenda raised her eyebrows.

"I'll let you know in few hours." He winked at her and smiled.

Brenda laughed as she pulled down the visor to check her makeup in the mirror. Kellogg turned on the radio, immediately cutting off the conversation.

The maître d at the Palace Arms recognized Kellogg and escorted the couple to a private table in the corner of the restaurant. Brenda became more animated as the five-course dinner progressed and after consuming three martinis and a bottle of wine, began to slur her words. Kellogg paced his alcoholic intake and after dessert, probed about her former employers. After further interrogation, she finally admitted to several sexual affairs with Casper Walsh, Al McDonald, as well as a one-night escapade with a Continental Divide Bank executive after a company Christmas party. After probing further, she revealed the bank officer was Willard Edwards. Kellogg invited Brenda to his residence for the night. All in all, it was an enlightening evening.

Still groggy from an active night of sex, Kellogg headed to the break room to seek a remedy from the coffee maker. Entering the break room, he decided to sneak up behind Penny, who was searching through the break room cabinets.

He pinched her right butt cheek. "Good morning, lovely."

She instantly spun around, dropping her cup of coffee, which spattered across the vinyl tile floor. Raising her right palm, she slapped Kellogg on his jaw. "Damn it! Never do that again or I'll quit on the spot."

Kellogg chuckled as he rubbed his chin. "I thought you heard me walk in. Most women would love a little tweak in the rear. Well…I guess you don't."

"You guessed right, Mr. Kellogg."

He pointed down at the floor. "Have the gal at the reception desk clean this mess up…her name is Sally, I think. Now, come to my office…I need you to deliver a contract to your husband, who's handling my Colorado Boulevard land purchase."

She raised her eyebrows and wrinkled her brow.

"Is there something wrong, honey?"

"Yes, there is…my name is Penny, not honey."

Penny followed Kellogg to his office where he handed the purchase contract to her.

"Nellie will be handing more legal work for me now. Nellie…that's what we called him at the frat in Boulder."

"I've heard the nickname. He'll be happy to hear about your trust in him."

Kellogg's phone rang, cutting off their conversation, although he signaled a thumbs up sign to Penny as she left the room. "Hello…X speaking."

"Collins speaking. I didn't know when to call you given our last conversation, but I have some news on the Seventeenth Street property."

Kellogg quickly asked. "What's the story with those sodbusters?"

"I received a call late yesterday afternoon from Pudge Bristol about the ground lease extension."

"Shit."

"Relax, Mr. X…the date for receipt of a written extension expired yesterday at 5 PM. He didn't understand the consequences of his failure to provide written notification of the ground lease extension to me as trustee…he thought a phone call was enough. I told Bristol I would prepare a simple document, acknowledging transfer of the leasehold interests to your KF Trust."

"Great news, Colly!"

"Not so fast…I received a phone call from Henry Buckingham a few minutes ago. Apparently, Bristol called him last night to contest the notice provision. Let's hope Buckingham doesn't try to muck this up with some legal bullshit."

"Not Henry Buckingham again! He's like a leach…I can't get rid of him." Kellogg paused. "Also, Buster called…Matt Morgan arranged a plea bargain with a year's probation. Call Morgan and have him arrange for Buster's probation to be served and monitored in Colorado…Buster is moving back to Denver soon."

Kellogg hung up abruptly and immediately raced to Rich Eastman's office. Although the door was closed, he burst through without knocking. Eastman was immersed in a phone conversation, but sensing Kellogg's impatience, cut the call short. "Looks like you need to speak with me, Mr. X."

"Since you grew up on a ranch in western Nebraska, have you heard of the Bristol Brothers…they're farmers from that area."

"Yeah…they own three huge ranches near our family homestead, including the place near Scottsbluff where we hunt pheasants. I've had a few beers with Pudge Bristol over the years and met Bud, his dumb brother, who lives in Cheyenne. When I was at Gabbert, I spoke to Pudge regarding their buildings on Seventeenth Street and was involved with a possible sale of their old gas station site on Colorado Boulevard, but he's more interested in bragging about rodeo bull riding competitions. Why are you asking about them?"

"I heard they missed a few ground rent payments under the buildings they own on Seventeenth Street…a default could result in a reversion of the structures to the landowner. There may be an opportunity to jump in the middle…see what you can find out." Kellogg immediately switched the conversation topic. "Any news on the meeting with SGB?"

"I arranged a lunch with you and Otto Blackmon at noon today. I assume you want to meet at The Platte Club."

"No…I want to see where he wants to meet." Kellogg relied on an old rule that a person's success was directly tied to the restaurant selection for an important business meal.

"Okay…I'll get back to you."

Kellogg spun around and left the office abruptly, smiling as he trotted toward Brenda.

"Thank you for a wonderful evening, Mr. Kellogg. I just got in."

He twisted his neck backwards toward her as he entered his office. "Let's do it again soon." Kellogg settled into his office chair and contemplated his next move, hearing a tap on the door.

Robert peeked in. "Good morning, kiddo. I heard you're about to sign a lease deal on West Tower with Sherman Grant and Blackmon…that's trouble plus they want some costly design changes too."

"Trouble…why?"

"Blackmon is a slickster…he weascled out of a Federal investigation on an insurance Ponzi scheme a few years ago with inside help from Congressman Walsh. Now he's running a maverick stock brokerage firm that has no track record. I heard the Federal authorities are watching them closely."

"My guys tell me they have solid financial background and they're hiring stockbrokers like crazy…it verifies people love to bet. I've also learned Blackmon is connected everywhere."

"Maybe…but you're gambling a two hundred thousand square foot building on a long shot."

The conversation was interrupted when Rich Eastman entered the room.

"Hey Rich…do you know my brother, Robert."

Eastman detoured toward Robert to shake his hand. "Yes, we just huddled yesterday to discuss the SGB tenant improvements for West Tower."

Robert suddenly turned to leave. "Watch yourself, little brother." Although Robert knew Eastman was a top office leasing broker, he now had reservations because of his connections to Blackmon, as well as his sole priority for the SGB lease consummation was to collect a large commission.

Xander smirked. "Have a nice day, Robert."

Eastman watched the elder Kellogg strode down the hallway. "What's his problem, Mr. X."

"He's in a bad mood...must be more problems at our construction sites."

"I spoke to Otto Blackmon's secretary...she's arranging lunch at the Palace Arms at the Brown Palace at noon.

"Excellent...let's drive there together."

Kellogg and Rich Eastman arrived at the Brown Palace at twelve fifteen. It had been Xander's long term negotiation strategy to arrive several minutes after a scheduled meeting time, even when he didn't have the upper hand. The maître d greeted Kellogg as he entered the Palace Arms restaurant. "Good afternoon, Mr. Kellogg...it's so nice to see you back so soon. How was your dinner last evening?"

"Perfect...perfect."

A gentleman with slick backed hair and dressed in a light green silk suit, hurried toward Eastman.

"Hi Rich...we've been waiting for twenty minutes...we thought we had our signals crossed."

"Good afternoon, Mick. Sorry...we hit some traffic along the way. I want to introduce you to Xander Kellogg."

Kellogg studied Poletti's features while he gripped Mick's hand with his classic twist. He skipped past Poletti's neatly trimmed black mustache and bushy eyebrows, focusing on the spaces between his teeth.

"Mr. X, meet Mick Poletti...the operations mastermind for SGB."

"It's an honor, Mr. Kellogg."

"Yes...yes." Xander glanced down at Poletti's shiny wingtip brown dress shoes.

"Otto's sitting back here in the corner." Poletti led the way to the table.

A shorter, rotund gentleman rose and greeted Kellogg with a warm smile. He wore a white dress shirt that was partially unbuttoned, revealing a mass of black chest hair. A dollar shaped medallion, imprinted with SGB, hung six inches below his neck from a gold chain.

"Good afternoon, Mr. Kellogg...I'm Otto Blackmon...call me Blacky. I guess we're here to cut a lease deal."

Kellogg stared directly into his beady black pupils, as Blackmon's strong grip controlled the handshake. "That's what they tell me." The two men continued to size each other up. Kellogg's eyes travelled down to Blackmon's shirt cuff, embroidered with the initials OBB, and then to his wristwatch...a prestigious Breitling Chronomat. He glanced at his own sleeve, tugging at it slightly to flash his Rolex Cosmograph in Blackmon's range of sight.

"Let's sit down...I already ordered a Vodka Martini. What are you drinking, Alexander?"

"Scotch...Glenfiddich...on the rocks."

Blackmon snapped his fingers at a waiter, signaling him to come to the table. "Garcon…my friend will have a Glenfiddich on the rocks, and I'll have another martini."

Poletti grabbed the waiter's arm. "Wait…this gentleman wants to order a drink too." He pointed to Eastman.

"Just an iced tea, please."

"Very good, sir."

Eastman tapped his knife on his water glass to gather attention and steer the conversation. "We shouldn't discuss business before we order lunch, but Mr. Kellogg prefers to get right to the topic at hand. Mr. Blackmon…West Tower will absolutely enhance your company's image and your three SGB signs on the top will be been seen by thousands every day."

"We already have a great reputation and a few thousand additional clients are always welcome." Blackmon confidently said.

"Blacky, you can call me Mr. X." Kellogg paused. "Tell me about your business…do you make a profit?"

"Mr. X…we offer a trading platform for stocks the white shoe boys on Wall Street ignore. We are well rewarded for creating a market…our fees are ten times what they charge. It's like shooting fish in a barrel…folks can own a piece of a company for a few pennies."

"Sounds interesting…but I need to see a financial statement on SGB. I never sign a lease with a tenant unless I know they're solvent. My construction lender will want to see your numbers too."

"We don't generate any official financial statements."

"Doesn't the Securities and Exchange Commission oversee your business?"

"Kind of…they know we run a tight ship. Some of the SEC directors and top brass are actually clients of SGB."

"How about seeing some tax returns?"

"We only started up last year and have been granted an extension from the IRS on filing our 1977 returns."

"There must be something you can give me…my bank lender is not as trusting as I am."

"Listen…we have two hundred brokers and adding twenty more every week, so that should tell you something. Besides, we've agreed to all of your lease terms and are ready to move in as soon as you can build out the floors and the features for my space."

Eastman broke in. "Mr. X, they've also agreed to pay for those special design items on their nickel as well as a ten percent override on their cost."

"We'll discuss that later, Rich." Kellogg glared at Eastman and turned to address Blackmon. "So Blacky…I understand you can raise capital for anything. How about a debt platform for a developer like me? Most days, the lame bankers in this cow town have a hard time finding their ass with both hands. The banks have no vision…no appreciation for dynamic ideas, like mine, that can transform this City."

"We've raised plenty of dough for startup companies, so I guess we could do it for a real estate outfit."

Kellogg was clearly irritated. "Listen pal…Kellogg Development Company is certainly not a startup and could never be labeled an outfit. I'm insulted by your insinuation."

Blackmon laughed as he held out his martini glass for a toast. "Congratulations for making it in the big leagues…Mr. X. Of course, we'd be honored to work out an arrangement to raise debt for your business…equity capital too. Here's my business card…call me directly anytime."

"I may take you up on that. Now…where's my scotch?"

The luncheon continued until two o'clock when Kellogg finally capitulated, failing to wrestle any financial details from Blackmon on SGB and its ownership structure. However, as a last-minute negotiating twist, Kellogg demanded the construction cost override be increased from ten to twenty percent, which Mick Poletti conceded with little resistance. On the drive back to the office, Kellogg ordered Eastman to press forward on the Sherman Grant Blackmon lease and specifically required a corporate seal on the lease document as well as on a corporate resolution authorizing the transaction.

Without any changes, the SGB lease for West Tower was executed by Otto Blackmon by the end of the day. Eastman delivered the signed lease and corporate resolution to Kellogg, who ordered Mike Peavy to deliver the documents to Willard Edwards at Continental Divide Bank.

Chapter Fifteen

The funds arrived for the West Tower constructions draw and Mike Peavy transferred the forty-thousand-dollar developer fee to Xander Kellogg's personal bank account at First National Bank. Kellogg immediately drove to their University Boulevard branch to withdraw ten thousand dollars in cash. On the way, Kell decided to meet Dusty at the bench in Washington Park again to repay the loan.

Dusty was more concerned about the robbery investigation. The police detectives, armed with a search warrant, had searched his residence, garage, and truck. Kellogg was relieved when Dusty reported he'd burned the clothes he wore the day of the robbery. Although Kellogg was still unaware of the stolen cash and Andrew's Oil Company rubber stamp, Dusty had removed them from his heating vent and stashed it under a row of brick pavers bordering a backyard garden.

It had taken three days for Rich Eastman to reach Pudge Bristol regarding the Seventeenth Street office buildings. Eastman knocked lightly on Kellogg's office door and entered without a prompt. "Mr. X, I spoke to Pudge Bristol this morning. He told me a trust owns the land and the lawyer trustee is pulling a fast one on them. Pudge called the attorney in time to extend the ground lease but was told a written notice was necessary. He is current on the ground rent payments, so there's no opportunity to take over their position. Bristol's two buildings may have just landed in the lap of the ground owner…what a colossal blunder."

Kellogg elected to withhold the background of his relationship to the KF Trust from Eastman. "Sounds like Bristol's been spending too much time riding bulls." Kellogg took a sip of water. "Rich, now that the lease has been signed with SGB, get the tenant finish work going on West Tower...I need cash flow ASAP."

"Right away. I've also prepared an invoice for half our lease commission for representing SGB...two hundred thirteen thousand dollars and some change. Should I give it to Peavy?"

"What!"

"You know, Mr. Kellogg...the industry practice in Denver is payment of half the leasing commission upon execution of a lease with the balance due upon occupancy. As the tenant reps for SGB, you agreed Curt and I would earn a three percent commission on the value of the lease." Eastman began reading from a piece of paper. "Start with one hundred ninety thousand square feet lease times fifteen bucks a square foot...$2,850,000. Then, multiply that by five, for a five-year lease term, which is $14,250,000... multiply that by our three percent tenant rep commission...$427,500. Our upfront share is half...$213,750."

"That's highway robbery."

"I forgot about the three percent for representing the building ownership side of the lease transaction to be paid from our new Kellogg+Jamison+Eastman Brokerage Partners account. Curt and I will initially collect half of $213,750...$106,875. The other half remains in the KEJ Partners account. Curt and I should also collect a six percent commission on your twenty percent override for the special SGB improvement costs, which are about a million dollars...so another six thousand bucks."

"Screw you, Eastman. I'm not paying you a penny for the override...you're making enough dough on the SGB lease commissions." Kellogg raged as he punched some numbers into his calculator. "You and Jamison will be walking away with $641,250 in total commissions…that's more than my development fee!"

"That's how the numbers work out, Mr. X. Talented brokers, like Curt and I, are invaluable. And don't forget, Mr. X, we'll get a fifty percent cut of the KEJ profits from the commission paid from West Tower Partnership."

"Get the hell out of my office before I change my mind on our brokerage partnership arrangement."

Kellogg immediately started pacing, periodically glancing out the window to the west toward Mount Evans. He suddenly halted, deciding he deserved an annual salary as Chief Executive of Kellogg+Jamison+Eastman Brokerage Partners. After a short deliberation, he awarded himself a monthly salary of ten thousand dollars, which he could immediately draw when the SGB commission was paid via a construction draw.

Hearing a slight knock, Kellogg motioned Mike Peavy to enter. "Mr. Kellogg…I just met with Willard Edwards at Continental Divide Bank and gave him a copy of the SGB lease and company resolution. He was perplexed, wondering what happened to the oil company sale."

"Didn't you tell him their purchase violated the company's terms with their banks?"

"I did, but he doesn't seem to trust us…he wants some official documentation."

"I should go down there myself and tell him it's none of his business what happened to Andrews Oil. We have a lease with a great local company at the rent we always projected. West Tower is one hundred percent leased, so tell him to fuck off!"

"Ah…ah…maybe you should tell him yourself."

"He can kiss my ass…did you ask him about my loan on the Colorado Boulevard land?"

"No, but I called Middleton."

"And what did he say?"

"He loves the site…he wants the business."

"Of course, he does…now get him what he wants. Another thing…you need to set up an operating account for Kellogg+Jamison+Eastman Brokerage Partners, or KEJ, as a subsidiary of Kellogg Development Company. I'm the Chief Executive of KEJ and will receive a monthly salary of ten thousand dollars."

Peavy jotted down the details on a note pad as Kellogg continued.

"Eastman and Jamison have prepared an invoice for half of their three percent commission as independent tenant representatives for SGB on West Tower. You'll also need to prepare a KEJ invoice to be paid from West Tower Partnership for $213,750…the upfront owner's portion of the three percent SGB lease commission. Submit both invoices in the next construction draw. When the KEJ invoice is funded, open a bank account at First National Bank. As brokers under KEJ, Jamison and Eastman will split a check for $106,875. I'll also pull $60,000 for six months' salary in advance from the balance in the KEJ account."

Peavy thought for a few seconds. "So…you're sure there will be sufficient funds accessible to pay you sixty thousand salary? I assume that there are other expenses like Penny Nelson's salary and other KEJ business expenses."

Kellogg glared at Peavy. "There should be plenty of dough be in the account to pay me."

"Yes, boss." Peavy quickly left the office.

Kellogg elected to drive his Buick to Washington Park, parking three blocks away at his Eldridge Apartment building. Donning a blue golf cap and sunglasses, he popped two sticks of chewing gum into his mouth and trudged to the park bench where he and Dusty had convened a few days earlier. Kellogg sat down, canvassing the immediate area and surreptitiously separated the chewing gum into two grey wads and pressed them against the bottom of a metal seat slat with his thumb. He slipped the envelope from his coat pocket and smushed it against the globs of gum. Deciding the envelope was secure, Kellogg surveyed the park again, spotting Dusty fifty yards away hiding behind a clump of bushes. Kellogg rose from the bench and retraced his path to The Eldridge Apartment parking lot. As he opened the Buick car door, he noticed the Denver Police Chief, Mitch Johnson, slowly exiting the back door of the apartment building.

"Hey Johnny Boy…you're not in uniform."

"Hello X-man. I'm working undercover today, but I just spent an hour with Jackie Jones under the covers in her apartment. Thanks again for the introduction to your former maid…she just MADE my day." Johnson exploded in laughter.

"Seriously, Johnny Boy…thanks again for helping me get my car out of the pound. How's it going down there at the cop shop?"

"Same old shit…except an oil guy from Houston has been bugging me twice a day about a burglary at his office downtown."

"A guy from Houston?"

"Yeah…his name is Buck Andrews. He's moving a big oil operation here. Those Texas guys are pushy, like they own everything."

"What's the big deal? It must have been a big take if he keeps bothering you."

"Twenty thousand dollars in cash and a metal corporate seal…it must have been made of solid gold based upon his persistence. The burglar used a gun and assaulted his employee, who's in a coma at Denver General Hospital. We're anxious to question him about the assailant when he regains consciousness."

"Do you have any leads?"

"Yup…why are you so interested?"

"I'm a concerned citizen…that hoodlum could break into my office and attack me or one of my employees. I keep a lot of cash in my office too."

"This guy is dangerous…he broke into a private office in a luxury downtown building in the middle of the day when dozens of people were around to spot him."

"I hope you catch him…I gotta go." Kellogg jumped into his Buick and drove past Washington Park, observing Dusty opening the envelope while he sat on the bench. Kellogg now knew where Dusty had gotten the loot to cover his bet with Chubby Morrison.

John Collins phoned Kellogg early Monday, October 30th, to cover a multitude of legal issues. "Mr. X…since the Andrews Oil Company lease conversations have ended, the litigation threat with Reagan & Holbrook has concluded for now. However, Henry Buckingham informed me R & H is demanding payment of a commission for a lease you've apparently consummated with Sherman Grant Blackmon…I recall their name on the tenant registration document I subpoenaed for the Andrews Oil matter."

"Are you fucking kidding me? Those lying pricks…when Eastman represented SGB at Gabbert and Company, R & H told him West Tower was fully preleased and pushed them to lease the 1010 Building too. I'm not paying them a goddamn cent! What else?"

"Buckingham reiterated Jill is still disputing the authenticity of the prenuptial agreement because of her mental state at the time."

"I'm tired of hearing her bullshit. Haven't you arranged a psychological exam for her yet?"

"Yes…Mr. X, but she's resisting. Remember, the question of her mental state is when she signed the prenuptial agreement…not her current state of mind."

"Tell Buckingham to get his client under control…anything more?"

"As you know, Buckingham is also representing the Bristol brothers on the Seventeenth Street ground lease matter. He claims there is an inconsistency in the document for the renewal notice date deadline, which the lease clearly states as October 26, 1978. Since the lease commenced on October 27, 1938, Buckingham contends that forty years ends on November 6, 1978, adding ten days for the leap years. He delivered a written lease extension notice to me at 3 PM on the 27th and therefore, professes they're in compliance with the renewal date."

"You wrote the ground lease, Colly, so you'd damn better be right."

"I've already consulted with Judge Watson, who supports our position, but Buckingham may want to pursue this in court."

"Colly. I expect better news the next time we speak."

Kellogg immediately raced to Rich Eastman's office, bursting through the closed door without knocking. "Richie Boy…what's this nonsense about a R & H claim they're owed a commission for the SGB lease? I just spoke to John Collins...he says SGB was a registered tenant under the listing agreement he subpoenaed."

Eastman rose from his chair. "Pete Simpson heard about the SGB lease through the grapevine and called me over the weekend. He reminded me of a conversation we had about West Tower several weeks ago, although I recall he told me your building was fully leased and insisted SGB take space at the 1010 Building."

"But they never toured West Tower...right?" Kellogg waved his hands above his head.

"Not with me...but Simpson apparently drove Poletti around the parking lot one day."

"Call Simpson back right now and tell him to take a flying fuck. Those sleazy brokers tried to screw me with that oil company and now they're trying to backdoor me again...right up my ass." Kellogg's face was crimson as he pounded the desk, until a container of pens fell over. "Call Poletti and set him straight too."

Kellogg was incensed...Steve Nelson hadn't returned his repeated calls over four days. Nelson finally called him about his review of the purchase contract for the Colorado Boulevard site. "Good morning Xander, I received several message slips to return your calls."

"Nellie Boy, if you want to do business with me, I expect a return call within minutes of my message...time kills deals. Now, where and the hell were you for the past four days?"

"Penny and I drove to Santa Fe for a long weekend...I assume she would have told you."

"No...she didn't. What about the contract I sent over last week?"

"Oh…yeah, everything seems in order, so go ahead and sign the agreement."

"All right…I'll send the title work over when we get it from Remington Properties. We'll order a survey soon and let you know who our lender will be."

Xander immediately signed the purchase contract and ordered Brenda to drive it to Bill Douglas' office at Remington Properties.

Kellogg was confident Wes Wheeler would deliver on his aggressive loan request for the Colorado Boulevard site, just as he had always done in the past. However, as a precaution, he phoned Wheeler to obtain some preliminary feedback.

"Hello…Wesley Wheeler speaking."

"Wheeler dealer…what's up?"

Wheeler instantly recognized Kellogg. "Hi X."

"Pal, give me the good news on my land loan request."

Wheeler cleared his throat twice. "Um…our screening committee actually met earlier this morning on your Colorado Boulevard land loan. The group loves the site, but the consensus was to offer a million and eighty thousand…eighty percent of your contract price."

"But I need a million-three, buddy." Kellogg quickly did some arithmetic. "Damn…that's only seventy two percent of what Friedman was paying."

"The loan committee really wanted to go at a million even, but I talked 'em up by eighty thousand."

"You're killing me, Wheeler. What happened to our great relationship? My stellar loan sponsorship should be worth at least two hundred thousand more."

"Our loan committee doesn't like to lend on vacant land...they consider it to be speculative."

"Did you tell them a construction loan is forthcoming as soon as I can get the plans done?"

"Of course, I did."

"Damn it...you're really leaving me in a jam, Wheeler."

"How about Continental Divide Bank? You have a relationship with them."

"I was only talking to you on this...First National has always been our primary lender."

"Sorry...X."

"You don't sound that sincere...tell the idiots on your loan committee I won't forget this."

Kellogg abruptly hung up and immediately dialed Mike Peavy's extension.

"Peavy...did you hear back from Middleton on my loan request for Colorado Boulevard?"

"Yes...he said Willard Edwards is done doing more business with us until he gets to the bottom of the Andrews Oil sale cancellation. He's threatening to call them directly."

"Bring his business card to me...I'm calling the bastard myself." Kellogg was in a rage.

Kellogg intuitively knew Willard Edward's call to Andrews Oil on the purchase contract could connect him to the theft of the company seal. He slumped down in his office chair and threw his coffee cup against the wall, the brown liquid forming a semicircle pattern on the wallpaper. Hearing the thud and Kellogg's cursing, Brenda instantly raced into his office and peered at the stains.

"Problems…Mr. Kellogg? Do you want another cup of coffee?"

"No, but do you still have the contract I gave you earlier?"

"I delivered it an hour ago to Mr. Douglas' office. He sure is a nice gentleman. Do you need to see a copy?"

"Forget it, but how about another dinner date tonight?" Kellogg was plotting to learn more about her sexual escapade with Willard Edwards to find a way to steer him away from the Andrews Oil connection.

"That would be wonderful."

"Excellent…make a reservation at the Canterbury Inn at six-thirty."

"Is it all right if I leave early to get ready for the evening? If you can pick me up, I'll write down my address."

"I'll be there around six-fifteen. One more thing…call Fred Hawthorne's office and get an appointment to get my tooth fixed."

"He's your dentist?'

"No…he's my eye doctor." Brenda looked perplexed. "Of course, he's my dentist." Kellogg shook his head in bewilderment. "Just make sure his assistant, Pam, is working that day."

Kellogg finally connected with Willard Edwards after navigating through a battery of secretaries. Edwards tone seemed very formal when he answered. "Willard EDWARDS."

"Mr. Edwards…this is Alexander Kellogg. I understand you have questions about West Tower office building."

"We retracted our demand for a million-dollar loan paydown after we obtained a new appraisal based upon a purchase contract you submitted. Now, I'm told that there is no contract…I want to see written documentation for the sale cancellation."

"But we've given you a signed lease for the entire building…from a well-known local company."

"I'm not sure Sherman Grant Blackmon is a credit worthy tenant, especially for a lease of that magnitude. We haven't received any financial information on them."

"There aren't any financial statements. Believe me…I tried to get them myself."

"That's a major red flag, sir. We're holding up future construction draws until all these loops are closed."

"Mr. Edwards…I'd like to come downtown in the morning and show you what we have on them."

"Can you be here at nine?"

"That might be a bit early…how about ten o'clock?"

"That works…see you then. Goodbye."

Kellogg shuffled through the clutter on his desk, searching for Otto Blackmon's business card. Finding it, he called Blackmon's direct line.

"Good morning…Mr. Blackmon's office."

"Is Otto there…I mean Blacky…this is Alexander Kellogg."

"Can you hold for a moment, please."

Kellogg tapped his fingers on his desk, growing more impatient as each second passed until Blackmon finally picked up. "Hey there Mr. X…what's happening?"

"Just counting how much money I've made today, Blacky."

"What can I do for you…something with our lease?"

"Yes…there is. My construction lender is holding me hostage on your lease approval until he reviews your financial statements"

"I guess I wasn't perfectly clear at lunch…we don't prepare financial statements and our income tax filings will be delayed for some time." Blackmon seemed agitated.

"Yes, I recall that now. Rich Eastman told me you were a campaign chairman for Congressman Casper Walsh."

"Twice, but several years ago. I don't understand why you're asking that question…it doesn't relate to our financial statements."

Kellogg ignored Blackmon's comment. "How did you guys meet?"

"We worked at Bache & Company twenty years ago and became good friends before he entered politics."

"Do you still see him often?"

Blackmon hesitated. "No…he's pretty busy in Washington."

"Blacky…I'm meeting with my lender in the morning. Hopefully, I can convince them to accept SGB as a tenant. Can you give me any documentation that could satisfy them?"

"No…I can't, but I'm sure you can persuade them. Now, if there isn't anything else…I'm a busy man."

"Wait Blacky…there is. I wanted to follow up on your invitation to raise some money for us. I need a million and a half for a loan on a site I'm buying near I-25 and Colorado Boulevard. The seller is desperate, so I'm getting a steal for a quick closing, but my banks can't move fast enough."

"Do you have an appraisal?"

"We ordered one…it should be ready next week."

"Send me your purchase contract and the appraisal when you have it."

"So Blacky…how much can you lend me?"

"Maybe eighty percent of the value…if we like the risk."

"What would you charge?"

Blackmon pondered for several seconds. "Nine over the Prime Rate."

"Sorry, I didn't quite catch that…must be a bad connection."

"Fifteen percent…plus four points upfront for a term of one year."

"I could get a better deal from my bookie….there's a usury law in Colorado, you know."

"That's how we can afford to pay the exorbitant rent on your building…we're not a typical lender."

"I'll get back to you, Blacky." Kellogg slammed the receiver down on the cradle.

Kellogg immediately called Sandy Sanders, the appraiser he traditionally hired to value his properties.

"Sandy Boy…I need a rush job on a site I'm buying from Remington Properties on Colorado Boulevard. I need a real rubber band approach if you know what I mean. As usual, you'll be well rewarded on your fee."

"I get it…a stretch appraisal."

"I can't share the details, but I really beat up Bill Douglas on the price. A developer from Texas offered a million eight, as well as a few others."

"I heard Abe Friedman had the site under control…what was his price?"

"I'm not certain, but you can speak to Curt Jamison or Rich Eastman to verify it since they had the listing at Gabbert and Company. By the way, they're working with me under a new brokerage operation I just set up."

"Send over your information and I'll get on it right away."

Next, Kellogg called Mike Peavy. "Peavy…we need a survey…pronto!"

"Our guy is on vacation for two weeks, but I can call around and find someone else."

Kellogg recalled his chat with cab driver, Charlie Jackson. "No…I just met a guy who's hungry for some business. I'll take care of it."

Kellogg sorted through a stack of business cards stuffed in a drawer, locating one for Jackson Surveyors. After Jackson agreed to complete the work in five days, Kellogg verbally engaged him to survey the Colorado Boulevard property. He immediately instructed

Brenda to send Jackson a copy of the purchase contract which specified the site boundaries.

Brenda informed Kellogg that Bill Douglas was holding on phone extension two.

"Hi Billy Boy…what's new?"

"Alexander, I'm wondering if you're ready to close the sale in two weeks. I happened to speak with Wes Wheeler…I hear you're scrambling to find a loan."

"What business do you have talking to Wheeler about my finances? He should know my business affairs are confidential."

"Don't you recall you told me to use my influence with Wheeler to get the loan processed quickly?"

"So…pal, I need a thirty-day extension to close since First National hung me out to dry."

"The contract has no extension options…you need to close in it two weeks or I'll sue you for five hundred thousand dollars referenced under the specific performance clause."

"I guess you've forgotten about our little secret involving Linda Melrose. You're still married to Helen…right?"

"Your threats won't work anymore, Kellogg. I confessed the affair to Helen…we've started counselling and she's already forgiven me."

"You're lying."

"Hold on…Helen is right here."

A few seconds passed. "Hello Mr. Kellogg. I understand you blackmailed Bill on our property because of his indiscretion with a lady tailor. You're a dirty scumbag. I also talked to Jill and she told me your lies about her mental condition too."

"Did she tell you about trying to kill me with a pistol? You might want to investigate that."

"Who could blame her? We're starting a petition to remove you from The Platte Club...there's a morality clause in the Club bylaws for members."

Kellogg laughed. "You're joking...half of the members should be expelled then!"

"I never joke, Mr. Kellogg. I've already spoken to our board of directors...I have support from at least two of them."

"Like whom?"

"You'll find out soon...goodbye."

Kellogg heard a dial tone and hurled the phone receiver at the floor. He arose suddenly from his chair and began to pace. He picked up the phone and called George Clements. "Georgie Boy...good day. I just heard a viscous rumor Helen Douglas is trying to kick me out of The Platte Club."

"Mr. X...that's right. Our board briefly discussed it last week. I wouldn't worry though...the guys really like you. She's trying to lobby their wives and attack you that way."

Kellogg grunted. "Just what I suspected...keep me abreast of any developments."

"Sure thing...how about a drink tonight?"

"Can't...I have an important date. Say...I heard you were recently appointed to the board of directors at Continental Divide Bank."

"Yes...my two-year appointment begins in January. Why do you ask?"

"I just wanted to congratulate you...so CONGRATULATIONS!"

Kellogg's strategy on the date with Brenda worked perfectly. After suggesting a drinking contest with shots, he instructed the waiter to pour water in his shot glass, while Brenda consumed eight rounds of vodka. It didn't take long for her to become inebriated, while Kellogg probed the details of Willard Edwards' sexual behavior from the evening of the Continental Divide Bank party. In her drunken state, he carried Brenda to his car and drove to his residence, where he tucked her into one of his guest bedrooms.

Kellogg arrived at the Continental Divide Bank at ten fifteen, maintaining his tardiness motto. Entering Willard Edward's office, Kellogg quickly scanned his features. Edwards stood just over five feet in height with a slim build. He sported a brown mustache and was clearly balding, using an elaborate combover to hide it. Kellogg concluded Edwards was in his mid-fifties, detecting several grey patches in his thinning hair.

"Hello sir...I'm Alexander Kellogg." As Edwards reached to shake hands, Kellogg reluctantly reciprocated, using his large palm to squeeze Edward's fingers tightly for five seconds until he grimaced.

Edwards wrung his fingers repeated, trying to regain some feeling in them. "Good morning, Mr. Kellogg. It's well past ten o'clock...I thought you must have cancelled. I expect the courtesy of a call if someone is late for an appointment."

"I couldn't find your building...there's too many one-way streets downtown."

"You're a real estate developer and can't navigate the streets?" Edwards smirked, while Kellogg's jaw tightened instantly. "Mr. Kellogg...do you have more details on the background for your West Tower tenant, Sherman Grant and Blackmon?"

"Yes...Casper Walsh is one of the investors in SGB."

"So what?"

"Casper Walsh...the Congressman."

"I know who he is...he's a major stockholder of this bank. Is he going to guarantee the lease? If so, I'll need to see his financial statement and tax returns."

"No...he isn't going to sign on the lease and I'm not getting any more data on the company."

"Well... this meeting is over then." He got up to escort Kellogg out of his office.

"Hold on there, Willard. I understand that you enjoy kinky sex with your female bank tellers."

Edwards stopped in his tracks. "Huh?'

"Your carnal affairs."

"What are you talking about?"

"Brenda Dunston shared the whole story with me. You coaxed her to your office after the bank Christmas party a few years ago. Do you want me to go on?"

Edwards' face was pale.

"I'll embellish it a bit more to refresh your memory. You both disrobed and then you put on her panties and brassiere. I guess you must be about the same size." Kellogg chuckled for a few seconds.

"Then you chased her around the office on your hands and knees, barking like a dog. You finally pinned her to your couch and had sex...apparently without any protection. Don't you use condoms?"

"I...I...I...I deny it." He shook his head repeatedly until his combover flopped over on the side of his head.

"You're guilty Willard, baby. Brenda told me there were other women too...all bank tellers. I'm sure Casper Walsh would love to hear those stories...new board member George Clements too. Casper and George are close friends of mine."

Edwards collapsed in his desk chair and wiped his brow with a handkerchief.

"I'll tell you what...Edwards. Give me all your copies of the Andrews Oil Company sale contract and their board resolution too...their corporate counsel wants them back."

"That's it?"

"Not quite...approve the lease for Sherman Grant Blackmon and promptly fund the rest of my draws. I'll refinance the building as soon as SGB takes occupancy...deal?"

"What choice do I have?"

"None...really."

"You can't tell my wife," Edwards whimpered.

"You have a wife, huh? I guess I could keep that secret from her if you play ball...woof...woof."

Edwards opened a credenza drawer, opened a large manila file, and leafed through the tabs, finally pulling several documents clipped together. He touched his index finger to his lips and leafed through the pages, laying them out on the desk. "Here's what you want."

Kellogg snapped up the pages and scrutinized them, assuring their validity. He sprung from his chair and dashed to the door without looking back at Edwards. "Thanks Willard."

Kellogg arrived at his office and immediately burned the Andrews Oil Company contracts and corporate resolutions in the building's trash container, confident all connections to the robbery were eliminated.

He called Steve Nelson. "Nellie Boy...what the hell are you doing over there other than taking long naps?"

"Mr. X...I beg your pardon."

"The sale contract I sent you requires me to close the purchase in two weeks and there's no extension option...and even worse, the specific performance damages are five hundred thousand bucks. Why didn't you tell me?"

"I assume you knew the business terms...you negotiated the deal. I only reviewed the legal stuff...that's what you asked to do."

"Get your head out of your ass...Nellie. Did you prepare a brief?"

"No...you never asked for one."

"Jesus...John Collins never misses a thing. Did you get your law degree from a nursery school? You may be over your head on this one."

"Sorry...I've been distracted on a complicated case where I'm the arbitrator. I'm up for the challenge, Xander...I just need to understand your objectives more clearly. Now that I understand the entire scope of what you need, I'm on it."

"Okay...but you're on probation."

"Thanks for the vote of confidence."

Kellogg abruptly hung up and darted to Rich Eastman's office. Curt Jamison was conferring with him on another transaction when Kellogg busted through the door.

"Howdy boys…I'm glad you're together so you can both hear this. Sandy Sanders is appraising the Colorado Boulevard site…when he calls you to verify the other offers Bill Douglas received, tell him they were all in the million-eight range like the Dallas group proposed."

"Even Friedman's price of a million-five?"

"You'll have to fib a little on that."

Chapter Sixteen

A week passed and the details for the Colorado Boulevard property acquisition were coming together. Charlie Jackson completed the boundary survey of the site and Sandy Sanders appraised the property for one million eight-hundred thousand dollars. Desperate for a loan, Kellogg transmitted the appraisal, survey, title report, and facsimile of an amended purchase contract to Otto Blackmon at SGB. To avoid a potential problem with any loan to value requirement, he ordered Brenda to blot out the actual price on the contract and retype one million eight-hundred thousand dollars. As a contingency for unexpected delays caused by SGB, Kellogg ordered her to change the closing date, moving it up three days.

Xander hadn't discussed the Colorado Boulevard acquisition with Robert but reluctantly knew he had to disclose the details to him. He confidently strode to his brother's office. "Robert...we're buying an eight-acre office building site on Colorado Boulevard from Remington Properties...the parcel adjoins I-25."

"I thought Abe Friedman had it under contract."

"I used my inside information to wrestle it away for five hundred thousand bucks less than what Friedman was paying."

"I don't want to hear how you managed that. How are you financing this?"

"I'm using a private lender. We're getting a great deal to close quickly, and the banks can't move fast enough. I'm expecting to get a hundred percent loan to our price. First National will take them out in a few months with a construction loan."

"I hope you have a handle on this, Xander. What does John Collins think?"

"He's not on this…my old frat brother, Steve Nelson, is running the legal. Colly pissed me off by withholding information on Sherman Grant and Blackmon."

Robert leaned forward, squaring his jaw. "I heard you signed the lease with those penny broker hucksters. I'm trying to figure out how to build out those damn special features…thanks a lot!"

"Robert, they're paying for all the costs and we're getting a twenty percent override, which should be worth twenty-thousand dollars. I'm sure you'll solve the design issues. More good news…we now technically control the office buildings on Seventeenth Street. Those Nebraska bumkins are raising a flimsy objection on the ground lease extension notice, but Collins says we're in good shape from a legal perspective. As soon as we get this documented, I'm planning to build the tallest building downtown."

"That would have to be over forty stories!"

"The Kellogg name must be associated with the biggest and the best."

"Interest rates are headed up, so be careful…we don't want to get overextended with the banks"

"Rents are spiking up too…in step with oil prices. There are dozens of exploration companies planning on major operations here." Xander cast his right thumb upwards toward the ceiling.

"By the way, I received the final bids from the subcontractors and material suppliers for the AM Manufacturing building. We'll be lucky to squeeze out any profit, thanks to your brilliant negotiations."

Xander tapped his right index finger on Robert's desk. "Wait for the change orders and then chisel McDonald with markups...we'll be fine. I have some extra ammunition I can use if necessary."

"You always have a fix for everything, Xander."

"Yup...I'm a visionary." Xander signaled out the window toward the bright blue sky.

"Hopefully not an illusionist." Robert pointed his right index finger at an abstract painting hung on his office wall. "Right now, Denver is experiencing a boom, but you should know every boom is followed by a bust."

Xander snickered and left Robert's office abruptly, turning a corner just as Sally Tuttle strolled down the hallway. Kellogg jumped backwards, narrowly avoiding a collision.

"Hello Mr. Kellogg...how are you?"

"Perfect." He smiled, trolling her body. "I haven't seen you since Las Vegas."

"I had a wonderful bus ride to Denver, and I'm eternally grateful to you."

"Hmmm...I didn't realize that buses were that great."

"The most beautiful young man in the world got on my bus in St. George, Utah and sat next to me. We fell in love before we got to Denver and got engaged last week. We're going to have at least ten kids...he's a devote Mormon."

"Boy...isn't he the lucky one." Kellogg quickly turned away.

Kellogg was hungry, driving to The Platte Club to see if Chanelle had returned from her father's memorial service in New York. Sam was patrolling the porte cochere as he drove up.

"Hello Sam...I haven't seen you for a while. How's the job hunt progressing?"

"Still searching...you wouldn't need a young energetic guy, would you? I've heard a lot of great things about Kellogg Development Company. I would even work as an unpaid intern."

"I love your enthusiasm, kid, but we never hire trainees. I want real estate veterans who've been through a few wars in the trenches. I'll be happy to provide a reference for you...I know everybody."

"Thanks Mr. Kellogg...I'll let you know. I'm still hoping to land in Gabbert's mortgage banking group."

"Vic Gabbert is a good friend...I'll call him and give you a boost."

"That would be great...thanks."

Kellogg flipped the car keys to Sam.

Entering the dining room, Kellogg was delighted to see Chanelle tending a table on the far side of the room. As she strolled to the kitchen, he intercepted her.

"Chanelle...I'm so pleased to see you here again. How was the memorial service?"

"It was so sad, Mr. Kellogg. I already miss my Dad so much." She began to sob, using her the back of her right palm to dab her cheeks. As Kellogg reached for his handkerchief, she turned away. "Excuse me for a moment, sir."

Kellogg took a step back, wondering how to respond. A moment later, she pivoted around. "I'm so sorry."

Kellogg put his right arm around Chanelle's waist and gently tugged her nearer. "Honey…I'm here to help in any way."

She nestled her head against his shoulder. "Thank you for your kindness…it's been so hard. Mom and I feel so alone…we don't know many people in Denver."

"I'd like to take you and your mother out to dinner this week. Can you let me know?" He reached for a business card from the gold-plated case. "Call my office and ask for my secretary, Brenda…she'll make a reservation."

"That's so considerate…I'll check with Mom tonight."

"Great…I'm catching a quick bite in the bar today. "He pointed in the general direction of the grill room. "I look forward to our dinner." He waved and turned toward the exit.

Kellogg left the Club and drove directly to Fred Hawthorne's dentist office. He leapt up the stairs, two at a time, anxious to see Pam again. He opened the door and was instantly confronted by Carrie Hawthorne. "You're fifteen minutes late, Alexander." She tapped her foot on the floor.

"My assistant told me the appointment was for one-thirty."

"No…one-fifteen."

"Oh well…I'm here now. Where's Pam?"

"She heard you were coming and took the afternoon off."

He looked down the hall, assuming she was lying.

"She's not here."

"Well…that's just terrific. Shit…let's get this over with."

Carrie escorted Kellogg to an exam room where Fred was pacing.

Hawthorne glared at Kellogg. "Good afternoon…Xander. How are you?"

"You don't sound sincere, Freddy Boy."

"So…you've cracked your molar again, huh?"

"Yep…too much ice munching, I guess."

Hawthorne pressed his index finger against the tooth. "Let's take a look."

As Hawthorne pried Kellogg's mouth open, Xander became rigid, gripping the armrests tightly.

"Relax, Xander…I need to probe a bit." Hawthorne tapped on the tooth twice, sending a sudden shutter through Kellogg's body. "Sorry…must have hit a nerve there." As he stuck the instrument into the molar crack again, Hawthorne could see sweat beads forming on Kellogg's forehead. Xander contorted his body outward, as if being electrocuted.

Hawthorne leaned back. "A little painful, eh?" He chuckled. "Get a grip, Xander…next time I'll install a seat belt for you. By the way, Al McDonald invited us to join him on your private jet to San Francisco for our wine country tour. I hope you won't mind."

Kellogg grabbed Hawthorne's arm. "Get that fucking tool out of my mouth! Yes, I certainly mind. That trip was specifically negotiated under his warehouse construction contract. McDonald shouldn't have disclosed that."

"I guess I overlooked that provision for the agreement to build my new dental building."

"Robert was solely responsible for your contract. If you had worked through me, I would have been more accommodating."

Hawthorne probed the infected tooth again when Kellogg pulled his arm away again. "You can use my damn airplane if you quit torturing me."

Hawthorne grinned. "I have bad news…you're going to need a root canal. The treatment will take a couple of visits to fully repair."

"Shit…you can't fix this today? What am I supposed to do in the meantime?"

"I need to take an X-ray first and analyze the damage before I can begin a treatment. Carrie can get the image from our X-ray machine in the back room."

Carrie completed the process without uttering a word and Kellogg was too pissed to drive a conversation, quickly storming out of the office.

Curt Jamison trailed Xander from the Kellogg Plaza parking lot, anxious to inform him about a redevelopment opportunity he had uncovered. "Mr. X…I sniffed out a hot deal this morning. It's four old warehouse buildings on Blake Street between 16th and 17th Streets."

Kellogg was perplexed. "There's just a bunch of winos down there…I wouldn't even dare drive my car in the daylight west of Larimer Street. What could I possibly want with those old dilapidated buildings?"

"You can buy the stuff for less than ten bucks per square foot. The structures, which aggregate nearly one hundred thousand square feet, are solid concrete…they can easily be gutted to modify into some unique office space. I've been speaking to a few tenants who like the old brick walls, high ceilings, and large windows. They like the loft look."

"Those warehouses are dinosaurs…they should be blown up. There's a landmark committee in the City which wants to preserve the architectural character of those historic structures. That's all I need…wrestle for years with some lunatic preservationists to get a building permit while the meter is running on my holding costs. Shit…I can easily construct a new building that looks like an old one."

"Look, Xander…there's a lot of room for error. My preliminary ballpark cost estimates are thirty bucks a foot for retrofitting…that's half the costs you'd spend on a ground up four-story office building."

"All right…have Robert check it out and get George Clements' architectural team involved too."

"Good move." Jamison nodded beginning to estimate his brokerage commission.

Kellogg sauntered toward his office, checking with Brenda for his messages. "Mr. Kellogg, the employment agency sent photos of three housekeepers…their background and references too. Do you want to review them?"

"All I need are the pictures. I'm sure their credentials have already been screened by the agency."

He snapped the photos from Brenda's palm and sat down at his desk, shuffling through them in less than five seconds and cast them into the trash can.

"Do you like any of the housekeepers, Mr. Kellogg?"

"NO…I should have given the employment agency a dress size limit, but I have another candidate in mind."

"Mr. Kellogg, while you were at the dentist appointment, I spoke to a Miss Donaldson from The Platte Club. She told me that tomorrow night would be perfect for the dinner."

"Oh great…make a reservation for three at six at the Wellshire Inn and call her back to confirm."

Brenda was writing feverishly. "Let me read that back to you…dinner at three for six people."

Kellogg glared at her, speaking slowly. "NO…SIX O'CLOCK for THREE PEOPLE…GOT IT?"

"Yes…at the Wellshire Inn…the restaurant adjacent to the Wellshire Golf Course?"

"YES…on Colorado Boulevard near Hampden Avenue!"

Kellogg was irritated, evaluating whether to fire her on the spot. He took a deep breath and held back, deciding he needed Brenda for insurance purposes as blackmail fodder on her former sexual partners.

The phone rang, ending their chat. "Hello…Xander here."

"Mr. X…this is Otto Blackmon. Mick Polietti reviewed the stuff you sent over and we can offer you a loan on the Colorado Boulevard site…say a million spot four with a term of one year."

"What's a spot four?"

"Spot means POINT in bond lingo…we'll lend one million and four hundred thousand dollars."

"Blacky, you told me that SGB would lend eighty percent off value…I want forty-thousand more."

"We rounded at off at an even number and as I told you last week…it will cost you fifteen percent and four points upfront…that's fifty-six thousand to save you the calculation."

"What if I pay it off earlier than a year…will you rebate part of the four points?"

"Naw…that's our offer, Mr. X."

"That's ridiculous…I've never heard of that before. Can you fund by next Monday?"

"Sure…send over the survey and title stuff. You can work with Nick Poletti from here on out."

"We'll be in touch, Blacky. Send us your loan documents…pronto."

Kellogg called Steve Nelson. "Nellie Boy…I'm closing the Colorado Boulevard loan on Monday with a stock brokerage group called Sherman Grant and Blackmon. The contact over there is Mick Poletti. Send him the survey and title report, plus anything else he needs."

"Fine, X…did you notice the closing will take place at Western States Title Company?"

"Yeah…rings a bell. That's who Bill Douglas wanted to use."

"Your first wife, Janice, is handing the closing."

"Are you joking? I haven't seen her in years. I know she'll try to fuck me by screwing something up."

"I'll keep a close eye on everything…X."

"You'd better review the loan documents with a fine-tooth comb too. I don't trust those sleazy hustlers at SGB."

Kellogg next called Mike Peavy. "Peavy…I'm using that penny broker firm as my lender for the Colorado Boulevard site. Study the loan documents carefully when we get them…those guys may try to pull a fast one."

"When will the closing occur?"

"Monday, but the original contract specifies Thursday. I want a few days cushion in case something crops up…but don't tell anyone."

Kellogg sat back in his chair to relax. He shut his eyes, anticipating the dinner with Chanelle and her mother when his thoughts were suddenly interrupted by a phone call. "Hello…X speaking."

"It's Dusty."

"Dusty…I trust you picked up the money at the park."

"Yeah, worked out fine. Listen…the police detectives want me to report for a lineup tomorrow morning. They apparently have a witness to the robbery."

"A witness, huh? I thought you pulled your cap over the guy's eyes. Do you have an attorney?"

"Chubby put me in touch with a lawyer named Tobias Smith…he's a partner in the firm of Buckingham and Smith. He'll be at the lineup."

"Jesus, that firm follows me like the plague…are they the only law firm in Denver?"

"Say again?"

"Nothing…let me know what happens."

The phone clicked. Kellogg began to pace, considering options for an alibi in the event Dusty was arrested.

The next evening, Kellogg arrived promptly at six at the Wellshire Inn. Chanelle and her mother arrived a few minutes early and were seated on a bench near the maître d's stand when he strolled in. As they stood to greet him, Xander kissed Chanelle gently on her cheek. He turned and touched Maggie's right hand, slowly turning her palm over to peck it lightly with his lips. Maggie was more beautiful than her photo and Kellogg was immediately smitten, especially with her distinctive accent.

After brief introductions, Kellogg approached the maître d, discovering that Brenda had mistakenly made the dinner reservation for the next evening. Craftily slipping ten dollars to the host, Kellogg insisted the group be seated immediately in a secluded corner of the dining room overlooking the golf course.

With unparalleled charisma, Kellogg's could be the most engaging host when necessary. Before they even ordered dinner, he had mesmerized the women with his favorite stories, boasting about his varied accomplishments. As the evening progressed, he queried Maggie on her early life in England and her marriage. After Maggie confessed to her current financial hardships, Kellogg finally opened the discussion for his need for a live-in housekeeper. Offering Maggie, a weekly salary of five hundred dollars and the payment of Chanelle's college tuition, she accepted his proposal over dessert. Even better, Chanelle would be his permanent house guest with her own private room under the offer. To celebrate, Kellogg ordered the most expensive champagne to toast the arrangement.

Chapter Seventeen

The following morning, Kellogg was still euphoric regarding the arrangement he made with Maggie Donaldson, planning for her to move into his residence after the Thanksgiving Day weekend. When he arrived at the office, he ordered Brenda to engage a cheap maid from the employment agency to work three days to thoroughly clean his residence. Since Jill left, it was littered with beer cans, sandwich wrappers, pizza boxes, dirty laundry, and mustard stained walls.

Kellogg propped his legs on his desk while admiring a white blanket of snow that had fallen on the mountain peaks overnight. He took a sip of coffee, licking his dry lips, when the ring of the telephone startled him. He reluctantly picked up the receiver.

"It's Dusty…they gave me a chance to make one call, so I figured it should be to you, since you got me into this mess. Somebody picked me out of the lineup and the cops booked me for robbery, aggravated assault, and attempted murder. I told my lawyer, Tobias Smith, I was with you the day of the burglary…he'll call you."

"Can anyone hear you now?"

"No…I'm in private phone booth."

"Did you say attempted murder charges?"

"I didn't tell you I plunked the guy on the head with my gun…I guess I hit him just harder than I thought since he's still in a coma."

"That's serious…why didn't you tell me earlier?"

"I didn't think it was necessary. I knocked him out so I could get away without him seeing me."

"Don't worry Dusty…I'll straighten it out."

"Can you post my bail?"

"Sure…no problem, Dusty. Your attorney can let me know the details."

"I gotta go now, Kellogg."

Kellogg instantly rehearsed a series of credible alibis for the defense, ultimately concluding he would confirm Dusty was at his house the day of the robbery making repairs to the garage.

A few minutes later, Brenda announced Tobias Smith was holding for a telephone conference. Kellogg took a deep breath and picked up the receiver.

"Mr. Kellogg…this is Tobias Smith from the law firm of Buckingham, Smith and Associates."

"Yes, I'm familiar with your practice…the BS law firm, right?"

"Excuse me?"

"You're Henry Buckingham's partner, huh? What can I do for you?"

"I'm representing Dustin McKnight on a charge of attempted murder and robbery. He gave me your name as an alibi. Apparently, you were with him in the early afternoon on the Seventeenth of October."

"I'm afraid you're mistaken…I don't know that person."

"Perhaps you know him as Dusty…he's a cab driver for Mountain Taxi."

Sweat beads collected on Kellogg's brow as he tugged as his tie. "Oh…Dusty? I've never heard his formal name before. He did some work at my house last month. I'll check my records to be certain, but

I believe he was repairing a garage door at my home around that time."

"Okay, I'll need to speak with you in more detail about it. Can you come down to my office tomorrow?"

"No thanks...you'll need to come here, Charlie."

"It's Tobias, sir. I can make it there...say ten o'clock? Where's your office?

"Ten works for me...I'm in the Kellogg Plaza building on Belleview Avenue, just east of I-25."

"Dustin told me that you would post his bail...fifty-thousand dollars."

Kellogg had already decided to decline to provide Dusty's bail money. "Fifty-thousand...that's a little steep, don't you think?"

"The deputy city attorney, Franklin Kennedy, actually pleaded with the judge to hold him without bail. That young Assistant DA is a tough dude...especially on anyone using a gun in a robbery. Frankly, I think he's trying to make a name for himself."

"That's ridiculous. Did you say the DA's name is Kennedy?" Kellogg recalled Kennedy's name as the attorney who wanted to nail him for his Plan-It-Travel parking ticket and his subsequent flight from the police.

"Yes...Franklin Kennedy."

"Mr. Smith...tell Dusty he'll need to spend a few nights in the clink...you should have done a better job to reduce the bail."

Later, Kellogg accepted a call from Steve Nelson. "Hey X...I've been reviewing the property survey, the purchase contract, and the title policy on the Colorado Boulevard property."

"Yeah...that's what you're supposed to do."

"Well...they don't match up. The survey and title policy state the parcel is Lot 2 and Lot 3 of Colorado Remington Subdivision. I checked Denver's plat maps and see those lots are part of a master plan filed by Remington Properties in 1972. The purchase contract specifies the easterly three-hundred-twenty-seven feet of Lots 2 and 3. However, the site has a depth of three-hundred-thirty feet according to the plat map...there's a three foot separation between the proposed property line and the Colorado Boulevard right of way."

"You mean the site I'm buying has no legal access to Colorado Boulevard, the public street?"

"Yes...you'll be landlocked. Remington Properties would still own the land you need for a street connection and there's no access easement. Western States Title must have simply pulled the legal description from the subdivision record and didn't notice the purchase contract was different. The surveyor missed it too...never even considered the lack of any street access...pretty sloppy work."

"If my stupid first wife is involved, I'm not surprised about the title discrepancy. You should have discovered this before I signed the purchase contract. I'll sue you for negligence!"

"X...relax and take a deep breath. You only sent me the contract at that time...not the title documents and survey. I found the discrepancy once I had all the information."

"You take a deep breath, you damn idiot" He plunked down in his chair and slammed his open palm against his forehead. "That fucking Bill Douglas...he did this on purpose, just for spite.

"The lender, SGB, will probably miss the legal description inconsistency too. They haven't mentioned it so far, but Alexander...I..."

Kellogg slammed the receiver down...he didn't want to hear any more. He briskly strode to Rich Eastman's office.

"Eastman...when you had the Colorado Boulevard site listed at Gabbert and Company, did you look at the legal description?"

"Yes...it was two lots in the subdivision filing...very simple."

"Douglas purposely carved out a strip of land along the west side of the site in the legal description, so I'll have no street access to my property. My worthless attorney accidentally discovered it this morning. I'm screwed and if I don't close the sale, Douglas will sue me for specific performance."

"Wait a second...I have an idea. Last year, Douglas was under contract to purchase an adjacent site with a vacant gas station that borders the south side of the Remington lots. If you buy the gas station property, you can connect your land for access to Colorado Boulevard through it...plus you can design a bigger project. Coincidentally, it's owned by the Bristol Brothers from Nebraska."

"Why didn't it close?"

"Douglas was concerned about the underground gas tanks and some petroleum product spills. He was worried about the cleanup costs."

"Will the Bristol brothers sell now?"

"At the right price...three hundred thousand might get it done. The original offer was four hundred thousand until Douglas found out about the environmental stuff and demanded a discount."

Kellogg pounded his right fist on Eastman's desk twice. "Now you can earn the ten grand I got you."

"Thanks…the title company faxed me a closing statement…it shows a ten thousand commission for me and Jamison from Gabbert's cut."

"You're welcome." Kellogg lifted his right index finger and pulled it down, as if adding a digit on his tote board."

"Call Bristol right now, but you can't tell him who you represent. We'll use a straw buyer to close and assign the deed to me later. Call him from a pay phone or your home number. I don't want to risk he knows you're working here."

"Why the secrecy?"

"It's a long story, Richie Boy." Kellogg ran his index finger across the front of his lips, as if sealing them. "Remember…loose lips sink ships."

Kellogg returned to his office, contemplating options to seek compensatory damages for his dilemma. He could sue Western States Title Company for creating a title discrepancy, file a bad faith lawsuit against Remington Properties, initiate a malpractice claim for Steve Nelson's incompetency, and punish Charlie Jackson, the amateur surveyor, for negligence…maybe pursue all of them.

Mike Peavy knocked on Kellogg's door and pushed it open slightly.

"Peavy…what is it?"

"Willard Edwards approved the SGB lease for West Tower and funded all of the lease commission invoices. I've created a new bank account for Kellogg+Jamison+Eastman Brokerage Partners and cut a check to you for your sixty-thousand dollars salary for six months."

"Good…well done, Peavy.

Kellogg met with Tobias Smith on Friday morning. At first, Smith pressed Kellogg on the background of his relationship with Dusty. Kellogg explained they met on cab rides and bonded since Dusty was a Vietnam War veteran. Dusty appeared downtrodden, so Kellogg engaged him on a couple of odd jobs at his residence, including the garage door repairs the day of the robbery. After Kellogg pressed Smith repeatedly on the credibility of the eyewitness, Smith finally disclosed the person was a building maintenance employee who saw a burly man, wearing a red hooded sweatshirt, exiting the stairwell on the oil company office floor around the time of the robbery. The witness never saw Dusty's face, so Smith felt the identification was tenuous at best and his handwriting samples didn't match the notations made on the strip club business card.

Kellogg was pacing, still nervous about Dusty's arrest, when Rich Eastman entered his office. "Mr. Kellogg, I've spoken to Pudge Bristol...he seems unmotivated to sell, even when I hinted at a price offer of three-hundred-fifty thousand."

"Did he make a connection between you and me?"

"No...I called him from a pay phone."

"Call him back and get a number. I don't care what price...just get it!"

With his mind spinning, Kellogg called John Collins.

"Mr. X, what a surprise...all forgiven?"

"Colly...just checking in on a few issues. What do you have for me?"

"About your divorce...I have a shrink lined up for Jill next week, so we'll see. On the Bristol ground lease matter, Buckingham is proposing an arbitration hearing, which I'm certainly resisting, unless he agrees to use Judge Watson."

"How about the Reagan & Holbrook lease commission issue for West Tower?"

"Yes, I've assigned Clint Clements to the case due to my conflict involving Sherman Grant and Blackmon."

"He's George's son, right?"

"Yes, he's been with the firm for three years…You'll be well represented."

"Good…I've known him since he was a kid. I'll wait to hear from him."

Eastman reported on his latest conversation with Pudge Bristol. "Good news Mr. X…I got Bristol to bite at four-hundred thousand bucks."

"That's pretty steep." Kellogg thought for a few seconds. "Okay…let's get it closed Tuesday."

"One problem…he's in no hurry. He's on his way to a rodeo competition in Las Vegas."

"What a horse's ass…when CAN he close?"

"Maybe in ten days if we bump the price a bit more."

Kellogg tapped on his desk calendar. "If you can we get the contract signed by Thursday, I'll take the risk and close on the purchase of the Colorado Boulevard parcel that day."

"He's really curious who the buyer is, so you better let me know now."

"George Clements will be the straw buyer…he's helped me out before."

"I may have to fly out to Vegas to nail it down."

"Go then, but no gambling and stay on Bristol's butt. Fill out a contract form in advance and have someone witness his signature."

Kellogg immediately called George Clements, asking him to be the interim buyer for the Colorado Boulevard gas station property. Clements initially rejected the proposal, although Kellogg lobbied excessively, straining their long-term friendship. Clements reluctantly agreed to cooperate, although insisted to assign the contract to Kellogg to avoid taking actual title to the property. Since Clements was not an active real estate developer, Kellogg encouraged Clements to announce his sudden interest in acquiring old gas station buildings for their architectural uniqueness and historical preservation.

As he contemplated the necessary pieces to fall into place for the Colorado Boulevard property acquisition to close, Kellogg reluctantly called Bill Douglas. "Billy Boy…it's Mr. X."

"Hello, Kellogg…ready to close next week, pal?"

"Yup…everything is going smoothly, except my attorney noticed you're trying to sell me a site with no public access."

"I guess you didn't pick that up before you signed the purchase contract…you must be slipping, Mr. X."

"You're a fraud…Douglas. I'm suing you for bad faith."

"Good luck with that, Kellogg. You're not exactly innocent, you blackmailer…but to show you I'm a nice guy, I'll sell you the strip of land for a half-million."

"Screw you…I've got great connections with the City, so I'll get my street access when they condemn your fucking land."

Douglas roared in laughter before he suddenly hung up.

Kellogg poured a glass of scotch and closed his eyes, startled at the shrill tone of the phone. He instantly picked up the receiver. "Yes."

"Hey Dad…it's Buster."

"Buster…great to hear from you. Are you moving back here soon?"

"Next month…I've got a few things to wrap up. I'm slated to testify at the drug trial in two weeks and need some time to sell my stuff. Can you wire another thousand?"

"Sure, I'll have Brenda take of it on Monday. I'm lining up a position for you in my development operation."

"Sounds terrific"

"Buster, I'm planning to rent a large villa at La Costa over the Thanksgiving week. I'm inviting a few friends and I'd like you to drive up to Carlsbad and spend a few days with me."

"I should be able make it…send me the details. I gotta hang up now…thanks. Don't forget to wire the money."

On Sunday, Kellogg was awoken with a phone call at 7 AM from Rich Eastman at his residence. "Mr. X…an hour ago, Pudge Bristol signed an agreement to sell the property to George Clements for a price of seven-hundred thousand."

"WHAT PRICE?"

"I sat next to Pudge for twenty-five straight hours playing blackjack before he finally cracked… and only after I convinced him George Clements was a gas station operator."

"You said agreement…you mean contract, right?"

"Not exactly…Pudge scribbled a few words on a cocktail napkin."

"You're shittin' me! I told you to bring a contract form with you."

"That's all I could do, but I got a card dealer to witness it…she initialed and dated it, although the napkin has whiskey stains. I'll keep trying but he's pretty drunk and has to get some sleep before his bull riding event tonight."

"There's a lot riding on this too…Richie Boy."

"I'm on it, boss…go back to sleep."

Holding a stack of drawings, Curt Jamison stalked Kellogg in the hallway the moment he entered the office building on Monday morning.

"Mr. X…I have some feedback from an engineering firm I engaged for a preliminary estimate on the historical buildings on Blake Street. You should make at least five million on this…and you know the best part? Your pals at Reagan & Holbrook own it…they've invested over a half-million in cash and the interest carry on the loan is killing them."

Kellogg's eyes widened. "Really…when did buy it?"

"Three years ago, I got the inside story from a buddy at Gabbert. The bank is threatening to foreclose on the loan."

"What lender and how much do they owe?"

"Continental Divide Bank has advanced six-hundred-thousand dollars."

"Sounds interesting...can we buy the note from the bank?"

"Hmmm...never thought of that."

"That's why I'm a genius...I'll make a call and let you know."

Kellogg stood at Brenda's desk. "Wire a thousand dollars to my son, Buster, in California. He's joining Kellogg Development Company soon, so order business cards for him...his title is Vice-President."

Brenda scribbled a note on a yellow pad as Kellogg looked over her shoulder to be certain she had it right. "The name on the card will be Alexander (Buster) Kellogg IV...be certain a parenthesis is around Buster."

She asked, "Will he have a direct phone number on his business card?"

"Yes...set up at a desk for him in my office...it's big enough for two."

Kellogg hurriedly placed a call to Willard Edwards at Continental Divide Bank.

"Hello Willard...thanks for processing our last draw. I believe that we're on good footing since our meeting."

"I'm trying to be cooperative."

"I understand your bank holds a delinquent loan secured by some old buildings on Blake Street."

"Where did you hear that?"

"I have connections everywhere. Willard…I'd like to buy your note."

"At par?"

Kellogg chuckled for a few seconds. "Look…I've had my people look into the numbers and it's going to be a hundred miles of bad road to make those dilapidated buildings work economically. I'll pay you fifty-cents on the dollar."

"That's not acceptable…we have strong loan guarantors to sue personally for a deficiency judgement if we lose money on the loan."

Kellogg was on the prowl. "The word on the street is the borrower is preparing to put the partnership into bankruptcy, so you'll be in court for years." Several seconds of silence followed until Kellogg finally spoke up. "Think about it, Willard." He abruptly hung up, feeling confident.

Rich Eastman called from Las Vegas again.

"Richie Boy…talk to me."

"Mr. X, Pudge Bristol is in a coma at a local hospital…a bull kicked him in the head last night at the rodeo."

"Did he sign a formal contract agreement before his accident?"

"No…all we have is the cocktail napkin."

"Did you say he has a brother who lives in Cheyenne?"

"Yes, his name is Bud…I've met him a couple of times, but he's really clueless. He's out here for the rodeo…I spoke with him at the hospital this morning."

"That's perfect…a dumb brother. Show him the napkin and force him to sign the contract, even if you must grip his hand with a pen between his fingers to trace his signature…have a notary handy to witness it too. You can do it…Richie Boy. I'll double your fee!"

Even with the number of deals swirling, Kellogg couldn't get his mind off Dusty's arrest. He decided to press his relationship with Ivan Zimmerman for a favor and called the Mayor's office. Zimmerman returned his call within five minutes and agreed to meet Kellogg at his Eldridge apartment unit at two o'clock.

Kellogg strolled to the break room to freshen his coffee when Penny Nelson arrived a few seconds later.

"Good morning, Mr. Kellogg."

"Oh…hello Penny. What are you up to?"

"Working up the preliminary marketing brochure for Kellogg+Jamison+Eastman Brokerage Partners."

"I want to review the brochure before you finalize it."

"Of course." She paused. "I understand that you and Steve had words."

"Yeah…he needs to pick it up. His mistake will cost me a lot of money."

"He's a talented attorney…I'm sure he's doing his best."

"His best isn't good enough. He hesitated a few seconds. "Let me ask you something personal...is Steve hooked on drugs?"

Penny looked down at the floor. "I've never seen him take anything stronger than an aspirin. I know that he's been under a lot of stress recently with a challenging arbitration case."

Kellogg raised his eyebrows, immediately spinning out of the break room and intercepted Mike Peavy on the way to his office.

"Boss, I've looked through the loan documents from SGB for Colorado Boulevard. These are the toughest I've ever seen. There's no grace period and if we miss a payment, the late fee is twenty-five percent of the payment amount...that includes the principal payoff payment too."

"The entire one-point-four million repayment amount?"

"Yes...three-hundred-fifty thousand dollars if we miss it. Also, I poured over the note five times and I don't see any detail on how the interest is earned or paid...it just states a rate of seventeen percent. Standard documents would always specify the interest is paid on the outstanding principal balance at a defined period...like monthly, quarterly, or semiannually."

"Are these guys part of the Mafia or what?"

Peavy shrugged his shoulders. "There's no loan extension period either."

"What else?"

"Did you know this loan requires your personal guarantee?"

"There's no fucking way I'm signing...Blacky never mentioned that!"

"Those are the big issues, I think. Do you want to me to call the Mick Poletti at SGB?"

"No...I'll take care of it."

Kellogg retreated to his office and called Otto Blackman immediately. "Blacky, we looked at the loan documents. There must be some misunderstanding...you never mentioned a personal loan guaranty. I'll never agree to ANY recourse."

"We're using standard mortgage documents our attorney drafted with a few modifications. If you remember, this is the first real estate loan SGB has ever made."

"Your pricing isn't exactly standard for a bank, Blacky."

"This is what our board approved. If you want us to drop the recourse, we'll need to bump the interest rate by two percent and charge another two points."

"So…seventeen percent interest and six points upfront?"

"Sounds right."

Okay…I'll agree to that. By the way, we're shooting to close on Thursday now."

"I thought the sale had to close today."

"I got a three-day extension."

"Fine…I'll let Poletti know."

Having researched the background for the West Tower lease commission claim by Reagan & Holbrook for the SGB lease, Clint Clements was eager to speak with Kellogg, "Good morning, Mr. Kellogg…it's been a while since we've spoken."

"Hi Clint…I haven't seen you since your graduation from law school…time flies, I guess. Your Dad brags about you all the time, so I've kept up on your advancement in John Collins' firm…congratulations."

"Thanks Mr. Kellogg…Mr. Collins is a tremendous mentor. I appreciate your help in getting the clerk position during my summer breaks from law school."

"You're welcome…do you have some news on the bullshit claim from Reagan & Holbrook?"

"It's a frivolous matter in my opinion I've taken depositions from the two brokers at R & H, who represented you at the time, as well as from Mr. Mick Poletti of Sherman Grant and Blackmon. I've also spoken to Richard Eastman, who represented SGB at Gabbert and Company when the purported tenant showing took place. I found no basis for Kellogg Development Company to pay a lease commission to Reagan & Holbrook. I spoke to Henry Buckingham earlier this morning about my conclusion, although he disagrees and wants to take this all the way through a jury trial."

"Buckingham's crazy…vindictive too. If he wants a fight, I'll win. I amended the listing agreement to only allow a trial by a judge…no jury. If he wants to proceed, I'll gear up for a battle."

Feeling confident, Kellogg popped a breath mint in his mouth and ordered Brenda to come into his office.

"Lock the door behind you, Brenda."

"Okay…why?"

"I'm in the mood for a nooner…how about you?"

"A nooner?"

"A little round of sex…it's noon, right?"

Brenda glanced at her watch. "It's five til' twelve."

"Close enough…take off your clothes, baby."

After twenty minutes of love making, Kellogg ordered Brenda to drive over to McDonalds for three cheeseburgers and two orders of fries. Sex always built up his appetite.

Kellogg left a few minutes early for his rendezvous with Mayor Ivan Zimmerman at the Eldridge Apartments. He ducked in the rear building entrance and climbed six sets of stairs to Zimmerman's third floor unit. He tapped on the door lightly and grinned as if being photographed, expecting the Mayor to look through the peephole. After the door creaked opened, Kellogg slowly entered to greet the Mayor, who still wore his topcoat and leather gloves. Kellogg managed to shake his hand with the classic twist.

"Good afternoon, Ivan." Kellogg surveyed the room and glanced down the hallway. "Is anyone else here?"

"Just me…Alexander. It's nice to see you again…what can I do for you?"

Kellogg strolled toward the windows and peered out. "I forgot how nice the view is from this unit." He glanced around the apartment. "The furnishings are luxurious too, better than what I recall…nice and cozy."

"Yes…thank you."

"Ivan…I'll get straight to the point. A friend, Dustin McKnight, was arrested last week for armed robbery after someone erroneously picked him out of a lineup, even though the eyewitness never saw his face. His attorney believes a trial is pointless because of the weak identification. In addition, McKnight was working for me at the time of the robbery."

"Who's McKnight's lawyer?"

"Tobias Smith."

"I've met him and his partner, Henry Buckingham a few times…Smitty's a solid attorney."

"The best defense lawyer in the city from what I've heard."

"Who's the prosecutor?"

"Franklin Kennedy."

Zimmerman raised his eyebrows and checked his watch. "I'm late for a meeting, so I need to jump. I'll speak to the City Attorney when I get back to my office. Is that it?"

Kellogg hesitated. "How would you like to join me at La Costa over Thanksgiving week…I rented a large villa and many friends are joining, including a few beautiful single ladies?"

"I'll check my schedule, Alexander. Have a nice afternoon."

They shook hands and left the apartment together. Zimmerman adjusted his Fedora hat, tilting it to the right, buttoned his topcoat, and tucked his red scarf around his neck.

Rich Eastman called Kellogg again from Las Vegas. "Mr. X, I have bad news. Bud Bristol won't sign anything unless Henry Buckingham reviews the document in advance…Bud's not as dumb as I thought."

"Forge Pudge's signature on the contract."

Eastman let out a deep breath. "I can't do that sir…it would be illegal, and I could go to jail."

Kellogg hung up abruptly and called John Collins.

"Colly…if someone signed a piece of paper agreeing to sell a property at a set price, would they be obligated to follow through with it, even though a contract was never executed?"

"Tough question to answer without more detail…was a closing date specified?"

"I don't think so, but the note was dated and acknowledged by a witness."

"I'd have to research this further, but a judge might rule it was an enforceable contract if there were enough details and if signed by the buyer too."

"I see...thanks."

"By the way, Mr. X...I have good news on the Seventeenth Street ground lease. Buckingham agreed to use Judge Watson as arbitrator on the renewal date dispute. He should dismiss this quickly without a hearing, so you can soon proceed on your development plans."

"Great! Thanks again, Colly."

Kellogg hung up and surprised by a call from Tobias Smith a few seconds later. "Mr. Kellogg...I just took a call from Franklin Kennedy at the Denver DA's office with some unexpected news...they're dropping all charges against Dustin McKnight...you won't be needed as a witness after all."

"That's terrific news...what happened?"

"Kennedy was apparently ordered to drop the case...he seemed upset on our call."

"You must have been convinced someone down there about his alibi...well done!"

"I'm always pleased when a client is released...perhaps the witness wasn't strong enough."

"I'm happy for Dusty...I always support our veterans."

Kellogg poured a scotch, filling the glass, and raised it against the mountain backdrop in a toast to his relationship with Mayor Zimmerman, when the telephone rang again.

"It's Dusty…I just got sprung."

"I just heard…Tobias Smith called to inform me I didn't need to testify."

Despite being released, Dusty was irritated. "Why didn't you provide my bail money…I had to sit in the stinken' hole for three days with a bunch of perverts."

"Smith should have done a better job with your bail amount. Even then, Chubby should have posted your bail or you could have used the cash you stole from the oil company office."

"The cash I stole?" Dusty asked innocently.

"Yeah…twenty-thousand bucks. You should share the loot with me since I hired you."

"It wasn't part of our contract…you never mentioned the cash. It's my bonus for taking a big risk, man. More importantly, I never snitched about your involvement in the robbery, even though that jackass Kennedy offered a plea bargain to name the person who engaged me…he knew it wasn't a random crime of opportunity. My lawyer recommended I take his offer."

"How much did you pay that worthless cocksucker?"

"Three grand, but Smith convinced the DA to drop the charges."

Kellogg smirked. "Toby had nothing to do with it…I pulled the strings to get you off. I have a credit with you now…I'll let you know when I need you again."

Dusty thought about the rubber stamp with Andrews Oil imprinted on it. "No…I've got YOU under my thumb, Kellogg. I also swiped something else from that office that could implicate you in the robbery and the assault."

"Is that a threat?"

"You can count on it, Kellogg. It's my insurance policy."

"You're lying!" Kellogg slammed the receiver down and picked up another call.

"Mr. X…Eastman reporting in."

"Get your ass on the next flight back to Denver with the napkin."

"Listen for a second…Pudge Bristol just died."

"Even more important you get back here now."

"Don't you even care that he's dead?"

"Why should I…he can't help me anymore."

"I'll call you when I land at Stapleton Airport." Eastman hung up the phone.

The next morning, Rich Eastman braced himself against Kellogg's office door as Xander strolled down the hallway.

"Mornin' Richie Boy…I was waiting for your call last night."

"I landed after eleven…I didn't want to disturb you that late."

"You should know by now that I'm a 24/7 guy…a real estate magnate never sleeps. Let me see the napkin."

Eastman removed it from his notebook and carefully placed it on Kellogg's desk, pressing down on the corners.

"I can hardly read this gibberish, Rich."

"Start at the top left corner…it says, 'I agree to sell S. CO Blvd gas prop to Geo Clements for a price of $700K'…he abbreviated the letter 'K' for thousand. His initials are below with Sunday's date…November 13th. The blackjack dealer's initials are right here…ATV. Her name is Autumn and I think her last name is Vance."

"What's this lipstick smudge?"

"When I told her of the importance of witnessing Pudge's signature, Autumn thought her lip print would look like a seal on an official document."

"What's the gold 'A' in the upper right corner?"

"The initial for the hotel casino…The Aladdin."

Kellogg picked up the napkin and studied the black lettering closely. "The top part of the seven is tilted down a bit…it could be amended to look like a 1. Here's a black pen…draw the top line downward slightly and a short line perpendicular line at the bottom. I need you to witness this, so do that too…right under the ATV line with Sunday's date." Kellogg extended his pen to Eastman, who resisted for several seconds until Kellogg repeatedly tapped on the space on the napkin. Eastman held the pen gently, making the number alteration and carefully jotted RRE on the tissue without tearing it.

"I'll call George Clements to sign an acceptance acknowledgement under Pudge's initials. That's all Richie Boy…good job."

"What about the blackjack dealer…she may remember the number seven."

"Richie, those dealers aren't that smart…we can always bribe her if necessary." Kellogg pressed his nose to the liquor stains on the napkin. "Smells like bourbon…I guess Pudge liked whiskey…maybe he was still drunk when he tried to ride that bull."

Kellogg drove to Clements' architectural office, where George scribbled his name on the napkin, acknowledging the purchase price, as well as today's date...November 15th. Kellogg promptly sped to John Collins office to show him the napkin, disclosing George Clements was acting as his straw buyer. Collins vowed to research similar court cases to determine if the napkin notes were an official offer to sell and to run the details past Judge Watson.

Mike Peavy reviewed the preliminary closing statement from Western State Title Company for the Colorado Boulevard acquisition, noting the surprising amount of cash required from Kellogg Development Company to settle the transaction. He intercepted Kellogg when he arrived in the office., holding a white sheet of paper in each hand. "Mr. Kellogg, I analyzed the closing statement...you'll want to review this immediately. You need to come up with two hundred sixty-six thousand dollars to close the deal."

Kellogg snatched the paper from Peavy. "There must be a mistake!" He studied the lines for a few seconds. "What's this...two hundred thirty-eight thousand for interest?"

"Mr. Kellogg...SGB is pre-funding the interest carry for one year at a rate of seventeen percent."

"Shit...I was counting on paying the interest monthly, especially since the construction loan should repay SGB in three or four months."

"Mr. Kellogg, did you ever ask SGB when the interest was to be paid or earned? I told you I didn't find specific language in the mortgage note that defined it."

"I forgot to ask Blackmon. And what's this outrageous legal bill of ten thousand from Steve Nelson...he's done nothing!"

"You'll have to ask him, Mr. Kellogg."

"SGB is charging five thousand in legal costs on top of their six-point origination fee? Outrageous!"

"The title charges look reasonable though, sir."

"Really? My fucking first wife probably padded it somewhere to support her gambling habit. Where is the settlement statement on the sale transaction?"

Peavy extended a paper as Kellogg who snapped it with his left hand. He scanned it quickly. "Where's my broker fee for the land sale commission?"

Peavy shrugged his shoulders.

Kellogg immediately stormed into his office and called Vic Gabbert.

"Vic, Xander Kellogg here...how are you?"

"Fine...I've been waiting for a courtesy call from you after stealing Rich Eastman and Curt Jamison, my top brokers."

"You should have taken care of them better. Look...I can't waste any time talkin' about old business. I'm calling about my share of the land sale commission on the Colorado Boulevard site I'm buying. I told Bill Douglas to tell you I was the broker representative for Kellogg Development Company."

"All he told me was to cut Eastman and Jamison in on ten thousand dollars on our side of the six percent commission."

"Then I'm telling you now...I'm taking half of the total commission as the buyer rep." Kellogg punched his calculator. "That's forty thousand...and five hundred bucks, Victor Boy."

"That's absurd! You're making more on the commission than we are...I'm calling Bill Douglas."

"Be my guest...you should know that I'm a talented broker in addition to the best office building developer in Denver."

Kellogg hung up and dialed Otto Blackmon's number.

"Blacky...I just reviewed the closing statement and see the interest is prefunded for the entire year. My construction lender will take you out within weeks, so I'll pay you monthly interest as we go."

"No, we're booking the entire two hundred thirty-eight thousand dollars of interest upfront, just like the six-point origination fee."

"That's got to trigger a usury violation for sure."

"It's forty-five percent in Colorado...we'll take the risk."

"That's bullshit, Blacky!" Kellogg abruptly hung up and called Steve Nelson.

"Good morning, Alexander...I'm looking forward to seeing you at the closing on Thursday."

"You never gave me your review of SGB's loan documents."

"I didn't see any red flags."

"My controller picked out a bunch of problems. You're only concerned about grabbing your check for your appalling legal fee. What's your hourly billing rate?"

"Two hundred fifty."

Kellogg punched several buttons on his calculator again. "That's forty hours...you need to take a speedreading course, pal."

"My paralegal spent some time on the deal, and we had some out of pocket costs too."

"Look Nellie, I'm a charitable guy, but you need to cut this down or I'll never use you again."

"Ah…well…I guess I could knock off two thousand."

"Send your revised statement to the title company."

Kellogg hung up suddenly and briskly strolled to Robert's office, tapping on his door.

"Mornin' Xander…what's up?"

"Brother…I need to tap the company funds for about three hundred thousand to cover the purchase of the Colorado Boulevard land."

Robert pounded his fist on the desk. "I thought you had this under control."

"Our lender, Sherman Grant and Blackmon, ambushed me this morning."

"The penny stockbroker lends money too? What kind of manure have you gotten us into?"

"They're jumping through some hoops to close the loan fast and lending more than the purchase price. However, they're charging the entire interest upfront for a full year. We can get back at SGB by padding the buildout costs for their improvements on West Tower."

Robert rolled his eyes and shook his head. "Xander…?"

"Robby Boy, we're getting a steal on the land and I'm working on the assemblage of an adjacent site that will double the overall value with more density…we'll build more than a million square feet of office space there by the time we're done."

"I'll make an exception to release the company funds if you truly believe this is a such a great deal…are you telling me the whole story."

"Absolutely."

"I'll call Mike Peavy."

"Excellent decision, Robert!"

"I understand Curt Jamison has you hooked on buying those old buildings on Blake Street. I told you before...be careful on how many irons you have in the fire."

"I AM an iron man! I'm plotting to buy the note at a big discount and foreclose on those Reagan & Holbrook shysters who own those buildings. Jamison projects we can make at least five million bucks there."

"I don't like rehabbing historic buildings...you never know what's buried beneath those old timbers and concrete."

"Like a vault filled with gold?"

"That'll be the day...old buildings are a money pit filled with fool's gold."

Xander returned to his office where he picked up a call from John Collins. "Mr. X, I believe there is ample case background to support Bristol's offer to sell the gas station parcel on Colorado Boulevard to George Clements. I spoke to Judge Watson...he also agrees it's enforceable, provided the witnesses to Pudge's signature come forward."

"Very good, Colly...I'll keep you posted."

Judging there was a legal path to buy the Colorado Boulevard gas station site for only a hundred thousand dollars, Kellogg closed the purchase of the Remington parcel on Thursday. Avoiding his first wife, Janice, as well as Bill Douglas and Vic Gabbert, Xander drove to Steve Nelson's building to sign the documents two hours before the scheduled closing at the Western States Title Company office. He dispatched Mike Peavy to the closing session and provided a power of attorney to Nelson to execute any final document changes.

Kellogg was delighted to note the settlement statement reflected his forty thousand dollars land sale commission. Together with the sixty thousand-dollar KJE salary draw, it had been a profitable two weeks, personally cashing in on company business transactions. To celebrate, he reserved the company jet to fly a few friends to Carlsbad, California for the week of Thanksgiving, where he rented a villa at La Costa Resort. The invited guests included Linda Melrose, Brenda Dunston, Bunny Byers, Jackie Jones, Rich Eastman, Curt Jamison, George Clements, Ivan Zimmerman, Mitch Johnson, Congressman Casper Walsh, and Buster.

Chapter Eighteen

Brenda Dunston, Bunny Byers, Jackie Jones, and Linda Melrose partied with Kellogg on his jet to and from California and stayed at the La Costa villa for the entire ten-day vacation. The male guests came alone and their staggered days at the resort enabled them to exchange partners with the single women.

On the first morning before the male guests arrived, Xander and Buster were randomly assigned to play golf with Salvatore Parzinni and his burly associate, Angelo Caccio. Kellogg discovered Parzinni was a financier from Chicago and his company, Illinois Gold Coast Associates, represented a consortium of investment vehicles which had funded equity capital for a variety of major office buildings and hotels throughout the United States and Mexico. Over cocktails and dinner, Xander established a rapport with Parzinni, who expressed interest in exploring future investment opportunities in Denver with Kellogg Development Company. Caccio, who Kellogg assumed was Parzinni's bodyguard, said little throughout the golf round and dinner, but listened intently to every conversation.

Buster sat next to his father at every meal and group discussion, as his Xander conducted the conversations like a puppeteer. Kellogg forbade Buster from socializing with the women, so later each night, the young man drove to a nearby bar in Carlsbad. where he hooked up with a different young lady for a rendezvous in his room. Buster was ruggedly handsome, an ideal model for a male surfer, with piercing blue eyes and blonde hair that hung down to his shoulders. Standing six feet in height, he had a muscular build after years of dedicated weightlifting.

One afternoon, Kellogg hired a limousine to drive himself, Buster, Ivan Zimmerman, and Mitch Johnson to the Del Mar racetrack in San Diego. On selected races, he recommended bets for his guests, who collected over ten thousand dollars in winnings. Zimmerman and Johnson were astounded by his acumen, although Kellogg had called Chubby Morrison earlier in the morning for tips, knowing the bookie had connections with several horse trainers at Del Mar. Staking Buster with two thousand to gamble, Kellogg was pleased to see his winnings double. Kellogg garnered fifteen thousand on his personal bets, sharing thirty percent with Morrison.

The day after Thanksgiving, Buster, Zimmerman, and Johnson departed, although Casper Walsh, Rich Eastman, and Curt Jamison joined the La Costa party. Kellogg invited the three men for an overnight excursion to Tijuana, Mexico where they spent the early evening betting heavily at the Agua Caliente Greyhound Dog Track. Later, Kellogg arranged a lavish party with four prostitutes at a boutique hotel, where the group reveled into the early morning hours consuming several bottles of tequila. The excursion to Tijuana was a success for Kellogg…Casper Walsh promised to steer Kellogg Development Company to the top of the developer list for the Department of the Interior building. To comply with the GSA requirements for developing a project of that scale, Walsh encouraged Kellogg to fabricate the project submission qualification forms.

Since Walsh was a major shareholder in Continental Divide Bank, Kellogg informed him about the delinquent loan on the Blake Street properties. However, Walsh's bank involvement was limited to quarterly stockholder meetings, knowing few details of the bank's lending activity. Nonetheless, Kellogg simply planted a seed about the sale of the delinquent bank note.

As soon as Kellogg arrived in the office on Monday morning, he strolled to Robert's office, informing him of Casper Walsh's intervention in the bid process for the Department of the Interior office building. Xander also provided Robert with the name of the GSA contracting officer in Washington, DC to obtain the project package, which included the building specifications and developer qualification details.

Kellogg greeted Brenda as he approached his office. "Honey, did you enjoy the trip to California."

"Oh yes…thanks for inviting me. I'll never forget the private jet flight…I didn't even know we were flying with the party atmosphere. It was also nice to get reacquainted with Congressman Walsh, but he didn't remember me."

"Did Mr. Walsh share anything with you?"

"He shared his penis with me."

Kellogg chuckled. "Did he share any stories about his businesses?"

"He's an investor in a stock trading firm. He told me it was minting money, so I assume it involved counterfeiting. He wants to see me on his next trip to Denver."

"Let me know when he calls you again."

Later in the morning John Collins called, informing Kellogg of the psychologist's evaluation of Jill's mental state. After extensive interviews and testing, the doctor concluded she had split personality disorder, evidenced by hallucinations, amnesia, and signs of depression. Upon hearing the prognosis, Kellogg jumped up and clapped his hands.

Collins also confirmed Judge Watson ruled against the Bristol Brothers' timing claim for the renewal notification of the Seventeenth Street ground lease. Watson ordered them to immediately deed their leasehold interests to the KF Trust, placing Xander and Robert in complete control of the property.

In addition, Judge Watson opined to the enforceability of Pudge Bristol's intention to sell the gas station site after reviewing the notes on the Aladdin Casino Hotel napkin. Bud Bristol was surprised to learn of the bargain price, curious if Pudge was coherent when he scribbled the offer to sell the property. Bud engaged Henry Buckingham to investigate the matter. Buckingham, skeptical of Rich Eastman's involvement, hired a Las Vegas private detective to interview the blackjack dealer and other Aladdin casino employees who may have interacted with Pudge Bristol.

Upon hearing Collins' report about Buckingham's detective, Kellogg sniggered.

"Buckingham is hallucinating…just like Jill. Say Colly…you seem to have a close relationship with Judge Watson. It seems very convenient to have a judge at your disposal when you need a favor. What's the story there?"

"He's my wife's nephew and clerked for me many years ago."

"I get it now. That's great news on the ground lease. I'm meeting with George Clements to review ideas for my office tower, so get the deed executed right away before Buckingham appeals Watson's ruling."

"Mr. X, I've looked at the old property survey and believe we can petition to vacate the alley to increase the density. The zoning allows roughly seven hundred thousand square feet depending on how you design the parking. I'm sure George will optimize the design, so have fun. One more thing…you should be happy to learn Judge Watson was assigned to preside over Reagan & Holbrook's SGB lease commission hearing, which is set for December 6th."

"Excellent…great work Colly!"

Kellogg met with George Clements later in the day. "George…here's an old survey to start your design analysis on my Seventeenth Street downtown site. I want this building to be the tallest tower in Denver. I don't care how much the construction will cost me. There's no limit…whatever it takes. My friend, this will define your architectural legacy too."

"Mr. X, the office will require dedicated parking…one car for every thousand square feet, so we'll look at an underground garage or an attached parking structure based upon the economics."

"Who cares about the parking…they're plenty of surface lots within three blocks and several garages too. I'll speak to the mayor about bending the zoning code."

Clements chuckled. "Good luck with that idea…your tenants will certainly demand onsite parking for a signature building. How's the Colorado Boulevard deal coming along?"

"You should know…the land assemblage involves your purchase of the gas station. Get cracking on the downtown tower design…I want to break ground in the spring.

Kellogg was eager to get home to greet Maggie Donaldson. As he turned into the driveway, he observed a dirty, white Ford Galaxie parked near the front door. Kellogg tooted the horn and waved to her as he eased his Mercedes into the garage. Kellogg hurriedly strolled to her car, opened the driver door, and lifted his right hand to help her out of the seat. He looked directly into her hazel eyes and kissed her lightly on the cheek. "Welcome to my humble abode, Maggie. I'm so happy you're here." Kellogg checked the rear seat, piled with several boxes which obscured the rear window.

"I loaded as many things as I could in the back…my luggage is in the trunk. Chanelle can bring her things later."

Kellogg opened the car truck…it was completely packed. "Where's Chanelle?"

"She has a class now…she'll meet me at our apartment later to load up."

Kellogg escorted Maggie into kitchen. "I'll call someone to help with your possessions and Chanelle's stuff."

Unable to contact Robert for a construction crewman, Kellogg decided to call Sam at The Platte Club. Fortunately, Sam's shift had just ended, and he immediately drove to Kellogg's residence to help with the move.

Kellogg took Maggie's hand, leading her through the first floor of the mansion and then to her second-floor bedroom at the far end of the hallway. "Maggie…you and Chanelle have private bathrooms connected to each of your bedrooms. Her room is next to my master suite."

"Mr. Kellogg…this is so luxurious. How can I ever thank you?"

"I'm sure we'll work something out."

Kellogg smiled and peered out the window as Sam parked his old green Volkswagen Beetle on the driveway. "There's my friend, Sam…he can haul your luggage to your room and bring Chanelle's possessions over here in my truck."

Kellogg greeted Sam in the driveway. "Sam, thanks for coming over so quickly. I'll pay you two hundred dollars." He gestured toward the backseat of Maggie's car. "Unload this stuff and drive my lady friend to pick up more things at her place…you can use my truck."

"Thank you, Mr. Kellogg…that's very generous of you."

Sam stacked the boxes and luggage on the driveway, carried Maggie's possessions to her bedroom, and then drove her to the apartment in Kellogg's truck. When they returned an hour later, Kellogg greeted Chanelle with a kiss on her hand and escorted her into the kitchen. He immediately hustled back to the truck and slipped two hundred bucks into Sam's hand.

"Thanks again, kid…please carry Chanelle's things to her bedroom. Is there any news on the job front?"

"I had a third interview at Gabbert Financial…I'm keeping my fingers crossed."

Kellogg didn't hesitate to lie. "I called Vic Gabbert…he thinks you're a terrific candidate."

"Thanks so much, Mr. Kellogg. If there's anything ese I can do for you, please let me know."

After Sam left, Kellogg escorted Chanelle through the house. After touring her bedroom, he led Chanelle to his master suite, hoping she would soon share it with him. She thanked him for his thoughtfulness but insisted on taking a bedroom next to her mother's room.

After ordering a large pizza for dinner, Kellogg led Maggie and Chanelle to the spacious family room to watch television, although Kellogg continually interrupted the programs by recounting the hunting stories behind the animal trophies mounted on every square inch the wall.

The following morning, Kellogg was surprised by a phone call from Willard Edwards. "Willard, what a surprise…what can I do for you?"

"Are you still interested in buying our mortgage note on the Blake Street Buildings? Our loan committee authorized its sale at four hundred seventy thousand dollars…that's a twenty-five percent discount on our balance, which includes accrued interest and our legal fees."

"I have a lot on my plate…" Kellogg cleared his throat. "But I might be interested at two hundred thou."

"Sir…you implied three hundred thousand in our conversation the other day."

"That was two weeks ago, Willard…fourteen days is an eternity."

"So…two weeks from now, you could be interested at our price?

"Two weeks from now, you might have to pay ME to buy your loan."

Willard grunted. "Goodbye…Mr. Kellogg."

At La Costa, Casper Walsh gave Kellogg his apartment telephone number in Washington, DC. Kellogg elected to call him, spinning erroneous details on the Blake Street properties.

"Casper…great to have you out in California for a few days."

"Thanks, Mr. X…I really enjoyed the excursion to Tijuana."

"We'll do it again soon…I promise. Casper, I just heard a story you will need to hear. To refresh your memory, it's about a delinquent Continental Divide Bank loan on some deteriorating buildings in lower downtown on Blake Street. A friend told me the buildings are ready to collapse due to some structural damage…in fact, bricks have fallen off the parapets, nearly hitting some people. Your bank could be liable for damages if someone were injured or killed."

"Our board of directors should be alerted and reprimand the mortgage officer who originated that loan."

"Bank officers will never raise an issue on a problem loan in fear of being fired, but someone in the mortgage department is trolling to sell the note. Given the property condition, my friend says the price is way too high and suggested discounting the note even more."

"Are you interested in taking over our loan?"

"My friend is intrigued, but you should know by now I only develop new high image office buildings…not own some old rat infected decaying warehouses inhabited by winos."

"Damn…I had no idea we make loans on that type of shit. I'll call some board members right away and get this off our books fast. Thanks for the tip."

Kellogg was optimistic he would ultimately be in position to buy the Continental Divide Bank note at a bargain and punish the loan guarantors, Lawrence Reagan, and Marty Holbrook, for their devious brokerage tactics, as well as the frivolous SGB lease commission lawsuit.

The next morning, Kellogg received a desperate phone call from Willard Edwards, who seemed out of breath. "Mr. Kellogg, I've been ordered by our board of directors to sell the Blake Street note immediately. I have two other buyers ready to close on Monday for three hundred thousand but thought you should have first crack since you're a valued customer of our bank."

Several seconds passed before Kellogg responded. "I'll tell you what, Willard… I'll buy your note for two hundred thousand bucks and close by the end of the week."

Edwards tapped his desk with a pen. "Okay…it's a deal. I'll tell my board expediency is more important than the extra hundred thousand."

"Let's proceed on a verbal agreement for now. Send everything you have in your files to John Collins, my attorney. He'll need to review the documentation, especially the personal guarantee language. Marty Holbrook and Lawrence Reagan signed full recourse…correct?

"Yes…and their spouses too."

"Good…even better. Call Reagan or Holbrook and tell them I'm purchasing your note. They will certainly plead to buy the note themselves, so don't forget about our little chat about your cross-dressing escapades. I'll need to get access to the buildings for a physical inspection right away…have their representative meet my brother and I at the property at one o'clock.

After Kellogg notified Curt Jamison and Robert about the Blake Street warehouse inspection, they instantly rearranged their schedules. Next, he phoned Wes Wheeler at First National Bank about providing the funds to purchase the note. After hearing the details from Kellogg, he expressed a strong interest in the transaction. Kellogg expected a new appraisal would be high enough to eliminate any cash investment, lobbying Wheeler to engage Sandy Sanders for the valuation assignment. Understanding the legal issues for documenting a note purchase would be complicated, Kellogg also called John Collins, alerting him of the pending transaction.

Xander joined Robert and Curt Jamison on the inspection tour of the Blake Street buildings. As they approached the structures in Robert's truck, Xander observed a Reagan & Holbrook for-sale sign nailed over the entrance of the largest building comprising the loan collateral. Graffiti was plastered over the sign as well as the wooden boards covering the front windowpanes. In addition, Kellogg noted the glass windows in the upper floors were all broken. Avoiding the potholes along Blake Street, Robert maneuvered his truck next to the broken concrete curb. Robert grabbed a baseball bat from beneath his seat and handed it to Jamison. The group approached three bums stretched out on the concrete steps, strewn with broken bottles and cigarette butts.

Jamison held up the bat and shouted. "Get the hell out of here fellas...you're trespassing."

A tall vagrant stood up, tugging at his long greasy hair and then his straggly beard. A faded Denver Broncos football cap was perched sideways on his head, revealing two purple scars on his forehead. He wore a faded army jacket, ripped flannel pants, and muddy cowboy boots. He stumbled on the step, fell on the sidewalk, and rolled over. "This is my home, fucker...get your ass off MY sidewalk."

Jamison raised the bat at the bums, ready to strike them. "Boys...do you want me to call the cops?"

A second tramp awoke from his stupor and spit at Jamison. "I am the law... see?" He flipped open a black blanket, revealing a silver badge pinned to a stained yellow t-shirt. "Now, leave me alone...I'm trying to sleep."

The altercation was interrupted by a loud car horn. Xander spun around observing Lawrence Reagan parking a white Cadillac behind Robert's truck. Reagan briskly walked toward Xander, refusing to initiate a handshake. "Mr. Kellogg...I hear you're trying to buy our loan from Continental Divide Bank."

"Larry…from what I've seen so far, I'm not so sure I will. I thought you guys had brains…why would you own a dump like this?" He pointed up at the buildings.

"It's Lawrence, sir…I'd appreciate if you'd address me as Lawrence." Reagan pointed in both directions on Blake Street. "My partners and I are visionaries. These blocks will be radically transformed within the next five years."

"Yeah, all the buildings will crumble, if not torched…leaving a bunch of vacant lots. I hear you've missed a few payments and the bank has initiated foreclosure proceedings."

"Just a misunderstanding…we'll straighten it out with the bank soon."

"I may be your lender in a couple of days…LAWRENCE. Even if you pay up, my yield will be incredibly attractive. From the outside, it seems there's been a lot of deterioration on the structures. In legal terms, I believe it's called waste…something I can sue you for."

"These buildings look exactly the same as the day we bought them."

Xander twirled toward the vagrants, who had settled back on the steps. "Reagan, these bums have probably lived here for a while…maybe they can fill us in."

The third hobo pulled a dark green bottle from his coat pocket, took a swig, and coughed for several seconds. "When we moved here last year, there was running water and no rats either…they should condemn this garbage pit."

Sandy Sanders rolled up in a rusted tan Oldsmobile, waving to Xander through the front windshield. "Reagan…our appraiser just arrived. Lead us on the tour, so you can clear out the rats."

Reagan shoved the bum aside and meticulously unlocked the heavy metal door of the southerly four-story building. The four structures were each separated by common brick walls, at least eighteen inches thick. Twelve-inch vertical wooden beams, spaced in a square grids every twenty feet, were anchored into thick concrete pads. The ceilings ranged from fourteen to sixteen feet, also supported by the large oak beams. The old maple wooden floors were worn and covered in an inch of dust. The plumbing fixtures were ripped from their wall supports and most were smashed into pieces. Each structure had a basement, although the clearance was only six or eight feet. The odor of urine and defecation was overwhelming, despite smoke residue created from several small fires. The tour lasted nearly two hours since Sandy Sanders insisted on photographing every room in the four buildings.

As Lawrence Reagan prepared to leave, Xander had a few departing words. "Beautiful properties, Lawrence...for a minute there, I thought we were touring a Siberian prison."

"Screw you...Kellogg."

"I'm looking forward to the trial next week...I'm not sure why you're wasting your time trying to sue me."

Reagan's faced turned crimson. "See you in court...dirtball." He strolled to his car and turned toward Xander, extending the middle finger of both hands.

Before Reagan could close his car door, Xander screamed... "Classy, Larry...very classy."

As Reagan clomped down on the Cadillac accelerator, gravel bits shot out from behind the rear tires at the group. Xander bent down and plucked a few pellets from his pant cuffs, tossing them at the tramps.

Robert turned to Xander. "The bum is right...these buildings should be condemned. Even if they were blown up and turned into parking lots, no one would dare park here."

"Relax…Robert. I'm only paying two hundred thousand for the note. I'll sue their asses for a deficiency judgement, plus waste on the asset and whatever else I can nail them for."

"I wouldn't exactly call these buildings an asset…little brother. What do you think, Curt?"

"This is a grand slam home run, Robert. It may take a few years, but Denver's downtown will definitely grow in this direction."

"Yep…so everyone can be closer to the noisy railroad lines? Let's get out of here before we get mugged."

After an exhausting afternoon, Kellogg looked forward to the first dinner prepared by Maggie Donaldson. To his delight, Chanelle was also assisting in the kitchen when he arrived. "Smells wonderful…ladies. What are you cooking?"

"It's Cottage Pie, Mr. Kellogg…one of my mother's favorite dishes from the British Isles."

"Maggie…call me Xander." He cozied near Chanelle, touching her shoulder. "How was your day, cutie?"

"Fine…I had classes at DU all morning and worked at The Platte Club for lunch."

"I had to settle for fast-food cheeseburgers…I was on the run all day."

"Can I prepare a cocktail for you. Mr. Kellogg…I mean Xander?"

"Sure Maggie…I'll have a scotch on the rocks. Do you know where the liquor cabinet is?"

"Yes…I took an inventory of the liquor supply this morning. You need more gin and vodka…I'll pick some up tomorrow if you can tell me where to go."

"I have an account at JHG Liquors on Evans Avenue…they'll add the charge to my bill."

"I went grocery shopping this afternoon at King Soopers and paid with a personal check. Do you have another grocery store preference?"

"No…whatever place you like. Some food store delivered groceries here every couple of weeks, although we ate out most nights. I'm not accustomed to home cooking…this will be a real treat. Make a drink for yourself…and Chanelle too."

"I need to study for an exam tomorrow, so no alcohol for me, Mother." Chanelle smiled as she left the kitchen.

Kellogg frowned. "That's too bad…what class is it?"

"French Literature, but I love my European Art class too. I assume you went to college, Mr. Kellogg…what was your major?"

"Business, although I had a minor in English…fiction writing and poetry." Kellogg fabricated his background, hoping to establish a closer bond with Chanelle.

"You'll have to show me the poems you've written."

"Unfortunately, my mother threw them all away."

"You can always try to rewrite them."

Maggie returned to the kitchen, placing a napkin and glass in front of Kellogg. "Scotch on the rocks…Xander."

Chapter Nineteen

Hour by hour, Kellogg was growing more impatient on the progress to acquire the Colorado Boulevard gas station property. Henry Buckingham hired a handwriting specialist to prove Pudge Bristol's squiggles on the Aladdin Casino napkin was a forgery. The expert was instructed to closely examine the $100k inscription, determining whether the "1" was the original digit inscribed by Bristol. Buckingham also deposed Eastman, having the graphologist observe Rich inscribed his initials on a sheet of paper multiple times.

Bud Bristol's detective discovered Autumn Vance, the Aladdin Casino the blackjack dealer who also witnessed Pudge's scribbling, had been fired. With the help of the local police department, the investigator discovered her body in the Las Vegas morgue, her death attributed to asphyxiation by the coroner. The detective talked to at least two dozen Aladdin cocktail waitresses and bartenders, none of whom could remember Pudge Bristol, even though he always wore a cowboy hat.

Having learned Kellogg Development Company had recently acquired a land parcel adjacent to the gas station site, Henry Buckingham began to connect the dots, especially with Rich Eastman's involvement as the sole witness to Bristol's napkin jottings. Buckingham also suspected Kellogg was using his close friend, George Clements, as a pawn in the scheme, although knew Clements had a stellar reputation.

John Collins countered Buckingham's handwriting specialist by assembling his own team of experts. Collins petitioned using Judge Arthur Watson as the mediator to resolve the dispute, although Buckingham vehemently objected. The impasse was resolved when both attorneys agreed to mutually choose an arbitrator. Unaware of the connection with Xander Kellogg, the attorneys selected Steve Nelson, who had an admirable reputation for adjudicating complex cases over two decades. Kellogg was ecstatic when he heard the news and instantly plotted a strategy. To start, he phoned a few old fraternity brothers, who confirmed Nelson was addicted to cocaine. He also decided Penny Nelson could provide some valuable insight.

"Good morning Penny…I've missed you." He lightly touched her shoulder.

"I heard you've been away in California."

"Yeah… a well-deserved vacation. How's Steve doing?"

"He's terribly busy and was just appointed as an arbitrator on a new case by a team of attorneys, although he hasn't shared any details with me. Steve has built a solid reputation in the State of Colorado as an arbitrator. It's not very lucrative, but he enjoys the challenge."

"Oh really…I had no idea. I'd like to learn more about the process."

"It's like a trial where the parties provide evidence…except he's the judge."

"Interesting…well, I'll see you later."

Kellogg quickly left to call Steve Nelson. "Hello Nellie…we haven't spoken since the day of the closing on the Colorado Boulevard site…I wanted to tell you how much I appreciated your help."

"Are you saying you'll write a check for the two-thousand-dollar fee I agreed to waive?"

"No…but I'll send some valuable clients your way soon."

"Thanks, Xander. By the way, my paralegal is assembling a closing book with all the documents…we'll have it bound and send to you next week."

"Great…Penny tells me that you've made a fine reputation as an arbitrator for legal disputes."

"Yeah…kind of an interesting departure from the normal attorney bullshit."

"What types of arbitration cases have you worked on?"

"Real estate disputes, bankruptcy liquidation disagreements, divorce settlements, contract conflicts…many variations. One just came in, although I haven't read much of the background yet…apparently a dispute about a signature authenticity on a nonconventional document."

"What type of evidence will you need in your deliberation for a case like that?"

"I'll certainly depose all witnesses to the actual signature, review the person's actual cursive and printed examples, plus hear from handwriting experts engaged by the respective parties. I will likely need to engage a third-party graphologist."

"Wow…that really sounds interesting."

"X…I need to jump on a conference call, so have a nice day."

Kellogg quickly trotted to Mike Peavy's cubicle. "Peavy…I need the entire file on the Seventeenth Street ground lease property. Now that we've prevailed in the dispute, I'll soon have title to the leasehold interest and want to review any information we have on the buildings."

Peavy sauntered over to a green filing cabinet, opened the top drawer, and pulled out a thick accordion folder, and placed it in Kellogg's arms. The binder instantly crashed to the floor, scattering the contents.

Kellogg glared at Peavy, expressing his anger. "Peavy, I didn't have a good grip...pick up those papers and carry the file to my office."

"My fault, sir."

Kellogg began to sort through the file pockets, which included several of Pudge Bristol's printed correspondence letters. Kellogg became encouraged, observing Pudge Bristol's initials on several pieces of correspondence, which matched those on the cocktail napkin. He finally found two pieces of correspondence where the number '1' was inscribed, although neither figure matched the napkin. In addition, Kellogg discovered several '7's' like the original '7' printed on the Aladdin casino napkin. Assuming the unsophisticated Bristol Brothers failed to maintain any copies of the original correspondence in their files. Kellogg decided to alter each figure to match the "1' on the napkin.

After ordering Brenda to photocopy Bristol's letters, Kellogg placed each page next to the Aladdin Casino napkin copy and snagged a magnifying glass to study the figures more closely. With careful precision, he altered each "1" and meticulously changed every '7' to a '1', perfectly matching the '1' on the napkin. Finally, Kellogg dispatched Brenda to make a photocopy of the forgeries and deliver them to John Collins for his graphologist team.

Xander accepted a phone call from Robert. "Xander... I spoke with the contract officer in Washington DC regarding the Department of the Interior office project in Lakewood. He sent the application documents to me although we can't qualify based upon the size of the buildings we've built."

"Robert, Walsh said we could add a hundred thousand feet to the West Tower building and include the Colorado Boulevard project with an estimate of five hundred thousand square feet."

"We haven't even designed that project yet. I'm not signing anything that's a fabrication, especially US Government forms…the FBI could investigate us."

"Send the forms over here and I'll sign them." Kellogg had no reservations in falsifying the documentation.

"You're incredible, Alexander."

"That's right, Robert…I am incredible."

"I didn't mean that as a compliment, Xander. I know you've played fast and loose with numbers before, but this really bothers me. I'm also concerned about the Blake Street buildings too…they'll require several hundred thousand dollars to renovate, although I seriously doubt any company would locate there in the next ten years."

"Those R & H brokers may be stupid, but they're not dumb…they must know something we haven't anticipated."

"Brokers are just salesmen…all they ever see is blue sky. What do they know about location and economics?"

"Nothing, but I just spoke with Sandy Sanders, who appraised the buildings for five hundred thousand. We won't need to provide any cash to buy the discounted note with collateral worth a half million…the two hundred-thousand-dollar price is only forty percent of the appraised value. Even if Reagan and Holbrook resume payments on the loan, our annual yield on our note basis will be at least twenty five percent."

"Shit…go ahead then. You can sleep down there if we ever own those dumps."

"Robert, I'll look forward to that… especially after I convert the structures into a luxury boutique hotel."

"Yeah…more like a homeless shelter for all those bums."

Kellogg called Sandy Sanders instantly. "Sandy...X here. Do you have an appraised value estimate on those Blake Street buildings for the bank?

"Maybe four hundred thousand if they were repaired to acceptable condition where they could be leased as storage space...they'll need at least two hundred thousand bucks in immediate work."

"Buddy...I need you to stretch the value and repair cost by at least another hundred each."

"Mr. Kellogg, I could easily adjust the cost of repairs, but I'm already bending over on the valuation estimate...there aren't any sales to justify a value of a half million dollars."

"Get more creative, Sandy...you've always come through before."

"Hmmm...maybe I can use the cost approach to base my final value. It will be tricky with the age of these structures. I've stretched numbers for you before, but this bordering on fraud. I can't afford to lose my appraisal accreditation."

"It's a layup, pal. These lenders are lazy...they'll only look at the first page for the value and won't even read your mumbo jumbo."

Sanders sighed. "I'll give it a shot."

"Atta boy! I'm on a short leash to close this deal...call Wes Wheeler with the number before three o'clock. I've got a full schedule this afternoon and can't be reached. I know you won't let me down."

Kellogg grabbed his overcoat before he passed Brenda's desk. "Brenda...I'm heading to the Platte Club for an afternoon poker game. If there's an emergency, you can reach me there...see you tomorrow."

"Good luck!"

Kellogg turned and laughed. "Luck...I don't need luck."

Kellogg left the Platte Club at nine o'clock, his pockets stuffed with cash after winning two thousand dollars playing seven-card stud. Dante, Kellogg's inside man, was the dealer in the poker game and flashed signals to him at critical times, enabling Xander to bet heavily on five hands with large pots. For the past two years, the duo had relied on two marked decks to help Kellogg's odds of winning at the club's monthly poker game. In return, Kellogg rewarded Dante by sharing twenty percent of his winnings with him.

Kellogg smothered the last three inches of his Romeo and Julietta Number 1 cigar into the Mercedes ashtray as he parked in the garage at his residence. Upon entering the kitchen, Kellogg discovered Maggie slumped over the counter, weeping uncontrollably. He circled the room, getting a panoramic view of her short red nightgown. "Maggie…what is it?" Kellogg put his arm around her.

Shaking, she uttered a few words. "I'm in serious trouble. I knew my late husband had a gambling problem, but I didn't know how addicted he was until his bookmaker called me an hour ago about his debts…twenty-five thousand dollars. His bookie threatened to kill me unless I come up with the money by Monday. I don't know what to do."

"Did he tell you his name?"

"He called himself Chubby."

"Chubby Morrison? I think I've met him...do you have his phone number?"

"Yes…I wrote it down on this piece of paper." She handed it to him. "Mr. Kellogg, I hope you can read it…I was trembling so much, I could hardly write it legibly."

"I'll look into this in the morning. Now…go to your room and try to get a good night's sleep."

"Thank you, Mr. Kellogg." Maggie faintly smiled, dabbing her tears as she turned to leave. "Please don't mention this to Chanelle...I don't want her to worry."

"I won't say anything to her. Is she home yet?"

"Yes...she's studying in her room."

Kellogg instantly recognized the phone number, waiting five minutes to call Dusty McKnight. "Hey buddy...it's Mr. X. I'm glad I caught you at home."

"Just leavin' for the strip club, Kellogg."

"Do you know about a twenty-five thousand-dollar debt a guy named Donaldson owed Chubby?"

"Why do you want to know?"

"A hunch...did you make a call here tonight pretending to be Chubby?"

Several seconds of silence passed by. "Yeah...Chubby made me the collector."

"How did you know Mrs. Donaldson was at my house?

"Chubby ordered me to track her for the past two weeks. I staked out her apartment and followed her to your house the day she moved in."

"Mrs. Donaldson didn't borrow the money, so why threaten her?"

"It's a lot of money...her husband's death doesn't cancel the debt."

"Did Chubby have Maggie's husband killed?"

"That's a good question for Chubby." Dusty coughed three times. "Why don't YOU pay the debt off ...you've got lots of dough from what I've seen? You moved on the widow pretty fast…her husband only died a few weeks ago and now she's living with you."

Kellogg chuckled. "Twenty-five grand, huh? Goodnight, Dusty."

Early Friday morning, Kellogg received a call from Wes Wheeler on the Blake Street properties. The Sanders "as is" appraisal value was two hundred fifty thousand dollars, resulting in an eighty percent loan, barely enough for First National to advance two hundred thousand for Kellogg to buy the Continental Divide Bank note. Sanders "stabilized" value estimate was five hundred thousand, so the bank's loan committee required Xander and Robert sign an unsecured note for three hundred thousand representing Sander's repair cost to restore the buildings to a leasable condition. On hearing the news, Xander blew up, screaming at Wheeler for five minutes about the committee's sudden bureaucratic overkill. As a minor concession, Wheeler agreed to remove Robert from the guarantee, although Xander continued his verbal assault for another five minutes. Knowing he needed the loan to close the Blake Street property transaction by the afternoon, Kellogg reluctantly acquiesced, notifying John Collins and Mike Peavy to meet him at First National Bank at 2 PM to sign the loan documentation and then accompany him to Continental Divide Bank at 3:30 to close the note purchase.

After a tumultuous afternoon of signing documents, Kellogg decided a weekend of skiing would be a perfect escape, driving to his Vail home with Bunny Byers. Kellogg also invited Curt Jamison and Rich Eastman, along with their girlfriends, to join him for the weekend at his house. After dinner on Saturday evening, the men gathered in Kellogg's den to smoke cigars and drink cognac to discuss business, when Jamison directed the conversation to the Blake Street buildings.

"X, you may recall I gave you a heads up on the Blake Street property…that tip should be worth some consideration, especially with Reagan and Holbrook's involvement."

Kellogg snickered. "Curt…you thought the buildings were a steal at a million-dollar price tag."

"Actually, nine hundred thousand."

"Excuse me, Curt…but through my masterful maneuvering, I'll soon control the buildings through my…" Kellogg cleared his throat. "…my TWO HUNDRED THOUSAND note purchase. The best part is it didn't require any of my cash to buy it. The only tip you gave me was the identity of the building owners…those R & H rats. You haven't seen anything yet…just wait until I start punishing them. Curt…your reward will be the big brokerage fee you'll earn when you land a buyer for the buildings who'll generate a lucrative profit for me."

"Very clever, Mr. X…very clever."

"Yes, I am…so let me propose a toast to my shrewd negotiating skills." Kellogg lifted his cognac snifter clinking Eastman and Jamison's glasses. "Kellogg rules!"

On Monday morning, as Maggie prepared pancakes and scrambled eggs, Kellogg reviewed his notes for the Sherman Grant and Blackmon lease commission trial set to begin at ten o'clock. Although he expected to be called to offer testimony, he had no direct involvement with SGB prior to the termination of the Reagan & Holbrook listing agreement.

"Mr. Kellogg, have you had a chance to check into my husband's debts? I'm so worried, I can't think of anything else. Should I go to the police?"

Kellogg rose and embraced her, shaking his head. "Maggie…Maggie…" He pulled her closer until her breasts pressed against his chest. "I'll cover the debt, but I'll pay you half your salary until we're even."

"I can get by on that…thank you so much."

Breaking custom, Kellogg arrived at the courthouse twenty minutes prior to the scheduled starting time. Anxious for the trial to begin, he scurried up the worn concrete steps of the historic structure. He pulled the heavy steel doors open and ambled down the long corridor, studying the marble floor pattern, finally arriving at Courtroom 5. He surveyed the room…it was much smaller than he had anticipated. Two walls were covered in purple tapestries while sunshine streamed through three gothic cathedral shaped windows on the east side. A fifteen-foot wide desk was anchored atop a two-foot platform, the seal of the State of Colorado attached to the wall above it, with the U.S. and Colorado flags to the right. Three rows of wooden benches were situated at the back of the courtroom and a few chairs were clustered around two small tables, which flanked each side of the aisle. He observed an oversized high back chair to the right of the bench, where he assumed the witnesses sat, as well as a small table in front of the bench where the court reporter would be stationed. Kellogg tilted his head back studying the high ceiling, covered with a mural depicting an ancient Roman tribunal scene. He was startled with a tap on his left shoulder, turning to see Clint Clements. "Good morning, Mr. Kellogg."

"Clint…nice black pinstripe suit."

"It's my traditional courtroom attire…you look pretty dapper in your three-piece suit too."

"Where do we sit, consigliere?"

Clements pointed forward. "At the table on the left. I want to remind you again this is a bench trial. We've gone over everything several times, so keep to our script and don't get personal."

Rich Eastman and Curt Jamison entered the courtroom and surrounded Kellogg and Clements, forming a tight circle. Clint spoke to the brokers for a few moments and instructed them to wait in the hallway until he called them as witnesses.

The Reagan & Holbrook entourage, consisting of Pete Simpson, Nathan Allen, Lawrence Reagan, and Marty Holbrook, entered the courtroom, accompanied by Henry Buckingham. Kellogg glared in their direction as they huddled in the far corner of the courtroom.

As Jeff Cohen appeared in the entryway, Kellogg smiled and waved, taking two steps toward him. Cohen instantly looked away, setting a path in the direction of the R & H team. Finally, Mick Poletti arrived, immediately shaking Pete Simpson's hand, and exchanging pleasantries. Kellogg was alarmed, instantly instructing Eastman to pull Poletti away from the enemy camp.

Clements escorted Kellogg to the defendant's table and emptied a thick file of notes from his brown briefcase, carefully arranging them in the order of the witnesses. Kellogg tried to get comfortable in the wood chair, leaning back a few inches on the back legs. Hearing the courtroom doors close loudly, he twisted, observing Rusty Affenson taking a seat. Kellogg glanced at Clements, gripping his arm. "Clint…the CFO from Andrews Oil Company just came in. What's he doing here?"

"Relax…he's our witness. I'm using him to testify the R & H brokers steered him away from West Tower, just like they did with SGB."

"Are you sure he's on our team?"

"Absolutely...I took his telephonic deposition last week after learning of the oil company lease commission dispute from John Collins. He didn't have the best things to say about you, though."

As Judge Watson entered the courtroom with the court stenographer, the bailiff called the court to order and everyone stood at attention. Kellogg estimated Watson's age in his late fifties. He had a dignified presence with his perfectly groomed silver hair. Watson promptly called the trial to order and instructed the parties on the procedures to be followed. The process began with Buckingham presenting his case, emphasizing that Sherman Grant and Blackmon was registered as an official tenant prospect prior to Kellogg's listing termination. Buckingham repeatedly scowled at Kellogg each time he called his witnesses and objected several times when Clint Clements cross examined them.

After a lunch break, Clements called Eastman, Jamison, and Cohen as witnesses, all swearing they had no knowledge of any R & H action to consummate a lease with SGB on West Tower. The most damaging evidence against R & H surfaced when Eastman, as SGB's tenant representative at Gabbert and Company, confirmed Pete Simpson and Nathan Allen falsely stated West Tower was fully leased, steering them to the 1010 Building in downtown Denver. Rusty Affenson also confirmed the same story involving Andrews Oil. A critical discovery was revealed after Clint Clements delved into the ownership structure of the 1010 Building, when each R & H employee reluctantly confirmed personal investments as limited partners.

After closing remarks by each counsel, Judge Watson surprised everyone by quickly announcing his decision to dismiss the case, condemning the actions of the R & H brokers. To Kellogg's delight, Judge Watson admonished them for the lack of ethical behavior and promised to report the brokerage company violations to the State Division of Real Estate and to the Colorado Board of Realtors.

After Watson pounded his gavel ending the court session, Kellogg instantly stood on his chair, shaking his fists at the R & H brokers, shouting a flurry of expletives. Lawrence Reagan charged across the courtroom and tackled Kellogg like a rabid football linebacker, pinning him to the marble floor. Before Eastman and Jamison could drag him off, Reagan rapidly fired a series of punches, at least two landing on Kellogg's jaw. With no security in the courtroom, the bailiff jumped into the fray, holding Kellogg on the floor while Judge Watson screamed for order. After tempers subsided, the bailiff finally released Kellogg from his grip.

Kellogg stood, rubbing his sore jaw. "Judge...thanks for dismissing the frivolous claim. I lost my cool, but I was so pissed at those guys...they've caused a lot of damage with their unethical business dealings."

"Your behavior is inexcusable...both of you." He also pointed at Reagan. "I could easily issue a contempt of court citation, but I won't. Take this as a warning, Mr. Kellogg...never display emotions like that in a court of law again." Judge Watson pivoted toward his chambers.

"Yes, your honor...thank you."

Clint Clements brushed dirt marks from the back of Kellogg's suit. "Mr. Kellogg...I understand you were pleased with the outcome today, but frankly; your outburst was embarrassing...your inappropriate behavior reflects on me. You were lucky to escape the judge's wrath."

"You handled the hearing well, Clint...I'll be sure to tell John Collins." Kellogg checked the courtroom, observing Rich Eastman and Curt Jamison were the only people remaining. "Where did Rusty Affenson go...I wanted to thank him for his appearance today."

"He left immediately after his testimony."

Kellogg pointed to Eastman and Jamison. "Clint...join me and my boys for a celebratory drink at the Ship Tavern...I'm buying."

"I'll take a rain check...I've got an important trial coming up soon I need to spend more time on...have fun."

After a late night celebrating his court victory, Kellogg was intent on inflicting more punishment on Lawrence Reagan and Marty Holbrook. For two hours, he called the broker executives every fifteen minutes, although neither would accept his calls. Frustrated, he phoned John Collins.

"Colly...your man Clint Clements was terrific in court yesterday. You should give him a bonus."

"Mr. X, your invoice for our legal services will reflect that."

"No...he should be paid from your firm, like more stock."

Collins sighed. "I'll consider that. I received a call from my nephew last night about your behavior in court. It sounds like you really lost it...Clint mentioned it this morning too."

"Maybe I got a little too excited, but those assholes needed some payback. I got the message from your nephew."

"Judge Watson is a fair guy and only concerned about justice, so you were fortunate he didn't cite you."

"Since I control the mortgage on the Blake Street buildings, I've phoned those R & H shitheads ten times this morning, but they wouldn't accept my calls. I don't believe they'll bring the note current, so initiate foreclosure action today and sue them personally for property waste under their loan guarantee...their wives too."

"How much deterioration would you estimate?"

Kellogg decided to lie. "The appraiser listed a half million in immediate repairs in his report."

"I'll need a copy of the report to document the legal action."

"Sure...no problem."

Kellogg had reviewed the original appraisal, photos, and engineering report from the Continental Divide Bank loan file and knew the buildings were in substandard conditions when the R & H brokers purchased the properties three years ago. Nonetheless, he wanted to pursue a claim the collateral had significantly deteriorated since the original loan had been closed.

After his brief discussion with Collins, he hurriedly called Sandy Sanders.

"Sandy Boy...amend your Blake Street appraisal right away. You need to increase the property damages to five hundred thousand dollars."

"What? I already jumped it from two hundred to three!"

"You heard what those bums said about the terrible condition and saw it with your own eyes...you can build a good case."

"Five hundred thousand in repairs would create a palace. It's hard to believe those buildings were ever in good shape...maybe after they were built seventy years ago. Shit...I'll need to engage an engineer to help me on this, but I can't guarantee anything."

"Get cracking, Sandy."

Chapter Twenty

John Collins and Henry Buckingham submitted an array of physical evidence regarding the authenticity of Pudge Bristol's initials and his handwritten scribbles on the Aladdin Hotel Casino napkin regarding the Colorado Boulevard gas station property sale offer. Over several hours, the attorneys paraded their expert graphologists into Steve Nelson's office to render opinions. Once again, Rich Eastman testified to witnessing Pudge Bristol's actions in the Las Vegas casino and inscribed his initials in Nelson's presence several times. John Collins also submitted several examples of Pudge Bristol's initials and number '1', all of which were provided by Xander Kellogg.

Without another available witness of Bristol's written offer, Buckingham was stymied, but vehemently questioned Rich Eastman about his representation of George Clements, a well-known Denver architect, who was not an active real estate investor or developer. Knowing the property background from his prior sale effort, Eastman testified he sought a potential sale commission, representing George Clements as the buyer and Pudge Bristol as the seller.

Buckingham also questioned Clements, who was not present in Las Vegas when he acknowledged the offer by jotting his initials on the napkin. When questioned about his motivation to purchase the gas station property, Clements articulated his mission to preserve historical properties with unique architectural design elements.

Knowing the property had been under contract a year earlier at four hundred thousand dollars with Remington Properties, Buckingham insisted Pudge Bristol was drunk and unaware of his actions to sell at a price of one hundred thousand. However, Eastman explained

Remington Properties had lowered their offer to two hundred thousand dollars after discovering petroleum contamination at the site. After Buckingham pressed Eastman on the negotiation details, Rich admitted Bristol rejected the offer and the sale discussions ceased.

When badgered by Buckingham, Eastman reluctantly confirmed the gas station parcel abutted the property recently acquired by Kellogg Development Company. However, Buckingham was unable to make any connection with Kellogg and the gas station property, other than through Eastman's partnership in KJE Brokerage Partners.

Steve Nelson was suddenly troubled with the conflicts of interest possibility, exposing himself to scrutiny if questioned in his role as an independent arbitrator for his connections to Kellogg and his long-term friendship with Eastman. In addition, his wife's employment with Kellogg's brokerage group was potentially problematic. Convinced the conflicts were serious in the aggregate, Nelson decided to recuse himself as the arbitrator and called Xander Kellogg at his residence.

"Good evening, Xander…it's Steve Nelson."

"Nellie Boy…what's up?"

"I was recently appointed as an arbitrator on a complicated real estate sale transaction involving an offer to sell a gas station property on Colorado Boulevard. I understand Rich Eastman and your brokerage group will collect a fee if the sale closes. My wife, Penny, has also mentioned it, which should have initially alerted me to a conflict of interest. In addition, since I know you and Rich personally, I'm recusing myself as the arbitrator in the case. I also represented you on the Remington property acquisition and it poses another possible conflict."

"Nellie...I have no connection with the gas station property. I didn't even know about the background until Rich Eastman mentioned the details to me in passing."

"Rich Eastman is a partner in your brokerage group and is the expert witness to the seller's offer to sell the property."

"Eastman told me the seller is Pudge Bristol and his brother. I know them...they lease our Seventeenth Street land parcel."

"Yes...Pudge Bristol was involved in the disputed offer to sell. As you probably know, Pudge tragically died after a rodeo accident in Las Vegas."

"I heard about the accident...very sad." Kellogg cleared his throat. "Listen Nellie...Eastman and his partner, Curt Jamison, represent many buyers and sellers in the real estate industry. They're well connected brokers and Eastman instinctively knew he could collect a fee connecting Bristol and the buyer, whoever that is. Eastman nearly closed the sale with Remington Properties last year, so had the benefit of the property history and had apparently known Pudge Bristol for several years."

"I understand, but attorney John Collins, who represents the buyer, provided samples of Pudge Bristol's handwritten initials and his inscribed number '1' from Kellogg Development Company files."

"Collins in the trustee of a Kellogg family trust that owns the land under the Bristol's Seventeenth Street office buildings. He has access to every piece of correspondence and the payment history related to the ground lease, but I was never asked to provide any information from our files."

"I see."

Kellogg sighed. "Nellie...you missed a lot of critical issues on my land purchase and the loan documents. I was concerned and did some checking and know about your addiction problem." Kellogg waited several seconds for a response, but not hearing one, pressed on. "Some of our old frat brothers confirmed you're addicted to cocaine. If the story ever got out publicly...it would probably ruin your career."

Nelson sounded desperate. "Xander...you're an old friend and I need your support. I've been to several treatment centers for my cocaine addiction...it's been a struggle for a few years. I think I've licked it, but I can't afford to let this story get out."

"I hear you, buddy. Reputations are everything, especially for a well-known lawyer and mediator. You should also know I'm considering suing you for malpractice on the Colorado Boulevard deal...not only did you miss several sale contract issues; you never spotted the problems in the private loan. I really don't want to pursue that action, so I hope you change your mind about recusing yourself and making the right call in the arbitration case to rule in favor of Rich Eastman's client."

"I've got a lot of material to review tonight and a few things to think about. Good night, Xander."

The next morning, Steve Nelson officially ruled Pudge Bristol committed to sell the gas station property for one hundred thousand dollars to George Clements. He ordered Henry Buckingham to prepare a formal sale contract using the standard Colorado Real Estate Commission form, designating the sale to occur within ninety days. In addition, he instructed Buckingham to provide all available information on the property from the Bristol files for Clements' due diligence analysis. Buckingham protested vehemently to the ruling, threatening to appeal to the State Supreme Court. However, Collins reminded him the outcome was subject to binding arbitration, which Buckingham had acknowledged in advance.

Hearing the news, Kellogg wasted little time to uncork a bottle of champagne in the breakroom, which he shared with Rich Eastman, Penny Nelson, Curt Jamison, and Brenda Dunston. In a surprise stunt, he opened a second bottle and shook it, spraying it over his staff. Returning to his office, he called George Clements for a lunch date at The Platte Club.

Kellogg was even more excited when Buster entered his office an hour later.

"Hi Pop…I'm home."

Kellogg sprung from his chair with his arms extended. "Buster…what a terrific surprise." Xander hugged him for several seconds and then shook his hand tightly.

"Buster…why didn't you call me in advance?"

"I wanted to see the look on your face."

Kellogg beamed, exposing his perfect white teeth. "Welcome to Kellogg Development Company…Mr. Vice-President. I've got three big deals teed up for development next year… you're here just in time to help me out."

"Where should I store my stuff?"

"Right here." Xander pointed to the far corner of his office. "That's your desk…you'll learn the business faster when you know exactly what I'm thinking."

"Like at La Costa…huh?"

"That's right!" Xander slapped Buster's shoulder.

"Dad…you haven't lost your taste in hiring beautiful women." He signaled toward Brenda's desk

"Yeah…and when you move back into the house, you'll see two more. Maggie, my new live in housekeeper, is gorgeous and her daughter, Chanelle, is even more stunning."

"A mother-daughter ménageàtroi"?

Xander chuckled. "I hadn't thought of that…but an interesting idea. I'll call Maggie and let her know you're moving in later."

"Pop…I'll stay there for a few days until I get my own pad. I need to take care of a few things now, so I gotta go."

"Whatever you prefer, Buster…see you at home tonight."

Brenda buzzed Xander. "Mr. Kellogg…a gentleman named Holbrook is holding for you."

"Let him wait for a minute."

Kellogg collected his thoughts before finally lifting the receiver.

"Marty…what's up?"

"Mr. X…just checking on your jaw today. Lawrence got a few licks in yesterday, didn't he?" Holbrook snickered.

"Just glancing blows…I hardly felt it."

"I know we've had our differences and I'd like to bury the hatchet." He paused waiting for Kellogg to respond. "I'm calling to see if we can work something out on the Blake Street loan. My attorney told me you've already filed a foreclosure notice and taking a separate action to sue us for damages to the collateral."

"You heard right, Marty."

"Those buildings were in total disrepair when we bought them three years ago, so they're not substantially any worse today. The original property engineering report and photos will verify that."

"The bums living there told us a different story."

"What bums…we've had the police sweep the place every day."

Kellogg chuckled. "When did you last tour the buildings, Marty?"

"I get down there all the time."

"Larry was on the tour with us last week, so check with him."

"Larry…who's Larry?"

"I guess he prefers Lawrence…Lawrence Reagan."

"How about giving us more time to sell the buildings…we've had several interested parties."

"Marty, you'll have plenty of time until the redemption period is over, or you can always bid on the foreclosure sale on the courthouse steps." Kellogg paused. "And about your suggestion about burying the hatchet…I'd like to sink an ax into Larry's head." Kellogg abruptly hung up the receiver, his adrenaline pumping. Kellogg never missed an opportunity to be ruthlessly punitive to people who crossed him, creating lifetime enemies.

Kellogg arrived at The Platte Club, ordering Rex Wilson to assign Chanelle to his table.

"Good day, Mr. Kellogg."

"Hello, Chanelle…it has been a great day, so far. My son, Buster, just drove in from California this morning. He'll be moving into the house for a while, so you'll met him tonight."

"I'm looking forward to meeting him. Would you like a Glenfiddich on the rocks?"

"Please...I'm waiting for George Clements, so get his favorite drink too."

After Chanelle trailed away, George Clements sat down.

"Georgie Boy...good news this morning. You're about to be the proud owner of an old gas station property."

"I told you I will never take title. I've never felt comfortable about this charade from the start and thanks to you, I committed perjury."

"George...don't worry. The arbitrator ordered the sale to close in ninety days, so there's plenty of time to put a little distance between us...I'll bring in another phantom buyer to cover the tracks. Now you can work on the master plan to integrate the three parcels and maximize the project density. I'd like each building to have fifteen stories...at least four hundred thousand square feet in each."

"We'll analyze it as soon as I review the surveys. We've been working on the Seventeenth Street site design, although I regret to inform you the project will need an attached parking structure...an underground garage is out of the question. The current zoning limits the building height by the size of the land area, so the structure will have no more than twenty-four floors, plus a one level basement."

"I'll tell you again, Georgie Boy...this office project must be the tallest building in downtown! Brooks Tower has forty-two floors and there are already two others around thirty stories. The Anaconda Building just topped out at forty floors and there's another one ready to break ground with forty-two stories...my project will be a dwarf if limited to only twenty-four floors."

"X...you should know we've carefully analyzed every possibility."

"I'll get a zoning variance…prepare some conceptual plans for a forty-five-story building I can share with Mayor Zimmerman and the planning staff. Also, I wanted you to know how brilliant Clint was in a hearing last week regarding a bullshit leasing commission dispute I had to defend. He's a sharp kid…just like his old man."

"Thanks, I'm very proud of Clint…Roger too."

"That reminds me…Buster is back in Denver and has joined the firm. He'll be working with me on these two development deals, plus those old structures you evaluated for us on Blake Street."

"We didn't do any work for you down there."

"I told Curt Jamison to hire you to estimate the costs to renovate four old warehouses."

"Never heard from him."

"Fuck!"

Kellogg hurriedly finished lunch, eager to speak with Curt Jamison.

Xander raced back to his office to find Jamison, who was having a snack at his desk. "Hi X…I had to go home and put on a new suit with all that champagne you shot at us."

"I should have thrown the bottle at you…you lied to me! I ordered you to have George Clements evaluate the Blake Street Buildings. He told me you never contacted him."

"I had an engineering firm look at the project. I told you the morning I first mentioned the deal." Kellogg now wondered if Jamison was rigging the numbers, anticipating a generous sale commission.

"Let me see the study?"

Jamison opened a credenza drawer, snapped a bound report from the file binder and placed it in Kellogg's hand. Xander quickly flipped through the first few pages. "They estimate eight hundred thousand in immediate repair work and a million to renovate into quality office space."

"Mr. X, that totals one point eight million…plus the note purchase of two hundred thousand gets your basis to two million. I spoke to several investment brokers and they believe the project could sell for seventy bucks a foot or seven million…a five million profit for Kellogg Development Company."

"Those morons are all smoking dope…seven million?"

"We're talking five to six years from now when downtown Denver explodes with demand from the oil and mining industries."

"Curt, I hope you're right, but this study will help me right now. Call Sandy Sanders and messenger a copy of this report to him."

Focused more on the damages for the property waste lawsuit, Kellogg forgot to lecture Jamison about ignoring his instruction to involve George Clements. He returned to his office to arrange a meeting with Mayor Zimmerman and the Denver Planning Director, Webster Fink.

Xander and Buster Kellogg entered Denver City Hall, heading to Mayor Ivan Zimmerman's office on the third floor. They passed through a hallway maze and endured a slow hydraulic elevator ride before being ushered into a small waiting area by a silver-haired secretary. The faded green carpet in the room was stained and well-worn from foot traffic. Xander slumped down in an unpadded chair which creaked as he twisted to comfort himself. He surveyed the grey walls, focusing on a black and white picture. Kellogg squinted at the inscription…'Mayor Benjamin F. Stapleton (1923-1931/1935-1947)'.

Xander pointed at the photo. "Buster…Stapleton Airport is named after that old mayor, Benjamin Stapleton. He was a member of the Ku Klux Klan when he was elected mayor in 1923. The Klan backed his candidacy although Stapleton denied he was a Klansman.

"The KKK?"

"Yes…Stapleton's first election win proved people will always get fooled by a popular promoter." Xander snickered. "We're here today to get some zoning accommodations from the mayor. I've invested a lot of goodwill in Zimmerman, like his apartment and the trip to La Costa last month."

"The Mayor leases a place from you?"

"He uses a furnished unit at The Eldridge for his extramarital affairs but doesn't pay any rent. Listen Buster…the most important thing you need to learn is how to capitalize on the weaknesses of influential people to obtain inside information and special favors."

The door to the Mayor's office swung open and Ivan Zimmerman stepped forward, his arm outstretched to shake Xander's hand. "Good day, Alexander…who's your handsome accomplice?"

"My son, Buster…you met at La Costa and on the trip to the Del Mar racetrack. Buster just returned to Denver yesterday to join my firm."

"Congratulations, Buster…you'll learn from the best." Zimmerman escorted the pair into his spacious office that overlooked downtown to the west. "Xander, what can I do for you today?"

"I need to speak to you about a few issues impacting my development plans. I thought your planning director, Webster Fink, would attend this meeting…I wanted him to hear this directly."

"I'll talk to Webster after I hear about your deals...he's tied up in meetings today."

Kellogg was irritated. "Ivan, I recently gained title to a site on Seventeenth Street where I want to erect the tallest building downtown...at least forty-five stories. I need a variance since the zoning code limits it to only twenty-four floors. My project will showcase the progress you've initiated to promote Denver as the most progressive city in the United States."

"Wow...forty-five floors, eh? That's a big difference from twenty-four stories...can't you acquire more land on the block."

"We've tried every angle, but I can't see a possibility unless a few people die." Xander coughed briefly. "I meant to say I'll deal with the estates after they die of natural causes, of course."

Xander placed a roll of drawings on Zimmerman's desk. Ivan, I'll leave you with some preliminary plans generated by my architect. I also recently acquired two parcels along Colorado Boulevard near the I-25 interchange. Unfortunately, I couldn't get title to a three-foot strip of land which abuts the street...technically, I have no public street access. The seller of that parcel is playing hardball, extorting me for an outrageous price."

"Who owns that strip?"

"Remington Properties."

Zimmerman raised his eyebrows. "We've worked with Bill Douglas and Helen's Remington family for many years...Billy is a reasonable guy."

"I want the City to condemn the land. We've engaged an engineering company to provide a traffic study for the widening Colorado Boulevard to alleviate congestion approaching the ramp to the interchange."

"Three feet will solve that?"

"You can take land from my property to create a full traffic lane. I'll send over our traffic study."

"I know Bill Douglas well. I'll call him and see if he can grant an easement to you...that seems like a simple solution rather than a complicated condemnation process. Is that all you need?" Zimmerman nervously checked his watch.

"One more thing, Ivan...I'm about to gain control of several old storage buildings on Blake Street near Sixteenth Street. Several vagrants are living there...the police should clean them out to help the image of the City."

"We have a small problem with a few bums, although they're harmless."

"The streets and sidewalks are in awful condition too. You should direct more funds to upgrade those blocks? The old elevated Sixteenth Street Viaduct is an eyesore too...tear it down."

"The city historical groups want the bridge to stay."

"If I ever want to demolish the old warehouses and erect new office buildings, I expect you'll control those preservationists."

"Sure...no problem, Mr. X." Zimmerman pointed to the wall clock. "I didn't know our meeting would take this long...I have an appointment with the City Attorney, but I'll check with our Director of Public Works on the street issues."

"What about Webster Fink?" Kellogg bristled in his chair. "Can you arrange a meeting with him?"

"I'll let you know." Zimmerman stood, pointing to the door. "Have a nice day, Xander...and it was great to meet you, Buster."

Xander immediately sprung toward the door, while Buster reached to shake Zimmerman's hand. "Thank you for your time, Mayor Zimmerman…it was terrific to make your acquaintance."

Buster trailed Xander by five paces until they were outside City Hall. Xander pointed up to the Mayor's office. "Zimmerman is an asshole…he didn't even want Webster Fink at the meeting. Did you observe his eye and body movements?"

"Not really, Pop."

"Kid…you have a lot to learn. Zimmerman kept looking at his watch and staring out the window…he hardly made any eye contact with me when he spoke. If the Mayor ignores my requests, I'll tip off one of the newspaper investigative reporters to stake out The Eldridge a few nights. I don't believe Zimmerman will enjoy seeing his photo taken with his mistress on the front page of *The Rocky Mountain News* or *The Denver Post*."

When Kellogg returned to the office, he phoned Police Chief, Mitch Johnson, informing him of his involvement in the Blake Street buildings. He requested a daily surveillance of the property, clearing out the vagrants inhabiting the structures. Johnson promised to cooperate.

Chapter Twenty-One

Kellogg refocused his efforts to pursue the title and survey mistakes on the Colorado Boulevard sites. With his lack of trust in Steve Nelson, he called John Collins to review the background.

"Colly...I believe I have cases against the title company and the surveyor for the land I bought from Remington Properties. I'd like to nail Steve Nelson for malpractice, although I understand lawyers don't like to sue other attorneys, so I'll let that slide for the moment. Western States insured my title to Lots 2 and 3 of the platted subdivision and the idiot surveyor used the official plat map dimensions too. However, the legal description in the sale contract excluded the westerly three feet of the lots, so they both missed it...Nelson too."

"Those are colossal blunders for sure. Offhand, you may have a claim against Western Title Company. Who ordered the title policy?"

"Remington Properties."

"Who engaged the surveyor?"

"Steve Nelson engaged Jackson Surveyors and provided the sale contract to him. We hadn't heard of Jackson before and relied on Nelson's recommendation since our regular surveyor was on vacation."

"Nelson is probably liable, although I would need more background to confirm the damages. His malpractice insurance carrier could provide restitution, assuming he has coverage."

"Colly...let's target Western States Title. My first wife, Janice, handled the closing and she's braindead...no wonder this happened."

"Send me everything you have…I'll start digging through it."

"Sounds great, Colly…goodbye." Kellogg stopped short of admitting he should have used Collins on the acquisition from the onset.

Planning nearly two million square feet for the Colorado Boulevard office complex, as well as the Seventeenth Street Tower, Kellogg needed a reliable source of equity capital and called Sal Parzinni at Illinois Gold Coast Associates in Chicago. After hearing the details about Kellogg's future developments, Parzinni agreed to dispatch Angelo Cacchio to Denver in January to review the projects first-hand. Regarding a construction lender, Kellogg could no longer rely on First National Bank after their loan committee ambushed him twice, changing his loan requests at the last minute. Continental Divide Bank was still on option as a lead lender for a sizeable construction loan, now that Kellogg had established a relationship with Casper Walsh, and had its chief lending officer, Willard Edwards, under his thumb. In addition, his close friend, George Clements, would soon join the bank's board of directors. Based upon their outrageous pricing and nontraditional lending policies, Kellogg was reluctant to use Sherman Grant Blackmon as a lender again, although didn't rule them out as a potential source of equity capital.

Kellogg was eager to complete the final visit for his root canal treatment. He arrived twenty minutes late for his dental appointment, incurring the wrath of Fred and Carrie Hawthorne once again. He was disappointed to discover Pam Vaughn had taken a position with another dental practice…even more depressed when he learned she was engaged to be married.

"Freddie Boy…this place will never be the same without Pam. Where did she go?"

"She specifically doesn't want you to know. Pam was a great assistant, but Carrie is still the best."

Kellogg chuckled. "Best at what…crosswords?" Hawthorne ignored the comment. "How did Al McDonald enjoy the trip to San Francisco?"

"He complained their suite at the St. Francis was too small."

"Al is never happy about anything. Oh well…what can you do?"

"Xander, our trip with the McDonalds was unbelievable…thanks for letting us tag along. I could get used to flying on private jets and using limos."

"No one is stopping you, Fred."

"Carrie and I are closely watching our spending since we're approaching retirement age. We're saving to buy a winter home in Phoenix."

"You'll make a big profit on your new dental building when you sell it in a few years."

"I hope so. I'm pleased that Robert has caught up with the construction progress."

"Yes, although I've had to prod him a few times…Freddy Boy."

"Xander, I heard that the construction crew found a unique metal object around the foundation when they were doing some soil compaction testing…some type of company seal."

Kellogg tried to remain calm. "Really…strange objects are always unearthed at construction sites. You wouldn't believe what they find in the ground. What did they do with it?" Kellogg gripped the dental chair arms tightly feeling his blood pressure rising.

"No idea, Xander...enough chitchat. Let's look in your mouth and get you on your way. Carrie, can you turn down the thermostat...it must be too hot in here...Xander is covered in sweat."

Xander raced back to Kellogg Plaza, heading directly to Robert's office. "Brother, did Al McDonald thank you for his trip to San Francisco and the wine country?

"No, but I have good news on his manufacturing building. Skip discovered a new steel supplier, so we've gotten the costs back in line...we're breaking ground next week."

"McDonald is an ungrateful creep...I'm not sure why we're wasting our time building his warehouse."

Robert rolled his eyes.

"Robby boy, I had a dentist appointment with Fred Hawthorne this afternoon...he mentioned the construction crew found an interesting object at his dental building site."

"Some type of metal corporate seal...I wonder how it got there. Bobby is the foreman on the job and may still have it at the construction trailer. Why are you so interested?"

"Just curious...that's all. Robert, I spoke to Casper Walsh this morning...he followed up on our submission for the Department of Interior project and it's looking good for us."

"You falsified the application and submitted it over my objection?"

"Robert, everyone fudges a bit...that's how the game is played."

Robert shook his head and pointed to the door, signaling Xander to exit.

On the way to The Platte Club, Kellogg stopped at the Hawthorne building construction site, anxious to speak with Bobby Kellogg. Observing only one workman at the far side of the site, he assumed the crew had departed for the day. After knocking on the trailer door, Kellogg discovered the unit unoccupied. Unable to locate the seal on the desktops, he rifled through the drawers when the trailer door suddenly swung open.

"Can I help you?"

"I'm looking for Bobby Kellogg."

"You won't find him in the drawers."

"Do you know who I am?"

"A robber?"

"I'm Xander Kellogg…I own Kellogg Construction Company. Who are you?"

"I'm the assistant foreman. I thought Robert Kellogg owns the firm."

"He's my brother…we're partners. Where's Bobby?"

"He left at four o'clock."

"I hear a corporate seal was found near the foundation recently…I'm looking for it."

"The company's name was on the seal…Bobby called the company and returned it to them."

"I see." Kellogg bolted from the trailer.

Kellogg was preoccupied with the seal, which could connect him to the robbery and Billy Norton's assault. His mind was racing, regretting he didn't dispose the seal into Cherry Creek or Chatfield

Reservoirs. He tromped on the accelerator of the Mercedes unaware he was driving well over the speed limit. Seconds later, he was startled by the shrill sound of a siren. Immediately checking the rearview mirror, a police car was quickly closing in. Throwing his arms up, he cursed and reluctantly coasted his car to the curb. The squad car parked inches behind his bumper and a skinny policeman emerged. Kellogg recognized Sergeant Perkins, punching the steering wheel five times. The cop slowly crept toward the driver's door when Kellogg lowered the window.

The cop started laughing. "Well…if it isn't Mr. Special. I see you've gotten the scratches removed from your car…the hood ornament and radio antenna have been replaced too."

"Funny you remember all those details…Sergeant. What's your problem now?"

"Can't you read speed limit signs? I had you at fifty-five in the thirty-five zone."

"Your radar machine must be broken…I couldn't have been doing over forty. You remind me of Barney Fife…why don't you spend more time chasing real criminals."

Perkins snorted, and pivoted toward his squad car after demanding Kellogg's diver license and car registration. Perkins radioed the Denver Police Department to check on Kellogg's driving record, discovering his probationary status. He briskly returned to Kellogg's vehicle, handing him the speeding ticket. "Mr. Kellogg…your shit out of luck. You've been on probation and this infraction will mean your driver's license will be suspended as soon as I process this ticket."

"Deputy Fife…you're forgetting about my connections downtown. YOU are the person who'll be on probation."

"Right…have a nice afternoon." Perkins tipped his cap.

Kellogg snapped the ticket from Perkins hand and promptly ripped it up, tossing the pieces in the air. He started the ignition when Perkins grabbed his arm through the window.

"Not so fast, Kellogg...I need to write you up for another ticket for littering."

Kellogg twisted away from Perkins' grasp and spit in his face. He shifted the car into gear and sped away on Colorado Boulevard.

Ten blocks ahead, Kellogg's Mercedes was surrounded by three squad cars, forcing him into the driveway of an abandoned gas station...coincidentally, the property he was attempting to buy. Perkins and two other policemen, with guns drawn, rushed to Kellogg's car. The officers dragged Kellogg from his seat and bent him over the car hood.

"Arms behind your back, sir." Two cops pulled his forearms backward, while Perkins attached handcuffs to Kellogg's wrists."

Kellogg shouted back. "You can't arrest me. This is private property...I own this gas station."

Perkins and a husky cop dragged Kellogg to a black squad car, hurling him into the backseat and slammed the door with a resounding thud. Kellogg flew across the seat, banging his forehead against the door handle on the far side of the car. Briefly stunned, Kellogg pressed his head against the seat cushion, noting blood oozing from the wound.

Kellogg yelled through the window. "Perkins...I have you for police brutality. I'll have your badge for this."

Perkins swiveled his head. "SHUT-UP, Kellogg...or we'll beat the crap out of you. I'm hauling you in for resisting arrest and assaulting a police officer."

Kellogg kicked the back of the driver's seat twice and turned his head, pressing it tightly against the seat cushion, attempting to compress the wound. He closed his eyes during the ten-minute ride to the police headquarters, avoiding any further outbursts. Perkins led him to the desk officer, who booked Kellogg for resisting arrest and assaulting an officer. Before placing him in a holding cell, Kellogg made his token phone call, fortunately reaching John Collins. Within an hour, Collins arrived at the jail, posting a five-thousand-dollar bail bond for Kellogg's release. Xander pleaded with Collins to contact his allies in the City Attorney's office to reduce the charges.

Seeking retribution for his arrest, Kellogg immediately raced to Mitch Johnson's office, although the police chief was unavailable. He then charged to Ivan Zimmerman's office at Denver City Hall, a block away, although the mayor refused to meet with him. Frustrated, Kellogg called Mountain Taxi, requesting Dusty McKnight's cab. Ten minutes later, Dusty pulled up in front of Denver City Hall, when Kellogg leapt into the back seat.

"Get out of my taxi, Kellogg! If the dispatcher had given me your name, I wouldn't have taken the call. You set me up for a crime that could send me away for a long time. But don't forget...I've got the other item as my insurance policy."

"Relax, Dusty. I have your back...I created a credible alibi and pulled the strings with the mayor, who arranged to drop the charges with the city attorney. Listen...I also have the money to repay Mrs. Donaldson's twenty-five-thousand-dollar gambling debt. Take me to my office and I'll grab the cash from my safe."

"You better not be bullshitting me."

After Kellogg arrived at his office, he retrieved an envelope from his safe and ordered Dusty to drive to The Platte Club. Dusty quickly opened the envelope and flicked through stack of C-notes. Satisfied, he put the car in gear and inched the taxi forward. Neither he, nor Kellogg, said a word on the fifteen-minute drive.

Sam was patrolling the front entrance of The Platte Club. "Good evening, Mr. Kellogg. How are you?"

"Terrific...Sam. I appreciate your help moving my guests' possessions."

"You're welcome. The best thing was meeting Chanelle...she's so cute. I had no idea she was a waitress here. I'm trying to get her to go out in a date with me."

"Good luck with that idea."

"I had good news today...I got an offer to work for Gabbert Financial. Maybe we can call on you and communicate what our mortgage banking team does. We represent several major insurance companies who lend on commercial real estate properties...we also broker loans to commercial banks and savings and loans."

"Sound interesting, but I only deal with lenders I can negotiate with directly...I don't trust middleman brokers. Congratulations on your new job, though."

Kellogg spun away, heading to the men's grill, where he positioned his personal stool at an angle to survey the entire room. He promptly ordered a Glenfiddich from Dante.

"Mr. X...you had a nice take playing poker last week."

Kellogg winked. "I got a lucky on a few hands." He pulled four folded C-notes folded from his pocket and covertly placed the wad in Dante's palm as Kellogg shook his hand.

"What's with the bandage over your forehead?"

"An angry guy attacked me in court last week after I won a big lawsuit against him, but I knocked him out with one punch." Kellogg simulated the blow by extending his fist toward Dante's jaw.

Dante chuckled as James Middleton sauntered into the room, pulling a barstool within three feet of Kellogg.

"Hello. Mr. X…did you have an accident?" Middleton pointed to Kellogg's forehead.

"Like I told Dante, I had to fight off an overzealous banker."

"Really?" Middleton snickered. "I hear you have a couple huge development deals on the drawing board. I hope we'll have a chance to bid on the construction loans."

"Peavy has you on the list."

"Last week, I had an interesting meeting with a potential bank client…the Chief Operating Officer of Andrews Oil Company from Houston. Wasn't Andrews Oil the company planning to buy West Tower?"

"They were going to lease it with the OPTION to purchase, but they were too greedy." Kellogg leaned away, watching Middleton's reflection in the backbar mirror.

"I recall the contract was a straight acquisition for twenty million dollars. In fact, Willard Edwards requested a corporate resolution and the company's seal on the documentation, which Mike Peavy later sent to me…that's why we rescinded the million-dollar loan paydown and funded the subsequent draws. I checked our files and I can't find the contract or resolution…I've looked everywhere."

"Like me, you're probably involved in so many deals, the tendency is to merge transactions."

"I have a perfect memory, so that's not it. Rusty Affenson, the Andrews' COO, mentioned a corporate seal was stolen along with twenty thousand dollars in cash from their Denver office...their employee was assaulted during the robbery and is still in an intensive care unit."

"Really...when did that happen? I hadn't heard."

"A couple months ago...the authorities arrested a cab driver, who apparently had a credible alibi and was released. Surprisingly, the seal was found on a Kellogg Construction Company site last week and was returned to Andrews' office by one of your foremen."

"What a coincidence!"

"Andrews Oil is putting a lot of pressure on the City Attorney to solve the robbery, so they're assigning another detective to the case."

"I would hope so."

The conversation ended when Bill Douglas strolled into the men's grill, shaking Middleton's hand, and positioned himself with his back to Kellogg.

"James...ready to head to our table for dinner?"

"I sure am, Bill." Middleton waved to Kellogg as he stood up. "Good night, Xander."

Douglas finally turned around. "Kellogg...I didn't notice you sitting there by yourself. With your shady reputation, it's not a surprise your only comrade is the bartender."

Kellogg looked straight ahead into the mirror. "Fuck you, Douglas."

As Douglas walked away, he flipped the bird at Kellogg behind his back, expecting Kellogg would see his gesture in the mirror.

Kellogg glanced at Dante. "Douglas has acted like an ass ever since I outsmarted him on a real estate deal."

Dante raised a bar glass at Kellogg. "Salute…how about a cigar?"

George Clements joined Kellogg for dinner in the men's grill… Xander didn't want to see Bill Douglas again in the dining room.

"Georgie Boy…I met with Ivan Zimmerman last week to request a variance to build a forty-five-story building on my downtown site. He implied I should buy more land on the block, so I'm betting he won't push the variance through Webster Fink and the Planning Department. I don't expect he'll help with the condemnation for the frontage on Colorado Boulevard either."

"Mr. X, speaking of Colorado Boulevard…I'm now reluctant to even sign the contract to buy the site…I'm concerned about the petroleum contamination. I've read about some pending legislation that could hold me responsible for cleanup costs…a possible financial black hole."

"George…if you never buy the site, you won't show up in the chain of title. I've already got someone lined up for you to flip the contract to."

"I'm still nervous about all of this…I wish I hadn't gotten involved in your scheme, Mr. X. I did a favor for you and this is much more complicated than what I signed up for."

"Let's enjoy the evening, George Boy…we have a lot to look forward to."

"Xander…The Platte Club board of directors is meeting next week and one item on the agenda is your expulsion as a member."

"That's still hanging around?"

"Xander…this is pretty serious. Helen Douglas circulated a petition signed by two hundred members…mostly women, although I understand thirty guys joined in. Jill provided a lot of background information Mrs. Douglas is using."

"Jill is a certified psychopath and I can prove it from our psychologist's conclusions. Technically Jill isn't a member at The Platte Club anymore…it's part of our prenuptial agreement. I forgot to tell Rex Wilson to drop her from my membership."

"Two of the seven board directors are women, who signed the petition to expel you…they demanded to put this to an official vote."

"I need to speak with the board members and show them Jill's psychological results."

"I don't recommend that, Xander. I've been lobbying on your behalf. There are three votes, including mine, to keep you, and three against. One director is on the fence."

"With only three votes out of seven…I'll be out! Who's the fence sitter, George? I need to talk to that guy immediately."

"Relax, Mr. X…keep a low profile and stay out of this. Let's have another drink."

"How can I relax when I could be thrown out of the Club?"

Kellogg arrived at his residence around ten o'clock and discovered the first floor was deserted. As he climbed the stairs, he assumed everyone had retired early. Upon reaching the landing, he peered down the long hallway, faintly hearing the song, "I Love the Night Life," playing from Buster's bedroom. Kellogg slowly closed his bedroom door, leaving it open a crack to observe any activity in the hallway. Seconds later, Buster's bedroom door opened and Chanelle appeared, clasping for the strings to secure her black nightgown.

Kellogg intently watched as she crept down the hallway toward her bedroom before glancing back at Buster, who blew her a kiss from his doorway. Xander quietly closed his door and crashed on his bed without removing his clothes.

Kellogg was startled with a phone call at 5 AM. Disoriented, he fumbled for the phone, dropping the receiver twice, before mumbling a response. "Yeah…"

"X-man, is that you? It's Johnny Boy…Mitch Johnson. I am here on Blake Street at a fire engulfing your buildings…it's a three-alarm call. There are at least thirty firemen pouring water on the structures, or what's left of them…it looks like a total loss."

"I'll get someone from my office down there as soon as possible."

"You might tell them to bring a frontend loader and a few dump trucks to shovel away the ashes and debris."

"Okay, Johnny Boy…thanks for the call, but I need to talk with you anyway. Your crack police Gestapo squad roughed me up yesterday. That overbearing Sergeant Perkins has it in for me…ever since I parked in the fire lane that day."

"I read the arrest report last night. X-man, I can't help you this time…I'm sorry, but you're going to have to deal with the consequences."

"I'm trying to contact Mayor Zimmerman…can he help?"

"I doubt it, but you can try."

Kellogg instantly called Mike Peavy to report to the fire scene. Still fuming about Buster's romantic encounter with Chanelle, Xander marched down the hallway and pounded on his son's door, also ordering him to drive to Blake Street immediately. He retreated to his bathroom, consumed four aspirin, and collapsed on his bed, trying to alleviate his headache.

Kellogg arose at eight o'clock, still groggy from his sleep disruption. After a quick shower, he shuffled into the kitchen, where Maggie was cooking eggs. She placed a cup of coffee on the table in front of him. "Good morning, Xander…you look tired."

"I am…I received a phone call at five o'clock and hardly slept after."

"I heard the phone ringing for several seconds. Is there a problem?"

"A fire was reported at one of my old buildings in lower downtown."

"I hope no one was injured."

"No one important…some hobos probably started the fire to keep warm."

Chanelle drifted into the kitchen and sat opposite Kellogg. "Good morning, Mr. Kellogg."

"Hello Chanelle…I hope you slept well."

"Yes…I had the most pleasant dreams." She stared out the side windows toward the rising sun. "One of my best dreams ever…"

"Did you enjoy the nightlife last night?"

"Yes…very much."

"I meant the song…I heard it playing from Buster's room when I got home."

"The song from Alacia Bridges? Yes…it's catchy. It's been in the top forty for several weeks now."

The telephone rang…Kellogg instantaneously jumped up to answer the call.

"Hello…Xander speaking."

"Mr. Kellogg…it's Mike Peavy. I'm calling from a pay phone a block from the fire. The buildings are a total loss…a few walls are still standing, but the roofs collapsed onto the wood floors, which crumbled into the basements. The fire is out but it's still smoldering. Blake and Sixteenth Streets look like a skating rink with all the ice and the police closed the viaduct to traffic."

"Is Buster there?"

"I haven't seen him, although Lawrence Reagan and Marty Holbrook were here for a while."

"Did you talk to them?"

"Yes…they seemed happy after speaking to their insurance agent."

"Do you recall the casualty insurance amount from reading the details in the loan file?"

"Yes…the casualty coverage was a million dollars."

"Shit…those assholes probably started the fire. I'll only get the six hundred-thousand-dollar principal balance from the insurance company and those guys will pocket the rest."

Yes…you're correct. The lender is named as additional insured but only up to the official loan balance of six hundred thousand in this case. Boss, that's not a bad payday…six hundred grand for a two hundred-thousand-dollar investment."

"Yeah…but I wanted to punish those jerks by suing them for the eight hundred thousand they caused for waste on the property. Robert will be happy though."

Kellogg hung up and sat down to eat his breakfast. Chanelle had quickly departed for class. He thanked Maggie and asked her to drive him to Kellogg Plaza where Buster was doodling at his desk.

"Buster…what did you observe at the fire?"

"What a blaze…fire trucks everywhere. They closed off all the streets within a two-block radius."

"Did you speak with anyone there?"

"A talked to a fire captain, although I didn't want to distract him for long."

"When did you get back here?"

Buster turned his wrist to read his watch. "About ten minutes ago."

Displeased with Buster's responses, Kellogg pointed toward the hallway. "Go over to Rich Eastman's office…spend a few days with he and Curt Jamison and learn how brokers operate, but you're on twenty-four-hour notice to drive me anywhere I need to go."

"I didn't move back here to be a chauffeur."

"A crooked cop cooked up a bogus speeding ticket and arrested me. I'm losing my driver's license but spending more time with me will only enhance your education."

"With my problems in California, I understand how the police operate. I'll help you out, pop…whatever you need." Buster crumpled a sheet of paper, casting it into a trash can.

As soon as Buster departed, Xander pulled the mashed ball of paper from the trash receptacle, noting a crude sketch of a surfer with the name, Chanelle, drawn inside a heart below. Kellogg turned the sheet over, reading the message slowly…'If you testify, you've signed your death warrant.' Kellogg crushed the sheet tightly before flinging it in the can. He tugged at Buster's top desk drawer and shuffled through a stack of papers, discovering a vial filled with white powder, hidden beneath. He shoved the drawer shut when Brenda interrupted his rage. "Mr. Kellogg...Mayor Zimmerman is calling you."

Kellogg plunged into his chair and snatched the receiver. "Good morning, Mayor."

"It's been a busy morning already. I understand those buildings you invested in on Blake Street burned to the ground overnight."

"Yeah...my guy has been down there before dawn and reported in."

"Well, you needn't worry about police surveillance now."

"No...but perhaps your crack fire department can find the arsonists, the building owners...Lawrence Reagan and Marty Holbrook."

"I can't believe that...they're civic leaders and are engaged in historical building preservation."

"Ivan...be careful who you spend time with. You know...when you sleep with dogs, you end up with fleas."

"That's interesting you would say that. I have good news, Xander...I spoke to Bill Douglas and he would cooperate by granting you an access agreement across his parcel."

"That's great, Ivan."

"You'll have to pay him five hundred thousand for the easement."

"Shit...I could have purchased his entire property for a half million. That doesn't help me...what did Webster Fink say about the condemnation?"

"Webster didn't see a need to widen Colorado Boulevard. He also rejected the height variance you wanted on your Seventeenth Street tower, even though I recommended your requests."

"That's very disappointing…can I speak with him directly."

"It wouldn't do any good…he was quite clear. That's all I have for you today, Xander…but please let me know about the next adventure you're planning. Thanks again for your apartment…I'm actually planning to use it tonight."

"Wait a second, Ivan…Your police arrested me yesterday on some bullshit charges. I need you to intervene to drop them."

"I'm sorry, Xander…the City Attorney already blocked my efforts. I understand your attorney, John Collins, tried to negotiate something with him. I can't help you but have a terrific day."

Kellogg ripped the telephone from the connection wall jack and hurled it against Buster's desk.

Brenda rushed into the office. "What was that?"

"A flying telephone…it happens sometimes."

Brenda picked up the device and plugged the cord into the socket. "I just read a sad story in *The Rocky Mountain News*. The burglary victim from the robbery in the 1010 Building died yesterday. The Chief of Police is quoted as having a new lead that recently surfaced. The City Attorney is promising justice for the victim…his employer is offering a twenty-five-thousand-dollar reward for a tip leading to an arrest."

"Only twenty-five thousand?"

"That's what it said. On top of that, I heard some buildings on Blake Street burned to the ground early this morning. The City doesn't safe anymore."

Kellogg called John Collins. "Colly, what happened to your great connections in the City Attorney's office?"

"The zealous deputy attorney, Franklin Kennedy, was assigned to your case again and my contact won't even discuss it with me."

"They didn't have the right to arrest me on private property...I was actually at the gas station site on Colorado Boulevard. I want you to press brutality charges against the cops who roughed me up...I have a laceration on my forehead."

"Xander...what were you thinking?" First it was alluding arrest to catch a plane; then the outburst in the courtroom; and now...resisting arrest and assaulting a police officer."

"I was distracted thinking about business problems...I couldn't have been driving more than five miles per hour over the limit. That police sergeant is another Barney Fife...he even ticketed me for littering? I'm surprised he didn't cite me for spitting on the street?"

"He actually did...that's in the police report too."

"Fuck...that's simply great! The only good news is Buster can be my driver until you can appeal to get my license back...he'll learn a lot."

Exasperated with the failure of the mayor to help, Kellogg drove to an older shopping center on Hampden Avenue. He plucked his sunglasses from the console and snagged a white golf cap, tugging the visor down. He wrapped a scarf around his neck and walked to a phone booth at the far end of the strip. He placed a dime in the slot and dialed the tip line for *The Denver Post* investigative team. Pulling the scarf over his mouth to muffle his voice, he carefully enunciating each word.

"Place a photographer in the rear parking lot of The Eldridge Apartments at Louisiana and Ogden after five o'clock this evening. A public figure will show up at some point with a guest."

To be continued…

CPSIA information can be obtained
at www.ICGtesting.com
Printed in the USA
ŁVHW110345300720
661928LV00001B/31